Baby Todd
AND THE
Rattlesnake
Stradivarius

Sherry—
When in doubt,
go left of center — at
least the view is interesting!

Tobsue

Baby Todd
AND THE
Rattlesnake
Stradivarius

TERESA KENNEDY

THE BODLEY HEAD
LONDON

A CIP catalogue record for this book is available from the British Library.

Printed in Great Britain for
The Bodley Head
32 Bedford Square
London WC1B 3EL
by
St Edmondsbury Press, Bury St Edmunds, Suffolk

First published by St Martin's Press, New York, 1987
First published in Great Britain in 1988

To those who believed:
Everything is possible—
pass it on.

CONTENTS

PART ONE

Fiddle, n. An instrument to tickle human ears by friction of a horse's tail on the entrails of a cat.

—Ambrose Bierce

Swans sing before they die. 'Twere no bad thing that certain persons die before they sing.

—Samuel Taylor Coleridge

This is work that concerns itself with two of the greatest mysteries of creation—Life and Death.

—Introduction to the movie Frankenstein, *1932*

You can go home again, but it will probably freak you out.

—T-shirt, The Sackcloth & Ashes Company

One

Atlantis County, Texas.
July 14, the Present.

LL IN ALL it was a pretty good funeral.

It was the middle of summer in the middle of East Texas
and, two days previous, one Ray Ed Strait departed this vale
of piss-ant tears by dropping dead right in the middle of a
bowl of lukewarm grits his grown granddaughter was trying to force-feed him for his own good. At the time, Ray
Ed was just eight days short of ninety years old and had no
more mind left in him than a cherry tomato, so despite the
speculation that went on about it later, the woman out-and-
out refused to accept that she'd been the one to do him in.
But Grace Ellen wasn't the type to go around taking blame
for the inevitable, no matter what folks expected otherwise.

3

The final moment came and went so fast it was hard to tell the difference, anyway. If Ray Ed hadn't chosen to speak, she might have missed it altogether. But instead he had, lolling his head and drooling farina, a death rattle going in his chest like a roll of drums.

"Destiny," said the old man. "Is not a blind armadillo."

It got her attention. She paused with the spoon halfway to his toothless gums, waved away a black fly, and studied the babyish, bald head and flat eyes that met her own with an accusatory, though entirely dead, stare.

Shit, she decided, life just isn't fair.

Half the county signed the Share Our Grief register set up near the front door and Uncle Dearest, Ray Ed's second-born, confided to Grace that if you counted the kids and those who didn't know how to write, there were more than three hundred milling over the lawns and through the house at the high point of it all. Dearest was a fairy who'd had a problem with the bottle ever since the physical education teacher from the high school ran away for a sex change and never came back, and so was prone to exaggeration. But the crowd was big enough, anyhow. People got to murmuring in the heat about how it did the old man proud with everyone turned out so nice, but Mammy Strait, the dead man's wife, just got a glazed expression when someone spoke about it to her and said it was a burying, thank you, not a damn bon voyage. Iris Lee Strait could more or less be counted on to be a rock in a crisis; she was just that kind. The rest of the family lined up with her to receive the mourners, all wearing the slightly fevered smiles of Moonies at an airport, but not Iris Lee. Iris Lee was a woman who knew how to make an example of her situation. To look at her, standing straight as a bone at the head of the stairs, eyes

dry as August, anyone would think she'd been a widow all
her life.

Privately, though, she was more than a little piqued at the
turn of things. According to his doctors, Ray Ed was supposed to have been dead six months ago. Anticipating his
end, Iris Lee had secretly signed up and paid a deposit for
a cruise to Alaska that was being sponsored by the Newly
Bereaved of the Methodist church in Queen City. She
wasn't Methodist herself, but Atlantis didn't have support
groups for the grief-stricken, only Kiwanis. Besides, she
figured she was entitled; Ray Ed hadn't ever taken her
anywhere while he was around. But the boat had sailed that
very morning, without Iris Lee and without the Methodists
giving her one red cent of her deposit back, either. To make
matters worse, when the man had finally expired, she hadn't
even been there to see it. She'd taken that particular afternoon to go to the Methodists about her deposit, but they'd
held firm while her mate of nearly sixty years breathed his
last for the sole benefit of a worthless granddaughter who'd
probably just used his illness as an excuse to run out on her
second husband, never mind what she told you.

After the mourners who weren't too tardy to bother
about had paid their respects, Iris Lee disbanded the receiving line, instructing the family to please mingle and not
embarrass her any more than was necessary. And, used as
they were to taking her orders, they promptly scattered like
ducks from a shotgun.

Except for Charles T., Iris and Ray Ed's eldest—he felt
more duty-bound than the rest and lingered a little, watching his relations disappear in the crowd. "Funny," he said.

Iris Lee squinted at him. "What?"

"This family," he continued dreamily. Seeing the Straits
all in one place after so many years left him a little per-

plexed. It was like falling witness to a Cheyenne war party.

Iris Lee made a little movement, as though she wanted to pinch him and had to restrain herself. It never failed to irk her that her eldest had turned out vague.

Charles T. smiled hesitantly. "I think Daddy would have approved," he said.

Iris Lee set her lips. Ray Ed would have been out of his tie and back to his plow before the coffin was covered up. But she decided to let Charles T. have his way about it, not having the strength to argue just then.

"Go to the kitchen, Charles T.," she told him. "See if the buffet is ready." She knew it was, of course, but she was tired of looking at him. "Charles T.?" she called sharply after him.

"Mammy?" he answered.

"Make sure those church ladies haven't got out my good Havilland. You know, with the flowers. The gold parts can't go in the dishwasher."

Charles T. nodded and moved away, raising little clouds of dust around his ankles as he went. Iris Lee sighed. The man was fifty-four years old and he hadn't yet learned to pick up his feet. Given Dearest's sexual proclivities and her baby Bubba dead in Asia, she might have counted her blessings in the son department, but Charles T. was her firstborn and, by virtue of a fundamental placidity, the easiest to pick on. He'd showed promise once, of course, before he took up with women and started looking at things wrong, but that was all misery under the bridge. Thirty-odd years previous, Charles T. had married for love, and ten years afterward, all he'd had to show for himself was a stack of bills and three homeless children. Charles T. had packed up the kids and come home like a prodigal, feeling like his life's adventure was through. And Iris Lee had been choking on I-told-you-so's ever since. He was smart, of course, but it wasn't the kind of smart a mother could take any pleasure in. Somewhere along the line Charles T. had learned too much to ever use it all and, as a result, was good at keeping life at a distance. And Iris Lee knew in her heart that anyone who viewed the world in such abstracted ways as did her oldest just couldn't help but be a little lacking in spine.

The old woman had got herself so worked up by the time Charles T. returned five minutes later with a plate of fried chicken and ambrosia salad that she was feeling short of breath. But she assured herself the mood would pass. She'd seen it time and again in families; there was just something about a death that made a person resent the living more than usual. After a moment, she raised her eyes and managed a little smile, determined to put a Christian face on the situation. She noted with some surprise that there were lines just beginning to deepen around her son's eyes, and that his graying hair fell thin and flat across his forehead. Folks said he was a handsome man, but she couldn't see it. Charles T. didn't look like anyone she knew.

"I brought you a plate," Charles T. said, unnecessarily.

"I can see that, Charles T.," she said, peering at it. "Is it the Havilland?"

Charles T. stared at it a moment, then held it aloft to better see the stampings. "No, Mammy," he assured her. "It's the stuff you bought at Walgreen's that just looks like the Havilland."

Christian or not, Iris was having some difficulty controlling herself. "Put it down somewhere. I don't feel like nothing."

Something like offense registered over his features, but he did as he was told, resting the plate on the stump of a holly tree he'd cut down while waiting for his daddy to die. He sighed. Charles T. liked to think of himself as a man misunderstood; most of the time, he was right.

"You want to sit down?" he asked.

"Don't stoop, Charles T.," Iris Lee told him. "And no, I don't."

"What?"

"I said, stand up straight."

Charles T. straightened a little and looked out over the company. He'd always done his best to help his family, but he knew better than to try to please. It wasn't his nature. He spied Grace Ellen by the pasture fence, and thought of how nice it had been of her to come all the way from New York just for a death watch on an old man who didn't recognize her. It made Charles T. feel good, having children with such a sense of family. Charles T. looked at Grace standing there in a silk dress and felt a stirring in his memory. Grace was a looker, all right, but it was more the combination than the parts. Since she'd moved up to New York, she looked more expensive perhaps, but she was still the same girl, rounded but restless, too smart around the eyes. Charles T. frowned, thinking of what he'd forgotten. Oh yes, the husband. He must remember to ask if Grace had left her husband or not. A father ought to be told.

He and Iris Lee flashed automatic smiles at a woman who shouted how awful it was as she passed by them with a plate of orange macaroni. "Well," Charles T. began.

Iris Lee scowled at him. She'd been thinking of the ocean again. "Well, what?" she demanded.

He stared at her uncertainly. So remote, his mother's face was like a relic of itself, etched in time and sacrifice— a kind of poor-white rendering of the Shroud of Turin. "Maybe I'll go find Davey," he offered.

Iris Lee almost smiled. As far as she was concerned, siring

Davey was the only thing Charles T. had done right in his life. "Tell him to come and see me please, Charles T."

Charles T. moved reluctantly off toward the pasture fence. He supposed Grace Ellen would know where her brother was. Grace kept pretty good track of things.

She was standing watching Dude Jenkins and his video camera taping the funeral guests and turning Ray Ed's last caveat over in her mind, destiny being a harder subject for her to contemplate than most. Thus far, she'd kept to herself on the subject of Ray Ed's last words, but she had a feeling that, in those last moments, staring down the business end of the cosmos, the old geezer had had something of a revelation. The problem being, of course, that she couldn't seem to get it to mean anything. She glanced up at her father's approach, determined to be well-adjusted.

"Well," Charles T. began. The look in her eyes was making him nervous, like she wanted him to mind his own business.

Grace closed her eyes. Never in her recollection had the man spoken an entire sentence on the first try. "Well," she replied.

"I came to see if you knew where Davey was. Mammy wants to see him." Charles T. paused.

"He and Uncle Dearest are behind one of the pickups getting drunk," she said matter-of-factly.

Charles T. nodded at the statement, as if he'd known it all along. "You know how she dotes on him," he said, in case she felt slighted. "Nobody can figure it out."

"Davey can," Grace replied evenly.

Charles T. smiled a little. Davey was practically famous for his charm, charm being something of an oddity in the family. Problem was, charm like that tended to hide more than it ought. Take the boy's homecoming, for example. Most of the time Davey toured with a band and might have been dead himself for all he called his family. He couldn't have known of Ray Ed's passing and yet, the day before, he'd arrived at the front door, big as you please.

"How do you suppose he knew to come home?" Charles T. asked aloud.

Grace shrugged. "I dunno. Maybe he's psychic."

All at once the two were surrounded by a group of old men in choir robes from the church who started in on a chorus of, "He Is Not Dead, He's Only Sleeping," in a last-ditch attempt to wring tears from the grieving relations. Grace bit her lip and stared at her feet, but Charles T. worked up a little mist for them, looking the tenor full in the face until the man got the point and steered the choir off to go upset someone else.

Grace stared after them in wonder. "The Good News Choir," Charles T. told her. "Mammy hired them special."

Grace looked at him. "What's the bad news?"

As he made his way to the pickup in question, Charles T. fell to contemplation. What if Davey was psychic? The children's mother had been psychic and so it was possible that their son probably was, too. In fact, the odds were probably in favor of something like that. Having lived through a bout of extrasensory powers with his wife, though, he found the prospect of having to do it over again with Davey almost too depressing to contemplate. Besides, it was more than being psychic that had brought Davey to the farm, Charles T. could tell. Being psychic was just a convenience. Something was up with Davey, too, just like there was with Grace. A pregnant girl, the law—something. It didn't matter which, Charles T. was a man who knew trouble when he smelled it. First the daughter, then the son. All grown up and full of inscrutabilities. It was too bad, really. The only one of his offspring Charles T. felt he could trust was the one who wasn't intelligent.

Charles T. swung suddenly down around the front of the house, avoiding the group by the pickup for the moment. Davey and Dearest would probably be well on their way to getting shitfaced, and much as he wanted to join them, Charles T. felt a certain obligation to endure the remainder of the afternoon sober. Boo was down by the mailbox playing with some dogs and Charles T. headed toward him gratefully.

Over by the pickup, Uncle Dearest spotted his big brother down by the mailbox and smiled. Privately, he had very little use for members of his family, but that didn't mean he didn't find them entertaining. Now that the formalities were over, he reached in his pocket and replaced a small silver flamingo in his left ear.

"I feel so much better," he said, winking at Davey. "Left means you're looking."

Davey paid him no attention, since he was staring at the array of bottles lined up in the back of the pickup and trying to decide what was going to get him drunkest fastest. It piqued Dearest a little being ignored, so he grabbed a fifth of Smirnoff, poured it into a gallon jug of cherry Kool-Aid, shook it a little, and pumped out a Dixie cup for his nephew, holding it out until the boy had no choice but to take it.

"I call it a Melanie Hamilton," he said. "You know? *Gone With the Wind?* The sweet one? My dear, two of these and you won't give a damn, either."

Davey took a swallow. "It's awful," he said. The concoction in the jug proved to be approximately the temperature of spit.

"Now, now," Dearest chided him. "Let's don't be picky."

"Get fucked," Davey said evenly.

"Gracious! A little respect, please," Dearest replied. "Besides, you may live to regret that you weren't nice to me."

Davey leaned easily against the side of the truck and faced Dearest with the same lazy, cool-eyed look that had been setting feminine hearts aflame since he'd been old enough to use it. "Why's that?"

Dearest, however, was unimpressed. He figured anybody born with Davey's looks couldn't help but turn out weak in character. "Such a pretty boy," Dearest mocked. "Pity you favor women."

Davey colored under his tan. "Pity you don't," he answered evenly.

"Can't miss what you never wanted, boy. Remember that," Dearest said lightly. "Besides, you have to be nice to me, I may turn out to be your rich uncle."

Davey threw back the rest of the Kool-Aid. "How's that?"

Dearest shifted a little and lowered his voice to a more discreet level. "Because of the money, of course!" he hissed.

"Money?"

"Daddy's money. I just know we're all going to inherit tons of money."

Davey had begun to take this turn in conversation seriously. "No shit?"

"Well, nobody knows for certain, of course. But the old man was always such a skinflint when he was alive, it only stands to reason he left us all enough to fight over."

Davey was about to pursue the topic further when he was thunderously clapped on the shoulder by a bleary-eyed man wearing what appeared to be dress overalls.

"Damn sorry about your granddaddy, kid."

"Thanks," Davey said.

"Taken in his prime," the farmer went on.

Davey bit his lip. Ray Ed Strait had been so old, it had come down to a choice between dying and sending out for parts.

"Damn shame," the farmer said, then fell respectfully silent as a long-legged blonde in a summer dress passed the group and smiled. Davey noted the shadows of her body moving under the dress and the flawless skin on her throat and noted, too, that she wasn't wearing much in the way of underwear. Her hair was beauty-parlor style in the manner of Texas city women, and the lines of her profile were as haughty and clean as a "draw-me" lady on a matchbook.

The farmer caught Davey's appraising glance. "World has changed since I was young. Women, too. Got to where they got to have rights." The farmer spat into the dust and shook his head. "Women are right this minute controllin' about half the money in the world."

Davey shook his head, never taking his eyes from the blonde. "Yeah," he said, a little sadly. "And all the pussy."

"Tut, tut," said Dearest, helping himself to the Kool-Aid and grinning. "That woman over there is spoke for."

Davey turned his attention back to Dearest. "You know her?" he asked.

Dearest grinned like a cat with a secret supply of sardines. "Sure do," he said, "her name's Luanne."

Davey glanced backward once more at the blonde and then back to Dearest. "So tell me more about the money," he said.

Down by the mailbox, Boo was trying to get his father to listen to a song from the radio that was playing in his head when a long, low car came pulling up the drive, going slow

as a limousine. Charles T. abandoned Boo for a moment
and strode to meet it, arranging his face in an expression so
sad it nearly did justice to his tie. His Aunt Baby Todd had
come calling.

She was Iris Lee's sister, younger, prettier, and a woman
who moved through the world like a debutante at a tea
dance. She called herself Baby Sheba Todd, more for the
sake of convenience than anything. Todd was the name on
most of her bank accounts, Baby was the name by which
everybody knew her, and Sheba the name she got when she
was born. Thrice-married, elegant to her aging bones, the
old woman emerged from her Buick in a knock-off Chanel
suit and a hat with a veil, looking for all as if she'd just
dropped by on her way to somewhere nicer. In her day,
Baby Sheba had been a beauty, though that, like her multi-
ple husbands, had pretty much gone the way of recollection. Only an ineffable lightness of attitude remained, along
with a pretty good wardrobe.

Over under the fig trees, Clara Cannon, publisher of the
Baptist newsletter, leaned over to Maivis Johnson as they
watched Charles T. escort his aunt to the house, the old lady
gliding along like she'd been greased someplace.

"I don't care if she was Miss Crepe Myrtle of 1923,"
Clara said sourly. "She looks like hell on a plate."

Maivis leaned forward and squinted in response to
Clara's comment. She couldn't tell which was giving her
more trouble this afternoon, her varicose veins or the rub-
berized hose that was holding them in. "Everybody gets
old, Clara," she answered mildly.

Clara surreptitiously slipped a plug of chewing tobacco
into her cheek. "Well, both her and Iris Lee was always vain
about more than they had, if you ask me," she replied.

Maivis studied a scaly-looking liver spot on her left hand.

Seemed she got a new one every time someone was buried. "Maybe," she agreed doubtfully.

"If I'd chose men with money the way Iris Lee and Baby Sheba did, I'd be a happier person today," Clara went on.

Maivis was using her tongue to rearrange her teeth. Clara Cannon had been a virgin for eighty years.

"And you can't tell me they didn't make sacrifices for what they got, either. You take Baby's last one, Preacher. The one who was so rich."

"Preacher?" Maivis put in. "Preacher Todd was a nice fella."

"Humpphh. Had a glass eye and false teeth, too. Used to take 'em out at parties. That's what I mean about sacrificing. Why, it makes my flesh crawl to think of lyin' down with a man who's half-missing like that."

"You never got to lay down with anybody, Clara, part or whole. Can't take your opinion."

Clara shot a polite stream of tobacco in the general direction of Maivis' shoe. "And Charles T.'s children are the same way, too. Vain as anything. Did you see that slithery dress the granddaughter had on? That man she married ain't nowhere in sight and her wearin' silk, flaunting herself. And that Davey—ain't right for a man to be that good-lookin'."

Maivis smiled a little as she recalled Davey Strait. He made her wish she were sixty years younger. Maivis lifted her left leg a little, testing the misery in her knee. "They're sayin' the granddaughter from New York was the only one here when Ray died."

"I think she kilt him."

"Clara!" Maivis glanced around, making sure no one had heard.

"Well, it would have been easy enough. He was all but

gone already. Had been for months. Way I got it figured, there's enough in Ray Ed's will to make somethin' like a murder worthwhile. If you know what I mean."

Maivis shifted uncomfortably in the webbed lawn chair. Clara's train of thought was making her squirm. Maivis had a granddaughter herself and a couple of CD's that weren't anything to sneeze at. "You're getting old, Clara," she said after a moment. "You're makin' up stories."

Clara spat again. "My mind is exactly the same as when I was eighteen, Maivis Johnson, and so's yours. And I don't have no insanity in my family, neither." She paused and nodded meaningfully toward the Strait house. "Not like some folks."

Maivis sighed. For a churchwoman, Clara had more barbs than a wire fence. "The Straits are just folks, Clara," she said. "Just like anybody."

"Sure, if you're not counting trashy women, light boys, and fools."

Maivis glanced around the yard. "Now that you're speakin' of it, where is Boo? I thought Iris was going to make him play his fiddle for the folks."

"Who knows?" Clara said irritably. "Probably doing somethin' he shouldn't."

"Well, you kin say what you please about the rest of them, Clara," Maivis put in. "But you can't fault Boo. Sweetest child I ever knew."

Clara snorted. "Course he's sweet, Maivis. He's an idiot. You got to have sense before you can make any real trouble."

But Maivis held firm. "Well, you're wrong about Boo, Clara. I jest bet you he turns out to be one of them idiot courants. Like that boy they had on Donahue last week. The one with the piano."

"You'll believe anything, Maivis Johnson. Besides, that genius stuff is just tricks."

Maivis fell silent as Grace wandered by, holding a Dixie cup of Kool-Aid and smiling a little. "I wish you'd tell me how that girl could wear silk in this heat without sweating it up."

"She gets that fine skin from the Quades," Clara put in. "Iris had it and so did Baby. They got no pores at all, none of them."

Maivis thought it over. Not having pores was a medical phenomena she had yet to come across, on Donahue or anywhere else, but she decided to let Clara have her way on it. The truth was, she wanted to get a crack at that buffet before it was gone.

Half an hour later, full of casserole and greens, the two old ladies made their way through the rapidly dispersing crowd, not wanting to leave without having properly expressed themselves. They found the widow standing near the front door with Baby Sheba Todd nearby, who was frantically waving a hankie at the departing company like it was glued to her fingers. Clara peered at them, glad at last for a close-up look. Her rather rheumy eyes roved from Iris Lee's to Baby's face and back again, and she decided once and for all that there was a case to be made for the use of expensive moisturizers, no matter who you had to marry to be able to afford them. Baby, from the look of her poreless, inherited skin, might have been a daughter. And yet, Iris Lee couldn't have had more than five years on her.

"Thank you both so much for coming," Baby cried, too enthusiastically, tears shining in her eyes. "Sad times are so much easier with people to share them with. I was just saying to Iris that she should count her blessings, not her sorrows. Wasn't I just saying that, Iris Lee?"

"Only just," said Iris Lee, a little flatly.

Maivis and Clara blinked at each other, then at Iris Lee, who responded with a closed, tight-lipped smile, like someone steeling himself to have a tooth pulled.

Clara cleared her throat. She didn't know what the two sisters had been discussing before they approached, but she'd bet her tobacco it had nothing to do with blessings. "Well, it was real nice," she said. "I just wish Ray Ed could have been here to enjoy it with us."

"That's the truth," Maivis put in.

"But you've got your family, Iris Lee," Clara went on. "And God, of course."

"God?" said Baby, from behind the hankie.

"Jesus," Iris Lee reminded her sister, as civilly as she could. "The Savior."

"I know who Jesus is, Iris Lee." Baby replied. Abruptly she laughed a little. "My sister treats me as if I were profoundly retarded. Always has. But then she has a serious nature. Don't you, Iris Lee? Ray Ed always said that about you. That you were the most serious woman he ever saw. I never had a husband like that myself. Not one that took me serious, did I, Iris Lee?"

Iris Lee's eyes went flat gray, like someone gone blind. "Pardon us," she said abruptly. "We have to see to the other guests." And, gripping a surprised Baby by the elbow, she all but hauled her sister away.

Maivis and Clara clucked their tongues all the way to Maivis' Chevette, parked a little way down the drive. Clara helped Maivis into the driver's seat and slid in the other side, slamming the door with a satisfactory thunk of disapproval.

"Well, if that don't beat all I ever saw," Maivis mused aloud. "Iris just walked her out of there like she had no more sense than Boo. Did you see, Clara? Her own sister?

And that look she give her when she did it. Made me want to quit livin'.''

"I got eyes," Clara muttered, rummaging in her handbag for another plug. "I tell you, Maivis, there's something not right about every last member of that family. Mark my words. The whole bunch is cursed."

Maivis thought it over. "Well, maybe it was just the grief made Iris act so funny back there."

"Or maybe Iris Lee Strait has more to hide than we thought," Clara countered.

"Like what?"

Clara faltered a moment. "I dunno, but sumpin'. You could see that well as me."

"Now, Clara. Iris Lee Strait is a good woman. Not warm, especially. But Christian."

Clara buckled her seatbelt tight across her skinny hips. Maivis drove like a terrorist. "Oh, sterling," she said mockingly. "Lives so nobody could point a finger."

Maivis keyed the ignition. "What's that supposed to mean?" She'd found, over the years, that gossip about one's neighbors was one of those dishes that might be enjoyed cold as well as warm.

"Nothin'. Only that it ain't hard to be good when you're old. It don't mean she was always that way."

Maivis made a sucking sound with her dentures as she floored the accelerator. "Oh. Is that all."

Clara squinted out over the fields, reviewing the afternoon. "Cold," she pronounced after a moment.

Maivis reached for the dashboard. "What's cold? Too much AC? I can turn it down if you want."

"Iris Lee Strait is what's cold. Got her guts on ice. And I just bet there's some besides me who wishes she'd been the one to go first, too."

"Clara Cannon, you shut your mouth. The Lord's the one who decides and not you."

Clara's withered cheek bulged and she spat into a Dixie cup she carried with her for that purpose. "I reckon the Lord knows more about Iris Lee and the sister and the rest of that family than anybody," she said evenly. "I just wish he'd let a little of it slip once in awhile, that's all."

Maivis edged up her speed; she liked it just on the high side of seventy.

"Well, you'd better save your breath for prayin', Clara Cannon. The Lord only sends revelations to those who ain't prepared."

Two

DESPITE CLARA CANNON'S opinion as to the family's general cursedness, things went on pretty much as might be expected at the Strait farm after the company had gone. As is frequently the case in families, the Straits found themselves gathered in the kitchen after the funeral guests had gone, straggling in one by one as if by some prior arrangement. Given the circumstances and the fact that they were basically nice enough folks, they were making something of an effort to be nice to one another. But, as is also the frequent case in families, effort alone is never quite enough.

Thanks to the tireless ministrations of the ladies of Atlantis county, the kitchen table was laid out like an anorexic's

hallucination—an arrangement of victuals so rich and inviting that almost no one had been able to bring themselves
to eat anything. When Charles T. brought Boo in to feed
him, the sight of all those leftovers left him agog. Excess in
most forms made Charles T. uneasy. It was just the way he
was.

"Christ," he said to no one in particular. "We should've
got us a sin eater."

Maejean Strait, wife of the long-dead Bubba, was already
up to her elbows in dishwater, having decided earlier not
to risk Mammy's Havilland, real or imitation, in the dishwasher. On the lanky side, Maejean had a face as round and
pretty as a frosted cake and a stunning capacity for work that
more than once had led to speculation that there might be
something amiss with her thyroid. She also had a world-
class case of the hots for Charles T., an aspect that was
obvious to nearly everyone but him. When he wandered
over to the sink in search of a plate for Boo, she dried her
hands, smoothed her hair and tried to quiet a sudden lurch
of her innards.

"What that's about sin, Charles T.?"

He lowered his voice. Mammy and Baby had begun to
squabble over by the freezer, and he didn't want to attract
any undue notice. "I said," he went on, in a whisper Maejean chose to mistake for intimacy, "that we ought to have
a sin eater."

Since he seemed to be in a talkative mood, Maejean
allowed herself a little more proximity. "I don't know what
that is," she responded in a honeyed voice.

Charles T. was eyeing Boo, who was over at the table,
having decided, apparently, to eat only white food that day.

"In the Middle Ages, when somebody rich died, the
family would go and hire a peasant to eat a banquet right
off the corpse." Charles T. paused as his other son, Davey,

and Dearest came in from the yard, drunk on their butts from the look of them. The sight of Davey, flushed-faced and glassy-eyed, cheered him a little. With Davey plastered, he could stall awhile on that heart-to-heart he'd been planning.

"They figured the dead man's sins went into the food first, then the peasant," Charles T. went on, turning back to Maejean, who was batting eyes at him like it was her life work. Maejean was a nice woman, Charles T. thought suddenly. Pretty, too. Except for that tic. "Hell's full of peasants, I guess," he finished.

Maejean blinked again. Charles T. could be the most unexpected person.

"What a perfectly revolting idea," Baby Todd put in as she crossed back from the freezer. Baby never missed anything. "Did it work?"

Charles T. considered it. "I don't know."

"Boo!" Iris Lee's voice shot through the kitchen like an arrow.

"Don't eat that, honey," Maejean intervened, rushing over to help Boo with his plate. "It's bad."

"What?" Charles T. came to the table, suddenly concerned. He peered over the array of food, trying to spot the problem. It never mattered how much a father paid attention, something was always going wrong. "Did he get the Havilland?" he said anxiously.

"It ain't nothin'," Maejean called brightly, piling up a plate and hustling Boo out the back door to sit on the porch. She loved the boy as much as anybody, but you didn't want to watch him eat.

"Only that Clara Cannon is trying to poison somebody," Iris Lee said darkly, her head inside the Frigidaire.

Now that the company had gone, Baby removed her hat and sat fanning herself. "Clara Cannon?" she asked idly.

"The one with the chewing tobacco," Iris Lee answered. "She had her friend with the rubber stockings with her."

"I know who she is, Iris. I got eyes, same as everybody else. Except Preacher, of course. He only had one." Baby nibbled her bottom lip for a moment. "But I'm sure you're exaggerating about Clara, anyway."

Iris Lee chose to differ. "Maejean was working her shift yesterday at the Safeway and swears that Clara came in and bought twelve Le Menus, just so's she could take the chickens out and put them in her own casserole. And everybody knows frozen diners are full of poison. All you have to do is watch TV."

"I make a very nice Le Menu myself," Dearest put in from his place in the corner. He'd thought about rousing himself to help the women, but decided against it; he was too drunk, anyhow. "Put some parsley on the plate and nobody would know the difference. And they ain't poison either, Mammy." Contradicting Iris Lee's opinion on things comprised one of Dearest's reasons to live. "Except maybe the cacciatore ones," he said, after a moment's further consideration. "What kind did Clara bring?"

Wordlessly, Maejean held the dish aloft for him to see the cacciatore on her way back to the sink, where Charles T. was tying on an apron over his suit in a way that threatened to break her heart for good.

"Oh," Dearest replied, straightening his Sunday toupee.

"Well, if she was trying to kill anyone, I'm sure it wasn't intentional," Baby insisted. Baby looked for the best in people, even if she had to invent it.

Just then was the moment that Grace chose to join them. Hearing her great-aunt's last remark, she colored up and tried to look demure.

"We weren't talking about you," Charles T. told her, clearing his throat. "It was the cacciatore."

Grace glanced at him. "Pardon me?"

Maejean blushed and tried to smile. "We were just discussing how you can't tell from looking at a person whether they're killers. But it—uhhm—wasn't anything. . . . It was Clara Cannon's chicken cacciatore that started the whole conversation. The point was in their being frozen in the first place." Maejean trailed off helplessly. She couldn't recall having strung so many words together in front of the family before, and Grace was staring at her like her brains were leaking. Thoroughly embarrassed, Maejean lowered her eyes and went back to dishwashing.

"Forget it, Grace," advised Dearest. "No one really thinks you killed the old man, no matter what they say otherwise."

Grace met his eyes. "Look, he just died, all right? One minute he was here, the next, pffftt! That's all there was to it."

Well, not quite all there was to it. There was still that business of the armadillos.

Dearest nodded sympathetically. "The way I look at it, you did us all a favor. I mean, someone had to be here when he kicked. Might as well have been you. If it'd been me, I know I would have been skinned and fried."

Iris Lee stood in the center of the floor, smoothing an apron over her widow's outfit, a tasteful little beige knit. "Dearest," she said sweetly. "Won't you please shut up?"

Dearest did.

"Could you tell it was coming? Other than it being so obvious, I mean." Baby fixed Grace Ellen with a bright, bird-eyed stare.

Grace didn't need to think it over. "Nope."

Baby was clearly disappointed. "Oh. I thought you might have got an intuition about it. I've found that if there's one thing this family all has in common, it's intuition about things. So I just thought you might have seen it coming. Which reminds me, did anyone hear from Gloria?''

At the mention of the long-gone Gloria McSaxon, things fell so silent in that room you could have heard chickens breathe. Charles T. leaned against the sink and refused to look at anything, having had the poor sense to have married the woman in the first place, while the rest of them looked embarrassed for no reason at all.

Baby went on as though nothing was amiss, but then, Baby usually did. ''I guess not,'' she said, answering her own inquiry.

''I guess not,'' echoed Iris Lee. ''Besides, there's no help for the past anyhow,'' she said, shooting Grace a little switchblade glance. ''What's done is done.''

Grace decided to take up the gauntlet—anything was better than discussing Gloria. ''Would you mind telling me what that's supposed to mean?''

Iris Lee met her eyes without flinching. ''It means that I ask you to do a simple thing like give Ray Ed his supper and what happens? Now, maybe it was your fault and maybe it wasn't. I can't say and neither can anybody else.''

Charles T. leaned against the wall, thinking of his dead father and his ruined marriage and of how life just wasn't all it was cracked up to be. ''Oh Lord,'' he said.

''Oh be quiet!'' Grace snapped. She turned away and started drying plates with a fervor that put the gold leaf in serious jeopardy. ''Obviously, there is no point in discussing a simple thing like death with you people,'' she said bitterly. ''Obviously, you don't know that people die whenever they feel like it.''

''Me and Charles T. saw Uncle Otie die, didn't we?'' Dearest put in. ''Out in the oil fields. He was the one who blew himself up.''

Charles T. nodded. ''Didn't look real,'' he said to no one.

"We are not discussing blowing up," Iris Lee said sharply. "Blowing up is accidental. What we are discussing is more serious."

Since he'd decided for certain that it wasn't his butt, Davey rose drunkenly to his sister's defense from a place in the corner. "Grace couldn't kill anybody with chicken," he slurred. "Grace can't even cook!"

"Shut up, Davey, there's a good boy," Baby said soothingly. Like many things about her sister, she considered Iris's favoritism of the boy a rather tragic lapse of taste. She turned back to Grace. Grace was the only one in that branch of the family who knew how to dress.

"You're very wise to ignore this whole affair, my dear," Aunt Baby went on. "Whenever anything bad happens Iris just lays the blame on somebody else. Does it to me all the time. She can't help herself." Baby studied her manicure. "The way she carries on, some people would say she had a guilty conscience. It's pure psychology."

"Pure bull, you mean," answered Iris Lee. "And I will thank you to keep my conscience out of this. My conscience doesn't have anything to do with anything except Jesus."

"See what I mean?" said Baby. "It was unfortunate, of course, Grace being the only one here when Ray Ed— uhhm . . ." she trailed off.

"Bit the big one?" Dearest suggested delicately.

Baby ignored this. "But I told everyone I talked to this afternoon; Grace Ellen couldn't hurt a fly, so they might as well just forget what they were thinking. Didn't I say that, Iris Lee?"

Iris Lee emerged from the Frigidaire with a complex expression playing across her care-worn face, like a nun praying for an Uzi. "I am no longer talking to you," she replied.

There was a little silence. Grace abandoned the Havil-

land, only to find herself face-to-face with what appeared to
be a casserole of cheese doodles in cream sauce.

"Cover that," Iris Lee directed, thrusting the dish at her.

Grace made to do as she was told, deciding that for the
moment at least, she'd been forgiven.

"Tie an apron on first, Grace. You don't want to ruin
your dress," Baby said.

"Hmmphhh," muttered Iris Lee from the cupboards,
and headed out into the hall. "Them that wears silk do
dishes same as everybody else."

"Pay no attention to her, Grace," Baby hissed. "She's
just eaten up with green envy about that dress. She told me
so."

Grace was trying to pick an edge off a roll of Saran. "She
did?"

"Yes, she did. It was when you were standing on the
porch earlier. She leaned right over to me and said, 'I wish
I didn't have anything to spend my money on but designer
clothes and my own selfish pleasures like some I could
mention.' But you know what she meant. It's just that she's
rather close about giving out compliments. Aren't you, Iris
Lee?" Baby called to the back hall where Iris Lee was going
after the reserve stores of Tupperware.

"A regular clam," said Dearest, lighting a cigarette.

Iris Lee reemerged with an armload of Serve 'n Seals and
the rest suppressed a kind of group groan.

"Oh good Lord, Iris," Baby put in. "Why don't you just
throw all this stuff away?" She gestured at the table. "The
way you carry on, you'd think it was the Depression and
they didn't have supermarkets."

"You know very well I can't do anything like that." Iris
Lee scowled, remembering too late that she wasn't talking
to anyone.

"How come?" Charles T. took off his apron. Maejean

had been trying to hold hands with him in the dishwater and
he figured he'd better move before she got any ideas.

"Because people would get the notion that the Straits are
too proud to take from their neighbors, that's why. You
start giving people ideas like that and before you know it
you can't go to church."

Charles T. tried to puzzle out how those ideas followed
one another and couldn't. He motioned to Davey and
Dearest to make room for him on their bench, hoping to
get intoxicated by association. Davey woke up and smiled.

"Hiya, Dad," he said cheerfully.

"By the way, I wanted to ask you all what you thought
of Brother Heck's eulogy?" Iris Lee asked them.

Brother Heck was a recent theology school graduate
with no lips and soft hands whose sermon had been an
attempt to link live goat offerings, crucifixions, and the
death of an East Texas farmer with some larger notion of
sacrifice, and so provide the necessary comfort to the bereaved. The rest of the family looked at one another, then
back to Iris Lee.

"Frankly, Iris Lee," Baby answered for all of them. "I
couldn't make head nor tale of it. But it was nice anyhow."

Iris Lee smiled a satisfied little smile. "You didn't understand it, Baby, because you don't know anything about
salvation. Brother Heck is the smartest preacher we ever
had around these parts," she went on. "He said everything
I told him to."

Dearest snorted. "If you ask me," he began.

Iris Lee scowled at him. "Nobody did," she said.

Maejean was drying up the remainder of the dishes, trying to recover from her rejection. "What if you took the
leftovers over to the nig—I mean, the black section,
Mammy?" she suggested, trying to change the subject.
Maejean was superstitious. And discussing salvation, she

felt, would almost surely jinx the possibilities. "I expect folks over there would be happy to have it."

Baby sniffed, temporarily abandoning the die-away drawl she'd mistaken for refinement back around the time she was queen of the flowering shrubbery. "Hmmphh," she said. "I went over to Feed the Hungry Day last Thursday at Black Baptist and those niggers wouldn't hardly touch what I brought. I couldn't understand it. Charity has got so unpredictable."

Dearest got unsteadily to his feet. "What'd you bring the poor folks, Baby?" he inquired in as innocent a tone as possible.

"Two platters of crudités. I made it look nice, too. Put doilies on the plates."

Dearest grinned. "Did you make 'em your salmon mousse? I simply adore your salmon mousse."

"You do? Well, let me give you the recipe, you take a can of tomato soup and some gelatin and some cream cheese, and . . ."

Iris Lee interrupted, her hands on hips. "Sister, we'll manage the food all right. I don't think you need to worry about it." It was, in fact, an invitation to depart, but Baby wasn't buying.

"Iris, honey, I am trying to have a conversation here. Why don't you find somewhere to light?"

"Well pardon me, Miss Crepe Myrtle. I thought this was my house."

"Now, now," said Charles T.

"Shut up, Charles T. Nobody asked you." Iris Lee turned her attention to Grace, who was wrapping up mayonnaise sandwiches and trying to be invisible.

"Grace," her grandmother said in that patient tone usually reserved for the half-witted or born-again, "Do you mind not pulling out that tin foil by the ream the way you do? This is not New York and I am not an aluminum baron."

The roll slipped from Grace's fingers and went unreeling across the linoleum. "Yes, ma'am," she said helplessly.

"Pay her no mind, Grace," Baby put in. "She's been ornery since the day she was born."

Iris Lee shot Baby a withering look as she stopped to pick up the roll. "Putting this food up needn't take the rest of our lives," she announced. "Providing some of us keep our minds on it."

But Grace had ceased to pay attention. Her eyes were intent on something beyond the house, as though she were trying to see through the walls, and her ear was cocked to a faraway sound. "Listen," she told them.

Over in the corner, Davey perked up for a moment. "Boo?" he asked.

Charles T. nodded with a wistful expression. "What's that song?"

Outside, the music rose, stretching and shuddering like some beast awakening.

Maejean sighed a little, suddenly thinking of her future. "Someone ought to put that child on the stage."

The tune shifted then, settling into a sad, familiar waltz, the refrain rising, finding its way through the open windows.

Iris Lee had frozen in her tracks. "He can't," she said in a strangled voice.

Charles T. stared at her. "What is it?"

"I said he can't!" The old woman's face went positively crimson with repression.

"Oh Iris, let him play. It's all he has," Baby put in in a bemused voice. "Besides, I think that must be the 'Anniversary Waltz.' Doesn't it sound like the 'Anniversary Waltz' to you, Iris Lee?"

Iris Lee slammed the roll of foil on the edge of the table with a force that made them all jump. "I don't care if it's Mozart. He can't be playing—not tonight. Davey, go and get him."

Davey rose from his place, a little surprised at having been asked to do something. "How come?"

The music swelled.

"Just go," Charles T. told him. For the first time in thirty years, wings of rebellion fluttered against the cage of his ribs.

Baby sighed luxuriously. "Oh, how that takes me back!" She hummed a little snatch of the song in a sad, wavery soprano. "Remember when I first got married, Iris Lee?"

"I do not. And if you had any sense you wouldn't either."

Baby smiled dreamily. "Don't be silly, Iris Lee. Memories can't hurt you."

Iris Lee turned away. "No," she said. "Just make you old before you're ready."

Baby sighed. "I wish you could have known my first husband, Grace. You could have appreciated a man like that."

"Along with anything else in pants," Iris Lee said under her breath.

"He was a man to whom beauty was not an enigma."

"Pardon?" said Grace, who was finding the turn of conversation a little odd.

But Baby only looked bewildered for a moment, then began to pin on her hat.

The music drifted around the room like a spirit looking for rest, the last notes trembling like colors for the hearing.

Dearest roused himself after a moment and saw Baby to

her car, and Charles T. watched them through the shadow
of the screen.

"Did you know," he said to anyone who'd listen, "that
the violin is the instrument closest to the human voice?
Some of the sounds are almost the same."

Three

Aytolles Parish, Louisiana.
1830 or Thereabouts.

MARY FAITH BEAUDINE lived eighty-two years, during which time she spoke only a single syllable. Her father's was the biggest house in Aytolles Parish, perched on a vast network of marshlands bordered by the Great Red, or Blood Bayou (what you called it depended on who your parents were), on the east, and on the west some land so fraught with mosquitos and moss that it was thought to be uninhabitable by anyone but free niggers and Cajuns. When she was a child, Mary Faith had been checked by all the usual specialists for an appropriate deficiency, but each came up empty. The girl was completely normal, they said—certainly intelligent, and if it was generally thought that the real reason for her lack of speech was some Indian blood heretofore unsuspected, few ever said so aloud. More than one person, in fact, suggested delicately to her parents that the problem might very well have a brighter side. A rich girl who kept her mouth shut might prove to be popular later in life.

Her parents, after some discussion, decided that since the girl could not talk, it might very well prove useful to teach her to read and write, singular talents for young women of the day. The girl grew very proficient at each of these and so, to show his appreciation of Mary Faith's efforts not to become a burden to her family, her father presented her with a small tablet and gold pencil, strung to a diamond-studded chain. Her mother thoughtfully provided the paper. The back of the tablet was engraved for her birthday:

To MFB
Still Waters Run Deep
3rd June, 1822

Roland Beaudine was not an original man. Still, the child must have found some use for the gift, for as far as anyone knows she wore the tablet around her neck until the day she died.

Contrary to what might have been hoped, Mary Faith did not grow into a beautiful woman. Her forehead was too wide, her eyes too close, and her lips too narrow to be of any real interest to the young men of the neighborhood. But she had a proud bearing and a taste for finery, though her choice of colors and frills was often considered a bit toney for a virgin. And, by the time she reached the age of twenty-two, when her parents passed on in the nastiest buggy accident anyone could remember, Mary Faith Beaudine was also richer than God.

She didn't take up the violin until the age of thirty, when

all hopes of marriage (and so, most of her social life) had pretty much bit the dust. Not that she minded so much. All told she found the rituals of social behavior rather trying. Even those young men brave enough to affect an interest tended not to differentiate between one's being dumb and one's being deaf and spent the evening shouting at her, or worse, found her shy, penciled messages altogether embarrassing. Ten minutes of flirtation tended to leave them with handfuls of paper and no more pockets to stuff them in. So, with the prospect of forty years of genteel solitude stretching out before her like dunes on a desert and no temperament whatever for philanthropy, Mary Faith decided to dedicate her life to music in general and the violin in particular.

At first she was content to teach herself, learning what she could from an assortment of books and diagrams she ordered from The Prodigy Music Publishers in Boston. But though she studied hard and practiced many hours a day, it wasn't long before she found that self-discipline, like masturbation, is not without its limitations. Thus enlightened, she set about the business of hiring herself an instructor.

The teacher hailed from Hungary and came to her by way of Ohio, where he ran a small musical agency. Miss Beaudine's letter arrived on a Thursday, two days, as it turned out, before Hedwig Biedle, daughter of the town's only laundress, informed him that she was expecting. Sunday morning saw Maestro Stepan Scheuelchinskaya on the train to New Orleans, his Stradivarius under his arm.

As is the frequent misfortune of women used to thinking of themselves as realists, poor Mary Faith was head over hoopskirts from the first time she set eyes on him. Wavy black hair, eyes that were blacker still, the man had the utterly irresistible look of someone going to hell in a hand-

basket. He alighted easily from the hired carriage, flicked
the road dust from his lapel with a graceful hand, and, as
an afterthought, smoothed his mustache. Mary Faith waited
on the veranda in cherry silk and ruffles, shocked and not
a little enraged at the twist in her solar plexus that left her
trembling somewhere between ecstasy and nausea.

Realism, though, dies hard. And Mary Faith so resolutely
denied the truth of her attraction for him that all she succeeded in doing was to give it a strength that was well-nigh
unendurable. But if her heart was made for passion, her
stomach was decidedly not. She promptly installed him like
a servant in a room off the kitchen, where aside from her
daily lesson, she would have as little contact with the man
as possible. In fact, it was three months before she fully met
his eyes. They were in the music room on a chilly April
morning, adjusting her fingering.

"Your hands are so cold," the maestro commented, giving her the full benefit of his gypsy's eyes. "You cannot
make music with such hands. They will not do what you
want."

Mary Faith stared at him, absorbed in an effort not to
faint from his proximity.

"May I get you a shawl?" he asked.

She laid aside the violin and wrote him an answer on her
tablet.

"Circulatory problem." Abruptly, she handed it over.

The maestro read it and put it to his lips, kissing it slowly
at first, then giving the helpless thing the benefit of teeth
and tongue until he had swallowed it entirely. The blood
drained from Mary Faith's face so fast it was as though she'd
been gutted. Helplessly she watched him, open-mouthed
herself. He covered her icy hands with his own and the rest,
as they say, is merely history.

They made love two hundred and eighteen times before

he left her. She'd felt it coming before it did, and was not distraught. If the truth be told, Mary Faith had grown a tad weary of feeling as if the temple that housed her spirit had been turned into something more resembling an amusement park, and was—quite simply—sick to death of the man.

The night before he was due to leave they lay together on her canopied bed, he snoring, she staring at the ceiling. She took it all in, the warmth of him, the hairs just beginning to spread over his shoulders. He sighed and rolled over, murmuring in his foreign tongue. The sad, sour smell of them both left her wanting to weep, with a taste in her mouth like bad meat. If she had smoked, she might have lit a cigarette. Instead, she got up and went to his room, now adjoining her own.

His bags were already packed and standing by the door. She thought wildly that he might never have unpacked them, knowing with an eerie, post-orgasmic clarity just how quickly the space created by his leaving would close. And, not surprisingly, she found she wanted more substantial comfort than his memory alone might offer. The Stradivarius was packed in its woman-shaped case, leaning against the rest of his things. He'd told her over breakfast once that it had been a gift from his grandfather, a concert musician whose greatest compositions had been stolen by the Germans. Soundlessly, she took it out and held it to her like a child, never letting it go again until the violin was safely in her case in the music room and her own rested comfortably beside the maestro's bags.

When he opened the case again, prepared to entertain a company of riverboat passengers bound for Illinois, the maestro found a folded note tucked between the strings of Mary Faith's instrument.

"My love," it read. "Still waters run deep."

Four

Atlantis County, Texas.
July 15, the Present.

THE STRAITS had been in Texas for a hundred years, an accomplishment which, in that particular part of the world, more or less qualified them for the makings of a dynasty. The first of them were part of that vast migration of outlaws and bushwhackers who had headed for the Texas territory after the Civil War. Those pioneers assured themselves and each other that they were heading west for adventure and wealth and freedom. The truth was, most of them were going because they had nowhere else to go. Christian or criminal, Texas was the place to be in those days: It was close enough to imagine, big enough to get lost in, and most importantly, it was new enough for promises —most of the promises in the world having been exposed or shattered or forgotten in the war. Emigrants, though, are always the same. Whatever moves them to a new place, they bring with them some of the sadness that goes with losing the old. They pack up their secrets and sins along with the wagons, piling up their hearts and tying the burden down with ropes woven of resentment and ambition, cherishing each loss as a foundation for gain. On the lam or merely on the move, they arrived in the Texas wilderness encumbered with their histories, the hills of Georgia and Tennessee, the cotton fields, the battlefields, all chiseled in memory, carried along like tablets of stone.

Founded by a soldier who'd had to change his name just to get across the Mississippi, and a bayou wife he'd won in a card game, the original Straits promptly went about the business of getting properly settled down. Great-granddaddy worked, swindled, and stole enough land to get them quietly and powerfully rich, and his wife bore enough tight-fisted sons to keep them that way. Each of those lived long enough to see their children grown, and by the time Ray Ed Strait met his Maker that July, blood relations were spread over three counties and beyond. And if there was a quality of temperament right from the beginning that was a little at odds with such stability, it was the best-kept secret in Atlantis, and one that was never quite bred out. For before he'd come to Texas, that patriarch soldier had been a soldier for money, a hired assassin. He'd arrived with his wife and his secret and no need for its telling, for they all had mysteries in those days. None of his progeny ever knew and yet, somehow they all knew, for the thing that set the Straits apart from the rest, the thing that showed out of their eyes and made them shy from the bland Christian inquisitions of their neighbors, was a form of the same obloquy: In each beat a heart that remembered the calculated purity of violence. And it made them violent or afraid or ashamed

in turn. It drew them to women with secrets of their own
and so could be trusted. Their unions brought forth children who had an obsession with privacy that bordered on
the occult and a nameless guilt that drove them to sin for
proof of it. And yet it all spent itself innocently enough for
awhile, in drinking and cards and bastard children. Until,
of course, Ray's boy Charles T. went and started World
War II.

Charles T. could read the future, he told his children
later, and he'd known ahead of time that the only way he
was going to get out of East Texas and being a farmer was
if there was a war. He'd prayed, he told them, for one to
come along. When it did, it eased his burden of unformed
culpability by increasing it, for he had no choice but to feel
personally responsible. As far as he could remember,
World War II was the only prayer he'd ever had answered.
And so he went to fight with a lighter heart than he'd had
in his life. To get killed, of course, would have absolved
him completely, but destiny had other things in store. He
said for years after it was over that he'd been a fighter pilot
in France and looked death in the face a number of times,
but it was only to make himself feel better about having
gotten no further than doing paperwork on a base in Illinois. Along about then was when he met the mother of his
children on a blind date, but it was awhile before he knew
it, the business of the war having left him a little hesitant
to wish for anything. Besides, being responsible for a war
was one thing, being responsible for a woman was another.

It was nearly seven years before he got back around to
Gloria McSaxon, life being what it is. After the war, Charles
T. went to college and learned the art of submerging the
weight of his heritage in that of the rest of the world, while
Gloria, afflicted with a natural unconventionality and a
steamy reputation, began dunking her identity in the waters

of religion. She got his letter while making a retreat. It came just as she was in the midst of a novena to the patron saint of hopeless cases to send her a husband. So when she got up off her knees to look at the mail and the envelope from Texas had trembled in her hand like something alive, she just naturally took it as a sign that the saint had come through.

Their evolution was evident in the children. Grace had been conceived in passion, driven and yet afraid, sex that rode the fine edge of union and doubt. As a result, she grew to be a woman with her heart in one of two places—on her sleeve or in her mouth. And when unity was no longer a question, it had been replaced for a time by the closest the couple would ever come to friendship, mostly expressed in uneasy attempts at flattery and seduction. Davey was born wanting to seduce the world with no real idea of why. And Boo was the last, a product of the wordless understanding that had, finally, done away with the rest of it. On the night he was conceived, Charles T. had struggled back from the swamp of orgasmic resolution to find Gloria fully levitated, lying six inches off the sheets, and smiling a faraway smile.

"This one will be your salvation," she told him.

Charles T. hadn't known quite what to make of it at the time. He had only stared at the cascade of long, reddish hair that hung down to the pillow slip, wondering why it was that her hair had not risen along with the rest of her. For the rest of it he decided to reserve judgment. It was only recently that his wife had begun to be aware of her true vocation and, like a lot of her prophecies at that time, the truth of it was yet to be revealed. After she'd descended, Charles T. had swung his legs over the side of the bed and lit a Lucky Strike, knowing deep within himself that he'd finally lost her. But whether it was for better or worse, no one could be sure.

So, when she'd announced over breakfast a year later that a vision of Christ had impelled her to go to the Amazon in order to learn psychic surgery, she hadn't met with much of an argument. They weren't to worry, she told her little family, it was just that God had her in mind for better things. It never occurred to any of them to disbelieve her. The business of the prophecies and visions aside, the woman had a gift for saying aloud what others could only think about.

And it was his lost wife that dominated Charles T.'s thoughts as he staggered into the kitchen the morning after Ray Ed's funeral, possessed of a dim, pointless rage.

Five

That Same Morning . . .

GRACE AND IRIS LEE were already up, drinking coffee and staring into their respective spaces. He peered at them; whether or not they'd exchanged more than the usual courtesies at so early an hour was impossible to determine. He poured himself a cup of coffee and sat down.

"I feel like I have the old man of the sea astride my shoulders," he said.

Nobody said anything—the two appeared to have their minds fixed on other things. Charles T. took a deep breath and sipped gingerly, hoping against hope that Grace had made the coffee. His mammy's version could float an iron wedge.

Iris Lee got up and started wandering from thing to thing like some fretful old butterfly.

"How's everything this morning?" Charles T. was determined to be pleasant. Pleasantness, he figured, was underrated as a builder of character.

His mother scowled at him. "Fine," she said. "You ask. Maybe she'll tell you."

Charles T. raised his eyebrows. "Tell me what?"

Iris Lee started pulling things out of the Frigidaire. "Don't play ignorant with me, Charles T. Now that Ray Ed is gone you're supposed to be the head of this family."

Charles T. started a little. Until that moment, the thought had never occurred to him. Thoroughly intimidated, he decided to take it out on his daughter. "What aren't you telling your grandmother?" he demanded, fixing Grace with what he hoped was an expression of slit-eyed disapproval.

Grace stared at him. "Have you got something in your eye?"

"Just answer the question," he told her.

Grace stared morosely at the jar of fig preserves in the center of the table and allowed herself the momentary luxury of wondering what it would have been like to be an orphan.

Iris Lee held an egg up to the light to see if she could tell how old it was. "We were just sitting here, nice as you please, and all I did was ask about Larry. Right away she gets real evasive. If you ask me," Iris said, cracking the egg for emphasis, "something isn't right."

Grace toyed with a biscuit. "Mammy," she said patiently. "I was not being evasive. Not in the least bit. I said he was fine, didn't I?"

Iris Lee pursed her lips and narrowed her eyes. Between

her and Charles T., the place was starting to look like a Chinese summit conference.

"You had an evasive tone," Iris Lee said. "Don't you think I know evasive when I hear it?"

Choosing between the rock and the hard place, Grace gave up and looked at her father. "Larry is fine," she said again. "I guess."

Charles T. shrugged. It all sounded reasonable enough to him. "She says he's fine, Mammy. No reason to lie about someone being fine, is there?"

Iris Lee waved her spatula at them, flinging little bits of scrambled egg over the linoleum. Having burned the biscuits, she commenced burning the eggs. "When a person has gone and got herself a husband, a person should not have to guess how he is, a person ought to know for certain. Besides, if he's so fine, where is he? That's all I want to know. Why isn't he here with people who love him?"

On the day of her wedding, Iris Lee had told Larry in no uncertain terms that all Grace Ellen needed was a man with a firm hand and plenty of money. Larry, having neither, had been convinced the old woman was trying to run him off. Grace smiled. Well, she supposed, love was peculiar.

"I told you," she said aloud. "He's in New York. New York is where we live."

Iris Lee nodded. "You see? What kind of an answer is that? Talk to her, Charles T. She's your daughter."

Charles T. was wishing Davey would get up and join them so they could harass him instead. The problems of sons were generally more serious than those of daughters, but not so hard to address.

Grace caught his expression and tried not to betray herself. She'd found over the years that her family generally did better when guessing about her life than they ever had with the truth.

The fact was, of course, she had left him. Larry Egger was a fine, decent man who, up until a couple of weeks ago, thought the sun rose and set on Grace Ellen. But she just wasn't the kind who could live with a man who never gave her an argument; it grated on her nerves. So when the call had come from her father, telling her that Ray Ed was due to buy the cosmic farm, she'd just naturally taken it as a sign that her marriage was done. To give him the proper credit, Larry had taken the whole thing pretty well. But that, she figured later, was because he was in therapy and felt good about himself. Toward the end, there'd been no talking to the man. He'd done her the favor of explaining her feelings for her as she packed her suitcases, telling her that she was only disguising her fear of death by pretending she was sick of him. He'd told her she'd be back when she realized her mistake. She'd told him to fuck himself and take care of the Pekingese. Her lawyer would be in touch.

Charles T. leaned across the table. "So," he said. "You and Larry getting along?" He waited for her answer, proud of himself. It was as direct as he ever got.

Grace shot him an oblique look. He hated that look, she'd got it from her mother.

"Actually, we're getting divorced. I plan to file for a no-fault next week," she replied mildly.

Charles T. thought it over. In making himself be direct, he hadn't somehow counted on directness in return.

Iris Lee sighed wearily. "I knew it," she said to the floor. "I knew it from the moment you showed your face."

Nobody said anything.

"Will someone please tell me why none of you people can seem to stay married? Me and Ray Ed was married for sixty-one years."

Charles T. added it up in his mind. "Actually, Mammy," he corrected her. "It was only just sixty. Well, fifty-nine, actually. September would have been your anniversary."

"Thank you very much, Charles T. I'll be sure to call you if I ever need a calendar."

"Sorry."

"Anyway, that is not the point. The point is that this daughter of yours doesn't seem to know how to keep a husband."

Grace shrugged. "Some you keep, some you throw back."

Charles T. fidgeted a moment. "I'm sorry, Grace," he said, hoping he sounded sincere. Already the memory of his erstwhile son-in-law was fading so fast he couldn't for the life of him recall what the man looked like.

Iris Lee appeared as though she were about to spit. "Oh, fine. I suppose that's all there is to this, then?"

Charles T. shoveled some eggs onto a plate. "Now, Mammy," he said. "When you got married, the world was a different place."

"Different, my foot," she said dourly. "The only difference is, some people know what it means to make sacrifices and some people don't."

Grace was making a perfectly good biscuit into a pile of crumbs. "You live with Larry for a month or two," she said. "You'll know what sacrifice means."

"Larry Egger was a perfectly good husband," Iris Lee countered. "Had his faults, of course, but what man doesn't? Look at your father."

Charles T. turned red.

"As I recall," Grace replied. "He isn't married either."

Charles T. turned redder.

"In fact, almost no one in the entire family is married," Grace went on in her own defense. "Why pick on me? At least I tried. Look at Davey. He never got married."

Iris Lee's face softened for a moment. "Your brother is

younger than you, and has plenty of time," she said. "Besides, Davey is different."

"Really?" Grace had begun to ooze sarcasm like sap from a tree. "And just how is he exempt, may I ask?"

Iris Lee looked away. "He just hasn't found the right woman. A man like Davey needs to look around some before he can settle."

As if on cue, Davey picked that moment to enter the kitchen, rumpled, half asleep, and handsome even at that. Grace shook her head. Of all the other things she found unfair about being related to Davey, the fact that he could look so suspiciously handsome first thing in the morning was near the top of the list.

Iris Lee got up with as much alacrity as her seventy-nine-year-old knees would allow. "Can I get you some coffee, honey?" she asked him.

"Mammy was just telling us all how you haven't found the right woman yet," Grace told him.

Charles T.'s voice was patient. "Don't start with your brother, Grace."

"I used to be jealous of my brother Otie," Mammy put in an innocent tone. "He got all the looks in the family, too."

"He was the one who was blown up," Charles T. put in.

"He looked a lot like Davey," Mammy replied, gazing fondly at her grandson.

"Before or after?" Grace asked pleasantly.

Davey glowered at her. His hangover that morning was making it difficult to form words, as though sometime in the night his tongue had been replaced by some other organ entirely. "Fuck you."

Charles T. asserted himself. "There's no reason to go offending your grandmother's sensibilities with that kind of language," he said.

Iris Lee smiled at Davey. "Ray Ed used to curse first thing when he woke up, too," she told them. "I think I'll miss it."

Grace resigned herself. One thing about life with the family; it was unfalteringly consistent. "I believe I'll see to the garden," she said. The garden was Iris Lee's pride and joy. Grace figured with any luck at all she might arrange to trample something precious.

Iris Lee stared at her suspiciously. "You figure you forgot how to garden, living in the city?"

Grace smiled innocently. "No, ma'am," she said. Bitch.

"Well, all right then," the old woman said after a moment. "Just don't ruin anything. See if you can find Boo to help you. He's around someplace."

"I'll help her," said Charles T.

Boo was indeed around someplace. As the two headed into the garden music swelled up from somewhere beyond the pasture fence like a serenade.

Grace bent down over the tomatoes and her father, after making sure there was no one to hear him, sidled up beside her and spoke in a whisper, his voice choked with hope and apprehension.

"You haven't heard from your mother, have you, Grace?"

Grace looked at him. The death had hurt him worse than she thought. Whenever Charles T. started missing Gloria, it meant he was in a bad way. "Just a postcard last Christmas. From Peru," she answered carefully. Boo had stopped for a moment to retune the fiddle, dragging bow over strings in sounds like the echoes of damnation, so that the cattle in the fields twitched their ears.

Charles T. held up the globe of a tomato, staring at it as if it were a model of the earth. "What did it say?"

Grace straightened her back and passed a hand over her eyes. "Just a poem. Something about Athena."

"Anything else?"

"No."

Charles T. let the tomato fall. "I'm glad you're here, Grace. You're my oldest and, well—I'm just glad. Seeing your children all grown keeps reminding you that life goes on."

Grace tried to think of some way to respond and couldn't.

"It's just that I miss her sometimes. Your mother, I mean."

Grace squeezed her eyes shut and lied. "Me, too."

He swallowed hard. "Do you know what you're gonna do now? I mean, will you be leaving again, or what?"

She looked at him. "No," she answered. "As a matter of fact, I have no plans at all."

It pleased him, knowing that. "Then you'll stay? For awhile?"

Grace stared at the bean vines, thinking of her grandfather's dying breath. "Sure," she said. "For awhile."

Charles T. wet his lips. "There's the will, anyway," he said seriously, and dropped his voice to just above a whisper. "Dearest thinks Daddy might have left a lot of money."

"A will?" Grace stopped what she was doing and stared at him. "Why would he need a will? Doesn't Mammy get everything?"

Charles T. looked uneasy. "Well," he said, "Daddy always believed in security. And providing for his family. I think it's possible he may have left quite a little money. And maybe Mammy won't get it all. Not that she doesn't deserve it, of course."

"Well, when's she going to read it?" Grace hadn't considered the possibilities of inherited money before. She was starting to feel more cheerful than she had in days.

Charles T. coughed nervously. "I'm not sure. Daddy only just died, you know."

Grace blushed a little. "Sorry," she said.

"But money is money. And since you and Larry—" He broke off in midsentence as the slam of the screen door brought them back to the tasks at hand. Iris Lee came out to the yard and squinted at their progress from beneath the brim of a battered straw hat, tied under her chin with fabric so sun-bleached it had lost all trace of its original color, like the skin of the terminally ill.

"You doin' all right?" she called to them.

"Fine," Grace answered, still thinking about Ray Ed and his money. It was just possible that her time at home wouldn't prove so thankless, after all.

Mammy nodded briefly and raised her head to stare out over the land, cultivated in strips that shimmered like colored ribbons in the heat. Boo started up again, trying to find his way to another song. "I'm trying to think. Fiddles," she said. "Boy ought to learn something useful."

She turned to stare at Grace as though she might know the secret, then remembered herself. "You haven't been to the corn," she said.

"I didn't think it was ready," Grace told her.

"You got to check the ears."

"Yes ma'am."

"Charles T.?" The old woman's voice rose querulously. "Yeah?"

"I want you to drive me to the cemetery. I want to look at the flowers some more."

"Okay." He walked out of the garden slowly, like somebody hearing the call of heaven. Grace watched them until they had disappeared down the road, then bent back to her task, picking up the rhythm of Boo's new arrangement. Money, she thought.

Sweat ran from her forehead and into her eyes; the muscles in her back pounded protest. Her manicured hands grew raw with harvesting. Then, without thinking, she began to sing.

"Satin on my shoulders and a smile on my lips. How lucky can you get?"

Six

IF MARY FAITH BEAUDINE ever regretted her small
revenge on the maestro, it didn't show. In fact, it rather
improved her playing.

When he had been a full week gone and Mary Faith
reasonably assured that he would not return, she removed
herself from the breakfast table and proceeded to the music
room, where she planned to allow herself the luxury of a
more detailed examination of her treasure. After taking it
from its case, she chose not to play it immediately, but
brought it to the window, where she might have a better
look. Whatever the maestro's other personal habits, the
violin had been lovingly kept, and the surface of it shone

in her hands like so much moonlight. Quietly, almost without breathing, she ran her strong fingers over the bridge and neck, around each of the tuning pegs and back down. She closed her eyes and the maestro's face swam up momentarily and was gone. The violin was hers now. Then the bow was in her hands. She ran it experimentally across the strings, and it shuddered like something alive. In love or not, she had gleaned more than a little from her teacher's haphazard instruction, and began to play a piece from memory.

Dovie Celeste was forty-three years old, and the head of Miss Beaudine's rather modest housekeeping staff. She was in the dining room when the music began, listlessly changing the tablecloths for lunch. The sound stopped her dead in her tracks, her normally beautiful and immobile face contorting with something very close to pain. She stood there helplessly listening, wringing the damask in her hands and lifting it to heaven.

"Sweet suffering Jesus," she whispered. "Why'd you hafta bring him back?" The poor woman had yet to recover from the last of the maestro's attentions—a bit of playacting that had entailed threatening her with horsewhips and watching while she smeared her ample body with lard and preserves, as though she were a ham.

Silently, she crept to the door of the music room and listened there for some hint of voices to confirm her fears. But there was only the music filtering out into the morning, sweet as syrup and sad as tears. That white man was crazy, she thought, dabbing her eyes with a corner of her apron, but he sure could play. For a moment she almost understood her mistress's weakness for him.

Mary Faith ended the piece and went to the door, the Stradivarius still in hand. Dovie barely had time to straighten her back before the door was thrown open. Her mistress stood before her, eyes shining and homely, arrogant face flushed with triumph.

Dovie gulped and made an effort to sound casual. "I—I, uhhh," she stammered, trying to read the new expression in her mistress's eyes. "I heard the music and thought that teacher might have come—" She waited breathlessly, knowing the impertinence of her remarks and what it might cost her should Miss Beaudine decide to take offense. When she dared to raise her face again, she was astonished to find Mary Faith smiling, more to herself than her servant. Their eyes met—her own wet and black as olives, her mistress's shining with pale fire. And for one instant they understood each other wholly, without question. Dovie struggled for some remark.

"Uh, that was real pretty playing, Miss Mary," she said, nodding and moving aside to let her pass. "Real nice."

Mary Faith gave her a long, even look, her eyes still showing that strange light. She took up her golden pencil and began to write on the tablet that hung around her neck, handing Dovie the paper when she had finished. Dovie took it and squinted with concentration. She could read, but she had to go slow.

"Dovie," it said, "have you watered the ferns?"

Seven

*Atlantis Township. July 30
and Times Previous.*

ERNEST EARL FAXTON, director of the town's only mortuary, formally advertised as Faxton's Funeral Emporium, and informally referred to by potential clients as Ernest Earl's, sat silently at his desk, going over the month's accounting. Feature for feature, he was a handsome man (for an undertaker) who kept his dark suits and formal bearing even when there was no one to look at him. At seventy-nine, his shoulders were yet square, and the line of his jaw only a little fallen from what it had been. And if the soul that stared so long out of those deep-set eyes had been made of anything other than what it was, Ernest Earl might have been a popular man. As it was, he was content to be necessary.

He had inherited the business from his father after spending twenty months in one of the more notorious branches of the Texas State Penitentiary for refusing to participate in the patriotic madness that made up the First World War. Though he never fully recovered from his time in prison, most of his youthful energy having been used up in abuse and disillusion, the man who had returned to his father was smarter about the workings of the world than the boy who'd gone in. Though to give credit where credit is due, Ernest Earl was no slouch to start with. Had not the taint of pacifism clouded his prospects, young Ernest might have made the state legislature. God knows his father was owed enough favors. Old man Faxton had served his community twice over, both as coroner and mortician, and had possessed the good sense to falsify an official document here and there with regard to the circumstances surrounding the demise of a number of powerful corpses—particularly when the truth might have proved embarrassing.

Other than his talent for petty corruption, the elder Faxton had one other notable trait. When it came to his chosen vocation, the man was an artist of the highest order. He could fashion serenity in the faces of his dead where none had existed in life, restore beauty and even innocence where it had been obliterated by decades of bad luck and envy. But if he was an artist, he was also an idealist, and a bit temperamental to boot. More than once had the young Earl been sent to soothe the ruffled feelings of mourners who could not recognize their waxy-faced loved ones disguised under the elaborate benefits of false teeth and store-bought hair.

As Earl came into the business then, he learned to temper art with realism, and though no less of a master mortician than his father, his work was generally thought to be more predictable. But then, Ernest's quirks took another turning.

He built his business as his neighbors built the town, growing along with the community until his reputation for fine, reasonably priced undertaking had spread throughout the county. He relied on word-of-mouth for advertisement, shunning the advances of television and radio, and for this delicacy was known to lay out entire generations of one family after another. His was, after all, the only game in town.

But tonight he could not concentrate, caught up as he was in the weary treacheries of memory. Ray Strait's itemized invoice lay like a summons under the lamp. He had known the Straits for sixty years, burying their dead and nodding to their survivors in the street. But this particular demise unsettled him greatly.

The towering clock that dominated the Emporium's lobby ticked away unrelentingly; Ernest checked his watch. It was nearly nine. He got up and paced the office, wondering at himself. He hadn't felt this bad when he laid out his own father. However used he was to death, it seemed he was something of a stranger to grief. In his nonprofessional life he thought of himself as providing no more than a comforting show for the bereaved; all the religion that went along with it was just so much custom in Ernest Earl's view of the world. Sending for a minister was like sending for a florist; the comforts of each were equally transitory. He recalled the brandy, locked in a cabinet in the corner, supposedly kept to fortify his more hysterical clients. He poured himself a shot, tossed it back, and took another. It was the funeral, was all, he thought. He'd seen her again at the funeral, looking beautiful as a memory, never once giving any notice to the man who wore his unrequited passion for her like a cross on his back. She'd never seen him watching her from the lawn, his heart in his eyes. He thought he'd seen her nodding once, with the brief, vaguely grateful smile reserved for men of Ernest's profession, but there had been no feeling in it, any more than when he'd buried her own husbands. He'd never mean anything to a woman like that—except perhaps when he laid her to rest.

As he stared once again at Ray Ed's invoice he felt betrayed from all directions, as though someone had been telling his secrets in the street. He was old and the cross of unrequited love was too heavy for an old man. He poured another brandy and managed a halfhearted smile, thinking of the locked chifferobe upstairs. There was one thing he'd kept from everyone. Right from the beginning.

In their salad days, Iris Lee and Baby Sheba Quade were considered among the prettiest girls around, despite Iris Lee's later contention that her brother was the one who got all the looks in the family. By the time she was eighteen, Iris Lee had turned down three genuine proposals of marriage, enraging her father and driving her mother to the comforts of an occasional belt of paregoric for some imagined injuries. But Iris Lee, catching a whiff of the liberation that was to come with short skirts and bobbed hair, cherished a belief that perhaps she was meant for better things than spending the rest of her days breaking her back and spirit on some worn-out farm. She was not entirely wrong, but her timing was lousy, for with the advent of the Great War, most of her prospects for life in another place were quite efficiently shot into oblivion.

She knew Ray Strait on sight, but his presence on the planet did nothing much in the way of lighting her fires until it began to be apparent to the young ladies of the neighborhood that he was one of the only whole and unmarried men left in those parts. She considered him thoroughly; he was shorter than she and already losing his hair. But while it is true that the Straits were a taciturn lot by nature, they were by no means impervious to the charms of a pretty face, and with his brothers gone to the war, Ray was thoroughly lonesome. Less than two months after the practical Iris Lee set her sights on him, the two were married. It was some time before they fell in love.

Ernest Earl had first encountered the Quade girls when their father died two weeks after Iris Lee's wedding. He remembered that encounter for two reasons: the first being that that morning in June was the day he fell for a woman he would never get over, and the second being that Ezra Quade, the patriarch, had apparently departed this world as a direct result of spontaneous combustion.

Baby Sheba, then seventeen, found her daddy by the chickens. She'd been attracted by a smell of burning that wafted in the kitchen window and, thinking the chicken house had somehow caught fire in the heat, came out to investigate. By the time she got there, there was nothing left but a heap of overalls and a charred pair of boots. She stared at the smoking mess without comprehension. It was fully fifteen minutes before she went into the house to call her sister, deciding not to wake her mother from her belladonna dreams for the moment. Iris Lee would be able to figure it out, she was sure. Iris Lee was good at that sort of thing.

The sheriff stopped by the Funeral Emporium on his way to the Quade place. He opened the back door that led to the workroom a little gingerly and called out.

"Hey Faxton! Got one for you over to the Quades'!"

There was no immediate response, and the sheriff pushed the door open a little further with the toe of his boot, convinced that he heard voices coming from the back. He was not superstitious, but it didn't pay to go courting bad dreams, either. "Hey, Faxton, you there?" He peeked around the edge of the door cautiously. Someone's foot was just visible from beneath the edge of a sheet. The sheriff put his hand to the butt of his pistol by reflex. Ernest Earl came from an adjoining room, wiping his hands on a towel. His normally grave brown eyes were alive with amusement. "No need for that, Sheriff," he said evenly, "They ain't goin' to hurt nobody."

The sheriff made a huge effort to look fierce and succeeded pretty well. "Where's your daddy, boy?" he said, lowering his voice ominously. He had no use for old man Faxton's convict son and his sissy-livered politics. Somebody who'd refuse to go to war would do anything, and the sheriff felt it his bound duty to make sure he didn't.

Ernest Earl, for his part, made an equal effort to look bland. One thing about being in prison, you learned not to mess with the Man. "They got the influenza in Smyrna," he replied, focusing his eyes somewhere on the sheriff's forehead. It was true, too. Since early that spring, folks had been dropping like hogs with the cholera. "Daddy went to help. Is there something I can do?" He paused to let the sheriff make his decision.

The sheriff cleared his throat. "Nobody else here?"

Ernest shifted his eyes. "No."

"I thought I heared. . . . Never mind. Your old man learning you the business?"

"Yessir."

The sheriff chewed the inside of his cheek. He may as well have the boy bring the wagon. Couldn't leave folks lying out in the heat. . . . "All right," he barked, "come on."

When they reached the Quades', Ernest Earl was the only one who ventured a theory on Ezra's demise. The sheriff sent the women into the house while Ernest thoughtfully explored the ashes with the toe of his boot. After some minutes, he stooped and picked a small object out of the ruin of charred bone and dust. It was the old man's wedding ring. He clutched it in his hand, then lifted his face to the sun. When he lowered it again, he met the sheriff's piggy eyes straight on. "Spontaneous combustion."

"Talk straight, boy," the sheriff answered him, fingering the butt of his pistol.

"I am talking straight, Sheriff. I read about it in Ripley's when—I read about it," he said. "The internal temperature of the body goes up and they just—just burn up."

The sheriff pushed his hat back off his forehead. For the first time in his fifty years, he was starting to sense that there were things in the world he knew nothing about. He examined the boy's face for some sign of deception, and couldn't find any. "No shit?" he said at last.

"No shit," Ernest answered.

The sheriff hunkered down for a better look at Ezra's remains. "Why ain't his clothes burnt?"

Earl stuffed his hands in his pockets. "It happens real fast, like a sort of explosion."

"Well, good God." He was genuinely awed.

Ernest squinted down at him. "You gonna tell 'em?" he asked, gesturing toward the house.

The other man stood up, shaking his head. "You're the expert." As Ernest Earl started toward the house, he stopped him with a beefy hand. "Hey," he said and broke off.

Ernest turned around. "What?"

The sheriff gestured toward the heap of empty overalls at his feet. "This kind of thing happen a lot?"

Ernest didn't smile. "No," he answered. "It's very rare."

"You be nice to them ladies, you hear?"

Ernest looked in the direction of the house, wondering what he was going to say. "Yessir."

He was utterly unprepared for the force of Baby Sheba's

charms. Iris Lee answered his knock, while Baby sat perched on the edge of the kitchen table, quietly weeping into a corner of her apron. At his first sight of her fragile, newly waved blond head, bent to expose a portion of her neck, the tether that held poor Ernest's heart snapped so completely that he was afraid for a moment it might have been audible.

He cleared his throat and nodded to Iris Lee and the widow, roused from her bed for the emergency. He made his explanation and offered his sympathies as best he could. With the initial shock already subsiding, Baby began to howl in consternation. She raised her wet blue eyes in appeal. Ernest Earl felt his veins filling with hot syrup.

"If people find out about this, I'll never get married!" she cried, and the spoken horror of it set her off on a fresh bout of weeping.

Iris Lee sniffed, rife with newlywed superiority. "Pay no attention to Baby," she told him. "She was born jealous."

Try as he would, Ernest Earl could not tear his eyes from Baby's face. For one wild moment, he thought he was going to propose right then and there. "Uhh—" was all that came out.

Miz Quade was trying to decide if she was dreaming this. Her miraculous release from thirty years of wedlock was almost more than she could comprehend. It made her feel a little like praying. But the sharp voices of her children interrupted her reverie. "Girls," she intervened.

"Well, it's true!" Baby cried. "If anybody finds out my daddy was a human torch, I'll never find anybody to marry me. I'll have to live with Mama the rest of my life!" She began to pace the room, wringing her hands. The rest of them watched her in silence.

Mrs. Quade spoke again, suddenly alert to the gravity of the situation. "You know, she has a point."

Iris Lee stood up all at once, like she itched someplace. "Oh my God!" she nearly shouted. This entire affair made her feel like spitting on the floor.

Ernest Earl felt as though he ought to say something—anything. But thoughts were flying through his brain so fast he couldn't get hold of one long enough to make it into words. He picked up his hat as if to leave, when all at once, he froze in his tracks. It was as though his mouth had been borrowed by a spirit. The solution presented itself with such unexpected clarity, it made him wonder later if he might not have a mystical tendency.

"I'll say it was a heart attack," he told them in a strong, clear voice. "And that he was cremated—at your request, of course."

The three women gaped at him, and Baby ran to throw her arms around his neck. "Would you?" she said. "Oh, would you really?" The shock of her so close sent him reeling—he could only collect little snatches of what he sensed about her for remembering. She smelled of oranges mostly, a little of sweat. The skin of her scalp was pinkish. He could feel the bones of her spine through her dress. All at once his hand fell away from her and he took a number of steps backward, horrified at himself. He had begun to weep. A shiver swept through him and he turned away. "If you have something to put him in—" he said.

Iris Lee was the first to answer. "Just a minute," she told him. "I'll get a shoebox."

As the wagon drove away, Baby stood at the screen door, wrinkling her pretty forehead. "Iris Lee," she said idly. "Do you s'pose that boy is all right?"

And yet he had never spoken for her. Instead he chose to live with passion throbbing in his chest like an open wound, relentlessly picking at the scabs of memory and longing when it threatened to heal. He allowed the years to pass in bitter silence, convincing himself that the stingy fear that ate up his soul was merely good sense; she probably wouldn't have him, anyway. He was a convict, after all, and dealt with the dead. Prison didn't end just because there weren't any bars on his windows, and no wife would want the stink of formaldehyde coming to her bed. And so, over the years, his hopelessness became a kind of comfort of its own. He had watched with secret contentment as her tiny figure spread and the bright blond hair darkened to a kind of rat-color with the years. He clipped the announcements of her marriages from the newspapers and laid out each of her husband's corpses as though they were his own. These days he drove past her house sometimes and parked his car down the street, watching as she came and went, the burden of his obsession growing by the days, until, without being able to say what it was, a means to his heart's desire took shape in his mind. She would be his before long.

Ray's invoice lay before him and the sight of it shot a little pain through his guts. Ernest Earl reached in his vest pocket and felt the shape of the key, hard and comforting against his heart. Ernest Earl rubbed his forehead, fear crawled up his spine like a trail of ants, and a rotten little giggle rose in his throat. He totaled the bill, put it in an envelope, and dropped it in the mailbox on his way home.

Eight

Atlantis County. August 1.

H E SUPPOSED if he'd had his druthers, Davey
Strait would have been long gone. But the truth of it was,
he'd arrived in Atlantis County a man on the run and his
conscience at his heels. Yet, after two weeks on Mammy's
fold-out sofa with regular meals under his belt, his reasons
for coming were seeming less important and reasons for
moving on less important still. As any outlaw will tell you,
men on the run have a limited momentum; once they get
safely away from a threat, it may take them awhile to get
going again.

In Davey's particular case, the threat in question was a
waitress named Carlene Dinkins. Back in Arkansas, Carlene
had taken a shine to him one evening when he sang his solo

with the band, and had been shining ever since. She'd
moved him into her apartment above the restaurant early
the previous spring and for awhile at least, Davey had believed himself in love with her. Carlene was quiet and ran
to the blonde, she was good with money, and before he had
known what hit him, had got herself so firmly entrenched
that he found her all but indispensable. And she was almost
as pretty as he was.

But it hadn't taken Davey long to get suspicious of his
contentment. The time when love begins to pale and the
road starts to look good again came and went, but things
between him and the waitress stayed the same. He watched
her for the sidelong looks and listened for the wistful sighs
that are the natural by-product of love with no plan at-
tached, but the looks and sighs never came. It got to be
downright weird. He developed some lines in his flawless
forehead and talked to himself when she wasn't around.
When the passion was right, he figured she was trying to
trap him, and on those rare enough evenings when it went
sour, he figured she was taking it someplace else. He'd
never pretended that things were forever, and in the end
had been forced to prove himself right. For shortly before
he turned up at the farm, Davey had at last begun to glean
that there was more than the light of romance making up
those stars in Carlene's eyes. The fact was, the girl had a
sense of her own destiny, a quality that, up until then,
Davey had never encountered in anyone.

The girl knew what she wanted, and Davey was it.

She had given him no pressure, but that, he assured
himself in retrospect, had all been part of her game. Like
her carelessness with his emotions, the way she laughed.
Such confidence, he'd figured, had to be some kind of lie.
But he'd finally seen through her whole, treacherous
scheme of things and the vision had shaken him more than

he liked to admit. For the truth was that in the brief interval between her first shy, appraising glance and her first sweet, noisy climax, Carlene Dinkins had decided she belonged to him. And there wasn't jack shit he could do about it, either. Because when it came to loving, Carlene was made from that rarest of recipes: she had just enough faith to believe that he would come around, just enough brains to make it easy, and just enough heart to see it through. There was nothing left for him to do but run.

So it was the need to prove his instincts that had shaken Davey out of her bed at three in the morning, packed up his clothes, and dogged him all the way from Arkansas to his grandmother's door, doubting himself with every mile. For in the end, Carlene had denied him any confirmation of his need to get free of her. In the end, Carlene had never said a word.

By the time he'd been back at the farm two weeks, though, his terrors of commitment had subsided a little and Davey was feeling himself again, except, of course, for not having anywhere else to go. Carlene may have sent him running home, but he began to think something else was keeping him there, something that tugged at the edges of his mind, made him anticipate days in a way that was new to him. It was more than the prospect of inherited money —romantic as he was, even Davey couldn't believe the old man had much stashed aside—and more even than the perennial comforts of home. No, something important was going to happen—all a man had to do was wait till it showed.

His car keys jingled as he pulled them from his pocket and all but crept out to the car, careful not to run into anyone. He'd found, in the past few days, that midmorning was generally the best time to head out. Hang around too long in the daytime and likely as not, someone would start giving out chores. Davey didn't think much of chores. It seemed to him like most of the work done around the farm was invented just to keep people out of each other's hair. And he didn't figure he needed to work to do that. Not as long as he had wheels, anyway.

He was just turning the ignition key when Boo came up and laid himself down in the driveway, effectively blocking Davey's escape route. Davey leaned his head against the steering wheel and closed his eyes. The kid was part bloodhound and part magician. No matter how carefully he planned, Davey couldn't get away without first getting past his brother Boo, and most of the time he wound up bringing him along. Wearily, Davey switched off the ignition and got out, coming around the front of the car to view Boo's current protest from a more direct angle.

"Get up," he said darkly.

But Boo only rolled his head from side to side and stayed exactly where he was, looking like a large fallen angel.

"You hear me? I said get up! I got to go to town." Just as he had on a number of mornings in the recent past, Davey leaned over and attempted to drag Boo from under the arms, but as was also the usual case, he gave up after a couple of tries. Boo had three inches and twenty pounds on his big brother and the uncanny ability to all but turn his body to stone whenever the mood struck him. Panting, furious, and utterly disgusted, Davey glared down at his brother.

Feeling the look, Boo opened one shiny, startlingly green eye, and Davey felt a rise of familiar frustration. Never, in his entire experience with his brother, had Davey been able to convince himself that the boy was witless. Perverse as hell, and spoiled to death, but not stupid. Not in the way people thought, anyhow. Davey sighed. He might as well give in right now. It would save time. So he swung back into the driver's seat and inched the car forward until he saw the top of Boo's white-blond hair appear above the grill.

Boo got up on his knees and propped his fiddle on the hood, looking at Davey through the front window and grinning like the fool he was. "Boo?" he said.

Davey glowered at him. "Well," he said after a minute. "You comin' or not?"

Charles T. was down by the mailbox and waved a little as the two sped past him and disappeared over a rise in the road. He smiled to himself. It was downright touching the way those boys of his got along. Davey practically hadn't let Boo out of his sight the whole time he'd been home. Smiling still, the doting father went for the mail.

Coincidence is a chameleon; it changes color once observed. Ernest Earl's bill was on the top of the pile, the postcard from Gloria McSaxon was on the bottom. Thankfully, it took Charles T. a minute to get to that, though— he was too absorbed in the black, scrolly return address of the Funeral Emporium. It took him a minute to recall that someone was dead. He toyed with the idea of opening the envelope, thinking it might be interesting to know in dollars and cents what death cost its survivors, but decided to leave it for his mammy instead. It had never paid to assume too much in the way of filial responsibility around the woman, anyway; she tended to take advantage.

But when he finally saw the postcard, it shook him to the marrow, the scratchy, penciled verse swimming eerily in his vision until the lines formed words and the words a message. He read it twice and stashed it in a pocket like a dirty photograph, with love and rage and guilt surrounding his intelligence like a circle of sharks. He ambled dreamily back to the house and into the kitchen, savoring his own trepidation. He presented the remaining mail to Mammy without comment and lit a cigarette. His mother noted the return address of the Funeral Emporium with her mouth set in a line.

"Already?" she asked him. "I don't know, it don't seem hardly decent."

"It's the first of the month," Charles T. said gently.

For a moment, she looked at him as though she couldn't quite place him, then shook her head and stabbed at the bill with her letter opener. "I declare, time goes by so fast you don't know if you're young or old."

Charles T. shrugged and gestured with his head toward the back porch, where Grace was addressing thank-you notes and cursing to herself. "You don't have to tell me," he answered.

Mammy studied the invoice skeptically. It wasn't as bad as she'd feared. Despite the fact that she'd known Ernest Earl Faxton for sixty years, she'd always found him too deserving of people's trust to ever be worthy of hers. Look at the way he'd made up that lie about her daddy. Easy as anything. Nevertheless, she made a mental note to put it all on MasterCard. That accomplished, she got back around to the business at hand. "You finished with those?" she called to the porch. For a reason none of them could really account for, the old woman had taken to shouting at her grand-daughter whenever they spoke, as though she might some-how make up in volume what she lacked in sentiment.

It was a moment before Grace could rouse herself to answer. "Soon," she called back, straining to put some conviction into it.

"That's good," Mammy said. "I was thinking about mak-ing us all some lunch."

"Oh," came the response. "That's nice."

As if she had just told a lie and had to make it look good, Iris Lee immediately went to the stove and started making a racket with some pans. A few moments later, she came into Grace's line of vision through the screen, her head appearing from behind the open door of the refrigerator. "Got to keep on," she yelled cheerfully.

"Yes, ma'am," Grace nodded firmly. "Got to do that."

"Have you seen your brothers?"

Grace told her no, which was practically true. In fact, she had seen Davey trying to run Boo down in the driveway a little while ago, but they'd been doing that quite a bit of late, so she figured it was nothing to worry about.

"They're in town," Charles T. told her.

Iris Lee look distracted. "Again? What do they find to do there?"

Grace gathered up the thank-yous and stepped inside. "Beats me," she said. Having been to Atlantis, she found she preferred the farm.

During lunch, Charles T., with the postcard still burning a hole in his head, tried to radiate to Grace some sense of the news in vain telepathy. Failing that subterfuge, he followed her out to the porch as soon as the dishes were cleared.

"I have something to show you," he began and glanced around furtively toward the kitchen. Mammy had begun the dishes and was humming hymns to herself in an old-lady soprano, steam rising around her like a protection. He groped in his pocket for the postcard and put a finger to his lips as he handed it to his daughter. He was a little disappointed that she wasn't more surprised to see it, but that was Grace for you. She could hide her feelings so well it made him wonder if she knew them herself.

She read it once and turned it over.

Unable to contain himself, her father bent over and whispered, "What do you think?"

Grace stared up at him with a bland expression. "Well, it's her," she said. "Nobody else could be that cryptic."

Charles T. read it under his breath:

> *"Destruction comes like a serpent gleaming*
> *Tighten the circle against the wind*
> *The weeping song of ages past*
> *Brings forth the remembering."*

Grace shrugged and tried to smile. "Don't look so worried," she said. "You know Gloria, she's the only one who really knows what she's talking about."

Charles T. wet his lips and made himself ask the question. "Do you think it means she might—well—come back?"

Grace refused to look at him. The man had a real blind spot when it came to the mother of his kids, a quality that alternately struck his daughter as incurably romantic or thoroughly irritating, depending on her frame of mind. At the moment, irritated was definitely tipping the scales. "No," Grace answered carefully. "I don't think so."

Charles T. picked up the postcard and waved it around as if to let loose its secrets. "But what does it mean?"

Grace sighed in frustration. Blind armadillos and all, she was running out of patience with the cryptic. It wasn't like it was the first time she and her father had had this conversation. Gloria's postcards arrived without rhyme or reason, marked with the stamps of any number of countries. It seemed to Grace, a veteran of such events, that the messages, though different, had a curious sameness to them. "This is your mother, having a wonderful time. Keep safe. I love you."

Quite unexpectedly, a mirror-clear vision of Gloria McSaxon swam up in her daughter's mind. "Well, anyway," Grace said, resuming her addressing, "her poetry's as bad as ever."

Charles T. laughed. "Well, your mother's poetic style always was sort of—umm—derivative." The smile faded to a kind of depressed wonder. "I'm smarter than I used to be, Grace. Your mother is a very gifted person. Special, even."

Grace stared at him. Destiny may not be a blind armadillo, but love sure was. "Daddy," she said, quite kindly, "she left you twenty years ago. Get over it."

Charles T. sighed and returned the card to his pocket. He worried about Grace sometimes. He found her keen sense of the obvious a little lacking in romance.

They sat for a time without speaking. Mammy continued with the dishes unaware of the silent disagreement that continued on the porch, absorbed in a pan crusted with something that resisted her sponge. When the car pulled up in the drive behind the house, no one acknowledged the sound. It seemed to be coming from too great a distance ever to be meant for them.

Maejean waved at them from behind the wheel. The sight of Charles T. changed her smile from friendly to dazzling. She switched off the ignition, availed herself of a fast hit of Binaca, and propelled herself to the porch. It was Mammy she spoke to first as she let herself in. "I can do that for you, Iris Lee," she said, and immediately snatched a spare apron from a hook on the door.

"Oh, Maejean, for heaven's sake. Put that away," Mammy said without turning around. "If you'd walked in the door ten minutes ago, I'd have let you, but you didn't." She finished rinsing the dishpan.

Maejean halted in the middle of the floor, too tall for her skin. Grace and Charles T. followed her in.

"Hi," she said cheerfully. Though her life's dearest wish

involved the man with the mustache standing to her left, flirting with a man in the presence of other women was a trick she'd never quite mastered. She looked at him, then looked away again, her heart hammering in her chest.

Grace came to her rescue. "Is that the paper?" she asked. Not that she expected to be told otherwise, she just felt an impulse to fill the gap in conversation. In truth, after the conversation about Gloria, Maejean was looking like the answer to a prayer; she was so—so—normal. Grace liked that in a person.

Maejean cleared her throat and blushed. "I thought your daddy might like to read it. And you, of course. And Iris Lee. I mean—everybody."

Charles T. took the paper from her trembling hand, smiling a smile that would last her a week.

Unable to look on him for long without wanting to put her hands on him someplace, Maejean moved away uneasily and turned her attention to the women. She put her hands on her hips and stuck out her rather bony chest for Grace's benefit. "Like my T-shirt?"

Grace had sent her a shirt last Christmas, adorned with a comic-book woman weeping on the front. The thought cloud above her head read, NUCLEAR WAR?! THERE GOES MY CAREER . . .

Maejean winked. "They adore it at the Safeway," she said. "We want to adopt it as the store uniform." Maejean was assistant manager there six days a week. "But Mr. Davis is afraid of Russians and said as long as he was running the place I couldn't wear it to work anymore, so I won't. I just kept my mouth shut about it and stole a six-pack at the end of my shift. He can't say anything about that. He makes off with half the inventory as it is, and he knows I know about it."

Charles T. took advantage of the momentary lull to get a word in edgewise. "Thanks for the paper," he said.

Maejean ducked her head like a girl half her age. "You're welcome," she said.

At the other end of the table Iris Lee rolled her eyes.

"There isn't nothin' in it really. The only thing that caught my attention at all was about that woman who brought roses to Valentino died. Let me see, Charles T."

Charles T. nodded and Maejean grabbed the paper and paged through until she found it. " 'Died. Ditra Flame, seventy-eight, one-time violinist and missionary who was known as the Lady in Black for her mournful visitations to the tomb of silent screen star Rudolf Valentino. Flame never tired of recounting that when she was deathly ill at age fourteen she was visited by family friend Valentino, who assured her she would survive and asked her to visit his grave if he should die, saying, "I fear loneliness more than anything in the world." After his fatal appendicitis at age thirty-one in 1926 Flame brought thirteen roses to his grave every day for three years and a single red rose on each anniversary of his death.' It goes on to say that when they went into her house, it had all kinds of pictures of him and some of his clothes and things like that. Like a sorta shrine." Maejean wrinkled her forehead. " 'A one-time violinist and a missionary,' " she said and paused. "And she still made it to his tomb all those years. Makes me feel like all I do is waste time." She shook her head and folded up the page.

"Sounds like a waste of roses to me." Iris Lee announced. "He never did anything for me, and I went to the pictures like everybody else."

Maejean assumed a bland expression and swiveled her neck in Mammy's direction. "Speakin' of clothes, I came to ask you what are you goin' to do with Ray's? Do you want to sell 'em? I can box 'em up for you, if you want. The Annual Resurrection Baptist Rummage and General Flea is coming up, they give you ten percent of everything that sells."

Mammy considered it with an unreadable expression in her eyes. "Seems like if I saw somebody walking around in his clothes, I wouldn't want to know them."

Charles T. cleared his throat uncomfortably. "Well, it is ten percent, Mammy."

"In case you haven't heard," she said carefully. "I am very well provided for."

"Uhmm. You know, I've meaning to ask you about that, Mammy. The will, I mean. You gonna read it soon? I mean not for me—but Grace. . . ." He broke off. Everyone was staring at him, particularly Grace, who looked ready to skin him alive.

Charles T. cleared his throat and started over. "Well, not just Grace. Everybody. I mean, if Daddy left them anything, they'll be wanting to know."

"It's true, Mammy," Maejean put in. "Half the town's got their heads together over how much money Ray Ed left you. I heard Clara Cannon and Maivis Johnson in the checkout line the other day, and Clara seems to think he had a million dollars."

Iris Lee started. "Well, good Lord. If he did, I sure as hell want to know where he got it."

"Do you know exactly how much he left you?" Grace wanted to know.

"I do not," Iris Lee said. "He left it all in his safe deposit box, and I didn't think it right to go traipsing down to the bank before the man was cold in the ground. It wouldn't look right."

Charles T. shifted nervously in his chair. "But it's been two weeks! Nearly. Couldn't we just go take a look?"

"When I get ready," Iris Lee said, "and not before. This is a will we're talking about anyway, not a state lottery."

Defeated, Charles T. lowered his head like a child and pretended to read the paper.

Mammy smiled a little. It was always nice to know she was still in control of things. Besides, she still had to come up with some way to replace that missing cruise deposit money, in case any of the rest of the family got too curious about the thousand dollars missing from Ray Ed's savings account. Not that she owed them an explanation, really. She just felt things ought to be in order before they got passed out.

She continued, though, to think aloud on the subject of the church sale. "I don't think Ray Ed would have approved of my just giving his clothes away," she reflected. "On the other hand, I wouldn't want folks to think I didn't have any charity."

Grace decided to put in her two cents. "Give them away to the sale and don't take the money."

Maejean supported her from out in the yard. Unable to sit still for long, she'd gone for her six-pack in the back of the car. "Hey, that's a good idea!" She stuck her head in the window and nodded approvingly.

Mammy pursed her lips. "That woman has ears like a bat," she said softly.

"I do not." Maejean said from behind her, making Mammy jump. She swept into the room with the beer. "Anybody else?" She lifted the pack in the air. Grace went for one, and so did Mammy, since Maejean had finally gotten around to asking. She sipped reflectively and devoted herself to the subject at hand.

"On the other hand," she began.

"You got three hands already, Mammy," protested Maejean.

Iris Lee silenced her with a look. "I can have as many hands as I please. They're my clothes, aren't they?"

Nobody said anything.

"Well, in a manner of speaking. Maejean, you go ahead and box up the clothes and make an anonymous donation. Then tell the reverend you want the check made out to cash and bring it to me. I'll give you something for your trouble." Mammy finished off her beer and popped another, pleased with her decision. "That way," she went on, "I can write the donation off on my taxes, and they can't trace the check."

Charles T. and Grace, for their part, went weak with admiration. It seemed almost dangerous to have blood like that running in your veins. Grace swallowed hard before she spoke again. "What if you see somebody—you know—wearing something?"

Mammy raised her eyebrows, then lowered them again. "I reckon I can stand it," she said, and sipped her beer.

Nine

Atlantis, Texas, the Center
of Town. August 6.

ALL THAT Travis Moseley, Jr., owned in the
world was a snow-white 1959 Cadillac that his grandmother
had bought him when he got home from the service. He
hadn't done, to the best of anyone's recollection, much to
deserve the present, not having been in an actual war, but
Cora Moseley couldn't be talked to on the subject of that
boy. When she died, Travis sold her house and all her
things to a family from Tyler, who would live to regret the
purchase—having moved east just before the big oil strike
made the remaining Tyler residents rich. He'd packed what
things he wanted into the trunk of the vehicle and drove out
of town intending to see the world, but somehow he never
got further than two hundred miles in any direction before

turning around like a dog who comes to the end of its chain.

Sometimes he went to Austin, running dope from Dallas into the campuses there. Other times it was north to West Memphis where the big river stretched a mile across, and he could work the factories when he chose. But mostly, he favored the small towns. He would pick one off a map in a gas station and drive through it until he knew it by heart, going slow as the police. It didn't matter that they were all the same, didn't matter that there was nothing to see—that was the best part for Travis. He'd make his way through the main street first, past banks and bars and hardware stores that eventually ran together in his memory the way colored paints smear into gray. Then into cool, tree-lined streets where the people had money, driving till the roads threaded narrow and hot and dirty children watched his car with their fingers in their mouths. Sometimes he followed a woman to see where she took him. When he got done with a place he'd gun the motor till he found the city limit sign and passed it, smiling to himself and turning up the radio. It was a great secret of his that he favored longhair music; the moaning and soaring and trembling of the strings reminded him of the thing he was seeking. The car had 145,000 miles on it when he slowed down in front of the Annual Rummage Sale and General Flea Market sign in front of the brick church on Laurel Avenue in Atlantis. Travis Moseley had considerably more.

It was a Saturday morning. Travis watched the station wagons pull up in front of the sale, unloading dozens of women in faded shorts and sleeveless blouses pulled tight across freckled chests. He stared intently through the heat waves that shimmered from the hood of the Cadillac. It was like he'd been in a desert and happened on the inhabitants of an oasis; he couldn't say for sure if they were real or not. He decided to join them and find out for sure.

Inside it was a great circus-colored jumble, with booths
and tables spread over the church basement till there was
hardly room to move and everyone who came to see it was
busily absorbing the remaining space with their bodies and
hollow, echoey voices. The air-conditioning was set so cold
it brought the hair up along his arms. He thought to leave
but was distracted by a table loaded with baked goods with
their prices stuck in the tops. He hadn't eaten since yesterday in Arkansas, and the sweets reminded him he was
empty. He ordered a dozen frosted doughnuts from a
blonde woman who had a child clinging to her thigh.

"Look around," she suggested, her hazel eyes thickly
bordered in strong makeup. "You might find something
else you like."

He chose to smile at her, exposing a line of movie-star
teeth and clusters of lines at his temples. "You know,
ma'am," he said, "you might be able to help me there. I'm
looking for a fiddle."

The woman smiled a little uncertainly. The stranger
didn't look like the musical type to her, but then you never
can tell. "Take a look over at Miz Hooten's," she said.

Iris Lee had seen him come in and was watching his
progress toward her table like an old cat. Maejean the Good
had sweet-talked her into minding the booth while she ran
to the drugstore, and Mammy was as close to mortification
as she ever got. She saw him eating doughnuts as he made
his way through the crowd, saw the way he hefted Bobby
Hooten's Cajun fiddle, crusted with dirt and cracked on one
side. Had she been made of weaker stuff, she might have
been startled at the eerie resemblance this cowboy bore to
a picture she had in her conscience, but as it was, she stayed
suspicious, noting with some satisfaction as the man drew
nearer that the face was missing some of the essentials she
remembered, like a cheap reproduction. When the man

finally got to her table and put his hands on her dead husband's tie, she allowed herself a kind of inward nod. That would be it, she thought to herself.

It was the color of a jonquil, with a woman painted on it who was wearing nothing but a pair of high heels. Her hips got bigger with the wider end. One hand cupped a breast and the other pointed to some blue script in an arc above her head. *"Souvenir of New Orleans."*

A sharp voice interrupted the beginning of his smile. "Don't get that all greasy," it said. Travis looked at the old woman standing on the other side of the table for the first time, then looked again. Her shoulders were drawn together in front of her as if she were perpetually chilly, and the skin on her face was florid and shriveled, like an apple no one got around to eating. He flashed an experimental grin before meeting her eyes.

"How much for this?" he asked her in a honeyed baritone he reserved just for those who had things he wanted.

She pretended not to have heard him. Their eyes met inadvertently and both sets narrowed at once. When the old woman spoke again her voice was so cold and flat that he couldn't be sure it hadn't come out of his own mind.

"I think I know you," she told him.

He waited a minute before answering. When he tilted his head for a better look at her his hat put a shadow on his face like a bad intention. "Anything is possible," he said.

The old woman was unmoved. She put out a bony finger in the direction of the scandalous tie. "You gonna buy that or you gonna try and steal it?" she demanded.

"Mammy!" Maejean came up at her elbow, all out of breath from running. "For heaven's sake, this is a church sale. For charity!"

"Yeah, well there's some that figure they're entitled to more than they get," she grumbled.

Maejean looked at the man and shrugged her shoulders in bewilderment. She knew Iris Lee was tough, but she rarely lost her manners in front of strangers. "I can wrap it up for you, if you want," she said aloud.

Travis pasted on a meek expression. The tall woman was pretty, even if she was a little on the craggy side. "How much?"

Mammy spoke up in a strong, clear voice. "Two dollars," she said, sure the extravagant figure would show him for what he was.

Maejean's mouth fell open.

Travis grinned. "Sold," he said.

He was watching for her when she came out of the church and made her way to a car parked in the shade. She took a tissue out of her purse and scrubbed at a flyspeck on the windshield before getting in. She drove a car easily, for a woman, with none of the straining forward that usually comes with age. He waited until her car had disappeared through an intersection that brought some county roads together in the center of town before turning his ignition key. He felt an itching in the palms of his hands and looked at them. Like his father and grandfather, Travis was born with a sensitive skin. It might not be a bad idea to find a motel for a few days, he thought, scratching reflectively. He'd seen something called the Mile-Away back at the edge of town.

Not a bad idea at all.

Iris Lee was doing some thinking herself. She'd carried her secret for so long that the force of having it return to haunt her so suddenly carried the weight of a penance. She rounded the curve of the road to the farm at forty miles an hour, startling some calves that lingered by a portion of fence.

"Trouble comes in threes," she said to no one.

Ten

Meanwhile . . .
Back at the Farm.

BABY TODD FOUND Grace arranging some new additions to the funeral plants grouped under the carport when she drove up to the farm on Saturday morning. Ray Ed's passing seemed to have left most of his neighbors without much in the way of a verbal response; everybody in the county seemed to have said it with flowers.

"Hello-oo," she called. "Is that you, Grace?"

Grace stood up with a reasonable muster of enthusiasm. In fact, she'd been attempting to flatten herself among the plants and hide, but since she'd been discovered, her dread had been so instantly replaced by a reflex of graciousness that she almost didn't notice the transition. But if she had to suffer some company, it might as well be Aunt Baby. As relatives went, Grace found her, if not exactly a kindred spirit, then at least not a hostile one.

The old lady was obviously in an unusual humor, she was wearing a light flowered print dress, decades too young for her, and was apparently fresh from the beauty parlor, there being no other way to explain the color of her hair. For one instant, with the sun in her eyes, Grace had glimpse of the girl Aunt Baby had been—Miss Crepe Myrtle come to call.

Baby's smile shone like costume jewelry. "How lovely to see you, Grace," she said, taking her hands in her own. "You ought to wear gloves, though, when you garden. They make all the difference." Grace took her hands back and put them in her pockets.

"But I know how you feel," Baby went on, "I just love flowers myself. They bring a person so close to nature, even the silk ones." Baby patted her coiffure. "I've just had my hair done," she said.

Grace studied the pattern of lacquered waves. "Lovely."

"I always have to drive to Queen City to get it done right. I had a girl who did it here in Atlantis, but she got run over."

Uncertain of what to say next, Grace, by force of habit, apologized.

"Oh, don't be sorry. She didn't die or anything. But she went on disability. I guess she figured there was no point in working if she could get paid for just sitting around in that wheelchair of hers."

Seeing Grace's look, Baby cocked an eyebrow. "I'm old, Grace," she said. "I can say whatever I want." Baby peered toward the house expectantly. "Is it just you? Where's everyone?"

"Davey picked Dearest up in town and they took Boo to the movies," Grace began.

"And you didn't go along?"

"I saw it already."

"Oh. Where's Iris?"

"Mammy's at the church sale and Daddy went to bush-hog the field back of the pond," Grace reported.

Baby smiled. "How nice," she remarked, "I've been hoping we'd have a chance to chat." She unsnapped her purse and drew out a hankie with an embroidered edge, so exquisite and fragile Grace thought instantly that it must've taken years off some French nun's time on earth. She caught a whiff of jasmine and closed-up houses. Eau de Claustrophobia.

Grace smiled.

"That's better, dear. You look so much prettier when you smile. Keep taking things so seriously and before you know it, you'll wind up looking just like your grandmother. You know those lines around her mouth? The direct result of taking life too seriously."

Grace gestured toward the kitchen door. "Do you want a glass of tea or anything?"

"Thank you, honey. That would be very nice. You always did have such wonderful manners. No one can ever tell what you're thinking. But it means you take after me, I guess. I could no more let a person go from my door hungry or thirsty than I could shoot something helpless."

Grace made a point of holding the door. "Lemon? Sugar?"

Baby eased herself down in the nearest chair. "Is that all you have? No mint?"

"I'll see."

Baby spied the writing tablet lying close to her elbow. "What's this you're doing, dear? Keeping a journal? My father always told us to keep a journal, and I always have. 'If life is not documented in some fashion,' he told us, 'life will cease to be.' Isn't that a beautiful sentiment? A little extreme, of course, but he was like that. Anyway, I've always kept a journal and I'm glad."

"Actually, I'm working," Grace told her, frowning into the refrigerator. "Back in New York I do some writing."

"Writing? What kind?"

Grace blushed. "T-shirts."

Baby didn't know quite what to make of this. "I see," she said. She didn't.

Grace retreated back to the refrigerator. "Just, you know . . . funny sayings, stuff like that. I figure as long as I'm here . . . No mint."

Baby made a disappointed noise. "No," she said. "Now that I think about it, Iris Lee doesn't care for mint. I guess lemon. What made you take up something like T-shirts? Isn't Larry working?"

"Of course he's working," Grace told her. "But women have careers too, now."

Baby sniffed. "Don't patronize your elders, Grace. I know women have careers. I read the magazines just like everybody else."

Grace removed a pitcher from the Frigidaire. "Lemon," she said.

"But it's natural that you would do something creative. You were always talented, even as a child. No matter what Iris Lee says about it. Like that time you glued the receiver to the telephone? I thought that was terribly creative." Baby paused and took a sip from the tumbler Grace set before her.

Grace sat down, smiling for real.

"Iris Lee damn near died, remember?" Baby giggled. "Her waiting to hear about whether or not she's the new president of the Azalea Society and the phone glued down like that. Lord! She picked up the whole thing and damn near knocked herself out. Me and Ray Ed like to kill ourselves laughing."

Grace laughed. "It's a wonder she didn't kill me," she said.

"Don't be silly, Grace. I never would have let her lay a hand on you. You're like the daughter I never had. Besides, I'm sure she's forgotten all about it by now. Look how well you turned out."

Grace blushed. It had been so long since she'd heard a compliment from one of the family that she clung to the implication of it like a person drowning.

Baby went on. "Don't be embarrassed, dear. I admire you. The only writing comes out of a place like Atlantis is the poetry you find on greeting cards. Did you see the big one Iris Lee got for the funeral? It was called, 'The Bosom of Jesus Is Broad.' Iris Lee practically wept when she saw it; the Jesus had dried flowers in his hair."

Grace nodded. "She gave it to somebody in town to decoupage."

Baby rolled her eyes. "Earline Monday, I bet. She makes her living polyurethaning things that ought to be burned. You should see what she did to the post office. But everybody's got to do something." She paused, thinking it over. "I've always wanted to write a novel, myself. People say I have the gift. Folks swear that whenever I tell a story, it's like they can just see it. You know what I mean?" Baby's eyes went a little dim. "I don't know why I never did it," she said. "Too busy getting married, I guess."

Grace nodded, momentarily seduced by the notion of writing a novel herself. Naw—she might be able to make them see it, but they'd never believe it.

Baby colored a little. "You shouldn't be shy about your talents, anyhow. You're entitled to them. Besides, being

gifted runs in the family—your father has done any number
of things with his mind, and you're a writer and Davey's a
singer and Boo—" Baby stopped and thought it over.
"Boo's a musician!" she finished, pleased at having thought
of something. "I still can't get over his playing the other
night."

Grace drummed her fingers on the table in waltz time.
"Mammy didn't like it much," she said.

Baby sighed. "My sister doesn't have the taste God gave
a mouthful of dirt. Never did. You should have seen her
take on about that stupid card." Baby sipped tea and smiled
a little. "Now that she's old, practically anything can set her
off."

Grace laughed. But she found herself wondering again
about Ray Ed's last revelation as she sipped her tea. It was
overexposure to the elderly, she decided privately; listen to
old people too much and you start to feel like you're not
yourself.

"Curious, though," Baby went on; she hummed a snatch
of the song. "That Boo would have chosen that song. 'The
Anniversary Waltz.' My first husband played the violin. Did
I ever tell you? He wasn't professional or anything, but he
was good at it. Cecil got up and played that on his fiddle on
the day we were married. Folks thought we should've
danced to it together, but I didn't mind. I just loved to
watch him play. It was so moving," Baby said, her eyes
glistening. "I think he wept. I think we both did."

Grace nodded, wondering if she would ever be able to
speak of a long-gone husband with any sentiment. She had
trouble, once they were gone, recalling what they looked
like.

"Have you ever been in love, Grace?" Aunt Baby asked
suddenly.

Grace started out of her reflections. Of all the families in all the world, she thought briefly, I had to walk into this one. . . . "I've been married twice," she said carefully.

"Grace dear, is there a problem with your hearing? I don't believe I asked you anything about being married. I asked you about being in love." The old lady's eyes twinkled like blue jewels.

Grace blinked. There it was again, that ghost of the girl moving across the old woman's face. "It's kind of a bad time to ask, I guess," she said finally. "Just now, it doesn't seem like it."

Baby nodded as if confirming something to herself. "I heard you were divorcing." She allowed herself a delicate pause.

"That's right," Grace told her. "I filed for a no-fault."

"No-fault?" Baby was puzzled. "That's the kind where you don't get any money, isn't it?"

"Yes, ma'am," Grace replied.

"Oh. That's unfortunate, but I suppose it's very modern of you," Baby said. "On the other hand, I happen to think you're well rid of the man, if you don't mind my saying so. I kept my peace at the time, of course, but I don't think you were ever right for each other."

Grace couldn't really think of anything to say to that; she didn't believe in arguing with facts staring her in the face.

"He was so awfully pale, wasn't he? Small eyes?" Baby frowned, trying to make sure of her opinion. "Poor dancer?"

Grace gave up any attempt at regret and snickered. "That's Larry."

Baby smiled at her fondly, sipping her tea. "We're so much alike, you and I, when it comes to men. Funny how it's always easier to find a husband than a lover, isn't it?"

Grace started. Having a finger put so precisely on the problem took her a little off her guard.

Baby saw the remark had hit home and nodded her satisfaction. "Well, take my advice, girl. Go out and fall in love. Right away. It's the best cure for a bad marriage. Maybe the only one."

Grace, still blushing, shook her head. "I didn't think I needed a cure," she said.

"Of course you do, dear. If people didn't need to get over their marriages, there wouldn't be any such things as promiscuity and credit cards."

"But before you fall in love, you've got to have someone to fall in love with, Aunt Baby. And the men around here. . . ." Grace faltered, having used up the entire strength of her protest. In fact, falling in love was starting to sound like a pretty good idea. Impossible as igloos in August, perhaps, but pretty good, anyhow.

"The dogs go barefoot everywhere, my dear, as my mama used to say. Besides, the place doesn't matter. The love is what makes you belong."

Grace fidgeted a little. "But what about your husbands?"

Baby smiled and beckoned for her tea glass to be refilled. "Oh, very nice men, all of them. But believe an old woman, Grace. Marriage is the least of it when you're really in love. I was lucky once. Lucky enough to marry for love. Maybe you will be, too."

Grace fetched more tea. "I don't know, Aunt Baby, I think I may have missed my chance. I'm over thirty, doesn't that make me overqualified?"

Amazingly, Baby laughed. "That's the truly wonderful thing about being alive, Grace. One never misses anything really important. The trick is not to abuse your opportunities." Baby looked Grace up and down. "I would say you're just the right age for falling in love. Not too young. I was too young, I think. When I fell in love with Cecil, him and his fiddle," Baby trailed off, then, unexpectedly, she giggled. "He used to come out in hives whenever he got nervous."

Grace stared at her intently, trying to reconcile herself to the idea of falling in love and pay attention at the same time. "Hives?" she asked.

"Bold hives, they used to call them in the old days," Baby answered. "They said if you let bold hives go too long, they broke out around the heart and killed you."

"Is that what happened to him?"

Baby stared at her hands. "No," she said quietly. "Cecil died of something else."

A little silence ensued while they finished their tea. Each in their own way seemed to be waiting for someone's entrance, as though the mere mention of passion could stir up a spirit and bring him through the kitchen door.

"Pay no attention to me, Grace. I don't mean to meddle," Baby said after a time.

"Of course you do," Grace told her, smiling.

Baby sighed. "I'm getting so old I want to live life over again, that's my problem. You do what you want."

Grace smiled, puzzling at the change of mood. "Oh, you're not so old as all that," she told her.

Baby smoothed her dress, her temporary wistfulness suddenly dissipating, the brightness returning to her eyes by degrees. "I appreciate the thought, honey. But I guess I know more about getting old than you do." Baby glanced at her hand again. "I went to a gypsy palm reader one time," she said. "She told me I'd die from a lover's bullet." The old woman shot Grace a wicked, bird-eyed look. "At the time, I thought it was the most romantic thing I'd ever heard. Now I expect I'll have to die in bed like everyone else."

She paused while Grace chuckled, toying with her diamond wedding ring. The ring had been a gift from the late

Preacher Todd. Grace stared at it for a moment, remembering that Uncle Dearest had said it looked like a prize from a Crackerjack box, while Iris Lee had insisted that the only reason the stone was so big was that once they saw how flawed it was, no one had seen any human reason to waste time cutting it down any further. Grace, on the other hand, had always thought it beautiful.

Baby caught her covetous look. "Preacher was so generous," she reflected. "And so very stinking rich."

Grace laughed a little. "Why, Aunt Baby, I'm shocked. Weren't you just extolling the pure virtues of love?"

Baby shrugged a little and patted her hair. "Of course I was, dear. And I meant it. But it's so very rare that love and money go together in a man. And believe me, money will get you through times of no romance much better than romance will get you through times of no money. So if you must have a husband, by all means try and get yourself a rich one."

Grace smiled. "May I quote you?"

"Not without giving me proper credit," Baby replied, gathering up her purse. "And not to that puritanical sister of mine. She'll have me run off for corrupting your morals."

Grace smiled. "I can corrupt my own morals, thank you."

"I imagine that much is true, anyhow." Baby stood up. "Well, I have to be off. Iris Lee won't move off this worn-out old farm and into a condo like everyone else, so every time you want to see her you have to drive halfway across the state."

Grace followed her out to the car. "Do you want me to give Mammy a message or anything?"

Baby smiled thinly. There was lipstick on one of her teeth. "Oh. Of course. Tell her I came to see how she was faring. And that—" she broke off. "And that she ought to get busy and read that will." Baby looked Grace straight in the eye. "The divorce rate being what it is these days, I imagine there's some who could use the money."

Grace winced a little. The subject of the will was getting touchier by the day. "Dad was going to ask her tonight."

Baby made a little clucking noise. "Charles T.? The last time Charles T. stood up to Iris was when he married your mama. He hasn't been any good at it since. Tell your daddy I'll speak to her. I don't imagine Ray had a fortune, but that don't mean it shouldn't be dealt out before everyone gets too old to care."

Baby beckoned Grace close as she started to pull away. "And I want you all to come to lunch one day next week. Hear? Tell her that. We'll have a party."

"Okay," Grace promised, smiling. Oddly, her heart had been a little lightened by the visit, as though something had been resolved. "I will."

Back in the kitchen, Grace rinsed the glasses and put them away, something undefined nagging at her. She slid her writing tablet across the table and stood with her pen in the air, not knowing ahead of time what would come. Then the words of Ray Ed's final revelation returned in force, and she printed the letters at the top of the page, to make them come real for her at last.

"Destiny," she wrote, "Is Not a Blind Armadillo." Then after a moment, she added some more.

"But it sure has a weird sense of humor."

Eleven

Aytolles Parish. April 9, 1877.

THREE DAYS before it happened, Mary Faith sent for Dovie to come to her in the parlor. It was an April evening, so clear and sweet-smelling it had set the whole household to longing for innocence. The Mistress Beaudine's dinner guests had recently departed; a small company of neighbors so old that they required only gumbo and pudding at the table. Everything else was too hard to chew.

Dovie knocked softly at the door. She was thinking someone had left something behind, perhaps a hat or a glove that would need to be sent along in the morning. She found Mary Faith sipping sherry in front of the open window. Dovie, well along in years herself, was fond of telling the kitchen maids that the mistress hadn't got so old as the rest of them. Her back was still straight as a nail and the hair she wrapped around her skull in thick plaits was only just dusted with gray. The hawkish nose had grown only sharper with the years and, when viewed in profile as Dovie saw it now, seemed to be holding the rest of the face up only by the sheer orneriness of its angle.

Mary Faith turned to her after a moment. Dovie nodded by reflex, noting with a shock the peculiar icy fire of her gaze. She knew that look. At first, it had shown out of the woman all the time after the teacher left—those terrible days when she played the violin so constantly they had feared for her mind. But as the years crept up on her and the misery took her hands, that funny light came on only in moments like this, when everything else looked peaceful. It came out of the soul, but never the heart, that light. Its fire gave no heat. Dovie had seen it only one other time in all her experience, in a preacher man who got too close to Jesus.

Mary Faith slowly picked up her gold pencil and began to write. The lace-gloved hands were so warped with arthritis that Dovie could see her jaws clenching with the pain. But she waited till the writing was done. You never could know what the mistress was after until you got that paper in your hand. When at last the twisted fingers tore the message from the tablet it made a slow, painful sound—like a heart breaking.

Dovie brought it close to the lamp and squinted at the shaking, spidery script.

"I am going to die," it said, and she read the words over again through tears that brimmed so quickly in her old eyes. "Please make up my room."

She did as she was told. She brought out some linens with tatted borders rescued from the hope chest that stood in a corner of the main bedroom, and fetched a pretty night-gown from the cupboard. She put some roses in a vase and some *gris-gris* under the featherbed in case the mistress should change her mind.

For three days nothing altered the routine of the house. Though confined to her bed, Mary Faith ate heartily, mak-ing her culinary requests known to the staff as she always had, by way of the gold tablet on the diamond-studded chain. She took pains to finish a novel she'd been reading and when she had done with it, spent her remaining hours gazing out the window watching the coming spring. But the light never for a moment left her eyes.

Only Dovie knew when the time had come. It was in the late afternoon, the dusk falling prematurely, the sky ob-scured by a storm that gathered to the west. She'd been dozing on the kitchen porch, lulled by the scent of lilac that had fallen over the world like a shroud. With the first smell of rain, she woke from a dream. In it, the teacher came to help her bury the violin, and the two heard music coming up through the ground.

She saw the mistress lying in the half-light, looking sud-denly skinny and old beneath the covers. There was a note already waiting when she got there.

"Bring it to me."

Dovie didn't need to ask what she wanted. She got it and brought it to the bedroom, holding the case like a baby to her breast. She lit the lamp and brought it nearer, then took it out and laid it by the mistress's hand. She herself had kept it polished, even after no one played it anymore.

Mary Faith let it lay close without yet daring to touch. She took the tablet from her neck and wrote her last. Dovie would keep that slip of paper for years as a charm against the Reaper.

"I cannot say good-bye."

Dovie read it and nodded. "I know," she said. "It don't matter."

The mistress raised her hand and half-waved her out of the room. The lamp was burning still and Mary Faith lifted the violin in front of her, watching the shadow it cast on the wall. She ran her crooked, aged fingers over its surface and around each of the tuning pegs, her breath rattling in her chest. She made her aching fingers pluck the strings as she tried the chin rest against her neck. Their music sounded, brief and cystalline against the rain. She held it to her and felt it shudder like something dying.

Her eyes searched the room, long with shadows in the corners, going over each of the furnishings in her memory —Mama's mirror, Father's trunk—then back to the beloved instrument clutched like money in her useless hands. The little gold tablet with its diamond chain glinted in the light with pale fire. She saw it even as the edges of her vision closed in, black and begging for rest. She remembered everything.

"Shit," she said, leaning her head against the fiddle. And died.

Twelve

Atlantis Township. August 6 . . .
in the Afternoon.

DEAREST AND THE BOYS never made it to the pictures in Texarkana. In fact, they never left town.

Of course, it wasn't the first time members of the Strait family had set out to accomplish one thing and wound up doing something else. The family as a whole had never quite got the hang of making plans. Life, after all, was so full of distractions. Clara Cannon and Maivis Johnson saw the Honda cruising down Laurel Avenue just as they were emerging from the Resurrection Baptist Flea Market, arguing over their purchases. Maivis had got some practically new walking shorts printed with flamingos on a field of blue that she was insisting would look just fine on her when she took off those pounds she'd been planning to lose, and Clara was telling her otherwise.

"You've been planning to lose that weight for five years, Maivis," she said. "If it ain't come off yet, it ain't goin' to."

Clara was convinced she'd got the better bargain. She was toting a porcelain lamp base encrusted with flowers, and feeling proud of the niggardly price she'd paid. It was far from perfect, but she figured she could turn the chipped part to the wall, and no one would be the wiser.

But when they saw the blue foreign car with Davey Strait behind the wheel and Dearest riding shotgun, wearing mirror sunglasses and a sable-collared cardigan too warm for the weather, Clara narrowed her eyes and hefted the lamp more securely onto her bony hip. The car disappeared down the road and Clara had one of the few moments of pure clairvoyance she was ever to experience. She stared disapprovingly after them, noting the outline of the idiot boy's shoulders in the back seat, suspicion growing in her breast like a weed.

"Hmmphh," she muttered to Maivis. "Probably going to a whorehouse."

Maivis set her mouth in a righteous expression. "Clara Cannon," she said, "your mind is in the gutter."

Up until the time Uncle Dearest opened his mouth to suggest it, though, the idea of taking Boo to a whore had never occurred to anybody, except perhaps the boy himself and he wasn't talking. When Uncle said his name, though, his sensitive hearing picked up the mention and a peculiar titillation went coursing through him like a devil on horseback.

"Davey," Uncle sighed, "I have an idea."

"Good," his nephew answered. "I'm fresh out." In the two weeks he'd been at the farm, his long errands had taken him over all the back roads and highways he could get to

without actually upping and leaving, but he'd managed, so
far, to stay stuck in Atlantis County, casting about for diver-
sions in the area like a sportsman stuck in a poor stretch of
river.

Uncle peered at him over the tops of the glasses. "I know
where there's a whore," he said.

Davey swerved to avoid something in the road. He'd
never gotten over the impression that armadillos were
really some kind of helmet with legs. He was so surprised
by the statement it took him a moment to respond. "You?
A whore?"

Uncle drew himself up as much as he could without
actually standing. "Well, don't look so pale about it, Davey.
As a matter of fact, me and your daddy used to go to this
little place over by Paris all the time when we was boys."

"Paris?"

"Paris, Texas. Your daddy had himself quite a reputation
back in those days."

Davey digested this new information as best he could;
that is, he related it immediately to himself. "I never did it
with a whore," he said carefully, pondering the possibilities.

Dearest lit a thin cigar and took a moment to practice his
French inhale. "Well, technically speaking, neither did I.
But me and the ladies would have dress-up parties. And
they had this little Creole faggot for a chef. But they fired
him after awhile. The girls was getting fat. He was real nice,
though."

Davey gripped the wheel and straightened his back.
"Forget the whore. I don't need to pay for it," he said.

Uncle clucked his tongue and grinned. "Davey, you
never disappoint me. You're so unfalteringly butch."

"Fuck you."

Dearest touched his spidery fingers to his face as if to

smooth it and brushed a little at the makeup he wore that made him so perpetually tanned. "See what I mean?"

Davey glowered out over the road. In fact, he found the idea of paying for a whore intriguing, but something he associated with men less fortunate than himself. That Dearest would even suggest it stuck a little in his gizzard. As it turned out, though, Dearest had other mercies on his mind.

"Anyhow, I wasn't thinking of you. I was thinking about Boo."

Davey didn't know whether to be disappointed or not. "Boo?" he said. His veneer of family homage worn so thin he could see through it, this new idea struck him as preposterous, and therefore utterly appropriate.

"Boo!" In the back, Boo sensed the tide turning and thumped the front seat with joyous enthusiasm.

"He is eighteen," Uncle put in. "And as far as I know—"

"A virgin," finished Davey.

"Boo," said Boo, by way of agreement.

Davey stared at his uncle, his mind decided. "Where's the whorehouse?"

Dearest laughed out loud. "Whorehouse? Where do you think you are? Paris? This is Atlantis, Texas, sweets. A one-whore town if ever there was. Now turn over at the stoplight up here."

"Okay." Davey was thinking maybe if the whore would do it with Boo—then he might go, too. Make it look like an afterthought.

"She's a very nice woman. And clean, too. Runs a nice little business out of her back door. Right up here," Uncle gestured. "Third from the corner."

"This?" Davey pulled up in front of the modest ranch-style house, all his visions of dens of iniquity ground to powder. "This? Are you sure?" he said, getting out of the car and flipping the seat for Boo, who was beginning to radiate excitement like it was Christmas morning.

Uncle stood with his hands on his hips. "Well, come on. Of course I'm sure. And don't you boys embarrass me, you hear? After all, I got to live in this town."

Boo was trying to decide whether to take his fiddle or not. He stared at his brother, the question in his eyes. "Boo?"

Dearest took him by the arm. "Leave it there, hon," he said. "You won't need it."

"Boo . . ." Boo fairly gurgled with delight and started up the walk.

Davey made a conscious effort to order his emotions, and by the time they reached the back door of the house, he looked as smooth as an ad for liquor. Anyone would think he'd been visiting whores for as long as he could recall. They waited at the screen door while Dearest rang the bell. A woman's voice rang out hollowly, telling them to hold on. Davey stuck his hands in the pockets of his jeans and tried not to look at anything, still reeling from the notion of a world where whores might be housewives and vice versa.

"Who is she, anyway?" he whispered.

Dearest inclined his head and grabbed him by the elbow as the door swung inward.

"Luanne Heck," he hissed. "The preacher's wife."

Thirteen

Aytolles Parish. May 4, 1877.

UNDER THE BEQUESTS SECTION of Mary Faith's rather lengthy Last Will and Testament there was an item that read:

> *It is my wish that that which I hold most dear among all my worldly goods, one authentic Stradivarius violin, shall be bequeathed to whomsoever among my friends and relations is the most deserving of its receipt. It is my express intention that the violin should continue after me in its purpose in this world. For it is a fine instrument, designed for a musician's hand, and further made for to give pleasure to those who shall witness its fine quality and tone. Therefore, it shall be given, at the decision of my Executor, to the one among you most talented and qualified to give it use.*

Mr. Willard, the attorney and executor of the document, gazed over the tops of his spectacles at the assembled company. "What that means," he told them, "is that she wants the fiddle to go to somebody who knows how to play it. Now, I don't think we need to talk about it too much, but I happen to have seen this fiddle before over at Miss Beaudine's and heard her play it, too. I'm not musical myself, but it appeared to be real nice."

Those gathered stared back at him wordlessly. In fact, they were all a little stunned—the piece of paper he held in front of him had altered the course of a number of lives that early summer afternoon. Nobody had the slightest notion about how rich the old lady had been. In fact, there were only a few of them who had ever met her more than a few times. In the face of the dispensation of what seemed to most of them an undreamed-of fortune, finding a home for her fiddle seemed a little ludicrous by comparison. More than one, in fact, wondered silently if the rock-faced Mary Faith hadn't gone a little soft toward the end.

The lawyer was still waiting. "Anybody?" he asked.

Cyrus Thomas, a second cousin from Mississippi, cleared his throat. "Sumpin' like that fiddle—well, what I mean to say is—is it worth anything? Moneywise, I mean."

"Well, Mr. Thomas, I don't rightly know myself. Don't seem like it would be. . . ." The lawyer frowned a little. "But you see that is not the deceased's intention, anyhow. I guess you could say she was kind of sentimental about it."

"So if I was to take it off your hands, you don't figure I could sell it for very much, huh?"

Mr. Willard closed his eyes. "Mr. Thomas, do you play the violin?" Having got an eyeful of Mary Faith's next of kin, he could understand why the family hadn't been close.

"No, sir."

"All right then."

He was about to proceed when he was distracted by a

sort of hissing toward the back of the room. Another man stood reluctantly up, apparently at the urging of the woman to his right. The lawyer checked his list of names. This one was from a parish up north, close to the center of the state. Calvin something—Purchase. Calvin Purchase.

"Uhh. Your honor, umm—well, my wife here—Belle, that's my wife." Belle had a face like a hatchet and she bowed at him from her chair. Calvin grinned foolishly and went on. "She was just reminding me that our boy plays the fiddle some. . . . I mean, he's just a boy and all. But he knows how, and I reckon we could take it for his sake."

"That's right," said Belle. She has been doubly blessed, the lawyer thought—a voice to match her face. "He kin play anything."

Mr. Willard had five pages of the will left to read. At this rate, it was going to take all day and most of tomorrow. He furtively scanned the faces in front of him for even a glimmer of objection. "Done!" he cried heartily, and took up his pen. "And what is the boy's name, please?"

Calvin shuffled his feet and looked solemn. "Victor."

The first thing Calvin Purchase did when he got home was to shorten the neck of the Stradivarius by two and a quarter inches with a handsaw. Victor was just a boy, after all, and long as it was, he found he couldn't get halfway through "Cotton-Eyed Joe" without getting tired. Besides, Victor played the fiddle held down alongside his arm the way the Cajun folks did, not up under the chin like a longhair. Calvin was a thorough, patient man and he did a good job. He really wanted it to be right. First, because it was not in his nature to do sloppy work, and second, because deep down he was keenly aware of the fact that he hated the kid.

If anyone had asked him to pinpoint a reason for his heart's recoiling from the only fruit of his loins, he probably couldn't have. The child was dark, serious, and thoughtful. No real trouble to have around. He had come as something of a shock to his parents, having been conceived after nearly twelve years of marriage, so perhaps that was part of Calvin's rejection of his paternity, the pitter-patter of little feet having had no small effect on the routine of the household. And, of course, there was the first niggling question of whether or not, after so long a period of childlessness, Victor was actually his child. But a number of sidelong glances at the stringy Belle had banished his doubts on that subject, and he put the whole thing down to wishful thinking.

No, the real problem was Victor himself. The boy had a cold streak in him, and his father knew from the time he was an infant that there was a part of his soul that no other human being would ever be allowed to see, let alone reach. It was as though son Victor was merely going through the motions of life; only imitating pleasure and pain where it seemed appropriate. When he first spoke, or took a step or climbed a tree, there was no joy in the discovery. It was as though the tiny child with the old man's face had known how to do these all along, and had merely waited his turn at doing them in public. In fact, the only thing that seemed to absorb the child at all was playing the violin. He had submitted to his mother's urging of lessons on him without reaction or protest. She wanted her son to be somebody, she was fond of repeating. And every truly great man the world had ever known, she was certain, had been "musical." In fact, Victor was not in the slightest bit "musical," though he practiced for hours at a time without fatigue or complaint. If his infrequent audiences of parent or neighbor paused to accompany his almost perpetual recitals with tapping toes or voice or clapping hands, the impulse died a-borning as Victor played.

"Sounds like music," Calvin once confided to Belle, shaking his head, "but it don't feel like music." He'd tapped his chest just once and stuck his hands in his pockets. Sadly, even his doting mother had agreed, and encouraged the boy to take greater amounts of fresh air.

Victor learned relentlessly, playing each passage over and over before attempting the next. The character of the music mattered little to him; he never showed a preference for one tune over another. It was more the difficulty of music that attracted him—the variety of fingering and pacing; the complexity of notes. More than once had Calvin caught Victor trying to stretch his chubby fingers on a nailed board until they were swollen and mutilated with effort. He tried scorching his fingertips in order to thicken his calluses and increase his tolerance for pain. But even Calvin's regular administration of a leather belt had failed to deter these covert practices. Finally, bewildered and weary, Belle intervened one afternoon in the woodshed.

"Leave him be, Calvin. He ain't goin' to hurt himself."

Calvin faced his wife, his kind eyes stinging with horrified, desperate tears. Defeated, he'd lowered the strap from its position above Victor's stony backside. "He was born to hurt himself," he told her miserably.

Half an hour later, Victor was fiddling on the front porch. He'd gone into himself completely, his face as dark and secret as the middle of the night. Calvin went to call him to chores and stopped dead at the sight of that pinched, fixed face above the fiddle's shining surface. But Victor was hearing beyond the frenetic strains that thudded over the landscape like hailstones. His dark eyes shone, glittering and implacable as a snake's.

Given the difficulty of his childhood then, everyone was more than a little relieved when, at the age of twelve, having possessed the stunted Stradivarius a little more than four years, Victor Purchase announced that he had spoken to God and was changing his name.

Fourteen

Atlantis Township. August 7 . . .
Sunday Morning.

I F, ON HER WAY back from church that morning, Baby
Todd had happened to see Ernest Earl Faxton slouched
behind the steering wheel of his undertaker's car, chewing
on his own bitterness and imagined wrongs, she might have
thrown decorum to the devil and invited him in for Sunday
lunch, for she was feeling lonely. But she didn't, and made
her way up the walk to her columned house without a
glance in any direction. Ernest Earl stayed put, though,
memorizing her movements and feeding his secret heart.

The bitch. No—whore. He said the word over and over
to himself, pleased at the sound of it. He'd found that it
quieted him a little when he cursed her, eased the sour

churning of his stomach. She'd come from church, he knew
that. He knew everything about her—knew that she got her
groceries delivered, but went to the liquor store herself. He
knew that she belonged to a museum. Once, a couple of
years ago, she'd gone to Hawaii and forgot to stop the mail.
He'd stolen every piece of it and steamed it open, going
over it all like a set of directions. And yet he only watched
her—watched her house and her life from the shadows of
her quiet little street, knowing all that could be learned in
fifty years of looking at externals, letting his hopelessness
turn on itself, until love and violence looked almost the
same.

And, twenty minutes later, when he had exhausted his
morning's inventory of imagined sexual espionage and
thwarted love, he drove on, intending to stop for a sandwich.

Baby sighed as she opened the door on the faux marble
of the foyer. A framed needlepoint hung to her right. She
unpinned her hat and put it away, noting the words of the
sampler for the thousandth time.

> *And we are here as on a darkling plain,*
> *Swept with confused alarums of struggle and flight*
> *Where ignorant armies clash by night.*

A B C D E F G H I J K L M N O P Q R S T U V W X Y Z

It was a gift from her mother, who had died shortly upon
its completion. Given that, Baby never felt she had a choice
but to display it. Whatever the sentiment, it was nicely
stitched, and she felt it looked well above the light
switch.

Today, however, she shook her head, unable to push

away the implications that resounded through the cool, silent hallways. She checked the time on the clock that sat atop the carved buffet. She poured herself a cream sherry from a glass decanter, surveying with some pleasure the cool elegance of her household, its heavy curtains drawn against the heat of the day. Sighing like a troubled wind, she kicked off her pumps, leaving them where they lay as she padded, glass in hand, toward the sitting room. She sank heavily in an armchair and stared through the shimmering amber depths of the glass. Maybe mother was right, she thought. Life is a bitch and then you die. But then, she'd been thinking on dying a lot lately. The old woman squeezed her eyes shut tight. After her conversation with Grace, Baby'd got to thinking of Cecil Moseley. And when Baby got thinking of Cecil, it might be days before she could stop.

The decanter was half-empty when the phone rang two hours later. Over seventy and a little drunk, Baby was still pretty fast on her feet and picked it up on the third ring.

"Hello?" she said, oozing pleasantry.

Iris Lee waited a minute before answering. "It's me," she said flatly. "Grace said you came by."

"That's right, I did. I wanted to see how you were." She paused and gulped at her sherry, thinking it peculiar that Iris had chosen to call. She was not in the habit of chatting on the phone. Especially not to her. "You know, Iris Lee, this is quite a coincidence. I was just going to ring you up and invite the whole bunch of you over to lunch on Tuesday!"

"Well, I'll have to ask them," Iris Lee told her. "But I imagine they'll be pleased enough."

"Of course they will!" Baby tried desperately to quiet the high, shaky note that crept into the reply.

There was a little pause at the other end. "You all right?"

She swallowed more sherry. "Fine," she answered. "You all?"

"Fine." Another pause.

"Iris Lee—I was speaking to Grace and I think—that is, well."

"Well, what?"

"Even Charles T. was going to speak to you about it. Now, I know that it's gonna be hard for you, Iris Lee. But you've got to be strong."

"Sister, will you come to the point?"

Baby gulped. "You've just gotta read that will, Iris Lee. It's time."

Well, Baby thought, she didn't hang up anyway. There was a breathing sound at the other end of the phone.

"All right."

"What?" Baby didn't quite know what she'd been expecting, but it surely hadn't been surrender.

"As it so happens, Baby, I picked it up yesterday outa the safe deposit box." Unbeknownst to anybody, she'd also sold off an acre of Ray Ed's prize bottom land to make up the missing cruise deposit money, but Iris Lee wasn't the kind who went around volunteering information about things that weren't anybody else's business.

"Oh, Iris Lee! That's wonderful! Did you look at it yet?"

Iris Lee's voice sharpened itself a little. "As a matter of fact, I haven't," she lied.

Baby had known Iris Lee too long to believe that, but she decided to let it pass—almost. "So when you going to read it to the rest of us, Iris Lee?"

Iris Lee was silent for a moment. "Since we're coming over there on Tuesday, we may as well do it then."

It took Baby a minute to gather her wits about her. "Here? Well, if that's the way you'd like to do it," she said, a little uncertainly.

"That's the way I'd like," said Iris. "What time?"
"I think about one. Sound all right to you?"
"Fine."
"Say hi to everybody."
"I will."

Fifteen

August 29, 1926.

IF, BY SOME ACCIDENT of history, the affections of these two sisters had come to represent two sides of some ignorant army or other there would, quite possibly, be nothing left of us. As it turned out, the consequences were far less serious. Nevertheless, when one Cecil Moseley blew into town on a dingy August day in 1926 in a soiled linen suit with a fiddle under his arm and a panama tilted over his eye, the female morals in Atlantis, Texas, took a decided turn for the loose.

He stayed but seven months. Should you be disposed to think it counts for anything, Baby saw him first, over a rack of movie magazines in Earley's Apothecary on Main—an establishment long since demolished. She was deep in the demise of Valentino, an idol six days gone, having left the world's camera to reel on without him. The tragedy hit Baby Sheba especially hard. The truth was, she'd been hanging around that drugstore waiting to be discovered for a star ever since the reign of Miss Crepe Myrtle had swollen her opinion of herself. But with the death of the Sheik, her visions of movieland had been subtly corrected. Baby had a lot of things in mind for her future, but dying young wasn't one of them. And from the way folks were carrying on over Tino, an untimely demise seemed a regular requirement of the movie star game. So Baby was pondering a magazine for solace when Cecil Moseley made his entrance. Things had come to such a pass that women were throwing themselves into the mouths of volcanoes to adequately express their grief, which, while affecting, struck Baby Sheba as a trifle unbalanced. Seeing your dreams bite the dust was one thing, killing yourself for a man already in the ground was plain foolishness.

When she looked up, still perturbed by the mysteries of such devotion, he was standing at the fountain, drinking lemonade. He was no Tino, true, but on the other hand, he was definitely the best-looking, up-close, flesh-and-blood human she had ever set eyes on. He stood nearly six feet, tanned and slim inside his creamy suit. The blondish hair was bright with Brilliantine, and his profile was as handsomely chiseled as any of those in her magazine. That was the first thing she noticed about Cecil Moseley. The second was that the druggist's daughter Hazel was giving him another lemonade for free and grinning at him like an idiot. Right then and there, Baby Sheba Quade decided it was time she got married. She pushed her waves into place, smoothed her dress, and gave the man a chance to introduce himself.

But his mama hadn't raised no fools. Cecil was as old as

the century and his face, linen suit, and panama comprised the principals of his worldly goods. The battered grip he hauled around with him held only an old preacher's coat, a spare shirt, and a Bible and was carried mostly for effect. The only other thing he owned was a certain violin and that he carried for his own sake, not having found, in the years of his wandering, a way to leave it behind him. Nonetheless, music had stood him in better stead than a lot of pleasures he could name. Faint hearts didn't win fair maidens, but a sweet, sad serenade had brought a number of them to his bed.

Cecil knew from experience what women could resist and what they couldn't, and one of the things they couldn't was a man on the move. And Cecil had been born with a wandering look and all the sadness of a man set apart from the general scheme. Though he'd been around some since, he'd been born not forty miles south of the spot where he stood and he was ready to see if there might be such a thing as home. Cecil was plain tired, and when the blond country girl with the china-doll face slid up next to him on a stool and pretended to drop her hankie, he was down to his last five dollars and a hitchhiking thumb. So he made a little bow and handed it back to her with a smile as wide and luminous as a summer moon. The girl was as good as any and prettier than most.

The two had been courting a full month before he met Iris Lee. Until he did, lust for Cecil Moseley had been a sort of impersonal obligation to his hormones; he was still a stranger to desire. He wanted women because he wanted to fuck, if it were possible to derive such satisfaction from doorknobs or guns or bottles of whiskey, he would have pursued them with the same dedication. Moreover, he'd been pleased to discover that women were generally very nice to him afterward and he appreciated that very much—

even though it distressed him a little to discover that the glow of their loving never lasted long enough.

It was the occasion of the sister's birthday—the last day of September. He and his Baby were invited to the Strait farm for supper. They stepped up on the porch and she clung to his arm like a flower. He smiled at her easily; she'd cleaned and pressed his suit only that morning and it made him feel like a brand-new man. Ray Ed Strait answered the bell.

"Birthday girl's in the kitchen," he told them, and was about to resume his chair when Baby dragged him back.

"I got me a present today, too, Ray Ed. Just look!" she squealed.

Ray Ed took in the speck of diamond on Baby's childish finger, and shifted his eyes in Cecil's direction.

"Aren't you gonna say nothin'?" Baby demanded.

Ray was cautious, but kind. "Course. It's nice, Baby. Real pretty," he said and went back to his chair.

Baby skipped to the kitchen to show off her treasure, leaving Cecil standing alone, panama in hand. He decided after a seemingly endless silence that he had better say something. He cleared his throat. "Uhh. Nice night."

Ray Ed looked up at him, his broad farmer's face studded with two startling eyes, black and shiny as beads. "Some rain wouldn't hurt," he said.

Realizing at last that he shouldn't have expected an invitation, Cecil settled his long frame into the only other available chair. "Well, I guess you're right there," he agreed, a little too heartily.

Despite what Cecil might have been thinking, Ray Ed was doing his best to be sociable. "Hear you're a fiddle player," he said. "You any good?"

Cecil cleared his throat. The palms of his hands were

heating up, and his neck itched under his collar where a rash was beginning to bloom. "Well, sir, I enjoy it, I truly do. I stood up at church last Sunday and played the recessional along with the organ. People seemed to take to it." He wiped his forehead with the back of his hand. "The Reverend Willis was real flattering. He seemed to think we could make it a regular thing."

"Don't get to church much, myself."

They fell silent. Cecil could smell chicken frying and heard high, screeching giggles coming from the kitchen. There was a baby crying itself hoarse somewhere in the back of the house. His throat felt like it was growing shut. He coughed again to clear it, deciding the tension he felt emanated from the farmer across the room. "I hope you approve of my betrothal, sir. I truly do."

Ray Ed shifted in his chair, stiff from the day's labors. "Not up to me," he said in a voice just short of a grunt.

Cecil finally let go of his hat. The way his hands were sweating had begun to warp the brim. "I just figured—the girls having no daddy and all."

Something like a smile played around the corners of the farmer's eyes. "Don't make no difference," he said. "Especially if the girl's a Quade."

Cecil tried to think of a good response, but found his wits had deserted him. He prided himself on his ability to speak well, and the other man's lack of the regular amenities was giving him the fidgets. "Well," he began again in a bright voice. "I want you to know I have Baby set on a real pedestal. She's a wonderful girl."

Ray Ed chuckled, a warm liquid sound in the back of his throat. "On a pedestal, eh?" Ray expertly rolled a cigarette on two fingers. He offered Cecil one, but he shook his head. The packet of tobacco disappeared once again into a vest pocket as though the man feared he might change his mind. "That's where I keep Iris Lee," he said matter-of-factly. "That way, you don't have to look 'em in the eye."

When he was done smoking, Ray Ed stood up. "You wanna eat, or what?"

They had fried chicken, pan gravy, mashed potatoes, yellow squash, and birthday cake with piped-on roses. And Cecil Moseley had to struggle to swallow his own spit. For the woman who stepped out of the kitchen with a plate of chicken in one hand and a boy child hefted on her opposite hip had set a fiery spirit to dancing in his guts. She'd stared at him curiously, a surprised, even amused expression playing across her features. But he felt more than saw the darker, more ominous look flicker across his body as she looked him up and down. To look at, the sisters seemed two sides of a thin coin, yet in Iris Lee, the prettiness turned to beauty, the softness to sensuality, and the clever light of the blue eyes was fashioned into a kind of greedy intelligence. It sparked a kind of rage in him, as though her glance alone had raped his private self. By the time Baby's suddenly grating soprano had done with the introductions and he'd taken the sister's hand, his balls were throbbing so badly he was afraid someone was going to notice the linen-clad erection poking through his suit. Hastily, he sat down.

He lost his mind over her. But he muddled through that narcotic evening as best he might, sure that the carelessness of her laugh or the way she reached up to repair a slipping hairpin were each secret signals apprising him of her plans for his destiny. Where, when, how, and yes-oh-please-my-love-my-darling—how often.

That night, on the long moonlit walk home, Baby squeezed his arm with a sickening proprietary air and asked him: "Well, honey, you haven't said hardly anything. Aren't you gonna tell me what you think of my family?"

He looked down at her stupidly, trying to think of the name of the snatch of music that played, over and over, around the vision of Iris Lee that danced in his mind. Baby's pretty, gentle face shone up at him with a childish, expectant expression that made him want to turn back time, to make it so the other's face and body would never happen to him. He wanted it to be yesterday, with him back on the road with his grip and his fiddle, back where he could feel again that nothing was inevitable. Abrubtly he took Baby's face in his hands and kissed her, his tongue desperately probing her mouth like something starving looking for food. She made a frightened little noise but he kept on kissing, letting his hands roam over the thin fabric of her dress like lost things, crushing her to him as though the timid warmth of her could fill the emptiness in him. That night, by the side of the road, Cecil Moseley took the silly virgin sister over and over again—until it was no use to try anymore. Until they lay in the long, sweet grass, sweating and sad and exhausted.

Just for spite.

Sixteen

PONDERING THE MECHANICS of taking a lover kept Iris Lee busy for days. The fact that the man she had in mind was about to marry her sister bothered her not as much as perhaps it should have. She figured anybody with one good eye and half sense could see the man was not cut out for marriage; she would leave sister Baby to make her own mistakes. But that didn't necessarily mean that he was good for nothing. A man like that could be good for a woman; the way he looked at her made her feel as though things were going her way. And that, perhaps more than anything else, was important. At the ripe old age of twenty-eight, Iris Lee Strait needed more than anything to see if, just for once, having something might not prove as good as wanting it. And she wanted Cecil Moseley very badly.

For awhile they were lucky; nobody found out. The preparations for the wedding went on and it was decided that Iris Lee would stand for her sister as matron of honor. Nobody could tell that the afternoon of the rehearsal had been spent with the two of them shut up in her husband's hayloft with the sun filtering over them like honey, and fucking like people possessed. Nobody could see that behind the bland, sweet rituals of the ceremony and the receiving line, two principal members of the wedding party were so gone on each other that desire hung sniffing at their heels like a starving dog when they were persuaded to dance. When the bridegroom, thoroughly drunk and unsteady on his feet, got up to play his fiddle with the band, no one paid it particular attention that he played the thing as though his life were slipping away, or that the smile he sent out through a sudden spurt of whiskey-fueled tears when he was finished was never meant for his brand-new wife.

Nobody saw the love or the sin that, given the day and age, would have undoubtedly enraged and disgusted the whole hymn-singing, Bible-thumping lot of them. Nobody knew anything. But then, people are stupid.

Too stupid, for example, to put together that the pale, rabbit-eyed woman who turned up in Earley's Apothecary with a child in her arms had anything to do with the suited dazzler who'd gone and married Baby Quade. The woman spoke to Hazel in a frightened, die-away voice and said she was looking for her husband, a man called Moseley. She said he'd never even seen the child. But Hazel shook her head—nobody like that had come through here, she said, though the name was common enough. But if the lady needed a place for her and the boy to sleep, there was a nice little rooming house just around the corner. Hazel had watched her go sympathetically—imagine a man running out on a poor little scrub heifer like that. The kid was pretty though, all them blond curls. And so she had only shrugged at the ways of the world and made herself a soda.

It was arranged that Cora (for that was the woman's name) could exchange light housework and some of the cooking for her room and board. Mrs. Bivins, who ran the establishment, figured it was the least she could do. Maybe it was the husband and maybe it wasn't—but that Mrs. Moseley had the look of somebody being eaten alive from the inside, and the good Mrs. Bivins knew there's nothing like some honest work to keep a body from thinking too much.

Having really nowhere else to go, Cora stayed in town an incredible three months before she caught sight of him on the street. She was out on the front porch, watering the last of the geraniums. At first, she was simply paralyzed, her arm halted with the watering can in midair, her mind and body frozen in a kind of dim wonder. It didn't seem possible that the figure standing in the street could be him. The image that she'd carried around in her brain was so familiar, so detailed, that once it came to life it didn't seem quite the same person. Then, all at once, she felt an absurd joy gushing into her sweet, colorless soul, followed just as quickly by a bitter, drowning disappointment. It was him all right. He wearing a wintry hat and talking to a blond woman who grinned and blew kisses at him before disappearing into the beauty parlor across the street.

Cecil looked at his watch, then hurried off in another direction. They were meeting at his house today. Iris Lee had gotten to complaining about taking all the risk for the two of them. Besides, she'd told him, folks might flap their tongues about his calling so frequently at the Straits, but nobody could fret at a woman dropping by to see her sister, could they? Cecil had only grinned and held her close. Iris Lee Strait was the smartest woman he knew. What he didn't know was that poor Cora had pulled on a sweater, gathered up her pretty baby, and was less than a hundred feet behind him as he turned the corner in front of his house.

Once she found him, poor Cora lost her nerve. She paced the block for almost half an hour before deciding to get on with things. The baby sobbed fitfully and a cold little wind sliced through her thin sweater, but she was oblivious to everything as she stepped slowly onto the porch, like somebody hearing the call of God.

Inside, things were quite a bit warmer. Iris Lee and Cecil were snuggled under Baby's wedding quilt like children, already glutted with love, yet unable to stop touching each other. Iris Lee had him in her mouth when the doorbell rang, and felt his penis wilt over her tongue like a wet cracker. She was already out of bed and pulling on her blouse when it rang again.

"Get up, goddamn you!" she hissed at him. "I thought you said she was getting a permanent!"

Cecil pulled on his pants, one leg at a time. To Iris Lee, it was like he was moving under water. Even the skin on his back had gone pale. Rage and fear and frustration were jumping around inside her, vying for position. Again the goddamned bell.

"Well, get out there! They're not just going to disappear!" She grabbed him by the arm and almost threw him from the bedroom toward the stairs. Two minutes later she was dressed and fairly composed. Enough at least, to crouch down by the banister to listen.

The voices rose and fell, his—a woman's, not Baby's. But there was a baby's voice too, first crying, then hushed to a cooing gurgle. Iris Lee nibbled on her thumb, trying to place the strangers' voices. But, quite unexpectedly, in the five minutes she chose to wait there on the stairs, the fire that Cecil Moses had lit in her heart went out. All the folly, all the emptiness showed itself to her at once in a clear, sweeping picture that showed him for what he was. It showed them both. And it chilled her to her bones. Coming so close to losing. (What? *What?* a desperate voice inside kept insisting. What would you have lost?) But it was too late. In five short minutes it was too late. The spell was broken. She rose and went downstairs, too empty even for weeping. No lover could have believed it got worse after that.

They were in the living room. Iris Lee stood listening, and it was a long time before the high-pitched keening of the woman made itself into words.

"I wanted you to know him. He's your son, anybody can tell that." There were sniffles, and the woman coughed and blew her nose. The tears reddened her pale eyes until they stood out on her face like fresh burns. "I named him Travis after my pa."

Iris Lee stared at the baby crawling across the floor. The woman fell to her knees beside it, rocking back and forth in misery.

"Please come home with us. Come home. I love you. It's just that I love you so much."

Baby threw open the door, flushed from the cold wind. "I had the most marvelous time . . ." she began, and stopped short as she took in the scene. Iris Lee moved toward her and Baby stared at her without comprehension.

"Hi," she said. "Well, hi. Did you stop to bring me those orange preserves?" Instinctively, Iris Lee put her arms around her and Baby just as instinctively returned the embrace. She looked up into her sister's face. "What is it? Iris

Lee? Honey . . . Who is this woman?'' She broke away and looked to Cecil for explanation. He stared at them stupidly.

"Baby, honey—oh, God—Iris Lee.'' He gestured help-lessly to the crumpled heap of mother and child. "This—this is my wife.''

It was Iris Lee who killed him. Above Baby's slow rising wail and Cora's wracking, hysterical sobs, her beautiful face was stolen and replaced by an empty mask; the eyes that met his gone dark and hard as stone. He loved her. She was the only one in the world, the only one who could touch him. He loved her and he lost her as soon as he looked into that cold imitation of a face. It was her face—and it was her mirror for him to see himself. In the moment he looked at Iris Lee his heart was cut out of him just as sure as if she'd held a knife.

The words came after, icy and flat and utterly final.

"You son of a bitch.''

That night, Cecil Moses sat by the side of the blood-red road that ran through the woods toward the cemetery and let the night settle over him like a comforter. He took out his fiddle and pieced together, for the first and last time, that fiery tune that Iris Lee Strait had conjured in his heart. When the last note had died away, he put the fiddle and bow carefully back in the worn, plush-lined case that had been the richest-looking thing he'd ever owned. Then he balanced the butt of a hunting rifle against the root of a tree, pulled the trigger with his toe, and forever ruined the hand-somest face the women of Atlantis County had ever seen.

The Stradivarius, however, was unharmed.

Seventeen

*Elijah Perdue's Musical Salvation Revival.
The Summer of 1899.*

I T SEEMED the handle God breathed in the child Victor
Purchase's ear that afternoon on the front porch was Elijah
Perdue, the Fiddling Prophet of Jesus. Thankfully, the news
didn't get out right away, for his parents kept him at home
three more years before turning him and his message loose
on the world. True to his mother's wishes, the fledgling
prophet did come to be considered (in some circles) a
"great" man, but there were never more than a few among
even his most fervent followers who would ever count him
as "musical."

Elijah hit the traveling preacher's circuit, which in those
days extended over a major portion of the continental
United States. The farmers and housewives and shopkeep-

ers who came to the revivals under the tattered, puce-colored tent that was Elijah's trademark came from a generation that rarely saw a newspaper, perceived the invention of the telephone and electric lights as instruments of the devil or the government, and never even dreamt of color television. The America of the day was clear-eyed, hardheaded, overworked, and sadly in need of entertainment. And, as any good preacher will tell you, God makes for great theater. They turned out by the thousands for the show, for the chance to see their neighbors, for the sheer release. For a revival was, first and above all, a chance to show feeling in public. To express, to the greatest degree possible, misery and joy and terror without the accompaniment of clucking tongues and raised eyebrows. It was freedom. And so they shouted and screamed and sang and wept and clapped their hands. They heard the Word and believed, if only for a day, that the God who sent drought and disease and taxes might be merciful. That if they raised their voices and believed, God could hear them, too.

So when Victor/Elijah struck out, at the age of fifteen, with a fiddle in his hand and Jesus in his eye, his audience was ripe for his harvesting of souls.

In the beginning, his gospel differed little from that of his fellows. After all, the fundamentals of salvation allow very little in the way of interpretation. And his age worked in his favor in those early days—a boy preacher was a novelty, and there are always those who confuse youth with purity. But if his youth and his fiddle were his bait to the faithful it was something else that kept them hooked. He said nothing at first, only sawed out hymns with his head bent and a strange pale fire in his eyes. When he was done, he held the Stradivarius aloft like a stone tablet and trembled.

"What have you heard?" he shouted.

There were very few among them who ever dared to

answer. Most were too stunned by the music and the incredible bellow that rose out of that scrawny chest.

" 'Sweet Bye and Bye'?" " 'Closer Walk with Thee'?" No one was ever quite sure.

Elijah never acknowledged any reply, only waited for a silence. "You have heard music," he told them, always a little sadly. "But I—when I pick up this instrument, it becomes the instrument of God."

Most nodded approvingly at this. Many even applauded, though on close examination it seemed a little deep for plain folks.

"You hear music!" Elijah screamed, jabbing a warped, accusatory finger into the crowd. *"But I hear the voice of God! Ladies and gentlemen! All of the faithful among you! I have heard the sound of the future!"*

Invariably, they went nuts.

It was a little to the south of Atlantis, on a hot June day, that Elijah met the devil. Naturally, he didn't recognize her right at first.

She was about fifteen then, and had been dragged to Elijah's revival on the arm of her portly and virtuous mother, who for years had known the girl to be afflicted. She sleepwalked, for one thing, and had more than once been discovered singing to herself in the hayloft when she thought no one could hear her. Elijah, on the other hand, was nearly thirty by that time and had become so thoroughly spiritual his disciples wondered under their collective breath why God hadn't called him to his bosom years ago.

Mostly, Elijah performed his revivals in a kind of stupor of righteousness. As the months of his travels stretched into years, he often had the sensation that he was watching himself from some distance when he was on the stage, and was always a little surprised at the grief, sin, and wailing that

he was able to produce when he confronted these hapless
congregations with the future of their souls. For when he
told them he had heard the sound of the future, he meant
what he said. Or at least, he meant it at the time. But it was
no whimpering world's end that echoed in the prophet's
mind—the future he heard was all the shuddering cacoph-
ony of heaven and hell; he fancied on those summer afternoons with the Stradivarius that he heard souls falling all
around him, snapping into oblivion like twigs underfoot; he
eavesdropped on the screams and chuckles of the damned;
he heard a chorus of angry angels and a few faint, breathless
voices of good crying out into the wilderness of life on
earth. Then the voice of the spirit would come and murmur
to him, quieting the madness in his head. He was never
quite sure what exactly God told him, but rather took it for
granted that His message was the same as had been heard
by all of his Chosen Ones.

Elijah Perdue was crazy as a bedbug.

As the sermons drew to a close, the healing began. When
they brought the girl forward to testify, she knelt before
him and bowed her head. Her mother stood up and explained her tribulations, enumerating the girl's afflictions.

"The falling fits is the worst, Reverend," she said. "She's
had it in her since the day she was borned. Her eyes roll
back and she foams sometimes. If you ask me, it's the Devil
wrassling Jesus for her soul."

Elijah had them lead the mother away, resigned as he was
to his mission. But when he placed his hands on her the
Fiddling Prophet of Jesus experienced something as close
to God's electricity as he ever got. Her shoulders were
smooth and round under her dress, and something about
the curious strawberry shade of her hair made his preacher's
collar suddenly unbearably tight. Almost experimentally,
he lifted his hands from her shoulders and raised them three

inches above her head. He could feel it still, the heat that coursed through his palms and up through his body, warm as another's blood. The crowd waited restively. "Heal 'er, Reverend!" "Bring her to Jesus!"

Elijah lifted his arms and waited for silence.

He placed one hand on the girl's head and felt a shiver go through her. He squeezed her skull in his hand like a melon as he raised his right arm to God. Her hair was silky beneath his fingers.

"Do you love God?" he demanded, words and thoughts and images dancing in his brain.

"Yes," the girl whispered, and Elijah noticed with a start that she had begun to weep. Tears were splashing over the tops of his boots like rain.

They were both trembling now. He departed from his usual formula and asked her a question. "What is your name, girl?"

"Ihmphdee."

He measured the crowd. A prophet is not allowed to repeat a question. He took the girl's chin in his hand and raised her face to him. Her kneeling brought her face level with his crotch and he felt the sweet, hot breath of damnation come over his manhood. Sweat poured down his forehead and the roaring began in his ears. Her eyes were the color of thin ice and her mouth leapt out of her pale face like stain on a bed sheet, full and red and riveting.

"SHOUT YOUR NAME TO JESUS!"

The terrified girl looked for a moment as though she might refuse, but his grip tightened and she raised her voice to heaven. "Icy Fee Moulder!" she cried. "And I Love Jesus!"

Eighteen

Autumn 1899.

IT WAS SHORTLY THEREAFTER that Elijah Perdue
made the decision to lodge his mission in Atlantis for the
winter. The folks there seemed more in need than in other
places, he explained to his manager, you had only to walk
the streets and notice their godless expressions. Never in
his travels had he witnessed such a forsaken people—they
might as well have named the town Gomorrah as far as he
was concerned.

More businessman than Bible-thumper, the manager, a
certain Mr. Sprayberry, had only nodded restlessly, figuring
that it would be wisest to give in right away, before the boss
got wound up too tight about it. The way in which he'd
arranged the Fiddling Prophet's accounting would keep

him comfortable for the rest of his life even if he decided
to depart this particular gravy train. It was a feat on which
he congratulated himself almost daily, though in truth the
books themselves hadn't been at all difficult to manage. The
choir and stagehands were so full of Jesus he never had to
pay them more than he would niggers, and as for the
prophet, well, he just never seemed to care. And if the man
was so busy tending the flock he never saw the wool being
pulled over his own eyes, some things just weren't his problem. Sprayberry bowed from the waist and told Elijah to
count on him for everything. The collection plate never
amounted to shit in the winter, anyway.

Elijah rose stiffly from the chair behind his desk, clad only
in the oyster silk choir robe he had taken to wearing in
private. "I'm glad you see the true light, brother. There are
lambs among the lions who have need of my poor services."
Elijah struck his breast and bowed his head. The movement
caused the robe to fall close to the preacher's body, giving
the other a glimpse of form and shadow through the fabric.
He hurriedly averted his eyes and took his leave, not daring
to snicker until the door had closed behind him. After what
he'd seen through the choir robe, Mr. Sprayberry found it
appropriate that Elijah had chosen to preach for a living.
The poor sonofabitch was hung like a cat.

That there was a particular bright-haired virgin lamb
among the flock that might require Elijah's poor services
more than the rest never got to be an issue, at least, not until
most of the damage was already done. Despite the hoopla
that surrounded his traveling show, religion to most of the
neighborhood was mostly a lick-and-promise affair, with
only a few believing in their hearts that they were so
diseased as to require more than the prescribed Sunday
dose of soul medicine.

But that Moulder girl was another story. If the preacher

felt he needed to spend more time at the tiny house by the woods than he did anywhere else, it was because of her and her alone, the poor creature having gained a reputation for being possessed of the devil. After Icy Fee's initial shouts of passion for her Savior the afternoon of the tent meeting, she'd pitched a kind of fit in front of them all, falling to the floorboards with her eyes rolling and her tongue lolling halfway to hell itself. So most felt that if the prophet was game to wrestle the serpent that dwelt in that childish body, he should have at it.

And, in his fashion, he did.

At first, the seizure had been so violent nobody could think to do anything but stare. Elijah himself had stood over her, clutching the neck of the Stradivarius in one hand and the front of his coat in the other, the tortured body writhing like a snake at his feet. That his timorous lust had precipitated such an answer from the Lord seemed ridiculously overstated, and he'd decided right then that another entity was responsible.

"Satan has stolen her!" he cried, raising the fiddle aloft. "He has crept into this holy place to mock us!" The girl had quieted some by this time, her lips stretched back as if in terrified agreement, her eyes rolled back to the whites. Elijah gazed down at her and another part of his mind took note that her blouse had come open. He raised his eyes again to the throng.

"WILL YOU LET THE DEVIL MOCK US?" he bellowed. Sweat ran into his eyes and blurred his sight; the audience churned before him like a thick, multicolored batter.

"No!" they cried. "No-no-No-no-No!" They began to chant and clap their hands.

Slowly Elijah sank to his knees, raising his arms for silence. "Then," the cracked, hoarse voice fell to a reverent whisper, "leave her to me." He scooped Icy Fee's quivering form in his arms, prepared to carry her. Two members of the choir rushed from the rank to help, but he shook his head and backed away as the curtain began to fall. The audience screamed and shouted their applause, and the prophet held her tightly to him, unable to tear his eyes from her now-unconscious face. "Suffer the children to come unto me," he whispered, and carried her away.

Icy Fee's eyelids fluttered open and darted around the strange room. She was on her back on a sort of table, and the cracks in the plaster of the ceiling told her that she was no longer where she had been. She hurt, she hurt so very much. Her body ached and strained everywhere, and she thought for a moment that she must have collapsed while hauling the washing for her mother like she did sometimes. But no—today had been the meeting, the preacher and the tent. There was something about the preacher. But it was too hard to remember—too hard to think. She closed her eyes and dozed for a time, fretting at the shadowy figures that danced on the edges of her rest, murmuring among themselves.

When she woke again, the preacher was with her, sitting in a chair with his head in his hands. He was wearing a kind of robe, light-colored and silky, wet here and there with dark perspiration. He was murmuring something to himself and she began to be frightened when she saw that he was weeping.

"Am I going to die?" she whispered.

He came and stood over her, his robe billowing. He wiped his face and stared down at her dazedly, a peculiar fire in his eyes. "No, child," he said softly. "Not yet."

Icy Fee returned the gaze. The preacher, a voice chided in her mind, there was something she wanted to remember about the preacher.

138

"Can you stand?" he asked her.

"I think so."

He took her hand gently and eased her up, supporting her under the small of her back like a baby. She made to get unsteadily to the floor, but he stopped her. "No, girl. Stand on the table."

She stared at him wordlessly, the question in her pale eyes, but swung her legs up despite her protesting muscles. She rose, her bright hair close to a lantern that swung from a chain on the ceiling. The preacher drew close to her and she could feel his breath against her stomach until he swept back to the safety of his chair. With the sudden shift in light, she could see that he was naked underneath that angel's robe. He was silent for a moment, his long fingers forming a steeple in front of his face as he watched her.

"Strip off your clothes, girl."

Icy Fee trembled, unable to move.

Elijah cleared his throat and elaborated. "I need to look for the devil's mark on you, girl. Strip off your clothes." He pushed forward a little in his chair, his eyes darting uncontrollably toward a corner of the room. She turned her head in slight modesty, and saw that a small cot had been made up there.

Then, for the first time, she looked him in the eye, a thin arm already reaching for the button on her skirt. She smiled a little as she remembered. There was indeed something about the preacher.

She drew a shaky breath and smiled again as the skirt loosened from her waist. And, seeing no particular reason to go to God a virgin, Icy Fee Moulder did as she was told.

Nineteen

Atlantis County. August 7, the Present.

OVER SUPPER that evening, Iris Lee announced her intention to read the will the day after tomorrow. It was a statement that wasn't as impressive as it might have been.

No, the rest of them just nodded and went on eating, as though she'd announced nothing more significant than her plans to spay a housecat. It was infuriating, really. Just because she liked the world in order didn't mean she was lacking a sense of the drama, and she was certain that a little more enthusiasm would only have been proper under the circumstances.

Grace cleared the dishes and began to do them, lost in dreamy contemplation. Iris Lee watched her with narrowed eyes and a can of after-dinner beer at one elbow. She figured Grace to be the weakest, or at least the greediest link in her little family chain, and thought that if she could get under Grace's skin on the subject of the inheritance, the evening might not prove a total waste, after all.

"Grace," she said sweetly. "Have you got any particular plans for your inheritance money? Assuming you get any, I mean."

Grace contemplated the soap bubbles for a long moment before answering. "I thought I'd donate most of it to the church, Mammy. Isn't that what you're planning to do with yours?"

Iris Lee sputtered. "God has struck people down for lesser lies, miss. I'd remember that if I were you."

Grace smiled to herself. Gotcha, she thought. "Yes, ma'am," she answered in as demure a tone as she could muster.

"Rinse that glass again. You've got soap all over it."

"Yes, ma'am."

All at once, Iris Lee felt old. She bore Grace Ellen no great love, but Grace had a way of keeping her honest in ways that the others couldn't, being, finally, just a little too smart for much pushing around. But, old or not, Iris Lee saw no reason to start giving up on her authority. She went to the sink and put a hand on Grace's soapy forearm.

Grace looked up with some surprise. They were not in the habit of touching.

"What do you really mean to do with the money, Grace?" the old woman insisted.

Grace met her eyes. It was a fair question, it deserved an honest answer. "I don't have any idea. Mammy," Grace dropped her voice to just above a whisper. "Did Ray Ed leave a lot?"

Iris Lee tilted her chin and turned away. "None of your business."

Grace dried her hands. "Mammy, what is all this about?"

"Nothing," Iris Lee said. "I just thought you might want to let your family in on your plans, that's all."

Grace studied the old woman. Nothing was a word that had rarely fallen from her grandmother's lips. When you asked a woman like that what things were about, she usually told you.

Iris Lee looked at her fingernails. "It's just that Ray Ed was always so partial to you." She hoped she sounded convincing.

To the best of her recollection, Grace couldn't claim knowledge to anything of the kind. "He was?"

"Well, he picked you to die in front of, didn't he?" Iris snapped. "That ought to count for something."

"It did," Grace said before she could stop herself. Then, seeing the greedy interest in Iris Lee's eyes, she had no choice but to finish it. "He said something before he died. But—it doesn't really make any sense."

Iris Lee was on her feet. "What? What was it?"

Grace drew a deep, faltering breath. "He said, 'Destiny is not a blind armadillo.'"

Weary to her bones, Iris Lee sank back in her chair. "Oh," she said finally. "That."

Grace stared at her. "That?"

"It was some saying Ray Ed picked up from a wetback who worked down at the Hooten farm. He used to say it all the time." Thoroughly disgusted, she drained the last of her beer.

"Oh," said Grace. And went back to the dishwashing.

Contrary to his expectations, the news of the will meant little to Charles T. He supposed his father would remember him some way or other, but in the past weeks he'd more or less given up any notion of birthrights. Returning to Atlantis and seeing his mother and children had so weighted him with a sense of the past that he'd simply given himself over to his role in things, no longer able to envision the possibility of buying his way back to identity with a dead man's funds. He had only nodded at the news and walked Boo off to the pasture fence to play a concert. The boy had been listless and fretful of late and the father in him figured a little guiltily that it was due to the lack of a encouraging audience.

In fact, poor Boo had a somewhat milder version of the disease that had run raging through his elder brother since their trip into town. The boy found this new aspect of the world fell just short of the miraculous, and had been despairing ever since that the fiddle he played might no longer be able to adequately tell the tales of his secret heart.

Davey, unencumbered by the past and unfettered by any sense of his future, could afford to relish his prospects more than could the others. And yet he was the least moved by his grandmother's announcement. Instead he was relishing his misfortunes. For since he'd first walked through the screen door and into the Reverend Brother Heck's immaculate kitchen, his thoughts had worn a groove around the sweet, ineffable memory of his wife Luanne and the astonishing body wherein she dwelt. Young as he was, he had never taken to the notion that a man's life could be altered by the presence of a woman in it, much less that a particular one could make a difference. More comfortable, certainly, but not different. He held himself up as his own best example, figuring that if women were able to change him, certainly one would have succeeded by now. Look at Carlene. And yet, in less than an instant, when he'd first encountered the tough and joyful spirit that shone out of the whore's emerald eyes, he spent the majority of his waking hours examining the memory and its effect on his spirit, enamored of the sheer impossibility of it all.

So he went out alone after supper, unable to bear the presence of expectation in his life. Instead, he spent that evening driving past her house in Atlantis, thinking of things he wanted her to know about him, until he found his way to a tavern on the state line and drank himself into a cheerful insensibility. When he finally made it back to the farm, the strain of having gotten there intact along with the beer under his belt put him to sleep on the spot. He never made it inside, but lay down on the front seat of his father's Toyota, smiling and oddly content. Tomorrow, after all, was another day.

He awoke several hours later, convinced that he was dead. That his relations had chosen to put him down in a car bothered him not in the slightest. He figured he would enjoy the prospect of an eternity spent drag-racing deceased Egyptians. But the throbbing of his bladder put him in mind of more important matters, and, as he sat up and looked out the window, he was more than a little surprised to find the ghost of Ray Ed Strait standing by the pasture fence, engulfed in only enough pale light to distinguish his spirit from the rest of the world.

When he was able to think about it again, Davey would say that the old man looked just fine—considering. As a matter of fact, it was one of the first things that occurred to him when the vision motioned him closer.

Ray Strait grinned and Davey could see that whatever else the afterlife had in store, false teeth were not in the inventory. "Well, do yer business, boy. That's what you got up fer, ain't it?"

Davey fumbled with his zipper, his bladder throbbing for attention. The spirit cackled appreciatively as Davey finished, steam rising around their feet in the dark. "Never had equipment like that myself. You got a real deluxe model whanger there, you know that?" The spirit moved around for a better look, shaking his head. "Enjoy it while you can, boy. Take my word."

Davey stole a downward glance at himself as he put away the equipment in question, having no real idea what to say. The ghost cackled again and looked out over the pasture, shoving his hands deep into the pockets of ancient, greasy overalls. Davey followed the gaze, then squeezed his eyes shut tight. Some dream, he thought. Some really bad-ass, beer-foam cocaine thing he was dreaming. He opened his eyes again, but the grandfather thing was right where it had been, staring out over the darkened, silent fields.

"Ain't no dream, boy," it told him, and sighed softly.

So much for the dream theory, Davey thought. He waited for more.

The vision murmured thoughtfully, "Place needs rain," and turned to face him, grinning again. "You can get away with a lot when you're dead, boy. Do a whole lot of things. . . ." The vision gestured out over the fields, still grinning. "Broke my ass workin' this place. Never got to do nothin' else and never wanted to." The grandfather ghost scuffed the broken toe of a work boot in the grass and peered toward the beginnings of light that flickered on the horizon. "Only thing I ever wanted was a little help—little sun, little rain . . ." he said, smiling like it was an oft-told joke. "Hell, now that I'm dead I kin do all kinda crazy shit—appear, disappear, all that shit." Ray paused and shook his head. "Found out all kinda things I didn't know before . . . but I still can't make it rain! Weird, ain't it?"

"Weird," Davey agreed.

"You're a good boy, Davey. You don't rush a person." The ghost reached out to clap a hand on his shoulder and remembered that he couldn't, staring down at what had been his hand in momentary surprise. He shrugged then and grinned as if it weren't important. The hands went into the pockets again.

"Came to warn you, Davey. You gotta be careful."

Having gotten this far, Davey decided to pursue it. "Why careful?"

"Snake's a comin'."

"Snake?"

Ray Ed was fading now, the faint light that filtered from the horizon diminishing his form by degrees. But he nodded again. "Snake," he said, the voice soft and whispery carried on the wind, voice and spirit blown slowly away, like dust caught in the coming light.

He left Davey still staring at the spot by the fence long after there was nothing left to see. But it was the last afterthought of words that came to Davey's mind before he turned toward the house that was the most bewildering of all.

"Take care of the women, boy."

Twenty

Atlantis County. August 1899.

THEY HAD A PLACE in the woods, the two of them.
Icy Fee led Elijah there by the hand, late in the summer.
She knew a place, she kept saying as he stumbled blindly
through the underbrush, it was cooler there.

In those days, the Moulder place consisted of nothing but
a tangle of trees and a small, no-account bayou that slithered
through it, quick and sparkling in the spring and grown so
brackish and slow by the end of August that people avoided
it altogether, convinced the place was full of typhus. The
farmers around liked to speculate about what those rich
acres might have amounted to if somebody with more natural gumption than old Vaughn Moulder had fallen into the
place, but as it was, they supposed nothing but trial would

ever come of it. Their wives warned them away from even minor poaching of the property, though the place was alive with good shooting; the women invented tales of bogeymen and snakebite to keep the children out. In those days, every mother in fifty miles took the same dark notion about the Moulder woods, and their spouses knew better than to argue. It was a shame though, wasn't it, they said, rising up from their plows and mopping at their foreheads and wondering at the clutch of trees rising up out of all that good farmland like a defiance. All grown over and going to ruin.

The girl carried a rolled-up bunch of newspapers under one arm. Walking behind, he could see the print smudging off onto the thin fabric of her dress, creasing in the sweat of her inner elbow. His black preacher's coat caught on a briar and she giggled at his helplessness, snatching it loose with one deft movement of her fingers. She ran lightly ahead of him, calling him to come on, to follow her invisible path.

When he came to the edge of a clearing a shudder passed through him, setting his teeth on edge. The wood ended so unexpectedly it was as if God had stuck his hand in to grope for something unseen and pulled it out again, leaving the place filled with some remembered light. He saw stones piled up in circles around the empty space, the arrangement so ancient that moss and flowers dared creep out of the spaces between them. He wondered at it, holding back even as he saw the crouching form of the girl, spreading her papers over a little hollow in the center of the circle, singing and smiling to herself. Elijah stood at the edges of it all, not wanting to come in. Icy Fee moved around easily, her lightness growing even less substantial in the clearing, as though she might float off and leave him should she choose. He realized with a start that she was saying something. Her thin, childish voice penetrated his mind so abruptly it was

as though she hadn't spoken at all, but instead that he'd
somehow heard her thinking.

"No one ever comes here but me. I've known about it
for the longest time."

She stood up then, flushed and excited. Her pale eyes
glinted in the sun like jewels on the velvet of her skin. She
held out her hand to him but he hung back, suddenly self-
conscious. She came to him then, encircling his narrow
chest with her arms.

"I missed you," she said simply, and leaned her bright
head against his coat. He struggled with himself, trying to
form some question even as he pulled her closer and caught
the subtle pollen smell of her hair. Abruptly she pulled
away.

"I almost forgot. I brought you something." She groped
in the pocket of her dress and dropped something into his
palm. Without thinking he stepped into the circle to better
examine the thing in the light. Icy Fee made her way to her
mattress of newspapers and smiled at him.

"Rattlesnake rattlers," she told him, reaching up to undo
a button at the back of her neck. "I killed it myself, right
near here. It was a big one. Fourteen rattles and a button.
I had to hit it over and over before it died."

Elijah stared at her, shivering a little as she pulled the
dress over her head and tossed it to the side. She stood there
and spread her arms for him to come to her, and he saw
suddenly that the silky tuft beneath her belly was the same
bright color as the rest of her hair. He slipped the things
in his coat pocket and plucked at his tie while she waited for
him.

"If you put them in your fiddle," she said, tiptoeing up
to kiss his chin, "they'll keep the little spiders out."

Twenty=one

SHE WAS ALL he ever wanted, and in the end it was just too much for him.

That year before the century turned, Indian summer stretched almost to December as if to oblige them, and Elijah Perdue began to think of that spot in the woods as the only place outside of heaven where he could feel he was alive.

He believed for awhile that he was trying to save her, though it never quite came clear that he wanted to save her for himself, Jesus and his instrument having a tendency to confuse themselves in the prophet's mind. News spread that he'd cast out her devils and cured her of the thrashing fits; there was talk of his building a permanent mission. But whether it was her devils or a lusty acquaintance with some of his own, anyone looking could see the change in him.

Though the revivals under the tent were held as usual, and the voices inside him screamed the same raw message and his congregation wallowed on the brink of damnation, another (Hers? Was it hers?) denied such unrelenting doom. One Sunday, raising his fiddle and bow, he'd heard that reassuring rattle inside it and fixed his congregation with an expression so unexpectedly benign they'd grown restless, thinking Judgment might have come after all.

It was she who coaxed them out of their clumsiness, working from some warm instinct that told her where the pleasure was hidden, surprising their bodies until it got to where he could no longer tell, when they coiled together in the grass, where his own stopped and hers began. It all bewildered him so much that he never quite realized the nature of it. Having no experience of women, lust, in his mind, was a painted whore and love was a pregnant wife. That was what he preached from his pulpit and that was what he believed. But Icy Fee Moulder was something else.

After they made love he would doze, full of peace and sun and the approving Miz Moulder's endless chicken dinners, his pale limbs heavy in the autumn sun. One afternoon toward the end, he woke to find his body covered in wildflowers, shaggy mustard and feathery milkweed and whatever else Icy Fee had been able to find, all torn so fiercely from the ground that they still had their roots, and Elijah had to quell the unbidden notion that she was decorating him like a corpse. He protested such wantonness, but she only laughed at him like a child. And she was a child still. He could see that even as he could see that she was growing, her hair had darkened to the color of blossom honey and her breasts were higher, rounder, hot to his touch. Sometimes he opened his Bible and read her the psalms and the Song of Solomon, quizzing her now and again as to God's intentions. She answered in earnest when she was able, but just as often he caught her glancing at him out of the corner of her pale eye, a child who knows the teacher has no power when school is done.

Yet she professed to love him. She listened devotedly while he rehearsed his sermons, came to him with the same unashamed passion. But later, when he was alone, he fancied there was some other creeping in—a knowingness—the way she had of answering his questions before he could ask them, or finding his hat when he was sure it was lost. She got to where she could tell when he was coming to see her and when he wasn't even before he could make some excuse, yet accepted his visits without question or comment or asking when he would return. But he was so in the habit of being apart he could not help but be suspicious of belonging. The better she knew him the less he understood her, the more familiar she was the more convinced he became that she was holding something back. He couldn't find a way to give himself to her and couldn't find a way to leave. When he found she understood him, it made him feel exposed, helpless, as though he'd been tricked out of something important.

He woke up one afternoon to find her in a seizure, her eyes rolling back, naked body wrenching and bucking in a horrible parody of love. He started for her and drew back, a tortured chorus in his mind taunting him, gleefully shouting that he'd been fornicating with a demon. But he fought them, pity and love making him grab her and clutch her to him long enough to force his fingers down her throat and hold her tongue. She bit him until he bled, but he held on fiercely, silently begging God and the devil both to let his love alone.

She regained consciousness around twilight, wrapped in

his arms and the black preacher's coat. Elijah was there, staring off into the distance, his lips moving in some calculated prayer. She reached up to touch him and he moved his face to look at her. His eyes were black and haggard and something in them made her afraid.

Icy Fee stirred and sat up carefully, waiting for her limbs to belong to her again, slowly obeying her brain. She stretched out an arm for her clothes and pulled her dress over her head. Elijah watched her, waiting until she buttoned up before trying to speak. Icy Fee met his eyes and for a moment they cleared; he was himself again. But just as quickly they filled up again with that blackness, illuminated only by some mad flickering that came from somewhere inside of him.

She touched his hand and he jumped as if he'd been scalded.

"What is it?" Icy Fee struggled to keep her voice from shaking. "Was it—was it a bad one?"

He was on his feet then, running his hands through his stringy hair.

"What are you trying to do?" he demanded, his voice rising through the trees.

Icy Fee clutched his coat to her. "What is it?" she kept asking him, "what's wrong?"

"I am a man of God." Elijah stood in the center of the clearing, the ground under him spread with newspapers. He struck his breast and made an odd, strangled sound in his throat. "And yet you betray me."

Icy Fee scrambled up next to him. "Betray you? I never—"

He whirled around and gripped her shoulders so tightly it hurt. *"You do!"* he bellowed at her, bringing his face so close to hers she could feel his breath. "I healed you! I called on the power of God! You let the devil get back in!"

She drew back from him, holding herself.

"You only pretended to accept Jesus!"

"No, I didn't! I believed! I did! I can't help the fits. It just—"

"You liar." Elijah's voice dropped suddenly to a whisper. "You thought you could keep me here with you, didn't you? All the time with the devil inside you." Elijah was pacing, his scrawny body doubling with each new agony. "You listened to him, didn't you? Let him tell you how to get me to marry you? Didn't you?"

"Married? Of course I want to marry you, I love you." She was so shocked, the tears started before she could catch up to them; it was almost a minute before she could sob.

Elijah sank to the ground. "Now I have to leave you, don't you understand that?" He pounded at the ground with his fist. "You let him in! Oh God! You wanted me to stay here, to rob me of my mission. To take the power of God from me!" At last it was too much and Elijah, too, began to weep. He couldn't help himself; even as he heard them, he knew his words for lies and cowardice and fear and could only scream them louder against the cold emptiness that was filling up his heart. His body shook against the awful responsibility. There was no God and no devil, he knew, there was only him, letting loose the cold destruction that was in him.

Icy Fee wiped at her eyes with the back of her hand. "Why? Why do you have to go?"

Elijah struggled to his feet and began to dress himself, groping for his clothing in the gathering dark. Icy Fee was whimpering, saying things through her tears that he would not hear. He knew she was waiting for him to right this thing, holding up the broken doll for him to fix.

He walked her back without speaking again. Icy Fee drifted along her invisible path like a sleepwalker, struggling to think amidst the numbing waves of pain. She felt as though she were almost literally beside herself, as if some other self were there, insisting that all she could do was follow that black form that stormed through the woods in front of her.

They stopped at the edge of the trees, a little away from the house. Elijah's buggy waited for him, and the horse tossed his head and stamped when it caught the scent of him coming. She flinched when he put a hand under her chin, but held on until she made herself look at him.

She thought wildly that his eyes were like an animal's, and suddenly some part of it came clear to her. He was leaving because he was afraid. There was no reason. He was afraid, frozen like an animal in a blinding light. She knew it as surely as if he had spoken the words. And with that knowledge came a hatred so fierce it was dizzying, and she began to strike him, thumping his face and bony chest until he caught her wrists and held her fast.

Elijah looked into her shattered face, tear-stained and streaked with dirt, suddenly ashamed. He felt it like a judgment on him, so much damage wrought in so little time. When she raised her face again the eyes had gone cold and pale, like moonlight in winter. Her mouth was set in a twisted, defiant line and he felt her contempt like a blow. He had to struggle not to embrace her, not to take her in his arms and beg her to believe it was all a mistake. And in the next moment he hated her for not making him do it—not seeing that she was breaking his heart.

He tried to smile and dropped her wrists. His voice came, mocking them both.

"Try to understand, I can't belong to you. I belong to God."

With that he turned and strode toward the buggy. She watched him go, shivering and hiccupping and trying to form some prayer—anything—enough to make God send her a gun. When the last of him had disappeared over the rise she crept along the path and through her back door, quelling her sobs so her mother wouldn't hear. Her bedroom was at the back and she stumbled into it, amazed suddenly that everything should look so much the same.

It might have been a minute or an hour that she stood there, playing it over in her mind, trying to make sense of it with anger and grief and desperate love vying for a piece of her crowded heart, each leaving her weeping and gasping for breath. She cried until she couldn't anymore, so emptied of feeling that the final idea occurred to her with a certain dull surprise.

Her hope chest stood at the foot of the bed, filled with linens and the beginnings of a trousseau. Her mother had added a quilt to it recently, worked in a dizzying pattern of colors she'd called The Wedding Rings. She'd finished it just last week, presenting the thing over breakfast one morning and telling her it was for when she and the preacher got married. Icy Fee had blushed about it and protested, but her mother had only shaken her head.

"I know when a man's in love and when he isn't," she'd said.

Icy Fee lifted the lid and looked in, the smell of starch and cedar wafting up at her, making her gag. She snatched out some of the nightgowns and dishes to make room, working swift and silent as a cat. The dark had come but she didn't bother with a lamp, she just stripped to the skin, mindful of the smell of love that clung to her like a guilty conscience. She spread the wedding quilt in the bottom of the chest and took a pillow off the bed. She clutched it to her and crept in, tormenting all her muscles until she found a way to fit. She pressed the pillow over her face, grateful for the cool of the cover and the brief, sweet clothesline smell in her nostrils. Then Icy Fee Moulder lowered the lid of her hope chest and lay motionless.

It was cramped and dark and full of the close, suffocating odor of cedar. She pressed the pillow tighter to her face and smiled behind it, giving herself over to the blackness. She was sure to be dead by morning.

Twenty=two

March 1927.

ERNEST EARL HAD had quite a time collecting what remained of Cecil Moseley.

When the sheriff called him out that cold morning to pick up the body on the cemetery road, he claimed he couldn't tell who it was, so much of the head was gone. But standing over the newly departed, surveying the mess of clotted blood and pulp against the soiled linen suit collar, Ernest Earl had to quiet the absurd notion that the lawman had only been teasing him, saving it for a surprise. Though to give the undertaker credit, he managed to pull himself together before voicing any appreciation, figuring the sheriff could not possibly have known it was his birthday.

He came upon the Stradivarius almost as an afterthought.

After seeing to it that the sheriff's men had got the long-legged, nearly headless form safely in his mortuary wagon, he spent some time going over the landscape for any missing parts, so absorbed in the search that he kicked the case a few yards before he realized what it was. He held the case by the neck as he made his way to the wagon, lingering fastidiously to scuff away some bloodstains in the road with the toe of his shoe. He rode back to town with the fiddle beside him on the seat, whistling.

He was naturally disappointed when Iris Lee and Ray showed up that afternoon to make the rather cursory arrangements. She identified the body with a look so shut up and mysterious, he'd had to ask her twice if it was her brother-in-law. Even then, it seemed to him that there was a great distance in her response, almost as if she'd known the corpse by some other name. They'd given him a deposit and told him to do what he had to, and it was only after Ray went to crank the car and Ernest made himself inquire after the widow's welfare that something of Iris Lee's rocky mask seemed to crumble away.

"Doctor says she'll get over it," she told him grimly. "But I can't say." She snatched at the strap of her purse and pulled it closer in front of her, holding on with both hands. "Some things don't ever come right, do they?"

They stood with the question hanging between them, but the husband returned and commenced patting her shoulder, leading her away before Ernest could make up a reply.

It was, of course, a closed-casket funeral. Ernest Earl had taken over the business almost completely by that time, and though his aging father may have had some fretful, swan-song inclination to rebuild the ruin that passed for the dead man's features, nothing ever came of it, even had the old man got his son to listen. For, twenty minutes after Cecil Moseley took his place on the workroom slab, Ernest Earl had another inspiration. It occurred to him all at once that the condition of this corpse afforded him a positively gilded opportunity to try his hand at mummification.

It was not as strange as it sounds. Ernest Earl had been among the thousands infected by an Egyptian fever that swept the world following the unearthing of Tutankhamen's bunker of the afterworld, his mortician's heart excited particularly by the ancient, gauze-wrapped carrion contained in the pyramid, preserved like something precious. He'd studied what he could about the process and, though not in possession of a proper recipe, he'd gleaned enough knowledge to warrant an experiment. Until then, he'd confined himself to the preservation of an occasional housecat, keeping the trophies under his porch where he could monitor the remains for signs of deterioration. And he would most probably never have considered such an historic undertaking of any human subject had not Cecil Moseley gone and blown his face away, and so cheated his family and neighbors of a last gander at his foolishness. As it was, Ernest considered the circumstances as a sort of professional birthday present; his only regret in mummifying Cecil being that he would have to wait until Judgment Day to know how well he'd done.

He worked far into the night in those two days before the funeral, wrapping the ruined skull in some raggedy sheets that he'd torn into bandages and drenched in a heady concoction of melted frankincense resin, ambergris, myrrh, and paraffin. Prior to the wrapping he'd cured the corpse like a piece of meat, eviscerating the body and packing the remains in a casket filled with sugar and salt. Two of the more exotic ingredients came from Deke Moseley's wife, a woman who dwelt in the woods south of town and was said to practice conjuring. The third he'd ordered some months before, from a mail-order apothecary in New York. The

paraffin he'd got from Mrs. Bivins, who ran the boarding-
house and had some left from her summer preserving. The
fruit had been poor that year, she assured him when she'd
overheard his asking at the general store as he purchased
the sugar and salt; he could have all wanted.

Somewhere in the middle of it all he changed his mind
and decided to keep the thing. Somewhere in the middle
of it, he realized that this was the body who had, those many
months, lain by the woman that should have been his. And
the pain of the realization was so exquisite he hated to part
with it all at once. So he weighted the coffin with stones dug
from his garden and carefully nailed them in, bowing his
head in reverence as the pallbearers lowered it into the
ground at the funeral. He wondered a little at what the
townsfolk would think should they ever find he'd kept his
mummy of Cecil, but he took what precautions he could,
locking the thing in an armoire in his bedroom, a place
where no human being but him ever set foot. It was after
the funeral was over and the scandal locked away with its
perpetrator that Ernest came in mind of the fiddle, toying
with the notion that he might have done better to put it in
the coffin, buried away like some pharaoh's trinket. He
thought then he should take it to the widow, even went so
far as to put on his suit and polish his shoes and rehearse
a speech for when she met him at the door. He cleaned the
case carefully and oiled the peeling leather, making sure
that what bloodstains there were could never be recognized. She might even be grateful, he told himself, even
offer her hand.

Then, to make a final inventory before he surrendered
it to Baby, he checked inside, swinging back the cover to
show the plush lining and sudden, breathtaking glint of the
Stradivarius in the light.

He could not tell how long he held it in his hands, how

long he stared into the depths of the warm, smooth finish, the wood grain undulating like a vision in a fortune-teller's ball. It wasn't Baby's after all, came the whisper in his mind. If it belonged to anyone it belonged to the bandaged shell that lay in his closet and his music-making days were surely done. No, Ernest Earl Faxton decided right then to keep it and make it his own, knowing with all the certainty of delusion that if its magic dwelt with him then she would be drawn to Ernest as she had been when Cecil kept it by his side. That if he kept the Stradivarius, she would have to somehow hear that tortured music playing in his heart.

And keep it he did, locked in the armoire along with the mummy, safe in his house. He kept it until the Tuesday morning when he returned from his doctors, knowing that he could not wait for Baby anymore. He took a key from his vest pocket, where it had lain near his heart for fifty years. And when he placed it, case and all, on the doorstep of Baby's house in town, twenty minutes before the rest of the family came to luncheon, he hoped some part of her would understand.

PART
TWO

If music be the food of love, play on.

Twenty=three

Atlantis County. August 10.

TRAVIS MOSELEY, JR., lay on his back on a single bed at the Mile-Away Motel, his arms raised above him, staring at his hands. The rash always started with the palms of his hands, a red, sizzling itch that crawled up his arms to the back of his neck and roared around his armpits, until the itch turned to living fire, until dwelling in that tender, swollen skin of his was like being eaten alive by invisible, hellish insects. There—he could see them now, those blisters, in the skin inside his elbow. He staggered to the bathroom, ripped off his clothes, and checked himself for the welts that had sprung up like flowers in the mist of his own sweat. There. They were starting there, too—blisters had begun to form a throbbing necklace under his collar; the hairs under his arms hurt. It would be a bad spell, this one, worse than he'd had in a long time.

His hands already a misery, he made for the things he'd purchased in town and began to mix the ingredients of a paste in the sink. Baking soda and witch hazel, a dollop of pink calamine—just till it was thick, the way his grandma had taught him. He mixed it with both hands, squishing it through his fingers, enjoying the momentary cool on the webbing between. Then he scooped up handfuls of it, smearing his upper body until he was white with it, the earliest layers already crusting next to his skin. Then he went to turn up the air-conditioning, standing with his back to the icy breeze until the paste had dried to a kind of chilly cocoon. Not knowing what else there was to be done, he took himself to the bed again, closing his eyes and holding still, lest he should start up the terrible itching a moment sooner than was inevitable. And after a time, he turned inward, searching out that chilly spot behind his eyes, making his mind as still as the rest of him. The paste on the front of him hardened by degrees as he lay, still as death, with his eyes closed tight, like a man in the process of turning to stone. Fucking hives, he thought.

It was like dreaming.

He could see himself naked under the light cotton blanket Nana Cora had wrapped him in, so skinny and small, half dead from the hives that rioted over his child's skin. It seemed the whole of him was raw. She'd tied his hands, finally, to keep him from scratching what skin was left. It was barely June. And the ancient truck roared over the rutted roads, each bump an agony to his flesh, each brush of his cover awakening some new needle of pain.

He was watching her, looking up through half-closed lids from his position on the seat, able to see the skin that was just beginning to hang from her neck. Skin that was cracked on her arms—leather skin, smooth as hide and tight across the bones. She was wearing a Sunday dress too, an old crepe print sprinkled with tiny flowers, darkened in spots where it clung to her in the heat.

"Ninety-nine degrees and only June," he'd heard the neighbors say to each other in the street. Ninety-nine degrees and he was on fire.

The boy wanted to talk to her, to ask where they were going, what was wrong, but he could not make words travel from his brain to his mouth. He was afraid because she was afraid, he could smell her fear in the mixture of sweat and sickness, dust and gasoline that mingled in the cab of the old crank-started truck, could pick his grandmother's fear from among the other scents like some noisome flower out of a withered bouquet. He was afraid because she was afraid— he had heard her talking to the woman who lived next door when she hung out the endless rags she used to bathe him, pretending she'd needed to cool them in the wind. But she was only getting away from his fretting and crying, he'd known that. He had tried to be good, hush like she told him, but in the end it was always too much and he would began to scratch and to cry and, finally, to scream.

But when Nana Cora talked to Emma who lived across the fence, it was she who had cried, the boy knew that, too. He could hear it in the choked sounds that traveled through the open window. She who never cried was crying then, crying because she was tired of him and the thing that had happened to his skin, crying because she was afraid.

"Dear Lord," Cora had wept. "Dear God, Emma! I'm gonna lose him!"

And that was when the boy had learned he was going to die. Dying like the rest of them had died. The people in little gold frames on his grandmother's dresser. The ones she called his parents. It was happening to him now, he would be like those in the pictures, gone away and never coming back. If his Nana Cora said it, it was true. She'd promised if he wasn't good, he'd turn out like them. And so he had tried to be the way she wanted, and raised his voice in church to sing. But the other part of him was too strong, he guessed. It had won out finally, and now the evil in his soul had come out for all the world to see, laying on his skin like a brand. He was turning out like those pictures, the man with the curly hair and the woman with the sick, terrified eyes. He was going like they had gone—going away and never coming back. The burden of knowing for those few minutes had grown too heavy in the end, and when he heard the creak of Cora's heavy step on the stair, he fainted.

But he was still alive. It surprised him when he opened his eyes expecting hell or heaven or just emptiness and saw the truck instead, saw his grandmother working the muscles in her jaw as she shifted the gears. He had not gone away after all, he was in the truck, and Travis Moseley, Jr., thought perhaps she had found some way to save him, after all.

It was like dreaming. Travis couldn't tell how long they had been driving, but it seemed long to him, longer than it took to get to church, longer than it took to visit Cora's cousins in Greenville. He shifted his eyes and saw trees on either side of the road as they sped by them, sunlight filtering through the leaves and branches like a moving picture. Wherever she was taking him was far away from Tyler, he knew, somewhere he had never been.

He'd dozed off by the time the truck pulled to a stop, and when he woke again he was in Cora's arms. She held him lightly, afraid to hurt him further, afraid to touch that suppurating skin except through the blanket. And mostly afraid to have him know how scared she was. But the pain and the rage on his skin had dulled a little as she lifted him from the seat and carried him like a baby to the house where they'd stopped. It was like dreaming, and in the dream the pain had not mattered so much, not so long as she held him close.

"You her?" His grandmother's voice, dim with years, came back to him.

But there had been only silence for an answer. Travis turned his head to look. A woman stood on the step, her arms folded across her chest. She had strange light eyes, like a blind man he'd seen once. But she could see him well enough. Her look seemed to swallow him whole.

"Set him down," the woman directed in a sharp voice, and amazingly, Cora obeyed. He was on his feet then, naked, his raw flesh searing in the sun as the blanket fell away. He was scared then, all right. His knees were watery, his head and vision swimming with heat and the woman's eyes looking at him. He wanted to pee and he wanted to cry but could not; Nana Cora would want him to mind, especially in front of this person.

Sensing he was about to be abandoned, he turned, shivering, to Cora, the question in his eyes.

His grandmother pulled at her fingers nervously. When she finally made herself look at the boy, her face was as helpless as he was.

"She's goin' to give you a conjure, Travis. To make you well."

He stared back at the woman on the porch. She seemed very tall to him, thin, like a weed in a field. And she was old, like Cora, except for the hair. The woman's hair was as red as a braided sunset, streaked with cloudy wisps of gray. She did not smile at him.

"You bring somethin' to pay me?" she asked.

"Some fine pullets," Cora answered timidly. "They was all we had." She stopped and half-gestured toward the back of the truck.

The conjure woman nodded. "You stay here," she told Cora, and took him by the hand.

Her house was ordinary, and it relieved him a little. It was like everyone's house. There were some blue chicory flowers stuck in a Mason jar in the center of a rough table and the blossoms shook as they crossed the floor. But there were different things too, a strangeness that seemed to come from everywhere at once, from the woman herself and from the dried things that hung from the rafters in the kitchen and the rows of labeled bottles lining the shelves on the wall, all colored like pickles. Only there weren't any pickles; floating in those jars were things he had never seen. Lines of sunlight filtered through the boards of the walls and the woman beckoned him closer. She pulled out a chair and sat down, never taking her icy eyes from his own. She touched him then, took him by the shoulders and turned him to face her, the fingers strong and cool on his blistered skin.

And oh, the eyes! Suddenly her eyes melted when she looked at him. They were like clear water, and the boy could see himself in tiny twin reflections as he saw into her eyes. Then, like a pool, the eyes got deeper the longer he looked; the water was deep and dangerous and dark, swirling, crowded with swimming things the boy knew no names for, things that lived in the bayou and swam in jars and the eyes got deeper and he could not look away. Then he knew —the knowing was like thunder in his mind. Nana Cora could not save him after all, him and his blistered skin. For he knew he had come to the place where people went who never came back. They drove you in a truck and gave some hens for you and you never came back. And still those eyes . . . always the eyes, eating him alive.

It was like dreaming . . .

It was like . . .

Dying?

Then he was in the truck again, feeling the sun on him. Cora was in the seat, too. The truck was moving, turning away from the woman's house, turning back on the road toward home. Cora licked the dust from her lips and sized him up out of the corner of her eye.

"Travis, honey." Her voice was bashful, changed. "You all right?"

Travis stared at her, then realized something. There was no blister on him anywhere, no itch, no fire on his skin. Only the sun and the light breeze coming in the open window. Only the little piece of root the conjure woman had given him, soaked in sorghum to make it sweet. He sucked it thoughtfully. He was well again. Whole. The blanket lay across his lap and he reached down to touch himself. Whole again. "Yes, ma'am," he answered seriously. "Fine."

Cora seemed to mouth some kind of prayer and he could see that there were tears on her cheeks. The road toward home sped by. After a minute, his grandmother spoke again, her voice shaky and odd, like she was telling a lie.

"Travis, honey. Uhhmm. What did she do to you, baby? Tell your grandma. How did she make it go away?"

Travis hesitated. He remembered nothing and everything, too. All at the same time. Slowly, the miracle began to sort itself into particulars.

He spat out a little piece of root and looked at Cora, his eyes round as plates.

"She rubbed my skin," he said simply. "She rubbed my skin and blew in my mouth."

Cora looked at the road. "Did she hurt you?" she asked.

Travis considered it strange. "No, ma'am. She made me better. Can't you see?" He extended his arms so she could. "I got no more marks," he said.

"I know, boy. Sit back."

"Grandma?"

"Yeah?"

"Who is that lady, back there in that house? She never told me her name."

Cora chewed her lip. "I told you, Travis. She's the conjure woman up here."

"But who is she?" the boy said, still sucking his sweet root. "Doesn't she have a name?"

"Name's Icy Fee." Cora said finally. "She's kin to you."

"Kin?" The boy couldn't believe it. "What kind of kin? How come I never knew her before?"

Cora sighed helplessly. "I don't know that, Travis. I can't answer."

"But how can she be my kin?"

"I'm your grandmother, right?"

Travis nodded.

"Well, that woman back there is your grandmother, too. Only she's your pa's grandma. So that makes her your great-grandma. You understand?"

Not entirely, he didn't. But he'd liked the notion. Great-grandma.

Great, indeed.

At the Mile-Away Motel, Travis Moseley, Jr., awakened without opening his eyes, sensing what he could. It was cool, and the color of his eyelids told him it was dark in the room. He shifted then, remembering the crust on his skin, waiting for the torturous itch to stroke him with its fiery fingers. But it had gone with his memory, as though it had never been. Except for the white, powdery crust that covered him, he never would have known those blisters had made a visitation. Smiling, he swung his legs over the side of the bed and sat up. He went to the bathroom and turned on the shower, letting it run until steam clouded the mirrors and he disappeared. Naked and trailing powder like a leaky bag of flour, he went back to the other room long enough to deposit a tape in his portable machine and turn the volume all the way up. Strings sang their way through a concerto and Travis Moseley, Jr., stepped into his shower, rinsing and lathering away the memory of the misery and the dirt and the road. He sang a little as the violins filtered though the steam, lulling him, making him whole.

It was like dreaming.

Twenty=four

June 1915.

BY THE TIME Elijah Perdue made his way back to
Atlantis County, with fifteen years of staving off damnation
under his belt and fifteen years of watching the realms of
the God-fearing hitting the skids, he was a man over the hill
and picking up speed.

Since the last time the Musical Salvation Revival had
worked the spirits of the town, poor Elijah's fortunes had
steadily declined. Little by little, over the intervening years,
the people had stayed home from the puce-colored tent,
preferring the more ordinary, and certainly less strenuous,
forms of worship than the Fiddling Prophet's revivals
would bring them. Besides, there was a growing feeling

among those who had witnessed Elijah's sermons that when it came to talking turkey about the Judgment, the man was plumb wrong about things.

For Elijah's fatal mistake had been in his failure to keep up with the times. Ignoring the advice of the Spirit and his implacable business manager, Mr. Sprayberry, he had continued to tell his following that he heard the sound of the future, only the future kept coming and life went on, and Elijah had yet to be proven correct on the Lord's plans for the disposition of the godly. If Jesus was planning anything so awful as Elijah kept promising, he was pretty slow about it. And after a time, most of the preacher's audience had simply grown tired of waiting for the brimstone and gone on to more amusing prospects.

For when the century turned, what many had feared most with that awesome occurrence, what those hellfire preacher's sermons had played on—utter annihilation—somehow never came to pass. The threat of destruction had never been followed up to the peoples' satisfaction, and after a time their attitudes changed. Whoever God was, he seemed to approve of the world he'd created these days, at least to the extent that he'd let it go on for awhile longer. It even seemed, to the more optimistic among the faithful, that God had seen fit to make life a little easier as the years rolled by, throwing in cheap electricity, telephones for those who wished to use them, and, miracle of miracles, the moving picture show. A God who saw fit to make Thomas A. Edison and Vilma Banky and the Gish sisters all alive in the same generation had to be merciful. It only stood to reason.

Elijah, in contrast to the rest of society, seemed in some unnameable way to have incurred his Lord's vengeance. For, shortly after he'd departed Atlantis the first time around, with the paint on Icy Fee's memory not yet dried, he had begun to be afflicted with a series of chronic skin ailments—rashes and hives and irritations that struck him without warning and tormented him until his already questionable reason was pushed still further toward oblivion. He never associated the coincidence of his misery with having done the poor girl wrong; he was not much given to psychology. But even if the prophet Elijah had put those things together in his mind, more than likely he would have seen his afflictions as God's punishment for ever having known her in the first place rather than his penance for having left her in the proverbial lurch. But there was something in Elijah didn't get smarter with age, and absorbed as he was in his plagues and trials, he had simply forgotten Icy Fee Moulder—put her in a place in his mind where even his conscience could not reach.

And so by the time he hit town so many years later, he was all but covered, neck to knees, with a sort of scaling— the results of fifteen years of scratching in his dreams. His skin thickened, but never healed, his soul was sinless but never grew. And without his clothes, the Fiddling Prophet looked like a freak of nature, something crawled up from the sea.

He'd been diagnosed by every medical man he could find; Wilmington, Atlanta, Des Moines, New Orleans, and a hundred towns in between, always risking his reputation as a healer by risking the doctor, always disappointed in the end. Over the years, he'd been diagnosed as having the shingles, the measles, suppurating follicles, smallpox, psoriasis, gangrene, and leprosy. But in the end it was a doctor in Kansas City who told him there was no hope.

Elijah could not speak at the time, in that particular episode, not only his outer skin, but the membranes of his mouth and throat had erupted in the same maddening disease. Mr. Sprayberry, fearing contagion, having broken out in a sympathetic bout of hives himself, had knocked the preacher on the back of the head and hauled him to a hospital there, claiming he was a Samaritan who found the suffering creature by the side of the road.

The morning that the doctor came, Elijah was steeled for the verdict, bathed from head to foot in stinking calamine, everything in his brain gone into hiding, except for that part that controlled the itch.

The doctor's name was Monday. He'd peered at the preacher closely, then at Mr. Sprayberry, who'd taken it upon himself to stay at the preacher's bedside.

Dr. Monday rubbed his mouth with his hand, ruminating for a moment on his own futility. "As near as we can figure out," he began.

Elijah and Sprayberry held their breath, each for their own reasons.

"As near as we can figure," the doctor said again, "this man here is allergic to himself."

"Pardon?" Mr. Sprayberry said.

Dr. Monday looked at him. "You heard me."

"But what can be done about something like that?"

Monday shook his head. "Nothin'. Not a damn thing. Near as I can figure, it all has something to do with his particular type of perspiration. More he sweats, the worse that skin of his is gonna suffer. Nothin' you can do about sweat, though, body needs to sweat to live."

Mr. Sprayberry looked at Elijah, who was pink with useless lotions and praying to himself. "So," he said, looking back to the sawbones. "There ain't nothin'?" He let it end as a question, more out of politeness than anything.

Dr. Monday shrugged. "Nope. Like I said, the man's got

a reaction to his own liquids. Nothin' anybody but God can
do about that, except . . ." The doctor trailed off—he'd just
given himself an idea.

"Except what?" Mr. Sprayberry was already counting
out the money for Elijah's hospital bill.

Dr. Monday shifted his weight and lowered his voice.

"You could take him to a preacher," he suggested.

And so Elijah had suffered. Itched his way down through
Missouri, had a letup for most of Arkansas, and been run
out of the northern corner of Louisiana, when an unusual
hot spell had forced him to reveal the condition of his arms
to three Presbyterian ladies who dropped by without warning to invite him to speak at a luncheon and caught him in
his shirtsleeves. Sprayberry had unexpectedly steered the
preacher's entourage toward Texas, and once again Elijah
Perdue, the Fiddling Prophet of Jesus, found himself in that
county of his undoing.

And out in the woods on the old Moulder place, the
conjure woman gathered herbs and watched the seasons
and bided her precious time.

Twenty-five

March 1900.

I CY FEE MOULDER did not die in the way she had expected. She got married instead.

On the morning after her vain attempt to take herself out, she'd awakened in her hope chest, tears of rage already on her cheeks from crying in her sleep. Not dead, she decided furiously, even before she'd opened her eyes, not even close. What she was, however, was rather violently sick to her stomach. So, allowing as to how she was still kicking, and seeing no point in ruining her mother's good linens with what was left of her bile, Icy Fee Moulder threw back the lid of her would-be casket, went to the window, and puked her guts out onto some jonquils that were just poking up through the ground.

179

Half an hour later, when the girl appeared at the breakfast table, tear-stained and shaky still, her gorge rose like a
fist at the sight of her mother's offerings of biscuits and
gravy and she was out the door and offending the flower
beds once again. Staring out the window after her bright-
haired daughter, Miz Moulder studied on this new development. Come to think of it, the girl was looking wan as an
early moon just lately, and filling out her calico, too. When
it came to being a mother, maybe she wasn't the cleverest
Icy Fee could have wished for, but she could certainly put
two and two together when it stared her in the face. Miz
Moulder sighed and poured herself more coffee, reflecting
on the turn of things, and almost immediately brightened
up a little. Maybe it wouldn't be so bad, she reckoned
silently. Having a preacher in the family.

When Icy Fee had pulled herself together sufficiently to
come back inside, Miz Moulder decided it was time for a
little heart-to-heart.

"The preacher comin' by today?" she asked the girl.

Icy Fee was experimenting with a couple of bites of dry
biscuit, seeing if she could keep it down. At the question,
she abandoned the idea. "No, Mamma." she said in a voice
like dying. "I don't think so."

Miz Moulder absorbed this. "I see," she went on.

"Yes?" Icy Fee answered, fixing her eyes on the plate
with an expression that threatened to wither the painted
flowers.

Miz Moulder sighed, privately damning the day she'd
ever let the girl's daddy pick out the child's name.
"Nothin'," she said aloud, "Eat your breakfast."

"No, ma'am, I can't," Icy Fee replied.

Miz Moulder settled her considerable bulk into a rush-
bottomed chair. "I was the same with you," she recalled,

smiling a little. "All guts and no glow, right up till the seventh month."

Icy Fee stared at her mother, thoroughly perplexed. "What's that mean?" she asked suspiciously.

Miz Moulder raised her eyebrows. Apparently, she'd neglected the girl's education on a couple of crucial points. That was the problem with being a widow so long, she decided in that moment. After a couple of years, you forgot about being a wife. Then all of a sudden it was your daughter's turn, and from the look of Icy Fee, anything by way of motherly advice was going to be a day late and a dollar shy. Miz Moulder worked her mouth, uncertain of how to break the news. "Icy Fee, honey, when was the last time you had your monthly?" she asked.

Icy Fee thought it over, counting time backward on her fingers. " 'Bout Christmas, I guess," she said.

"But it's just turned March, honey. Don't that mean nothin' to you?"

Icy Fee frowned. "Well," she admitted slowly, "I guess I ain't sure why you call 'em monthlies, seein' as how I ain't had one for awhile."

Miz Moulder smiled patiently. "No, Icy Fee. You see, hon, when a girl and a man been doin' some lovin', like you and the preacher, and the girl don't get her monthlies for a spell, it means—well—it means you better think about gettin' married."

Icy Fee's lips went white; her eyes narrowed to cat slits.

"Why?"

Miz Moulder blushed with a mixture of guilt and happiness. Now that the idea had sunk in some, she'd realized with a certain joy that she was due to become a grandma. "Because, Icy Fee," she said gently. "When a girl don't get her monthlies, and starts bein' sick in the mornin' the way you have, it means she's in the family way."

Icy Fee half rose, knocking her chair backward onto the floor. "What?!" she demanded incredulously, blinded by a sting of furious, heartbroken tears. It was the last time she would cry for a hundred years.

Mother Moulder stared at her daughter, wondering if the child, too, would have those pale eyes. "Sit down, girl," she instructed. "No point in wishing different. Fact is, come harvest you're gonna have a child."

Slowly, as if she were moving under water, Icy Fee righted the chair from where it had fallen and sat down. She sat without looking at anything, the morning sun admiring its reflection in the lights from her hair. The silence stretched itself to minutes, until Miz Moulder began to fidget, anxious to see how her daughter was taking the news.

"Honey, didn't you hear me? I said you was gonna have a baby."

Icy Fee met her mother's eyes. "No, Mamma," she said, her voice and eyes as cold as charity.

"I'm gonna have a bastard. Just like his daddy."

And so, little by little, Icy Fee's recent tragedy had come out, prompted by Miz Moulder's gentle questions. In the hours since Elijah's desertion, Icy Fee's heart had turned on itself, and, as she made it all come clear for her mother's benefit, she had regained a measure of control. Miz Moulder, on the other hand, had her bonnet on before the story was done.

Icy Fee stared up at her mother, whose very skin seemed to tremble with indignation.

"Where are you goin'?" Icy Fee asked dully, her heart so emptied of feeling she could barely form the sentence.

Miz Moulder squinted and set her jaw. "I'm goin' to have a talk with that preacher of yours," she said. "Hitch up the wagon."

Too tired to protest, Icy Fee stood up, intending to go to the barn.

"And Icy Fee?" her mother called, as soon as she was out the door.

Slowly, Icy Fee turned around, ignoring for the moment the quickening flutter in her belly. "Yes, Mamma?" she said, shielding her eyes against the sun.

Miz Moulder's form seemed to puff out in that moment, expanding until her bonnet and billowing skirts filled the entire doorway.

"Get me the gun."

But Fate is a gnarled orchard, full of twists and branches no one can count on, where the fruit of good intention falls unnoticed to the ground, and folks continue starving for that they cannot reach.

Miz Moulder never had her little chat with the Fiddling Prophet of Jesus, partially because he had packed up his puce-colored tent and skipped town in the dead of the previous night and partially because a farmer named Artie Moseley was too lazy to fill in the ruts in his stretch of the road and the intrepid Miz Moulder, traveling too fast for her rig, had broken a wagon axle and her best horse's leg not ten miles from her intended target.

After surveying the damage and shooting the horse in the traces, leaving its companion to marvel at its salvation, she righteously hoisted her gun and huffed off to the Moseley's farmhouse, intending to give that no-account Artie a piece of her mind. But by the time she arrived at the Moseley spread, most of her fury consumed by two miles of exertion, she was thinking clearly enough to notice that her grudge against Artie might temporarily be put on the shelf in the interest of more important things.

For the only one of the Moseleys who chose to be at home that day was Deke, Artie's oldest boy.

Miz Moulder spied him over by the horse trough—you couldn't hardly miss him, the way he was built. Deke stood six and a half feet tall, and filled out his height to the point of giantism. Though he wasn't yet eighteen, and from all accounts had the mind of your average tree frog, he knew farm work and, as far as the good woman knew, had no overt bad habits. The Moseleys were prospering, too, from the look of the place. The house had paint and there was a new plow leaned up against the side of the barn. All of which, as Miz Moulder examined the unsuspecting Deke from under the shadow of her sunbonnet, assumed the sudden aspects of a gift from heaven. The boy wasn't perfect, of course, but no man can be, and to someone in Miz Moulder's unfortunate circumstances, the boy's being a little light in the brains department might stand to advantage when looked at in the right way. So she laid down her shotgun and pasted on a smile, calling to the mountainous Deke to please bring his wagon to see her back home.

She nodded satisfaction as Deke bounced the wagon back past the Moulder woods toward their destination. "I must say, Deke, you're a fine-looking man," she said.

Deke blushed the color of the red dirt, not knowing what to do with himself. He knew this lady on sight, but adults hardly addressed him as a rule, except to give him orders and except for his mother—he couldn't remember the last time he'd spoken to a full-grown woman.

Miz Moulder leaned back a little and fanned herself. "I s'pose a strapping young feller like you's got himself a girl?" She stopped and looked at him, her heart in her mouth.

Deke shifted and stared at the horses. "No, ma'am," he admitted, remembering not to breathe through his mouth. "I cain't say as I have," he finished.

Miz Moulder laughed delightedly. "Lordy," she breathed. "It sure is turnin' out a fine day, ain't it?"

Deke considered it. The day looked like any other day to him, but if his mother was any indication, women in general were wont to say any number of extraordinary things.

He was trying to get his mind to work up an answer when the Moulder woman astonished him further by leaning over and touching him, right on the arm.

"Deke," she said mildly. "Have you met my girl, Icy Fee?"

Deke met her eyes for the first time that day, slowly shaking his head in the negative.

Miz Moulder smiled. It certainly was turning out a fine day.

Further down the road, standing on her own front porch, Miz Moulder's girl gnawed at her fingernails and waited, not daring to hope that her mamma, by some sweet miracle, would bring Elijah back to her.

But, as she spied the dust that signaled the wagon's approach, what little heart the girl had left in her was swallowed in bewildered disappointment. For it was no sallow, black-suited preaching man that rode beside her mother on the seat. Instead, her mamma had brought home a stranger —a boy who looked like a tree.

Twenty=six

WHETHER OR NOT Deke Moseley ever caught on to the fact that his firstborn son came into the world only six months and twelve days after the day of his mother's wedding, while all the rest of his children seemed to take a little longer is, ultimately, beside the point. The fact is, he doted on the boy from the morning of his birth as though God himself and not the dewy-eyed Miz Moulder had placed the child in his arms that particular dawn. They decided to name the boy Cecil, because neither one of them knew anyone by that name and mostly because Icy Fee had decided way back in her fourth month that this child, at least, would start his life with a name of his own. And if Cecil's proud papa ever doubted the baby's origins, he kept his mouth shut about it because that was his way about most things. He proved better than most as fatherhood went, and as he walked the floor with the colicky Cecil, he confided to the baby's ear most things that he knew about the world. Fortunately, neither his teachings nor the colic took all that long, and by the time another year had passed, with Baby Cecil already learning to talk and another little stranger in the works, it seemed to Deke Moseley that life was looking pretty good.

He and Icy Fee, at the insistence of her mother, had set up housekeeping on the long-neglected Moulder farm. Deke might have been dumb as your average post, but he knew how to make things grow, and the farm was cleared into thirty ordered acres of cotton and cows before any of his neighbors could convince him to change his mind. He put his mother-in-law in charge of a half-acre of vegetables in back of the house, while Icy Fee, who seemed to have no particular talent for more conventional forms of agriculture, was given the woods and bayou to keep for her own, allowing as how they weren't worth plowing. It was an equitable arrangement all around and for awhile, at least, there were no real complaints from anyone. There seemed, in those first years, nothing whatever to stand in the way of the young couple's bliss except backbreaking labor, fundamental deception, and of course the fact that man and wife had less in common than gravel and gravy.

On the plus side, though, Icy Fee's bargain with her giant boy was not without certain compensations. For aside from his talents for husbandry, Deke Moseley knew, with all the instincts of the uncomplicated, exactly how to fuck. And after getting over an initial adjustment to the sheer size of the beast, Icy Fee, not without some instincts of her own in that department, and after some minor instruction to her new spouse on some of the fine points, began to think of her sudden wedlock as something of a blessing in disguise.

Yet, too much of a good thing is never without some consequence, and in the fifth year of her marriage, with deliverance on her mind and four small children underfoot, Icy Fee Moulder found a vocation in sorcery.

It started as something of an accident. Not yet twenty, the poor girl was thoroughly sick of being, as her mother insisted on calling it, in the family way, and when a recent incident, wherein her terrified and solicitous husband had tried to cure her of one of her grand mals by undoing his pants and mounting her, had resulted in yet another pregnancy, Icy Fee began to inquire, as discreetly as possible, if there mightn't be some way of pursuing the more pleasurable aspects of life with Deke without paying the unreasonable costs of nearly perpetual childbearing.

On the advice of some women in town, Icy Fee betook herself to Chicken Young, a swamp woman of mysterious reputation who dwelt back in the bayou and conjured for her living. According to most, Chicken had the Sight and could cure anything from typhus to toothache, providing you weren't too squeamish as to how it was done. So enough, being in this particular instance, too much to be borne, Icy Fee left her children in care of her mother one cool morning in spring, tied on her Sunday sunbonnet, and went to see what she could find.

At the time, and at the age of eighty-seven, Chicken Young had come to the somewhat ironic conclusion that, after uncountable years of witching and healing, of interceding with the gods of the swamp and the woods, that she herself had fallen prey to the one malady that couldn't be cured with the right herbs and the proper intentions, and that affliction was her own old age. As it turned out, the conjure woman's disease was rapidly proving fatal, and she'd been on the lookout for some months for the proper person to take over her bustling backwoods trade. On the day that Icy Fee came for her help, one sharp look in the girl's nearly colorless eyes convinced the conjurer of a buried disposition for things magical, and Chicken Young decided in that instant that her witches' secrets might just as well go to the tired-looking red-haired woman waiting timidly on the front porch that morning in May as to anyone else in the world. So she smiled around her rotten teeth and threw open her ruin of a screen door, bidding the girl come in for tea.

Now, Icy Fee Moulder may not have known magic from macadamias, but she wasn't the kind to argue with what worked, and after Chicken's prescribed necklace of cypress bark and a cup of juniper-flavored tea appeared to have cured her of not only her fledgling pregnancy but her excessive fertility as well, she fell into Chicken's instruction like a pig in a wallow. Unfettered by religion (any predisposition for that having fled with the preacher) or much of a conscience (having borne her husband another man's child) Icy Fee was feeling the lack of more spiritual influences in her life about then, and reckoned that learning the tricks of curing the sick and raising the dead might prove just the ticket to her dubious salvation.

It all came in very handy. She rubbed lettuce juice on Deke's temples when his potency got out of hand, and put her children to sleep on pillows stuffed with rue and thyme to ward away their nightmares. When her oldest boy Cecil began to betray signs of his father, she soaked his head in chamomile to keep him blond and bathed his eyes in chicory water to change their color. By and large, her growing knowledge made motherhood come easier than it did naturally. There was an odd serenity that went with believing you knew what to do. By the time the horrific day came when her youngest, then nearly three, fell into the lye she used for soap-making, Icy Fee was able to pack him in wet comfrey to grow him a new skin and go to her circle of stones in the woods. Over and over, she was able to whisper to the night the words Chicken Young had taught her to say, without ever once recalling that as the child's mother, she was supposed to be afraid.

Word of her talents got around, and before too many years had gone by, Icy Fee had got herself a reputation with the neighbors. There seemed a never-ending supply of people needed curing, and all the things to cure them with to be found under the rocks and waters and branches and underbrush that grew in that wild medicine chest on the verge of the pasture. There was smartweed and chamomile for gangrene, motherwort for delirium, catnip for sleeplessness, violets for headaches, goat's weed for rheumatism, and sprigs of willow for those afraid to die. There were hemlock cones for barrenness; henbane for adulterers, red peppers for envy, and rosemary for stupidity. And there was too that special mixture she kept for her own consumption. Skullcap and lady's slipper, mistletoe and elder blossom, steeped in water, drunk everyday, so that, after awhile, the fits that had come upon her since her beginning never came again.

She kept in her cupboard special beans to rub on warts, bags sewn up with colored threads, filled with those leaves that would banish bad memories; she could cure an animal of an open wound by placing it in a circle of thistle flowers; she could turn your fortunes around by placing pennyroyal in your shoes. As conjure women went, she was pretty damn good. Some years the neighbors came in secret, trading her money or livestock or food; some years they came in droves with nothing at all. But sooner or later they came to her—with their ailing children, their illness and misery, their tired spirits and broken hearts. Sooner or later, all of them came.

And so when Elijah Perdue, fifteen years gone and layered with sores, finally came to her too, thumping up the front steps wrapped in his disease and a black preacher's coat, Icy Fee Moseley was as ready for him as a spider in a web.

Twenty=seven

Atlantis. August 14.

NO ONE HAPPENED to notice the snow-white '59 Cadillac that sulked at the intersection of Live Oak Street and White Oak Avenue that Tuesday afternoon, when the whole of the Strait family relations piled into town to have lunch with Baby Todd and discover what Ray Ed had left behind, if anything. No one paid any particular attention to the fact that the car had followed their little convoy most of the way from the farm, or that the driver with the absurd yellow tie sat peering at them all from under the shadow of his white hat like he meant to do someone some kind of wrong. Taped up to the dashboard was a clipping from a newspaper, decades old, and a woman's photograph stared back at him just the way she always had, confirming things with her eyes.

Iris Lee, in the car with Dearest and Davey, probably should have been the one to see that Fate was waiting for her a half-block away, after all, '59 Cadillacs weren't all that common in Atlantis or anywhere else, but she simply wasn't looking at anything but a compact mirror while she assured herself that she looked years younger than her sister Baby, no matter what people said, and trying at the same time to decide if that spot on her cheek was going to turn out to be skin cancer like Clara Cannon had just had removed or if it was something more serious. Davey didn't see because he was looking at the picture of Luanne Heck he carried around in his mind, and trying to figure a way to sneak away from the family after the will was read in order to lay down with her and tell her of the fortune he was planning to inherit. Uncle Dearest didn't see either, because he was looking at Davey and reading his thoughts and telling him out loud that he might as well not do any wool-gathering that way, because Tuesdays were the day Brother Heck and his other half went to the opposite side of town to perform certain charitable acts for niggers.

Boo didn't see it, because it wouldn't have made any sense to him if he had, and besides, the boy was absorbed in staring at his lap and trying to imagine the sound his fiddle would make should someone decide to throw it out the window of a moving vehicle. Next to him, in the driver's seat, Grace couldn't have noticed the Caddy because she could barely see over the steering wheel. She had promised Maejean, in a fit of goodwill, to drive her car so Maejean would be free to ride in the car with Charles T., and she couldn't get Maejean's driver's seat adjusted to the point where she could reach the pedals. Which still would have been fine, except that Maejean had taken advantage of a closeout on violet eyeshadow at the Safeway the day before and positively stunned the rest of the family by turning up with so much of the shadow rioting around her eyes that she looked exactly like a drug addict. So, Grace didn't see anything, because she was busy trying to see ahead to the car with Maejean in it, and wondering what in the world had possessed her, and Maejean didn't see because she was making violet-lidded eyes at Charles T., who, given the turn of things, could hardly stand to look at anything and besides, he was watching the road.

On the other hand, it didn't take anyone a minute to see the Stradivarius propped up against the front door. Grace and Boo were halfway up the walk when Baby opened the front door to wave them all in, and Boo had the case in his hands before it could fall backward into her house.

Having worn herself out completely ordering around a freelance white trash cook for most of the morning, in order to better be able to pretend she'd made the lunch herself, Baby had donned a pink organdy hostess apron and helped herself to a couple of shots of Ezra Brooks sour mash before the relatives showed up, so her vision was a little ᴘn the hazy side when she looked at the object Boo held up for her to see. She frowned at it for a long moment, as though trying to remember its name.

"That's good, honey," she said absently, trying to recall where she'd put her breath mints. "Iris Lee finally get you a case for your fiddle?"

"No, I did not," Iris Lee answered, making her way up the steps. "For your information, that fiddle case was sitting right out here on the porch for God-knows-how-long. A ratty old thing like that, too. What's the matter, Baby? You losin' track?"

Baby was momentarily distracted by Maejean's eyeshadow. "Uhmm," she said. "Maejean, don't you look exotic. And for your information, Iris Lee, I don't know where that fiddle came from. It wasn't here this morning."

Iris Lee scowled. "Probably a gift from one of your many admirers."

Baby smiled dreamily. "Why, Iris Lee, what a lovely thought. Only I can't think who it might be."

Iris Lee pressed her lips together. "Some people learn and some people never do," she said rather more grimly than was called for. "And if you don't mind my asking, are you going to invite us in, or do we just have to stand around on the porch expiring in the noonday sun? All this damn wisteria of yours is makin' me woozy."

One by one, they filed through the front door, except for Boo, who hung back on his own, trying to figure how to open the violin case.

"Oh, bring it along with you, honey," Aunt Baby told him. "We'll figure it out after lunch."

"Boo," said Boo and followed her in.

Baby clapped her hands like a teacher bringing a classroom to order. "Well," she said, brightening up a little, having remembered the mints were on top of the refrigerator. "Everybody find somewhere to sit." She managed a gracious, apologetic smile. "You all will have to forgive the appearance of my house, the nigger quit."

Iris raised her eyebrows and lowered herself into a frieze-covered Empire chair. "How long ago?"

Grace stared around her, stunned at the unabashed excesses of Baby's decorating scheme, which seemed to have begun somewhere prior to Mr. Heppelwhite and ended with sets from "I Love Lucy."

Dearest caught her expression and grinned. "Welcome to knickknack nirvana," he said.

Grace hid a smile. "I'll go help in the kitchen," she said,

seeing as how no one else was making a move to do anything of the kind. Charles T. and Davey were absorbed in
trying to get the fiddle away from Boo so they could look
at it, and Iris Lee was paging through a *Reader's Digest.*

"Oh, me too," Dearest whispered and winked. "I'll
make the iced tea."

So Grace, under Baby's direction, saw to the chicken
spaghetti while Maejean got out plates and Dearest poured
bourbon into tumblers, adorning it with enough mint to
make it look innocent.

"I don't know if I ought," Maejean said when Dearest
held out her glass. "I had real bad cramps before I came
over to meet you all, so I had some medication."

"What'd you take, puddin'?" Dearest inquired solici-
tously.

"Three Pamprins, a couple of diet pills, and a Lite Beer,"
Maejean told him. "You think if I had that mash, I'd get a
reaction?"

"Undoubtedly," said Dearest. "How much do you
want?"

Maejean took a tumbler. "Oh, this'll be fine. But if I go
into a coma, lie for me, okay? You never heard a word
about the diet pills."

Grace shrugged and went back to the stove. It accounted
for that eyeshadow, anyhow.

Baby was trying to unmold the Jell-O salad and cursing
because it wouldn't come loose when Charles T. made his
way into the kitchen a few minutes later, Boo and Davey
close at his heels. Charles T. held a fiddle aloft, his face alive
with some quality the old woman found hard to define. Like
wonder, maybe. Or youth. She caught sight of that face and
paused, with the Jell-O mold poised upside down over the
plate. Her salad plopped out with a wet, satisfying sound,
and there appeared on the plate a perfect imitation of a

fish, with bits of celery and banana suspended in its guts.

"Why, Charles T., you should see your face," Baby told him. "You look like a spring day."

But he was too excited to pay attention. "Baby, where'd you say this fiddle came from?"

Baby shoved some hair out of her face where it had come unglued from the rest of her coiffure. "Why, I don't think I did say, Charles T. I don't know. You all said it was on the porch."

"Yes, but how did it get there? Don't you have any idea?"

Baby smiled distractedly. "None whatsoever, hon. Why don't you get everybody set down at the table?"

"Not now!"

Grace turned around from her place at the stove, surprised. Just behind Charles T., Davey's eyes were also focused on the fiddle, dancing with some unfamiliar emotion.

"You gotta see this, Grace," Davey told her.

She crossed the kitchen, wiping her hands on her apron. "Nice fiddle," she said. "This the one from the porch?"

Charles T. stared at his daughter as though he were meeting her for the first time. "Listen," he said and tipped the violin softly from side to side. Something rattled softly from its insides, whispering to her.

"Is something broken?" she asked, already knowing that was not the case. She stepped over for a closer look at the thing—the smooth, syrupy finish rippling in the light like water in a pond. Something happened to her then, something like falling under a spell, and she found, like the rest of them, she couldn't look away from the wondrous thing her father cradled like eggshells in his callused hands.

Baby stood trembling along with her Jell-O fish, pale as death. "Do that again, Charles T."

Charles T. did, and again the rattle whispered its treacherous little song.

Baby's eyes went dark and round, like tunnels. "Give it to me," she snapped, then remembered herself. "Please," she said. "It's just that—my husband—Cecil had a fiddle like that. It had snake rattlers inside."

Charles T. handed it over reluctantly. "What kind was it?" he wanted to know.

Baby sat down heavily and held the fiddle close, looking like she wanted to weep, her face contorted with tears not willing to come. "Kind?" she asked bewilderedly. "Let me remember, he told me one time it might be valuable. He appreciated things, Cecil did. Fine things."

"When he played, it made you feel like you'd just been born. It sounded like angels. So many years ago. . . ." She glanced around as if she'd been roused from a dream and was surprised to find them all standing there.

Boo saw his opportunity. He sidled up silently and let himself touch the thing, just once.

"What kind was it, Baby?" Charles T. gently insisted. "Did he ever say the kind?"

Baby passed a hand over her eyes. "I think he said it was a Stradivuss."

Charles T. thumped the table joyfully. "Damn, I knew it! Didn't I tell you, Davey? Didn't I say?"

Grace moved around the side of the table where the fiddle lay in waiting. "What the hell's a Stradivuss?"

Charles T.'s brain was on fire. "Just look!" He fairly danced with excitement. "Look inside."

Grace picked up the violin, her fingertips tingling with the contact. She tipped it to the light, the better to see the label pasted therein, and there, too, the dried, grayish rattles that had settled in a shadow, silent for a time. Even the insides seemed to have a particular life, warm and a little dusty, like a woods in the autumn.

"*Antonius Stradivarius Cremonensis,*" she read slowly. "*Faciebat Anno, 1722.*"

Iris Lee roused herself from her chair in the front room and made her way to the kitchen, wondering what the quiet was all about. She stood in the doorway, her hands folded across her chest.

"If I'd known this was your idea of inviting someone for lunch, Baby, I would've eaten more breakfast."

Baby looked up from the fiddle. "Oh, Iris Lee!" she cried. "You're not going to believe it. It's Cecil's fiddle!"

Standing there in the doorway, with everyone who cared to look unable to miss the event, Iris Lee Strait's face fell completely apart. She put a hand to her throat and stared at each of them, trying to decipher which of them might be responsible for such cruelty. When her eyes lit on her sister, she managed, at last, to speak.

"It is not," she answered hoarsely. "It isn't because it can't be."

"But it is!" Baby insisted. "Listen." She lifted it up and shook it like a witch doctor's wand.

"Oh, my God." Iris Lee said the words one by one, like she was memorizing the words of a curse. Her mind told her feet to move, and she got herself around the table to look at the thing, standing with her head bowed, identifying the corpse.

"Well, if it's a real Stradivarius," Dearest put in, "it must be worth a fortune."

Iris Lee didn't look at him. "Oh, shut up."

"But where did it come from?" Charles T. still wanted to know.

"It came from Cecil," Baby insisted. "Didn't it, Iris Lee? You remember. Isn't this Cecil's fiddle? It even has those rattles."

Iris Lee ran a bony finger over the bright, immaculate finish, and it was like touching something unreachable—putting her hand through some hole in the world that led to things gone by, making all her guilty secrets rise up, shivering.

"It's his all right."

"NO!" A deep voice that everyone knew and no one could remember hearing before came from a chair in the corner, and they all turned around to see Boo Strait rise up from his place and cross to the table, fixing them all with eyes that were vivified with some unnameable fire.

A boy again, he grinned at their surprise, then gazed lovingly back at the instrument that lay between him and what he would become.

"It's mine," he said matter-of-factly.

Maejean fell on her knees. "Dear Lord," she said. "It's a miracle."

Grace said, "Davey, cut it out."

But Davey only gaped at the stranger in his brother's body. "Holy shit, Boo," he breathed. "When'd you learn to talk?"

Charles T. went and thumped Boo on the back, tears shining in his eyes. "It's his mother," he said. "Gloria must've found some way to heal him long distance."

Uncle Dearest, for the first time in the history of his life, couldn't think of anything at all to say and simply sucked on his bourbon like a man in the desert.

And Baby Todd stood shakily up, trembling like a leaf in a breeze. "I'll be the judge of who it belongs to," she said, snatching up her violin and staring at the boy.

So, as surprised as all of them were right then, nobody noticed when the stranger crept up on the stairs of the porch off the kitchen and slipped the gun from his belt and felt the cold, sure presence of it like an extension of his own hand. Nobody saw the way he licked his lips and tilted his white hat and strode the three steps across the porch, leading with his weapon like some trained assassin, his purpose shining in his head like holy fire. He splintered the rickety screen with a single, explosive kick and stepped inside with a pistol for a calling card and a little smile playing around his mouth. He stared at them, this family that had stolen from him all that his life might have been.

Nobody could think what to do when Travis Moseley, Jr., stepped into the kitchen, aimed, looked into Aunt Baby Todd's thunderstruck face, and said:

"I'll take that fiddle, ma'am, if you don't mind."

Twenty=eight

1915.

THE SPRING WAS WET, the summer dry. The autumn was mild and the mice and shrews bred fat, gnawing on the leavings of that one harvest that made the farmers smile and count money in their sleep. The barns and cribs and silos were busting, the man who ran the cotton gin got rich in a single year. Life was full of miracles—all the children got shoes for school and the women got calico and gingham and grosgrained silk to cover their bonnets with. Those who had something got confident enough to go out and buy more; those who'd had nothing finally had enough. And out on the old Moulder place, the conjure woman buried her mother in the land on the hill, watched her oldest boy turn almost to a man, and waited in a circle of stones, noting the signs.

The shrews and field mice and rodents ate themselves to death on that single, incredible yield, breeding in the millions. The predator snakes fed on millions of fat, furry dinners and in their turn bred themselves into greater numbers than anyone could remember—until the next year—that year when snakebite got to be common as mosquito, and the farmwives took to keeping wooden bats and hammers in the house, to better fend off the black snakes and grass snakes and puffin' adders and cottonmouths and rattlers that slithered over the land, sleeping under their porches and crawling unbidden through the cracks in the walls to sun themselves on farmhouse floors.

She'd known he was coming, but she didn't know when. Even the enlightened don't know everything, especially when the inkling that her preacher was finding his way back to her produced in Icy Fee a host of feelings that twined, serpentine, around her methods of magic, distorting vision with longing and knowledge with fear.

Icy Fee supposed she would still love him; as someone would say many years hence, some people learn and some people never do. And whether her continuing passion for the man indicated weakness on her part or a peculiar kind of faithful strength, she could not decipher. She knew she would hate him, too. Sometimes in the kitchen, chopping meat for the children's dinner, she would think of her Elijah lying cold in the ground or watching her contented life from his postcard heaven, wishing he could have been a man. And invariably, such thoughts would make her smile. She reasoned, in calmer moments, that she should have forgiven her preacher by now, and knew also that she could not. Not with fifteen years of wondering, sitting at the bottom of their love's ocean. But what the tide takes out, it always brings home, and that single jewel of a notion, glinting in and out of the years, that—above all—was what kept her heart beating and alive, and bleeding from its thousand wounds. So when she took herself to the woods and the circle of stones that had been their bed one morning and saw that rattlesnake-in-waiting, coiled like a spring on a smooth, flat rock, she sat down and laughed like someone gone mad. She laughed and clapped her hands and crooned to the serpent like a mother. Fourteen rattles and a button, she counted delightedly as the snake watched her sideways with flat, reptilian eyes. The Fiddling Prophet of Jesus had come back to her at last.

Cecil peered through the curtains at the preacher on the porch with something like fear crawling around in his belly. The man had to be a preacher, the boy reasoned to himself. From the look of him, he couldn't have been anything else. But that alone was puzzling; why would a preacher come to call? Like all of his brothers and sisters, he was old enough to know that people came to see his mother, and old enough, too, to know why. But a preacher needing a conjure was something the boy had not yet seen in his life, and he answered the man's knock with his heart in his mouth.

"Yeah?" He frowned at the man, trying to look older.

Elijah stumbled over his words. He was expecting a witch; this Moseley woman had a full-grown child. And several others, from the look of things. He stared at the handsome boy for a moment, trying to think what it was that made that beautiful young face so familiar to him.

"I came to see Miz Moseley, son," Elijah said after a moment.

Cecil puffed out his chest a little, to better intimidate this stranger. "What for?" he demanded.

Elijah looked at the boy helplessly, all his years of misery showing out of his eyes. "So she can give me something for my skin." With that, the man pushed up his sleeves a little and displayed the insides of his arms. Cecil blinked. The man looked like he'd been in some kind of fire.

"You stay here on the porch," the boy directed him. "I'll go fetch her. You got any money?"

Elijah reached into a pocket and withdrew some paper currency and two gold coins. "A little, son. A little," he said. Something in the boy's fearsome expression was making him want to smile.

Cecil glowered even further. With that face of his, the general effect was that of a kewpie doll in a bad temper. "I'll get her," he said. "And don't call me son, neither. You ain't my pa."

Elijah bowed his head. "Of course," he said. "My apologies."

A figure came toward her through the woods just as Icy Fee was recovering herself. With the sun in her eyes, it looked like some kind of golden-haired grounded angel thrashing its clumsy way through the trees. When she finally saw who it was who had come for her, she started. Cecil? Somewhere in her mind, she thought of Cecil as a child, still. This boy was nearly a man. And a beautiful one, too. It bothered her a little, to see such beauty in a man. She thought wildly that in diverting the boy's physical traits away from any resemblance to his real father, she might have overdone it some.

"A man come for you," Cecil told her. "He's got money."

Back on the porch, Elijah was starting to feel better about this errand. Not hopeful, exactly, but better nonetheless. The hard fact was, when following Mr. Sprayberry's scrawled directions, he had taken the turn that led to the road that led to the place where Icy Fee Moulder had dwelt in a rundown house with her mother so many years before, and his spirit had all but deserted him entirely. But Sprayberry had assured him that the place belonged to a family named Moseley now, and the truth was, Elijah almost wouldn't have known the place, things were looking so prosperous.

Then he felt a presence at the door and turned around to find the face of his single transgression from a spiritual life turned into a woman of flesh and of bone, who was standing at the door with her hands planted on the curve of her hips like Temptation come to the Garden.

"Victor," she said, and that was all. The sound of his name hung between them like an unfinished song.

Twenty=nine

August 14 . . .
a Little Later On.

LL IN ALL, it was a pretty good robbery.

Now that Boo Strait had demonstrated a heretofore unsuspected ability to express himself like normal folks, and with that fearsome, handsome stranger kicking in the screen door and pointing a pistol around like he planned to use it, it took a couple of moments for the little gathering in the kitchen to pull themselves together to the point where anyone could begin to think about the extraordinary turn the day had taken.

But, since no one apparently had any plans whatever to scream or overpower him, and having figured, too, that there were too many of them to shoot all at one time, Travis

Moseley, being a reasonable sort, politely repeated his request to the little old lady clutching his father's fiddle to her bosom in a way that threatened to render pointless any robbery at all.

The woman only stared at him with horrified, periwinkle eyes. Travis decided it was time to clarify the situation. "It's mine, ma'am. It belongs to my family."

Instead of turning the instrument loose, a response which Travis had rather innocently expected, Baby Todd began to weep and invoke the dead. "Cecil, dear God, Iris Lee, look! It's Cecil come to life."

"Oh, it is not either," Iris Lee answered irritably. "It's a criminal. Look at his tie."

Travis frowned at the sound of that word, and with the hand that wasn't holding the gun touched the offending neckpiece. He'd only worn it at all so she would know who he was. He motioned at the one called Iris Lee with the barrel of his gun. "Look, ma'am," he said, doing his best to sound menacing. "We can do this easy or we can do this hard."

Iris Lee looked him square in the eye. "Don't wave that thing at me, young man, I ain't as skittish as some folks. I bet you don't even play the fiddle."

Travis caressed the trigger longingly and narrowed his eyes. In fact, she was right. All at once, something important occurred to him. "Iris Lee?" he asked bewilderedly. "Isn't your name Sheba?"

Charles T. was edging toward the stranger with the gun. Whether it was the sudden presence of the Stradivarius in his mind or the certainty that his long-lost Gloria had reached out from somewhere in the wide world to unlock the mind of their youngest son, Charles T. found himself able, for once, to shake off his lack of definition and, coming from behind in a single, deft movement, he went for the gun.

They struggled only enough to shoot a hole in the ceiling while Maejean, in the grip of her medication and the sight of her passion in jeopardy, commenced to faint.

"Oh, my lord," Iris Lee said, running a hand across her eyes. "Now you have done it."

The bandit, horrified by the sound of a gun in so small a room and the woman lying prone on the floor, let loose of his weapon without another thought. Charles T. took cold steel in his hand and smiled a Pancho Villa smile.

Grace stared wonderingly at her father, then at the wondrously handsome character standing rather sheepishly in the center of the room. Things were looking up, she decided. Definitely.

"Daddy was in the war," she explained, in case the man needed comfort. "Fighter pilot." Blue eyes. She might have known. She'd always been a sucker for the right shade of blue.

Keeping the gun in careful aim, Charles T. shot Grace a sidelong glance. He must remember, now that the kids were grown, to have a little chat with them on the subject of his soldiering.

Iris Lee scowled at Grace, who was staring at Travis Moseley with a look in her eye that glittered with Jezebellian calculation. If history had to repeat itself, she thought bitterly, it could have the decency not to do it in front of a person's face.

"If it isn't too much trouble," she said out loud. "It might be nice for somebody over on that side of the room to check and see if Maejean is dead or not."

Grace nodded stupidly, too enraptured by the man's sheer physical presence to make any verbal response. She bent down and, unable to find blood anywhere, started rather vigorously slapping Maejean around the pulse points. "No," Grace announced for the benefit of everybody. "I guess she only fainted."

Having received that bulletin, Dearest helped himself to another nip of his iced tea to quiet his nerves. He looked at his big brother with newfound respect. "Pistol-whip him, Charles T.," he encouraged. "Knock him on the head."

"Why?" Davey put in irritably. "So he won't be awake when we shoot him?"

A few moments before, with his life passing before his eyes, Davey'd found himself thinking of Carlene Dinkins, that waitress back in Arkansas, and not of Luanne Heck at all. Completely disgusted with the workings of his own mind, he decided to take it out on someone else.

Dearest, not impervious to Davey's tone, puffed out like a barnyard cock. "Well, excuse me for living, Davey. Is it just the heartache, or does it hurt when you pee, too?"

Having decided at last that the man in her kitchen was not, in fact, a manifestation, Baby took the situation in hand. "No one," she announced, "is going to shoot anyone. Not when I've just redone my kitchen."

"I meant to mention that," Iris Lee said, looking around her. "What are those things on the wallpaper, anyhow?"

Baby smoothed her apron and drew herself up. "For your information, they're pineapples, Iris Lee," she said. "Impressionistic pineapples. Now, Charles T., I'm sure everyone appreciates your bravery, but I want you to stop waving that silly gun in this man's face so he can tell us who he is."

Travis kept looking from one old lady to the other, like there'd been some mistake. "Iris Lee?" he asked no one.

Charles T.'s face resumed its characteristic uncertainty. "Well, he better not try anything."

"It appears to me as though he's tried about all he was going to," Baby told him. "Haven't you, uhh . . . ?"

"Travis, ma'am," the man answered. "Travis Moseley. Uhh. Junior."

Baby looked startled. "Moseley?" she asked. "Well, there you are. I just knew you had to be related. That's why you gave me such a start when you first came in. Other than the gun, I mean. You look just like my first husband. His name was Cecil, Cecil Moseley. Isn't it just remarkable how much they favor each other, Iris Lee?"

"I don't care," Iris Lee answered. "I just want to know why he's still here."

Since no one was apparently going to shoot him, Travis pulled up a chair. "You mean, you were married to him too?" he asked Baby.

Baby went on as though she hadn't heard. "Give him a chance to explain, Iris Lee. My goodness, a man doesn't just go around stealing violins without some provocation, do they, Travis?"

"No, ma'am, they do not," he said and took off his hat. "Which one is Sheba?"

Baby looked surprised. "Why, me, of course. But nobody ever calls me that. Mostly, folks call me Baby."

"Baby," said Travis Moseley, thoroughly confused. The plan had seemed so simple back at the motel.

On the other side of the kitchen table, Grace gasped a little and paused in her effort of trying to get the semiconscious Maejean into a chair. There had to be some way to get that man naked before they sent him to jail. There just had to be.

Baby walked around the back of him for a better look. "I knew you weren't violent," she said. "You can always tell a serious criminal by his face, and you just don't have the face for a life of crime. Does he, Grace?"

"No, ma'am," Grace answered.

"Hmmpphh," said Iris Lee.

"Now, supposing you tell us what all this is about," Baby went on, scooting her chair up.

Travis tried to think how to explain himself. "Your husband—Cecil—was my . . ."

"Pa?" Iris Lee interjected. She was playing an old movie over in her mind, freezing the projector on the frame of a woman with a golden-haired baby in her arms. "Cecil was your pa?" she asked incredulously.

"Don't be silly, Iris," Baby chided. "He just got done sayin' he was a junior. There have to be two named the same thing before one can be a junior."

Travis was trying to think where to begin. "Cecil was my granddad's name. I was raised by my grandma. Cora, her name was."

"Cora?" Baby was putting things together. "Cora was the woman Cecil was married to before he was married to me, wasn't she? Well, technically I suppose we were both married to him at the same time, but I never knew it. Ask Iris Lee. Iris Lee is my sister. The one with the mean mouth," Baby said, indicating her sister.

Iris Lee folded her arms across her chest, feeling suddenly cold. In sixty years, romantic, addlepated Baby had never once guessed Iris Lee's true errand in her house on the terrible day when Cora Moseley had come to call. And Iris Lee had never told her, either. Iris Lee stared at nothing. Chickens and secrets, she thought bitterly. They both come home to roost.

"You remember," Baby prompted her. "That day when you came to give me those preserves and Cora was crying and Cecil . . ." Baby broke off, the terrible, aching loss that had never quite been obscured by betrayal threatening her heart with silvery knives. Even now. She smiled wanly at the strength of those recollections. Hurting, after all, is so much better than dead.

"I remember, all right," Iris Lee snapped. "I remember that man was trash right from the start. Marrying two women," she said disgustedly.

"Now, Iris Lee," Baby began. "Travis here can hardly be held responsible for someone else's mistakes."

"Don't Iris Lee, me. Trash begets trash, it looks like."

"Pay no attention to my sister," Baby went on for Travis's sake. "She doesn't put much store by social graces."

"Oh, excuse me," Iris Lee countered. "I was under the impression this man here just broke in to kill us."

"That's not entirely true." Travis spoke on his own behalf. "All I wanted was that fiddle."

Seeing as how the crisis appeared to have passed, Charles T. passed the gun over to Davey, who was looking like he needed something to do. "How did you know where to find it?" he asked. "Baby says she never saw it before we brought it in from the porch."

Travis opened his mouth to speak and closed it again as Charles T.'s remark sank in. "You mean it was on the porch? Here?" he asked incredulously.

"Well, only for a little while," Baby said comfortingly. "I imagine somebody left it there sometime this morning." She paused to think things over. "Would have had to have been after ten o'clock, too. Ten o'clock is when I go out and trim the dead blossoms off my wisteria. If you keep the arbors trimmed, wisteria will bloom most of the summer, did you know that?"

"But how?" he said to Iris Lee, who was staring at him like he was sprouting fur. "I thought it was with you!" Travis was starting to feel a little sick. All those hours, following the wrong woman. And all the time it had been here, on the porch of this house. In broad fucking daylight.

Davey eventually tired of playing with the gun and laid it on the counter. "With Mammy? Why would Mammy have it?"

"I need air," said Iris Lee. No one appeared to have heard her.

"Why in the world would you think something like that?" Baby asked. "Except that it was right of you. Obviously we do have it. It's just that we didn't until today. Unless, of course, Iris Lee was just teasing me and had it all along."

"And just what is that supposed to mean?" Iris Lee demanded. "What would I be doing with a dead person's fiddle?"

"It doesn't mean a thing, Iris Lee," Baby answered. "It was just an idea. What is wrong with you today, anyway?"

"Not a thing. I'm fit as a . . ." Iris Lee broke off in midsentence. Given the circumstances, it was a poor choice of words.

"Could you excuse me just a minute, Travis?" Baby asked. "I just remembered, I think I have a picture of your Cecil upstairs. Would you like to see it?" A little distractedly, Baby disappeared without waiting for an answer.

Travis looked across the table, where Grace was restlessly trying to get his attention by displaying just enough of the slogan printed on her T-shirt to be provocative.

"We haven't met," she said sweetly, when she'd finally caught his eye. "My name's Grace."

Travis promised himself to give that one a second look in a cooler moment. For now, however, he was grateful for the little smile that teased around the corners of her mouth.

"Are they always like this?" he asked her.

"Oh," she assured him, "worse."

He smiled distractedly. "What's that say?" He indicated, as discreetly as possible, the slogan printed in smallish letters above Grace's not-so-smallish bosom.

"Don't die wondering," she told him.

Travis was beginning to think he might be finally losing his reason. "Pardon?"

Grace's smile broadened. "That's what it says, the shirt, I mean."

Iris Lee shook her head. "Might as well be a tattoo," she said under her breath.

Grace mouthed her response across the table at Travis and he read her lips with an inappropriate fascination.

"I have one of those, too."

Maejean stood up at last and made her way to Charles T. She paused a moment before she could bring herself to speak, looking down at the Stradivarius where it lay on the counter and daring herself to touch his arm. And curiously enough, she did, laying her hand on him like a benediction.

"I wanted to thank you for saving us," she whispered, her eyes teeming with emotions that had nothing to do with the words coming out of her mouth. "You're the bravest man I ever saw."

At the sense of Maejean's cool, sure touch on his arm, Charles T. tingled with delicious, near-forgotten electricity. He looked in her eyes like he was meeting some intoxicating stranger. "Why, thank you, Maejean. I always wanted to rescue a pretty woman."

Having convinced himself that he was the only one in the family with any attention span at all, Dearest sat backward on a kitchen chair and tried to return to the subject at hand. "Look," he said. "I just want to know two things here. I want to know what made you think any of us had that fiddle and I want to know why you wanted to steal it."

Travis's palms were beginning to itch, and, when Baby returned from the front of the house, unable to find the picture she'd had, Travis told them what he knew.

"I was raised on that fiddle," he began. "But I never heard it played. Cora, the one that raised me, she said it was mine by rights. I know it belonged to Cecil and to his pa before him, but that's all. Cora used to say that fiddle was the whole reason she fell in love with Cecil in the first place."

"Oh, I can relate to that," sighed Baby. "Hearing it made you feel like you'd just been born."

Travis stared at her a moment before continuing. "Anyway, she—uhmm—she thought there was a conjure in it, but I didn't believe that part. Then again, when she said it was a Stradivarius, I thought it might be worth tracking down. That's why I showed up here."

"How did you know to come?" somebody asked.

Travis shrugged. "Cora told me some things. Cora was all I had. My daddy run off before I was born and my mama was dead before I could walk. I never knew my kin, really. Except for Cora. And then, a conjure woman. But her I only met one time."

"Beg your pardon?" Grace asked. If she was going to fall for a man not right in the head, she figured she ought to get all the facts up front.

"Sort of like your mother," Charles T. explained.

"Oh," she said, immediately depressed. "Swell."

Baby glanced at her. "Hush, Grace. The man's talking."

"Anyway," Travis went on, "the fiddle come through my daddy's side, like I said—three, four generations. And Cora made me think it should have been mine, too. Except that my grandpa run off and married this other woman and nobody ever saw it again."

"Oh geez," said Grace.

"I traced who my granddad married up this way through the records and from this. I found it just after Cora died." Travis took out his wallet and withdrew an ancient, yellowing clipping from some decades-old paper. "She had it hid in a desk."

They all gathered to glance at the picture and the headline over it. "Wife Testifies at Inquest," it read and there, underneath, Iris Lee's young, beautiful face stared back from the page.

Baby smiled a little. "I remember," she said. "I was too distraught to say anything, so you went for me. I guess the paper got it mixed up. Oh, my goodness, you certainly were a pretty woman, Iris Lee."

Davey picked up the photo, delicate as butterfly wings, and looked at it in the light. "Geez, Grace," he said. "It looks just like you."

Grace peered over his shoulder, then back at her grandmother, suddenly not relishing the prospect of what the next fifty years was going to do to her face. "Oh," she said. "Maybe a little."

"When I came into that church sale, you were the same lady as in the picture," Travis said to Iris Lee, who wasn't looking well at all. "I thought you was the one married to Cecil. On account of what the paper said. When I saw that white-haired boy you got had a fiddle with him today, I followed you all. I figured it was the same one."

"Well," Iris Lee announced suddenly, the weight of these sudden treacherous revelations gnawing at the edge of her secret heart like a mouse through wood. "That don't change nothin'," she said and made for the telephone.

Baby stood up. "Iris Lee! And just what do you think you're doin'?"

"I am calling the police."

"No, you are not." Baby said, equally firm. "This is my house and I get to say who calls who and what about."

The phone call having comprised her one last-ditch attempt to rid herself of some impending judgment, Iris Lee wearily sank into the nearest chair, pale as a winter sky. "Fine," she said. "Do what you want."

"Besides," Baby turned and addressed the rest of them, smiling like high noon. "This man here is family."

Grace pondered this, trying to reckon whether or not his relation was close enough to label the things she was planning for the man as incest.

But Baby had smoothed her apron and was already giving orders. "We'll get this all straightened out," she promised, looking at Travis and smiling fondly. "How about some chicken spaghetti?"

But, finally, it was Davey who noticed that something was not as right as it looked. As Travis told his story, Davey, with his extra sense, felt a sudden absence from the room and wondered at it without daring to interrupt. And, as the rest of them set the table and reheated the food and fell over each other, Davey held perfectly still, fear taking shape in his mind like some terrible, poisonous cloud.

"Boo's gone!" he said all at once, seeing the mild surprise in their faces turning to something different as he told them the rest of it.

"So's the Stradivarius."

Thirty

As SOMEONE WAS TO SAY, many years afterward, some people learn and some people never do. And
there was no doubt at all, in the moment when, after fifteen
years of waiting, Icy Fee Moseley looked into the eyes of
Elijah Perdue, the Fiddling Prophet of Jesus, in which cate-
gory those two reckless ones belonged.

There was a long moment in which, after the woman's
shocking utterance of his real name, Victor/Elijah couldn't
think of a thing to say. He tried his best to recollect if he'd
ever let on to her, at some point in their history, that Elijah
Perdue was not the name he'd been given at the baptismal
font and could not. He tried to give a name of his own to
the expression in those pale, implacable eyes of hers and

failed that equally. Finally, when the silence between them was stretching itself to the point of mutual embarrassment, he said all he could think of, uttering the single platitude that managed to climb the spiraling summit of his bewilderment.

"How've you been, Icy Fee?"

Something like amusement flickered in her face and was gone.

"The boy told me you needed a conjure," she said flatly, noticing at the same time how profusely she had begun to sweat and how the sudden temperature of the afternoon made her want to unbutton the top of her bodice. She narrowed her eyes and swung open the screen door in wordless invitation. "That right?" she asked.

The preacher paused as he passed her on the doorsill, close to her body, the pollen scent of that riotous hair working on him in a way he didn't think possible. "I don't know, Icy Fee," he said and went in. "I've been to a doctor. He said there wasn't any help for it." Elijah lost his train of thought, unable to explain to this woman who'd been his lover how desperate he was. How hopeless he felt. He swallowed hard and went on. "But if you could give me something for the itch, I think I could bear the rest. God sends His crosses to us all."

Icy Fee shot him an edgy look and let the door bang on its spring. "Set," she directed abruptly. Putting the kettle on the fire, she went to her cupboard and commenced to mix him an infusion.

Elijah watched her. His initial confusion having begun to waver a little and relax, it was rapidly being replaced by a cold suspicion born of his own helplessness. He looked around him; the place was well-kept and clean, light filtered through a window like a blessing. Moseley, Elijah repeated the name over in his mind. Whoever she'd married, he'd managed to provide for his family; there were even some pieces of store-bought furniture and rug on the floor. And he watched her at her working and wondered.

Icy Fee spoke, anticipating the question forming in his mind. "I learned from a conjure woman lived in the swamp," she told him, measuring some leaves into a teacup. "I needed a conjure when—I needed some help and we got be friends. She's dead now, so I took up the trade."

Elijah picked up the steaming cup she set before him and stared, hypnotized, at the roots and bits of green that floated in its depths. He sniffed at it a little, feeling his willpower slipping away. Any cure for his misery lay at the bottom of that cup, he knew, and yet he would not drink.

He set it down with a jittery noise. "This is witchcraft, then?" he demanded, with a trace of his old thunder.

Icy Fee turned to him and smiled evenly. "And God said, 'Behold, I have given you every herb bearing seed which is upon the face of the earth and every tree in the which is the fruit of a tree yielding seed; to you it shall be for meat.' "

Elijah leaned back in his chair, frowning a little. "Ezekiel?" he asked.

"Genesis," Icy Fee answered. "Drink your tea." She looked at him. "For it is written, Prophet. 'Thorns and thistles shall bring it forth to thee and thou shalt eat the herb of the field.' "

Elijah sipped a little. Whatever it was, it tasted like dirt. "Exodus?" he asked, forcing himself to swallow.

Icy Fee laughed. "Genesis again," she insisted.

And so at last, he drank, talking a little between sips as he let the burning liquid cool. He never came out and said why he had come to her; somewhere in his heart he already understood that the results of his cure would differ greatly from that which had caused him to seek her out. And understood, too, that somewhere between his first sips of Icy Fee's medicine and his last, that something about her changed—turned from taut to tender, from remote to revealing—as though she herself, like the leaves in his cup, were releasing her power as she steeped in his presence.

And when at last he was finished, he realized something else. He was hornier than King Solomon on a Saturday night.

She waited until he was done and looking at her in the way she had known he would, the taste of the stuff lingering in his mouth like something forbidden. Then she stood up and leaned over to him, placing her hands on his shoulders, her touch filtering a curious warmth down through his clothes to his skin. He looked in her eyes and felt her melting heat and looked deeper, believing in his innocence that the price of her touch might not be too much, after all. Then, before he could move, she came closer and blew into his mouth, three short, quick breaths that he swallowed without meaning to. And then, she was gone from him, standing straight and observing him with a look both wary and satisfied.

Elijah rose, blushing, never noticing that his itch had been replaced by some new need, and his terrible, scaled skin was smooth as an infant's under his clothes.

"Is that everything?" he asked, not wanting the miracle of her presence to fade again, still feeling her breath in his mouth, discovering with another part of his mind his own regrets, his own nagging incrimination at having to do what he'd done, so long a time ago.

But instead of letting loose any long-stored wrath, the conjure woman came to him, the secret challenge in her eyes. "Not everything," she whispered, tiptoeing up to kiss his chin. "We can go to the woods."

He stared at her, love and gratitude and fear tossing his

heart around for sport and the sudden, undeniable truth of the horror that lay under his clothes snatching it away to spoil the play of his emotions.

"I cannot," he said, his voice strangling in his throat. "I am not—" he hesitated, searching for some delicate way to tell her of the tragedy that had happened to his body. True, it hadn't been much to start with, but now . . . "I am not as I was. You would find me—repugnant." Elijah swallowed hard and reached for his hat, intending to get while the getting was still good.

But Icy Fee stopped him with a hand laid lightly on his arm. "I think not," she said.

Elijah, to date, had not had much by way of experience with women who wouldn't take no for an answer. In fact, her insistence on him was something of a first. He pleaded with her with his eyes, and finally, seeing no other way out of his torment, he unbuttoned his shirt, so she could see for herself the cause of his unworthiness. "See?" he said, anger and humiliation and thwarted love bringing him to tears.

She stared at him, already unbraiding that sunset hair and letting it fall around her shoulders like a halo of flame. "See what?" she said, and incredibly, she smiled.

"Elijah, see for yourself."

And, remembering the route like something out of a hallucination, he followed her form through the brush and the branches to that same bright, cool clearing with its circle of stones and its secrets and sorrows and he watched her undress and she came to his arms and he loved that sweet body till he thought he would die.

Thirty=one

ERNEST EARL FAXTON had a tumor in his guts and two more months to walk the earth. Possibly three, assuming he ate right, but what a sudden absence of fried foods in his diet was going to do to stop the growth of the thing at this late stage of the game was not only beyond his understanding but that, he suspected, of his physicians as well. When the doctor gave him the report, he'd closed his eyes, a sudden image of the cancer crowding the pictures in his mind. He knew exactly what it would look like, exactly the spongy, yet oddly resilient texture and the size. He ought to, he'd removed enough of those tumors in the course of his work to know what they looked like when they reached the killing stage.

So he reckoned on seventy days, tops, and began to keep a little calendar, crossing off sunsets as they passed him by. The poor soul adjusted so quickly to the idea of expiring that his doctors, unable to believe their own finesse, promptly drew up a medical paper on the strength of Ernest's example, informing others among their brethren just how they'd managed to tell the patient of his imminent termination without having to sit through a messy reaction. Ernest Earl hadn't even gone pale, but then, he was so wan to start with, it was difficult to tell.

The secret fact of the matter was, Ernest was not at all dismayed by the news. Being a mortician, he had long ago got used to the idea of dying, and learning about it ahead of time, he reckoned, only gave him the advantage. The doctors had assured him he'd go quick enough, with no more pain than could be handled by a prescription. And Ernest Earl, his ties to the living tenuous at best, decided at once he could ask for no more. He knew at least approximately when the Reaper was coming to call and had time, the way a death-sentenced criminal has time, to look his life over and tie up any dangling ends. Finding out about his cancer, then, didn't move him one way or another, really. He likened it in his own mind to getting a notice in the mail that a magazine subscription was running out. For good.

There were things he wanted to attend to, of course. The matter of his coffin, the instructions for his interment. Ernest Earl had just recently found that his corner on the county's traffic in death was not as secure as it once had been. A brand-new establishment for eternal rest had sprung up not a month before in the new shopping mall between Atlantis and Queen City. The place was being managed by some fraternal twins from Nacodoches named Beemish, and though it was as well or better appointed than Ernest's own establishment, he knew for a fact the twins were having a hard time drumming up a clientele. People, as anyone can tell you, cling to tradition when it comes to putting their loved ones down. But with Ernest dead and no son to replace him, the Funeral Emporium was soon to shut its doors. So in a burst of professional generosity, the old undertaker figured it might boost the twins' morale if they could get an advance booking and a confidential promise of more on the way. Three days after he'd received the news of his impending demise, Ernest Earl drove over to see the Messrs. Beemish and make himself some proper arrangements. True, the twins were a little surprised at the presence of the forbidding, square-jawed man in their showroom, and even more so when they gleaned the nature of his errand, but then, the Beemish boys were not yet twenty-five, new to the business, with much to learn. Ernest chose mahogany for his everlasting condominium, stained like rosewood and lined in blue. He would have preferred an apricot shade for the satin, but the Beemishes convinced him otherwise. The blue would prove the perfect counterpoint against Ernest's rather sallow complexion. He chose his Bible readings and his music, too, just something to put the mourners in mind of eternity without being overly depressing, he instructed. And the Beemishes promised to do what they could. By the time the afternoon was done, Ernest Earl felt himself a different man; he was so pleased with the outcome of his transactions, so confident in the talents of the Beemishes, that if it hadn't been his funeral he was planning, he might have sent out invitations.

In fact, the only thing that was really troubling the patient at all was the little matter of the violin. He'd expected, when he'd given it up to Baby Todd's verandah on the morning he'd learned he was practically a corpse, to have been released from the high-security prison that comprised his feeling for the woman. And for awhile he had fooled himself into believing that in giving back the violin, his heart, too, had been liberated. At first, the gesture made him feel like Scrooge on Christmas morning, the miser turned benign when the jig is finally up. But he found, with the passage of days, that giving up the Stradivarius was simply not good enough; when it came to hopeless love for Baby Todd, he was as bad off as ever. It pissed him off, and not unrightly, either. He figured it unseemly for a man of his age to carry on this way over something so impossible as love, and he figured, too, that after sixty years, there ought to be some way for him to be able to buy off his relentless heart and die in peace. He'd righted the wrong he'd done, returned what had been taken. So why then, after so many years of unfulfillment, did his heart race at the sight of her figure in the street? Why still did he drive past her house, more frequently than ever now, for the sheer pleasure of sending her those silent hexes? Most humiliating of all, why did he still wake sometimes, dreaming of her hands on his wasted flesh? Most loves, he realized, might have shriveled and dried from sheer lack of attention, but Ernest Earl Faxton was coming to the reluctant conclusion that his heart was made of different stuff. Fact was, loving Baby was the single thing that Ernest Earl Faxton was going to miss about being alive.

It was somewhere in the second week of his next-to-the-last month of living that Ernest Earl began to rely quite heavily on his pain prescription. And when Maivis Johnson died of a stroke as the brakes on her Chevette gave out in the Safeway parking lot that Tuesday and they brought her to his slab, it was not at all surprising that, through the fog of his anguish, she was speaking to him the following evening in the workroom, talking through the stitches he'd put in her lips.

"You'd be doing the woman a favor, Ernest," Maivis told him in a necessarily slurred little speech.

"And how would that be, Maivis?" he asked, gently combing out her hair.

"By killing her, of course," Maivis told him. "They couldn't send you back to prison. You're already dead."

Ernest paused and got some hair spray from a little table nearby. He shook the can and the mixing marbles inside clattered like laughter in the chill of the room. He closed her eyes and sprayed and when he had finished, opened them again. "I don't know," he reflected solemnly. "What would folks think?"

Maivis looked at the bright bare ceiling, being unable, really, to look at anything else. "Folks don't think, Ernest. If folks were thoughtful, like they say they are, the world wouldn't be what it is. Take my granddaughter. Was it thoughtful of her to bury me in this dress? I look like trash."

Ernest patted a cold, still hand. "The dress is fine, Miz Johnson. You look right pretty."

The corpse made a disgruntled sound in its throat. "Besides," it continued. "I said you ought to kill the woman. I ain't sayin' you should put it on the radio."

"Kill her?" Ernest frowned, reaching again for those pills that dulled his pain. It was seeming as plausible to him as rotting of cancer was. As deaths went, murder could be quick enough, and certainly more attractive. "How?" he said when he'd swallowed some.

The corpse's voice dropped to a breath above a whisper. "First her, then you. You could be together, Ernest. You and your lady."

Ernest's hand trembled a little as he applied some rouge to the withered cheeks, and not liking the effect too much, he dabbed a little on her nose to draw attention from the wrinkles. "I never killed anyone," he said. "I wouldn't even know how."

Despite his work on her face, the thing that had been Maivis Johnson kept on talking.

"That .41 Colt you got in your chifferobe upstairs is how, Ernest. It ain't never been fired, but that don't mean it can't be."

Ernest paused, recalling the old frontier-style pistol his father had given him for his eighteenth birthday. It would work, he reckoned silently. A single shot, clean and quick. At least Maivis had put him in mind of where to find the weapon. He himself hadn't seen the thing for thirty years or more.

"She's got so old, Ernest," the cadaver urged. "What's she got to live for anymore 'cept gettin' sick? You never give her anything, Ernest, not your love or your children or a home. You were too afraid to tell her you loved and now you're going to die," Maivis chided him. "All you ever gave her was that old fiddle. And that weren't even hers to start with."

Ernest smoothed the waxy Hide-a-Flaw Number Two into the shadows under the corpse's eyes. And somewhere in the middle, he began to cry, a tortured garbled sound in the back of his throat, too dry for real tears.

"At least give her death, Ernest. You wouldn't give her a good life. All you got left to give is a good death."

Ernest brushed a touch of youthful brown into Maivis's ghostlike brows, thinking it all over, thinking of the sense in the body's reasoning. Thinking that of anyone, he could do it well. "Murder?" he whispered, trying the word out on his tongue.

The voice faded to secret sound. "She loved you, Ernest

Earl. It was you she loved all along. Give her a chance to prove it."

Ernest gave a long, last look at his handiwork and the face of Maivis Jonhson stared back up at him, the eyes opened wide with all the depthless wisdom of the departed, looking better than she had in twenty years.

Thirty=two

IT NEVER WAS CLEAR precisely when Elijah Perdue gave up his last chance at living. It might have been the first time he crossed the threshold of the conjure woman's door, or the day, two weeks after his cure, when he'd thrown any vestige of discretion to the devil and, with nothing on his mind but red hair and white, white skin, he'd stood at the end of the Moseley's road like some miserable scarecrow, waving his arms until she came out and drove him off. Or perhaps it was that afternoon when he spoke to the boy Cecil in her absence, the day when Icy Fee had gone into the swamp to deliver someone's baby, and Elijah, possessed of the need to see her again, had come to the farm on the pretext of needing some insomniac's tea. Finding her gone, the preacher had passed the time with the blond, curly-headed Cecil, never once suspecting the boy was his own. Elijah, with all the elaborate pretense of sociability that goes with being guilty as sin, made quite an effort to draw the sullen, difficult boy into conversation, and that failing, had instead taken up his bow and filled the child's head with the treacherous sounds of those angels that dwelt in his Stradivarius. He even taught the boy to play a little, sixteen bars of an old-timey hymn.

No one, not even Icy Fee, who had a talent for such things, could measure when exactly the Fiddling Prophet of Jesus started to seal up his fate. But one thing was certain; it all ended because of the laundry.

All good gamblers have a system and Icy Fee Moseley was no exception. She had a knack for seeing her way around the impossible, and when it became obvious that Elijah was more willing by far to risk her security than she was, she devised a method for their madness that, for awhile at least, suited everyone concerned.

For reasons she preferred not to think about too much, the linens from her hope chest had gone unused and reeking of mothballs and cedar for most of her marriage. But as it happened, Elijah's return to Atlantis had more or less coincided with a need for some new towels, and so, shortly after his visit, it seemed to the woman that life was falling into place when she resurrected her dowry, gave it a good scrubbing, and put the things to their proper use at last. It was those very linens that gave her the notion, as she hung them on her clothesline in the sun one morning, of how it was going to pass that she could have her cake and her preacher, too. And before too much time had passed, the conjure woman had her lover trained to the workings of her household.

Elijah was to ride, the three days a week that she hung

out her washing, to the edge of the bluff in the woods and note the colors of the dish towels hanging on the left side of the clothesline. A red border meant Deke was around the farm and Elijah was to keep his distance. Green or blue gingham checks indicated she would meet him at their appointed place in the circle of stones; plain muslin cloths or those with embroidery meant a question mark—only that she would come if she could.

That the two of them should pick it up pretty much where they left it off seemed, in Elijah's mind, almost too much to pray for, but he found, to his everlasting wonder, that this new Icy Fee seemed to want him as much as did the old. Just why she did, however, was something of a mystery. The preacher was never to set eyes on her husband, but reckoned, given what he'd seen of the rest of the world, that the man almost had to be better looking. And given the condition of the farm and the number of children, Elijah reckoned also that this Moseley was also more prosperous. But, curious as he was as to the reasons for her desire, he never could bring himself to ask. The Fiddling Prophet of Jesus had come to a time in his life when he was no longer in possession of the necessary energy to look gift horses in the mouth. She wanted him, and as long as that held true he had made up his mind to be satisfied.

It was as though the couple had some silent agreement between them to fill what time they had with all the things that might have been, or at least, not to crowd it too much with regret. So, in the long afternoons they spent together in that clearing in the Moulder woods, neither of them chose to ask too many questions. Instead, they spoke of more innocent things. It was he who, at Icy Fee's bidding, brought the newspapers that made up their bed in the circle of stones. Deke, she had explained to her lover in an off-handed way, had never learned to read or count beyond five hundred, and she figured the man might get suspecting should too much newsprint suddenly start to appear around the house. So Elijah, anxious to please and perhaps to impress her, brought all he could, some from places as far as Dallas or, on one occasion, St. Louis, and after their love-making he would read to her all the news of the world beyond Atlantis County, and describe, in his admittedly limited fashion, what parts of that world he had seen. Sometimes, he even played the fiddle, not hymns this time but all the love songs he could learn, fiddling soft and low, so none but they two could hear.

But it is a rare human being who will not mess with perfection, and Elijah Perdue, while rare enough in some other respects, proved no particular exception in this one. After a month or so had passed, with Icy Fee's system working like a charm, the prophet began to think, in those terrible frustrating mornings he waited on the ridge, that perhaps she was hanging out the plain or embroidered dishrags more often than she had at first, or worse, the ones with the crimson borders—those red flags that told him to stay away. He began to think that she did not want him so much after all. That, couched as she was in the haven of her picture-book farm with her phantom husband, she felt she could afford to throw him some crumbs from her passion's table. He saw that she was was toying with him and perhaps she was, being, in the depths of her secret heart, equally unable to let well enough alone.

And so, when it happened that Icy Fee Moseley hung out three sets of bedsheets and no towels at all one fine Saturday morning, her lover squinted toward the clothesline from his position on the ridge like some great scavenger bird, rage and jealousy lodged in his gullet like pieces of carrion. And Elijah Perdue decided right then and there that enough was not going to be enough after all.

She never saw him coming.

And yet he took no particular pains to hide himself. He tied his horse to a tree and made his way through the woods and around the barn to the clothesline side of her house, his mind on fire. She was there, keeping up with the rhythm of her housework, bending down to take up the sheets, displaying the curve of her hips through the volume of her skirt, then reaching, her long arms raised, clothespins in her teeth and breasts bulging under her bodice. He watched her, desperately fumbling with the buttons on his pants until he had freed himself, swollen and stiff and urgent as a boy. The vision of her appeared and disappeared, hidden for moments in the flapping cloth. Elijah stood, his need for her burning a hole in his mind, and, making his way through the clotheslines, he waved the sheets aside, the scents of soap and bleach and sunlight filling his head like an aphrodisiac. She stood with her back to him as he panted and stroked himself, waiting his chance. And when she bent down to retrieve the last of the clothespins, Icy Fee Moseley, never famous for undergarments, had her skirt rucked up over her head and before her mind could put a name to what was happening, was entered from behind.

She fell on her knees with the weight of him, his breath and tongue and lips hot and wet on her neck. And the pain and rage of such violation dissolved with his breath and the feel of him driving deeper, straining to touch that part of her that no one else could reach. Then, so fast the sound of it seemed to come too late, his hands, tearing her blouse front and back, laying his face in the sweat that came up along her spine, licking it, reaching around to roll nipples in his hard fingers and squeeze. The hands sought lower, front and back, groping for her belly, feeling for her and him together and she grabbed, too, when those twin ribbons of fire that flickered from her breasts to meet at her gut burst into a roar and spread through the whole of her, taking his hand into her mouth to suck the sweetness from his fingers, biting the flesh to keep from crying out. And still they touched and pushed, groping for each other inside their embraces—concealed from the world in gleaming sheets that flapped and rippled around their bodies, smelling of the sun and the wind.

Thirty-three

BUT THEY had been discovered after all.

The boy Cecil had been in the cotton field with his father since dawn, picking and checking for weevils. He had a fifty-pound sack that he dragged behind him through the rows, picking fast and sure as any nigger could. The cotton came early and it was due to rain and the two were racing the weather, stripping twenty acres of bottom land at the far edge of the farm with their four hands alone, picking until their fingers bled and the sacks on their shoulders grew heavy as stone.

Cecil fared well enough working the farm, but his heart was in other places and everyone knew it. Everyone but the man who called himself the boy's father, that is. Somewhere along the line, Deke's love for the boy had grown fearsome and rigid, denying, with all the blind futility of fatherhood, those qualities in Cecil he could not understand. The boy had become Deke's right hand around the place since he had completed what education was available the previous spring. Deke was doing all he could think of to keep Cecil on the only road he knew, and in a last desperate attempt to keep what was his, set the boy to farming, hoping to work the wayward heart out of him, if necessary.

Plowing and picking and clearing till both were ready to drop should have cured Cecil of his wandering tendencies but instead it had made them worse. And as he bent and sweated and ached by Deke's side, part of his mind was always traveling, that part of him that was fatherless and homeless and dreaming always, stayed free to see the world as it was.

That morning they had left his mother alone in the house and it troubled the boy in his heart, though he couldn't have said why. Since it was Saturday, the little kids were allowed to town, with a penny or a nickel apiece, to gorge themselves on candy or buy what treasures they could find. But Deke gave Cecil a dollar, telling him he could have it if he stayed and picked the cotton. Deke wasn't fooling anyone by that time, but Cecil's blue eyes had widened nevertheless at the sight of so huge a bribe. A dollar, he figured silently, was more money than he could spend in a day.

And so they had gone to the fields.

The bag was half full and the boy could no longer tell where his fingers left off and the cotton began. He felt as though there were some kind of stone fastened to the base of his spine and he had passed the point in his picking where he felt any need to straighten his legs, those muscles, like the ones in his fingers, gone too hard and dead to protest.

He didn't mind it, especially. He'd found when working with Deke that it was better not to feel too much, just let the machine of his body do what it was bid while his mind dreamed away the day. Then, as he rounded a row and made to pick his way back up the other side, the whole world changed before his eyes.

Lines of white cotton expanded and shimmered in the heat, waving and flapping, like wings and then like curtains. They undulated, gleaming, blinding him until his pupils could adjust to so much light. Then, horrified, the curtains parted and he looked to what the cotton hid—there—at the far end, those figures writhing like reptiles. And the boy, frozen in the cotton, too dumbstruck to know what the bodies meant, too shocked to see what he was already seeing, too sick and fascinated to look away. The figures heaved and cried out and then there was music singing in his head, begging for his understanding. The boy felt himself begin to breathe again, felt water on his cheeks when he made himself see at last that it was his mother there hidden in the sheets, her mouth contorted and her eyes bulged out, her single red braid coiled in the grass. And he understood, too, that it was he, Cecil, somehow there with her, in black preacher's clothes with his hair hanging in his face.

Soon after, when the vision faded and the cotton was cotton again and the earth was merely earth, Cecil saw his mother climbing down the wagon at the edge of the field, bringing them their lunch. The boy straightened up for the first time in hours and went to her, unhitching his burden and biting his lip to keep his tears from showing in his eyes, wondering how it was that his mother could be in two places at once, bringing them dinner and back at her clotheslines at home, lying naked in the grass.

He never asked and she never said, but one look at the

handsome face, that up until that morning had still been a boy's, and Icy Fee understood without having to think about it that the time of the preacher was done.

At supper that evening, Cecil ate little and kept his eyes focused on his plate, not daring to look at anything. Deke was in an unusual mood himself, tickled half pink at Cecil's dedication to the harness and believing that he was the one responsible for the boy's lack of spirits.

"Hard work is the only kind there is, boy," he said heartily, noting Cecil's lack of appetite with no little satisfaction. If the child was too tired to eat, it meant that he was too tired for foolish notions as well. "And there's more of it where that came from. We got new fences by the south pond come Monday."

Cecil did look up then, contempt for the man's stupidity shining in his eyes like liquid poison. He made to speak, but Icy Fee intervened in time.

"He can't go with you Monday, Deke," she said quietly. "I need him here."

Deke frowned. No sooner had he done the boy some good than his mother wanted to come along and soften him up. Take that linen suit she'd gone and bought him for graduation. "Why?" he wanted to know.

Icy Fee stared at her husband, eyes as blandly innocent as thin ice on a river. "I need to get to the place up in the woods where I keep my plants. There's been a rattlesnake up in the clearing. A big one, and mean. I want Cecil to kill it for me."

Deke, his respect for the delicacies of women at war in his mind with his love for his son, sulked over the remainder of his mashed potatoes. "Well, stay out till he goes away," he said.

"Can't," Icy Fee replied, never varying her tone. "Miz

Jenks has got female trouble and I need some golden seal. Up there's the only place it grows."

Deke swallowed uncomfortably. He knew nothing of female troubles and didn't want to start learning, either. "Why can't he kill it tomorrow?" he asked, switching to another tack. "Ain't nothin' but a rattler."

Icy Fee smiled a little and made to clear the dishes. "Now, Deke," she said mildly. "You ought to know by now I don't hold with killing on Sunday."

Monday dawned clear, the sky wide open and blue. Cecil watched it happen from the tiny window in the loft where he slept, silently ticking off the routine of the morning as his treacherous mother made breakfast and sent Deke to build his endless cursed fences with two of the younger boys, while his sisters and the babies scattered like butterflies to the secret errands of their days. The house fell quiet and Cecil stared out his window, glad for his solitude, nursing that unnameable hurt that his mother had caused him, resenting the flood of change in his heart.

It was fully noon before she called him downstairs; the day's washing was out on the line. When he pulled on his overalls and sulked out to the yard, the vision of that wet laundry waving in the breeze sickened him and he had to turn away.

He could feel her eyes on him as he scuffed his toes in the grass. "Cecil Moseley," she chided him softly, "you take on like you'd never seen a dish towel before."

Cecil had no answer he could make into words. Maybe it was all foolishness after all, he figured, seeing the corner of a blue gingham cloth waving like a flag at the edges of his sight. Maybe he was wrong.

Icy Fee's face betrayed nothing. "I'm going up to the

clearing now," she told him. "I left you a plate of pone and greens on the stove. Get you something to eat and you can follow me with the rifle."

"Yes, ma'am," he said.

"You know the place I mean?"

Cecil nodded and went into the house, watching through the window as his mother's back disappeared through the tangle of trees at the edge of the garden.

Elijah was already there, as she had known he would be, spreading out his newspapers on the grass and rehearsing in his head what he would say to her. He could think of no way to explain himself or the madness that had made him take her like a criminal as she'd hung out her washing. He had needed to know—he guessed—that she belonged to him, and yet between the cool, exquisite dampness of the sheets he had learned that and more. He had no other questions of her and yet, when he turned and saw her smiling, standing at the edge of their clearing with the sunlight dappling her strange, bright hair, he knew, too, that she wanted explanations. And it relieved him so much he nearly laughed aloud as he took her in his arms.

What he didn't see were the leaves she crumbled quick as a thief into his pockets as he held her to him and kissed her, feeling her breath in his mouth. He caught a sudden waft of some scent he could not identify and in the time it took to blink and smile, he was overcome with an overriding need to sleep. As she backed out of his embrace, the preacher yawned copiously and stretched his arms, his vision growing dim. He smiled like a sleepy child.

"Lord," he sighed. "I need a nap, I guess. Must be getting old."

Icy Fee smiled at him with an expression distant as the moon. "No, Elijah," she crooned. "You won't be getting old."

Something in her tone struck him wrong, but his mind
was so fogged with fatigue he was unable to grasp just what
it was. He needed to lie down. If he might just rest his eyes
a minute, he figured groggily, then he would understand.

"Lay down, Elijah." she urged him, leading him by the
hand. "On the papers. Sleep a little while."

He frowned uncertainly, yet he was grateful for her presence, her cool comprehension.

"You don't mind?" he asked, stretching out and closing
his eyes.

"No, love," she whispered, leaning over to brush his lips
with her own as he relinquished the last of his consciousness
and slept. "I don't mind at all."

And the rifle was in Cecil's hands as he watched them,
cold metal pulled back hard and loaded quick. She who was
his ma embraced the scabby man who'd played the violin.
And the violin was there, too, a little off to the side as Cecil
watched them through the trees, his heart like a fist pound-
ing anguish in his chest. It made him want to scratch himself, that feeling under his skin. The rifle with a life of its
own raised to his shoulder as the man laid down. And Cecil
wanted to cry and his throat closed up and his itchy finger
found the trigger when his mother placed her kiss on the
stranger's sleeping cheek.

But he did not fire. He parted the curtain of leaves with
his rifle still aimed true and he passed into the clearing,
facing her—needing, in that final moment, to know the
reason why.

Cecil's voice was sure and clear as it echoed through the
clearing and the woods, certain as a man's.

"Who is he?"

Icy Fee looked up at her son, tall and straight and beautiful, holding his gun like a soldier. And she wished to God
in that moment that he had never been born.

"He's your pa." The voice was dry as wind.

And, there being no greater indignity he could think of, Cecil Moseley aimed his rifle and shot his father in his sleep.

When it was done, mother and son rolled the culprit up in his newspapers like some enormous fish, carried him through the woods, and threw him in the swamp. Cecil watched the bundle sinking and wondered, in the depths of him, how he could go on living with that sight so burned in his mind. And when he could think again, when he could speak, he looked to his mother. She held out the black preacher's coat and the fiddle case to him like a present.

"These belong to you, I guess."

And so he took the only things in the world besides himself that Elijah Perdue, the Fiddling Prophet of Jesus, had left to mark his time on earth.

And, three nights later, after Icy Fee had made him chew honeysuckle to take away his memory and burned black cohosh by the light of the moon to banish his boy's bad dreams, Cecil Moseley, cleansed of his conscience and handsome as sin, had packed up his clothes and his fiddle and his pride, and set out for those places he'd always wanted to be.

PART
THREE

THE PRESENT

Music is essentially useless, as life is.

George Santayana.

Some things in life are just like Myra Needles' punch.
Just because somethin' goes down easy don't mean you
can't get real drunk.

Anonymous

Thirty=four

WHEN LUANNE HECK and her preacher hus-
band got a load of Boo Strait running through the streets
of Atlantis like he was on fire someplace with a fiddle
clutched to his chest and his face flushed with exertion and
wonderment, it didn't really occur to them that anything
was not as it should have been.

Brother Harlan Heck had spent most of that day on the
wrong side of the tracks with the kind of sinners they'd
never mentioned in the seminary and was feeling close to
his limits as far as Christian charity was concerned. When
Boo huffed past them, little more than a blur, as Harlan was
parking the Hecks' Pinto wagon a little after two-thirty, he
rather irritably voiced the intention of having a good long

talk with Iris Lee Strait on the subject of where her duties lay. "That hellion ought to be in jail," the reverend finished, listening to the Pinto's engine knock as he switched off the ignition.

Now that she had finished with the day's tedium and was back on her own turf, Luanne seized the moment to stomp on her husband's already frayed sensibilities by lighting a menthol. "Oh, leave it alone, Harlan," she said. "If the boy wants to go jogging, let him."

Harlan thumped the steering wheel with his soft hands and what little lip he had disappeared altogether. "The boy is a menace, I tell you! He ought to be put away." His voice rose shrilly, to levels he used for the more inspired of his damnation sermons, but he broke off in a coughing fit as Luanne blew smoke in his direction. "Must you smoke those things?"

Luanne toked on her Kool, inhaling till her throat protested and her reverend husband turned a little green. "Yes," she said. "I must smoke these things." She paused a minute to contemplate the ember glowing at the cigarette's end. "I figure they'll get me used to hell." Having been married for nearly a decade, Luanne had long ago discovered that Harlan Heck was too much the psalm-sayer to beat on a woman. Nevertheless, she'd never tired of seeing to what miserable lengths his Christianity would bring him. She watched as the skin under his cleric's collar went purple with rage, and her made-up eyes narrowed with a secret satisfaction as she recalled her visit from the Strait boys the other afternoon. "And that boy," she said blowing a little more smoke up the reverend's sinus and smiling like a girl, "is as right as rain."

Unlike most of the people in the world, the distance between wanting and getting was a shortish hallway in Boo

Strait's mind, uncrowded with all the complex mental bric-a-brac that clutters more intelligent minds, collecting hesitation and insecurity and morality and unmade decisions like so much dust in a maniac's parlor. The boy had only to set his eyes on that wondrous instrument, announce his feelings, and take it, making away with the thing in no more time than it took to know he had to have it, no more time than it took to play eight bars of fast music, no more time than it took the rest of them to get surprised. For if the stuff of genius is just tricks, Boo Strait knew them all.

No one had seen him take the violin simply because he had not wanted them to. Boo had tricked the world into believing he wanted its attention for minutes at a time, and so, few ever questioned how he filled his hours. People have a way of believing what they see and go right on believing even after the picture has changed. The trick in tricking people was in being specific. Once you got someone to thinking they knew what you wanted, you could do pretty much as you pleased with the rest of your time. A little bit of thievery was nothing.

The family would notice he was gone eventually, they always did. And if he didn't show up, they would come looking, because they always did that, too. But the thing that no single member of his family had ever yet realized was that in all the eighteen years Boo Strait had been alive, none of them had managed even once to find him before he'd decided it was time to be found. He could stay free for as long as he chose. He could run faster than a car if he needed, and knew about hiding, too. If they should get near him, he could hide just right, and whoever was looking would never know he was under their noses, close enough to grab. Not until he let them, not till he was ready.

Boo grinned as he ran through the streets of the town, knowing how they would look for him—hearing their

voices in his mind, loud and distinct, shouting at each other
for not noticing what they never saw, not seeing what they
never noticed. Mammy would blame Grace and Baby
would blame Mammy and Grace would blame Davey and
Davey would blame Dearest and Dearest would blame
Mammy back and Maejean would wish she had someone to
blame but didn't, so she wouldn't blame anyone and
Charles T. would blame himself and the rest would, ultimately, let him.

And so Boo went his own way. Running not from fear
or urgency but carried by the rhythm of the movement
alone, legs and breath and sweat keeping time to the orches-
tra of sounds that played always in his heart. He ran harder
as he passed the drugstore and the Safeway and the place
where they kept the money, running till there were spots
dancing before his eyes and each breath was a fiery torture.
He would run till he fell, face down, in the clover that grew
in the fields at the edge of town, blossoms laid out in pat-
terns like crocheted doilies over the grass. And he would
get up again with that sweet green smell in his nose and run
some more. They might not ever find him, this time.
Maybe, finally, he had tricked them all for good. Because
none of them back there could hear the way he could; none
of them back there, their heads crowded with secrets and
wishes and words, could know what this thing was that he
had taken. None of them could know the sounds it would
make, none of them could listen. And so he ran with that
curved piece of magic under his arm, sweating music.
Music. Music that was pouring into his head like water from
a broken pump. And now, for the first time in all his life,
Boo Strait had a proper bucket to catch the water with. So
he kept on running. Running for all he was worth.

Suddenly he knew his direction, the name of the place he
wanted to be thundering in his mind like the summons of

an angel. He heard it and swung wide, around the corner
on Laurel Avenue, heading for another part of town.

The Greyhound station was past the Exxon and the funeral parlor, down by the part of Atlantis that was cloaked
in secrecy, as though the despair of those rickety houses and
dark, silent roads was something not to be discussed. The
station wasn't a whole place, just an ancient, locked store-
front with a bench in front and a greasy, flyspecked sched-
ule taped to the windowpane. But Boo knew about it, knew
where it was and how to get there. He knew from eighteen
years of spying on the world he dwelt in without having any
say. He knew when the buses came and went, knew from
watching and never speaking, from memorizing other people's habits, greedily saving them up like shiny pennies in
his head, knowing all about everything because no one
would ever expect it of him, and knowing too, how easy it
is to move around in a world when no one ever expects you
to answer a question.

He was playing a song when the reason for his going
there finally appeared, notes that first shimmered like rain-
bows in the fading daylight, then hung suspended in the
street like wishes. Boo's fingers were graceful and tapered
and strong, trembling with effort over the foreshortened
Stradivarius, the rattlers whispering inside it, singing secrets. The boy played on, not needing any but himself to
hear it, hoping, though, that someone would, the melody
meandering through his instrument like someone picking
flowers on a country road, pausing to exclaim over one
exquisite, fragile blossom, going on to take another—holding the whole arrangement back for a time to better admire
the beauty. Flowers of music bobbed in the light, not caring
or conscious that their perfection could not last forever.
Each moment of that wild music was content to sound, each
note added on a blessing, until the bouquet of song grew

finally, too perfect to hear without weeping. The soul is too proud a thing to reach, most times, too used to being alone. Touched, even by so gentle a magic wand as a country boy's fiddle, it is startled, and thinks it feels pain.

And so when the woman stepped off the only bus to come through Atlantis that day and saw that fiddling idiot playing his heart out to no one, it was through tears. She might have been forty, or seventy, or anywhere in between —she had the kind of face where only the eyes mattered anyway, one being decidedly blue and the other a murky peaish green. No matter the color, those eyes shone with an identical light and all the fanatic will that goes along with having to feel a little more alive than anyone else, and a little more alone. Meeting those eyes, most people looked away, feeling their own shame rising up in them like she had spoken an accusation. Others, of a stronger nature, looked back, meeting that gotch-eyed stare with a kind of sympathy, wondering in their hearts what a nice female like that could possibly be doing wandering around a place like Planet Earth. Eyes like that, they figured, couldn't help but be a little disappointed in what they saw, and most would leave her a little lighter in the heart, figuring their burdens less cumbersome than hers. For the woman who stepped off the only bus to come through Atlantis that day knew, as did her lastborn child, all the tricks it takes to work a human being. Yet, after nearly twenty years of running and twenty years of sacrificing all those things that running makes you leave behind, Gloria McSaxon Strait had found her bag of tricks running down to the lint in the bottom. And, with a suitcase full of foreign clothes, a heart full of fear or love or curiosity (she couldn't tell which), and a mind brimming with possible futures, she walked up to the boy on the bench and waited, trembling, until he finished the last of his incredible song.

Boo laid the Stradivarius down, set aside the bow, and looked up, meeting those eyes of hers with an expression neither surprised nor sympathetic, but one that was, in its own way, worse than something she might have been able to recognize. Glint for glint, shine for shine, the light that came out of her own son's eyes struck Gloria with a force she had yet to encounter in all of her desperate straggling around the globe: it was equal.

Boo moved his lips and, caught off balance the way she was, it took her a moment to realize that the mouth had sound coming out of it, words clear and well-formed, the voice impossibly deep.

"Hi, Mom."

Thirty=five

THERE IS NOTHING on earth, or possibly anywhere else, to compare with an old-fashioned family reunion.

When Boo and his prodigal mother made their mutual way up the front walk and onto Baby Todd's wisteria-draped porch, the old woman was peeping out from behind the parlor curtain to see who it was.

"Iris Lee!" she cried, the moment she'd recovered from her surprise. "Iris Lee! Boo's come back! And you're just going to like to die when you see who's come with him!"

Iris Lee was in the kitchen, eating cold chicken spaghetti out of a pot on the stove and counting her misfortunes. She'd stayed behind when the rest had gone out searching, not so much out of conviction that the lost would eventually wind up where he should have stayed in the first place, but because the events of the afternoon had left her utterly demoralized, unable to tell any longer what was important from what wasn't.

When Baby called to her, the voice bouncing off the kitchen walls and ringing in her ears, she ignored it for the moment and went on eating, thinking all the time of the ocean, of that cruise she'd wanted to take, thinking of Alaska. Alaska. The name itself sounded like snow in the wind. Alaska would seem like the Promised Land about now, she figured grimly. A whole, white, cold wilderness where you didn't know a soul to speak to and there were no such things as untold secrets and lies a half-century old. Even better than heaven, she thought blasphemously. You didn't even have to die to get there.

Baby commenced to holler again from the foyer. "Iris Lee! You just got to come and see who Boo's brought home with him. It's a miracle!"

Iris Lee squeezed her eyes shut and took another swallow from the sweating tumbler of bourbon still at her elbow, wondering in her heart whether the good Lord could possibly expect any mortal person to withstand so many miracles in one day. Well, she would just go to Alaska, she promised herself. And right under sister Baby's nose, too. Just as soon as things had calmed down.

"Well, Baby," she called from the kitchen. "You can scream if you want to. Just because I'm old don't mean I'm deaf." The whole mess was Baby's fault, anyway, Iris Lee concluded in the distance from the kitchen to the hall. Assuming a person looked at it right. If Baby hadn't been so starry-eyed her whole life, so full of her drivel about love, she wouldn't have ever got herself a husband like Cecil in the first place. She would have done right and got herself someone sober and hardworking, someone who never even whistled, let alone played the violin. If Baby had ever had any sense, she would have gone and got herself the kind of husband nobody would even think of stealing. Iris Lee started to feel a little better, as though the sudden appearance of Travis Moseley and the god-cursed fiddle weren't quite so much her fault. Somewhat cheered, she straightened her back as she went into the parlor, having managed to derive what comfort there was from having being born sensible.

"Didn't I say?" Iris Lee announced. She wished, suddenly, she'd gone a little lighter on the spaghetti. Her insides were starting to talk back. "I told you Boo always turns up. Just because he had some damn fiddle with him didn't mean he wouldn't." She hesitated just short of the foyer, realizing she still had her spaghetti fork in her hand. "Who came with you, Boo, honey?" she called in a syrupy, innocent tone, stashing the fork under a nearby cushion. In fact, she would have liked to strap the child right then and there, but since he'd brought company, she didn't see any point. All she could do was hope he hadn't brought anyone too unfamiliar; she'd had enough of strangers for one day.

Baby was already at the front door, weeping with relief and throwing her arms wide around Boo and the Stradivarius, whose finish glinted like a mockery as he held it out in Iris Lee's direction. Iris arranged her features to greet the mystery guest, who was still hidden in the shadows of the hall. But as soon as she got close enough to see that Jezebel standing just beneath the sampler stitched by Mama Quade's dying fingers, Iris Lee could only stand there and gape, all the air exiting her lungs in a rush of righteousness. Then, as soon as she got enough of her wind back, she proceeded to cuss Gloria out in a voice that might have peeled paint.

"I have lived too long," she intoned, as soon as she

began to run out of things bad enough to say, packing epithets together like sardines in a tin. "You just turn right around and get your carcass back to wherever you dropped out of. I ain't gonna have it."

Gloria's smile was breezy and cool and utterly unsettling, like the air before a hurricane. You didn't need to be psychic to figure where you stood with a woman like Iris Lee. "My carcass, old woman," she replied in a low, even voice, "is staying right where it is."

Iris Lee could have strangled on her own spit. "Fine," she said. "Don't believe me. But Charles T. won't have you, I want you to know that right now. Once a man's heart's been broke they don't turn fool so easy."

It was a rash sort of utterance, of course, considering what everyone knew about Charles T. and his general propensities for turning fool. Especially where his heart was concerned.

But Baby Todd, being more familiar with the workings of hearts, broken or not, than was her sister, fanned away her agitation with one corner of her apron and smiled. "You never know, Iris Lee. It might be just like that song, you know, the one about things being nicer the second time around? Charles T. might see Gloria and fall in love all over again. Like in the movies."

From the kitchen, where Boo had drifted, came the obliging melody. On a Stradivarius it sounded a far more serious song.

"Can't he ever be quiet?" Iris Lee said irritably and began to pace the corridor. "And you," she said, jabbing a finger in Baby's direction, "have got moonlight where your brains ought to be."

Baby stopped fanning long enough to think it over. "Why, Iris Lee. What a lovely thought." Ever the hostess, she nodded approvingly at Gloria. "I just can't get over how well you look, Gloria. Like those paintings of the martyrs they have over in the Catholic church. Spiritual, I mean. And I like your hair loose like that. It's very becoming." She swung around for a better look at Gloria's reddish hair, streaked with white and falling down her back.

Iris Lee sniffed. "Loose indeed. Like she was in a bedroom. She ain't nothing but trash."

Baby patted her arm in a way that made Iris Lee commit murder in her mind. "Now Iris Lee, Gloria is part of the family. Besides, I don't see how she could wear her hair some other way. I mean, if she's been in the jungle or wherever. Some places are very primitive."

Iris Lee narrowed her eyes. "Hhmphh. Looks like she's all set to weaken Charles T.'s will. Seduce him. Just like she did before."

Baby studied Gloria, who hadn't been listening at all, but concentrating instead on the brief bits of music emanating from the kitchen. "I don't think she can help that part, Iris. She just has that kind of face. But never mind. I'm just sure you haven't come back to break anyone's heart, have you, Gloria?"

Gloria started a little, then obligingly shook her head no, hoping it was the right answer.

"You see? I told you!" Baby said. "Iris Lee is just the suspicious type. Always has been. Maybe Gloria here just wants to see the children."

"Where are they, anyway? I thought they'd be here."

"Oh!" Baby smiled delightedly. "I always knew you were psychic. No matter what anybody said about you. Iris Lee never believed in any of it, but I did. The first time I set eyes on you, I said to myself. 'Now there is a woman with the gift.'" She paused. "Everyone's out looking for Boo and the Stradivuss violin that belonged to my first husband. It's really quite an interesting story, isn't it, Iris Lee?''

But Iris Lee thought it to her advantage to keep the subject on the subject at hand. She peered at Gloria. "If you're so nuts about them kids, why'd you leave town in the first place?''

Gloria smiled a little. "I hardly think it matters at this point. The past is past, isn't it, Iris Lee?'' She shot her mother-in-law an odd, meaningful look that made the chicken spaghetti in Iris's gullet rise and sit cold.

A little bewildered, Baby sought to fill the sudden chasm in the conversation. "After everybody gets back and we get Ray Ed's will read—oh, by the way, did you know Ray Ed had passed on?''

Gloria nodded. "I sent Charles T. a postcard.''

"Isn't that amazing, Iris Lee? It must be so nice to have second sight. You'd always know if anything important was coming up and could get a card off.'' She paused, suddenly hesitant to ask the question on her mind. Gloria met her look with her blue eye, shiny and kind.

Baby swallowed hard. "Could you read my future, do you think? I never had my future read. Except back when I was young.''

Iris Lee snorted her contempt. Baby and Gloria ignored her.

Gloria suddenly dropped her eyes and stared at the carpet. The future, indeed. "Sure,'' she answered quietly. "If you like.''

Baby turned positively pink with happiness. "As a matter of fact,'' she went on, "I was just reading about things of that nature the other day. Ion charges, I think they were called—they affect a person's biological rhythms and such.''

Iris Lee's jaw dropped in disbelief at the statement. Biological rhythms indeed. And from a church-going woman! She felt as if the whole of the world's pagan population might be gathering on the front lawn, preparing their attack.

"Anyway," Baby said, "from what I understand, these ion things can float around and make a person think practically anything. Sort of like vibrations. Right, Gloria?"

Gloria nodded, smiling with her eyes. Iris Lee made a little choking noise in her throat.

Baby smiled. "Well, I've said it before and I'll say it again. It's always the little things that wind up changing your whole life. It's like the whole world is a big secret. Then suddenly, you find out a little tiny bit of it and it's enough to change everything. Don't you agree, Iris Lee?"

She turned around for her sister's opinion and saw that Iris Lee's face had gone crimson all over and was working itself up to purple in spots, like a sunset.

"Iris Lee?" Baby raised her voice in a question, then trailed off, deciding she knew what the trouble was.

"Raving mad," Iris Lee pronounced. "Both of you."

"Pay her no mind, Gloria dear," Baby assured her. "It's just her imaginary angina. Iris Lee thinks she has has angina pectoris. It gives her an excuse to turn colors when things don't go her way."

"I think I'm dying," gurgled Iris Lee.

Baby frowned at her. "Don't be rude. You're not dying at all, you just need to sit down."

Boo appeared from out of the kitchen, still stubbornly ahold of the Stradivarius. He'd been amusing himself with Baby's Jell-O fish while the women argued.

"Boo, honey," Baby directed. "Fetch your mammy a chair."

Boo held the violin up to his ear and shook it, hearing the rattles inside. When he lowered it, he had slipped behind the veil of half-wittedness again and only stared at them, his eyes empty as the sky. "Boo," he said.

"Up yours," he might as well have said.

Baby drew back, a little surprised. "Well, my goodness."

Gloria hauled Iris Lee into the parlor and shoved her into a chair and was fanning her with the latest pack of lies from the Publisher's Clearing House.

"I could lay hands on you," she suggested out loud, never taking her eyes from Iris Lee's mottled face. "I learned to heal when I was in the Amazon."

She paused in her fanning and turned her hands, palms outwards, in the old woman's direction. Iris Lee cowered away as though she were afraid of being singed. For there was, in fact, a peculiar sort of heat emanating from those hands, pulsing through the fabric of her dress even at a distance of inches.

"You touch me and I'll scream," she said. "You got a devil in you."

Gloria dropped her hands and blinked her incredible eyes. "I got several," she answered. And smiled.

"Blasphemer!" gasped Iris Lee. "Yankee."

"Witch," said Gloria.

"Ladies—" said Baby.

It might have continued, but at that moment, Dearest and Davey came tromping through the kitchen and into the parlor like a couple of lead-footed children.

"I told you he was here," Dearest was saying as he spied Boo standing in the foyer and cradling the violin. "Hi, y'all," he announced when he saw the ladies. Naturally, he didn't notice Gloria right away; Dearest had other things on his mind. In the course of their search for Boo, Davey had taken the notion to go looking for him at Luanne Heck's house, and the only way Dearest had been able to deter him had been to snatch the keys out of the ignition right in the middle of Laurel Avenue, almost causing a pileup of half the cars in town. Since then, most of Dearest's attention was involved in not letting Davey get close enough to kill him.

"We saw Charles T. and Maejean kissing in the front seat of the Buick when we pulled up at the stoplight, didn't we, Davey?"

He glanced at Davey, who made a little snarling sound in the back of his throat. "That's the problem with young people." Dearest sighed wistfully. "No romance in their veins. Who's the company?" he asked, suddenly spying Gloria, who was standing with her back to all of them, staring out the window.

"You see?" Iris Lee's voice rose querulously. "I told you he'd never take you back. He's got himself a decent woman."

Dearest lit a cigarette. "What in the world are you talking about?"

Gloria turned around and let Dearest see what the matter was. He gasped. "Shut my mouth."

"Yes, please," said Iris Lee.

Davey's face had gone the color of dough. "Geez—" he put in, suddenly embarrassed for no reason.

Dearest eyed Gloria up and down. "My, my," he said. "Where've you been keeping yourself, Gloria? You look like you been to hell."

"Dearest, be nice," Baby intervened. "She had to come in on Trailways. Boo found her at the bus."

"Had any good visions lately?" Dearest wanted to know. Anticipating the dramas sure to be caused by Gloria's sudden resurrection, he could barely contain his excitement. "Down amongst the heathen?"

Gloria raised the eyebrow set over her green eye. "I never liked you," she said.

Dearest grinned. "I know," he told her. "I never cared."

Over in the corner, Davey couldn't think what to do next, afraid that any movement on his part might disturb the precarious balance of his emotions, causing him to weep.

Gloria crossed the room in his direction. "It's good to see you, son," she said.

"Disgusting," said Iris Lee.

Everybody was still getting reacquainted by the time Grace and Travis Moseley (who'd been busy getting acquainted themselves) came in the front door half an hour later.

"Anybody find Boo?" Grace called out cheerily. She hadn't been too busy looking herself, but the chance to be alone with Travis Moseley on the pretext of a search had been too golden to pass by. Davey was just coming out of the kitchen and she grinned at him. "Davey, you have got to see this man's car."

"Not now," Davey said, and something in his tone caught her up short.

"Didn't anybody find him?" Grace asked, suddenly concerned.

Davey's eyes didn't change. "She's come back, Grace," he told her in a voice like he was in church.

"Who?"

"Your mother," announced Gloria, coming toward her with outstretched hands. "You haven't forgotten your mother, have you?"

Grace gulped. She felt as though she were about to implode from the sheer shock of it, leaving nothing but a heap of skin and innards on the floor. "Of course we didn't forget you," Davey put in, seeing as how his sister seemed to be having some trouble moving her mouth.

Gloria turned her attention to Travis Moseley, who was standing between the wall and the door, trying to pick a good time to leave.

"Is this your husband?" Gloria asked.

"She's just like you," Iris Lee said bitterly. "Some people just think they can move all over the world and take up with men whenever they feel like it."

Grace colored like a rose. "Uhh," she said.

Gloria whirled around, "Jealous, Iris Lee? Too late for that now, don't you think?"

Iris Lee gasped.

"This is the one I was telling you about," Baby intervened. "The one who tried to rob us. Only when Boo disappeared, he decided to help look for him instead. Wasn't that nice? His name is Travis Moseley."

Gloria sized Travis up in one quick look from her green eye and nodded, like something about him was familiar. "I don't blame you a bit," she whispered to Grace. "Even if he isn't your husband."

Grace nodded. Now that the shock was wearing off, she was glad indeed to see her mother. "How long are you staying?" she asked.

Gloria's face went secret, like a flower closing up. "That depends," she said.

"Here he comes!" Dearest had posted himself at the window to watch for Charles T. "I just can't wait to see his face," he went on, clapping his hands delightedly. "This is better than pay TV."

Outside, Charles T. and Maejean emerged from the Buick that had become their lover's chariot, grinning like teenagers on a spree. Hesitantly, as if he were afraid of breaking her in two, Charles T. draped an arm around Maejean's shoulders as they headed up the front steps, determined, in the fashion of the smitten, to have this sudden romance appear as natural an occurrence as possible. Dearest tore open the front door as Gloria took a place in the center of the parlor, just in case he might not notice she was there.

"Surprise!" Dearest yelled.

Charles T., blushing like a bridegroom, led Maejean into the hall. When he saw Gloria, though, his arm fell away from Maejean's shoulders like a limb from a tree and he stood there, paralyzed, trying to decide if that figure in the middle of the room was genuine, or simply some manifestation of his own lack of reason, some projection out of his mind, like a picture on a screen.

But it was Maejean who was the first to react. Her outrage at this sudden wrench in her scheme of things was almost physical in its impact, like a fist in the teeth.

"Oh, *shit!*" she cried. She shot Charles T. a furious, wounded look, which he never saw, and ran into the kitchen, wailing all the way.

"Oh my," said Baby, and got up to see what she could do.

"I've been talking to the children," Gloria said. "You did a fine job with them, Charles T. I always knew you would." She fixed him with her blue eye while the other roamed over to the spot where Grace, Davey, and Boo had huddled together like orphans waiting for a train, looking half their ages.

Iris Lee glanced up from the magazine she had been stubbornly pretending to read. "No thanks at all to me, I suppose," she said bitterly.

Charles T. was smiling at Gloria like someone who's discovered that the fistful of rocks in his pockets were diamonds all along. "Mammy helped," he said.

"Damn straight," mumbled Iris Lee.

Something flickered in Gloria's eyes, and Charles T. saw that there was more than the hesitation of homecoming lurking in her expression. It was buried deep enough, but it was there. Fear, shiny and defiant as a ruby in a creekbed, glimmered at him from the depths of her eyes and made him want to cry out. He might have called this wife of his a lot of things in the course of his life, but never a coward. His mouth went dry.

"What is it, Gloria?" he asked. "Was it in the postcard? Me and Grace tried to figure it out."

Gloria shook her head slowly. "I sent that before," she said.

"Before what?"

Unexpectedly she began to weep, causing them all to frown at her, as though a woman like herself had no right to such things as tears.

"Before Atacuari."

"Where?" Dearest asked.

"It's a village in Peru," she began shakily, clutching Charles T.'s hand like a person drowning. She paused as the enormity of her secret swept over her. "Dear God, Charles T. I had to come back. I didn't know where else to turn."

Iris Lee opened her mouth to speak and popped it closed again as Charles T. silenced her with a look.

"What is it, Gloria?" he urged softly. "What's happened?"

Gloria shot them all a last, resigned sort of look. "I've had a curse put on me," she said. "Even the Indians can't cure it."

"Hmmphh." This from Iris Lee. "Serves her right."

"Mammy, shut *up!*" Charles T.'s voice thundered through the room, making them all jump.

Gloria drew a shaky breath. "It was a medicine man . . ." she said slowly. "The one who put on the curse."

Charles T. frowned, not knowing how much concern was

going to be appropriate. "What kind of a curse?" he wanted to know.

Gloria stared at him, the fear in her eyes no longer buried, but raw and living and overwhelming as she made the horror of it into words.

"He made me immortal."

Thirty=six

LIVING FOREVER was an idea that Icy Fee Moulder, on the other hand, had long ago got used to.

The summer that found Gloria McSaxon Strait fled to Atlantis with the intention of burying herself, figuratively or even literally (assuming that were still possible) in the collective bosom of her loved ones, found Icy Fee Moulder still in residence in the world, not forty miles to the south. She still dwelt in that house she'd been born in, still climbed, though not so often as formerly, the hill through the woods to that same circle of stones, and was approaching the age of one hundred and three.

Other than long, Icy Fee's life to date had been a peculiarly satisfying one, for she had succeeded in doing what

most of the true loners in the world never manage; to
outlive everyone they know. For despite what love she had
given in the course of her many years, despite that which
she had gotten in return, Icy Fee's had remained the solitary
heart, never overcrowded with too much affection, never
overburdened with too much pain. There was always that
part of her that remained untouched, unmoved—that part
that had survived what other hearts might not have, belonging only to itself and going on.

After Elijah, Deke was next to depart her life. A sudden
spirit of adventure had come over him in midlife when the
land on his farm got wore out with cotton, and he'd died
wildcatting in Oklahoma, flattened like an insect in a rig
accident. Icy Fee had sorely missed him for a time, and even
made one or two attempts to conjure him back, but with no
real results, except for discovering, after awhile, that perhaps it was not his absence that bothered her so much as her
own willingness to have him gone. One by one, their children, too, had passed away, each taking a turn at leaving
their mother a little more to herself—one with a cancer, one
in childbed, another died old, not five years before. And
one, the eldest, had died by his own hand. The suicide had
made for news all over the county, and word of it had
reached his mother even then—bigamy and scandal being
harder to come by in those times than now. At the time, Icy
Fee figured that they would bring him back to her or even
that she would make a trip to Atlantis to fetch him home.
Yet somehow neither had come to pass, and the child of the
only man she'd ever loved was buried in a criminal's grave
without his mother there to mourn him. It bothered Icy Fee
a little, even now, that Cecil had never come to rest in that
place on the hill that became, not by virtue of anyone's
decision, but only by practice, the family graveyard.

Instead, there was a cleaning woman between Deke and

one of the grandchildren in the place where Cecil might have come to rest. The woman's name was Irene, a transplanted Cajun Icy Fee had hired in 1956 to help with the heavy work. Irene had died one spring while cleaning out her kitchen cupboards, having come across some of her employer's conjuring preserves—two Mason jars of sectioned snake, packed like pickles in their brine, and a pint containing only the oddly deformed, floating head of a chicken, hatched twenty years previous. The contents of those jars were long past harming anyone, of course, but that hadn't mattered to Irene, who proved to be of an excitable nature and, upon dusting the jars enough to see what they contained, had given one high, sharp scream and promptly expired. Icy Fee, not seeing anything else to be done about it, had her duly buried along with the rest in the little cemetery on the hill. Not wanting poor Irene to feel the less for eternity, Icy Fee even went so far as to purchase a tombstone, inscribed at her own direction:

IRENE LAFITTE
Died 1957 of a weak heart.
Rest in Peace.

It wasn't clear, precisely, when it was that Icy Fee gave up the notion of dying altogether, but as she moved through the years with no more resistance than a swimmer in a pond, death had ceased, somehow, to be important. She continued while others did not; the specifics of it weren't worth thinking about. She was whole enough and well enough not to complain. She didn't have her own teeth, of course, those having loosened and fallen out sometime after her change of life. But even her dentures had outlasted a lot she could think of, and with use and time had become more hers than the originals, being, in the final analysis, easier to clean.

270

And quietly, with no thunderclap of revelation, no need to pinpoint where the change was coming from, Icy Fee Moulder had, during the course of her years and the passage of those countless hours she had spent in that clearing in the woods, come to the conclusion that the world was improving with time.

She kept her reputation as a conjure woman for those who still had need of such things, but as the world got easier to live in, the needs of folks seemed to lessen, too. She still had her teas and her potions and poultices, still had charms for lonelyhearts and magic for bad seasons, but conjuring, in the course of her long, long life, had fallen a little by the way. And, for a woman in semi-retirement, the occasional customer was enough. She wanted no more.

More might prove too repetitious, she reckoned. One problem might get to seeming too much like another, too much like all those that had gone before, and conjure recollections better left alone. The past was something Icy Fee preferred to keep at a distance. She had seen too many collapse with the burden of remembering and regret and was determined, for her own part, that if there was to be traffic between the two, the dead should envy the living and not the other way around. The halls of her memory were neat as a pin and carefully arranged, like a museum. For Icy Fee Moulder, of anyone still walking the earth, knew the treacheries in recalling too much.

As time went on, she came to view remembering as a vice of the weak—those who dwell on what is gone only do so because they cannot name what they yet want. And even at one hundred and three, Icy Fee Moulder knew for certain that there was a lot yet to get from the world, a lot yet to be wanted. Wanting meant getting and getting, to her mind, meant life got better. These days she saw the world on color television and thought of Dan Rather as one of her friends. She had a microwave oven in the kitchen next to her mother's old wood-burning stove and a freezer full of summer vegetables to eat when she took the mood. These days she did her washing in a jet-action Maytag and dried things in a dryer that was perched on top. The world was getting newer all the time, shinier and faster and easier, too. And as long as that was true, Icy Fee Moulder intended to stick around.

She knew that she would die, of course, everyone does. But somewhere along the line, death had lost its fascination with her and for her. After killing off her kin, death had grown tired of feeding in that one spot, it seemed, and refused to take her as well. It got to where death was like a picture hanging in her house, looked at so often it loses any significance. Death became another human habit that people around her repeated without thinking, like chewing tobacco or going broke or making love. She supposed one day she would look at that picture and see it for real; until then she was content to let it hang.

And so Icy Fee Moulder's was a fortunate life, freed, by virtue of her great age, of any need to know her limits. Freed of destruction and passion and longing and remembrance and even conscience. Icy Fee Moulder continued and in the course of continuance had discovered one of the more precious secrets to living well, the truth of which got up with her in the morning and lay down with her at night, shining like a jewel in her head and out of her pale eyes all the hours in between.

After murder, she would tell you, to be happy is the best revenge of all.

Thirty=seven

MONEY IS INFINITELY more interesting to imagine having than to actually get, its possibilities more infinite. In the refuge of imagination, it becomes the stuff of dreams, in reality it becomes just stuff again—a place to live, a new car, or a slap in someone else's kisser. But when the slaps are placed, the attitudes paraded, and purchases made, things—as things will do—go on pretty much as always. And so it was that the Last Will and Testament of Ray Ed Strait proved, in the grand scheme of things, to be neither here nor there.

Still, it all worked out pretty well. While Ray Ed had died with enough to fight over, it was not, after taxes, enough to kill for. Aside from a number of blue chips, a savings

account, and the farm itself, all of which was bequeathed to
Iris Lee, the old man's insurance policies had come to something in the neighborhood of a quarter million dollars,
divided among the rest of them.

Aunt Baby, the only one of them not secretly wishing for
something better, had not paused long enough to do the
long division involved, and, upon hearing the sum, had
commenced to sob.

"I just can't help it," she'd wept. "All those years of
sweat and sacrifice, just so's the man could died secure. It's
the most touching thing I ever heard of."

Thoroughly ashamed, the rest of them had hastened to
concur with her opinion, not having chosen up until then
to see things quite that way.

And so the rest of that summer spun out in the manner
of all summers, days bright enough to hurt the eyes, tem-
peratures hovering in the savage. East Texas in August is a
long heat sandwich, days of lassitude and dust pressed between slices of spongy night, breathed and swallowed and
digested by victims of the climate until, gorged on sun and
swollen with humidity, no one can tell any longer what is
real and life takes on the aspects of a dream.

Dreamy or not, the world is made up of specifics, and
before the first breath of autumn, life had changed to the
point where no one except a prophet might have believed
it.

Iris Lee, having gotten the business of the legacy out of
the way, tried to resume her hold on the family by her
out-and-out refusal to have Gloria under the same roof. So,
rather than listening to her carry on about it, Gloria simply
took up residence in Aunt Baby's house in Atlantis, and the
two women stayed up whole nights in séance, talking with
the dead. Charles T. had it in mind to move in, too, but
something had happened to his love for the woman in the

nearly twenty years they'd lived apart—something he could not explain. For twenty years he'd polished her memory, longed for her return, cursed her leaving, wept for her, and even, on a couple of occasions, prayed. Coming face to face with her so unexpectedly, he'd had no choice but to realize that the rituals of his regret had become a refuge of their own, that he'd clung to the memory because memory was a more faithful wife than any made of flesh and bone. It had surprised him a little, learning that, and embarrassed him a little more. Immortal, levitating, soul-reading Gloria was still just Gloria, after all. So having no real idea what else was to be done for her, he gave her some of his inheritance money and took to spending his afternoons in the library in town, researching the ways of Amazonian shamans and consoling himself with philosophy.

And Gloria, for her part, was grateful to him. Money may not be the first thing a person thinks of on finding theselves doomed to eternal life, but she reckoned it couldn't hurt. It never occurred to anyone to doubt Gloria's tale of being cursed. She had never been, to the best of anyone's recollection, much given to exaggeration. Even Charles T., when pressed, could tell a better story. So eventually, with varying degrees of enthusiasm, each member of the family accepted the situation for what it was, having come to the conclusion that no one, right-minded or not, would go to all the trouble of turning up in Atlantis and announce that she was never going to die for the sheer sport of seeing the expressions on their faces. And so, reluctantly or not, Gloria came to be accepted back in the family circle.

Grace and Davey fixed up an old house at the edge of the farm, the place that had been their grandfather's before he was married. It suited them well enough, Davey because he needed a place to be when he wasn't busy buying up Luanne Heck's free afternoons and Grace because she'd taken up with Travis Moseley in an offhanded way and was, as she told him, entirely too old to fuck in motels.

And Maejean, who'd lost her heart and her nerve with it, decided that if she had to live a loveless life, she might as well get rich doing it, and quit her job at the Safeway. She pooled her inheritance with some money from Uncle Dearest, who, having failed to obtain a blood sample from Gloria in the hopes of marketing a fountain of youth, was looking for a new line of work just then, and together they opened up a T-shirt shop in the Galleria mall outside of Queen City.

"Running a business means you got to know what the people need," Maejean told Grace one afternoon as she was trying to coax her back to work as a slogan writer. "And if there's anything folks around here need it's to have some-one sum up their feelings. Even," she finished a little sadly, "if the only place they ever do it is on the front of some damn shirt."

Travis Moseley, too, settled into life in Atlantis. And, for a wandering man, he found it appealing. He still had it in mind to wrangle the Stradivarius out of them if he could, but thought it better to bide his time, particularly since he had Grace to bide it with. The embarrassment of the rob-bery still made him blush when he thought of it, though none of the family had mentioned it since. And they took his keeping company with Grace the same way they seemed to take everything else, that is, more or less in stride. He planned, of course, to get moving again once he got that fiddle, but he was sure they would settle the matter honora-bly once they got to know him. The problem with that being only in getting it away from that idiot boy.

For since the day he'd first set eyes on it, Boo had at-tached himself to the thing like it was growing out of him. No amount of persuasion could get him to relinquish it, even when he slept, and when awake it seemed to the rest of them that the world was always filled with music, snatches of his songs following them around, floating through those days like wish fairies blown from a dandelion. Travis would wake from his dreams in the Mile-Away Motel hearing waltzes, and ten miles away, Grace would hear them, too, making her smile in her sleep and whisper her lover's name. Davey sat bolt upright one afternoon at Luanne Heck's, sweating and pale from his exertions, as a tune came bouncing through the open window.

"What the hell is that?" he'd wanted to know.

Luanne yawned and reached over on the bedside table for a Kool. She shook one from the pack and stared at Davey with an amused expression dancing in her green, green eyes. "If I know my fiddle players, it's your brother Boo," she told him.

Davey had frowned then, straining to hear as the last of the music echoed away and down the street. "I know it's Boo," he said after a moment. "What was the song?"

Luanne allowed herself a long, luxurious stretch and sat up.

" 'Turkey in the Straw.' "

Charles T., absorbed as he was in the study of curses, would hear them with only part of his mind as he poured over borrowed books at the kitchen table—Spanish songs and jungle lullabyes. Once, hearing music in a corner of his mind, the words on the page before him had started to swim in his vision, the letters forming themselves into a picture of Maejean, dressed as a senorita in a layered skirt and lacy veil. But he blinked again, and it was gone, and Charles T. broke off his studies for the day.

Each of them heard different, each heard right. For the rattlesnake Stradivarius, come down to them through so many different hands, the object of love and secrets and desire, could speak to hearts in more tongues than an apostle, singing its magic for any who cared to hear. Iris Lee, in odd moments, doing the dusting or cleaning the closets, would hear songs sixty and seventy years old, songs by which flappers had danced their fevered dances and winked at lovers from under tight cloche hats. Songs of all the sin and innocence of bygone times, until she spent whole days with a picture of Cecil Moses lodged in her mind, in a crisp white linen suit with half of his head blown away, the lips still moving in words she could not hear. *Toot-toot-tootsie good-bye.*

Late one night, when it was too hot to think of sleep, Baby and Gloria sat up on the verandah, the scent of Baby's wisteria falling over them like a dream of not being able to breathe. They had not spoken, but only sat in wicker chairs, thinking their separate thoughts. Baby heard it, and started a little, unable to think of the name of the tune that echoed around from somewhere in the back of her house, sad as some adagio, inevitable as a minuet. She'd shivered suddenly and drawn her old woman's wrapper around her throat as if she were cold.

"Is that Boo?" she asked, her voice shattering the spell. "I can't imagine Iris Lee letting him out in the middle of the night like this."

Gloria stayed in the shadows, her cat's eyes glowing in the dark, catching pinpoints of light from the street. Baby looked at her once and rose, crossing the porch and leaning out over the railing.

"Boo?" she'd called softly. "Is that you?"

But it was Gloria's voice alone that answered, calm and sure and comforting from the shadows of the night.

"Let's go in, Aunt Baby," it coaxed her. "There's no one here but me."

And Ernest Earl had finally heard the music, too, bent

nearly double over his workbench in the middle of the night, looking like he was being eaten alive. In less than a month, his eyes had gotten huge in his face, glowing like some evil darkness in the yellow leather straining over his bones. He heard the music, driven and urgent, calling to him, giving him the little more life that he needed. He heard the tune and began to hum in a gravelly, old man's voice, his hands keeping time to the urgent rhythm, loading and unloading his gun.

Thirty=eight

LOVE, AS ANYBODY'S Aunt Baby will tell you, is not so much many-splendored as many-faced. It is compelled to disguise itself most times, masquerading in the mind as need or rage or greed or even, as was the case with Grace Ellen Strait and a cowboy named Travis Moseley, that most modern of oxymorons—casual sex.

Grace screeched a fetching little red Porsche Carrera up in front of Baby's house one morning, the car made possible courtesy of blind armadillos and Ray Ed's insurance money, her face clouded up like a late summer storm.

"Men," she announced less than a minute later, plopping the new batch of slogans for Maejean's heat transfer machine in the center of Baby's fruited impressionist kitchen, "are mean and stupid."

Baby and Gloria were in the midst of their morning baking lesson. With the possibility of immortality staring her in the face the way it was lately, Gloria had decided in a practical moment to learn to cook, it seeming as necessary a skill for eternal life as any other. And Baby, her theories on the subject admittedly more dependable than their execution, had taken it upon herself to instruct her. When Grace walked in, they had just finished putting a coffee cake in the oven, and were busy admiring it through the oven door.

"Why, hello, Grace," Baby said pleasantly. "Stay for some of your mother's coffee cake, won't you?"

Grace stared at her; somewhere in the world, Aunt Baby had managed to find an apron to match her wallpaper. "Didn't you hear what I said?"

"Of course we heard you, dear," Gloria replied, lighting a cigarette. Grace noted the act, a little surprised. "Since when do you smoke? I never remember that you smoked."

"I've just taken it up," Gloria told her, coughing slightly. "I figure, what with the curse and all, it seems a little silly to worry about my lungs. Besides, who knows? Smoking might take a hundred years or so off my life."

Grace frowned, distracted from her own troubles for the moment. "I never thought of it like that," she admitted.

Baby pulled out a dinette chair. "Sit down, Grace, you look positively restless. What was it you were saying? Something about men?"

Grace sat down, then almost immediately was on her feet again. "Mean," she said darkly. "And stupid."

"Yes, dear, we heard that part. Now tell us the rest."

"It's Travis Moseley," Grace announced, as though that were anything new. Unbeknownst to her, Baby and Gloria had laid down a number of private wagers between themselves on just how long their Grace Ellen was going to be able to pretend she was something other than gone on that cowboy. Baby, being an optimist, had given her two months. Gloria, being less sentimental, had given her three.

"What about Travis?" Gloria put in.

Grace began to pace around the room, talking as she went. "I just want to know what I've gotten myself into here, that's all. The man is impossible."

"Oh," said Baby.

"Inconsiderate, boorish, self-centered, mean-spirited, complacent and . . ." Grace ticked adjectives off on her fingers and switched to the other hand.

"Vain?" put in Gloria, checking her cake.

"Oh, Gloria," Baby chided, "she hasn't gotten to the V's yet. How about loutish? Insensitive? Ignorant? Egotistical? Domineering?"

"Yes," Grace answered. "And stupid."

"You said that," Baby reminded her.

"He simply doesn't understand anything!"

"Anything?" Gloria inquired.

"Me," said Grace.

Baby was filling up the Mr. Coffee. "They never do, dear. I nearly talked myself to death trying to explain things to my second. Stupidest man I ever knew."

"Well, he is! Stupid, I mean." Grace sat down again, and got up again, furious. "He has no money, he drives that awful car, and he doesn't even own a suit! I have lived in New York City, goddamn it! I cannot be involved with someone who doesn't own a suit!"

"Involved?" asked Gloria in a tone that made Grace go positively pink with indignation.

"Well, of course not! Not involved, involved. Involved is not what I meant. I meant—well—you know what I meant."

"Probably," her mother agreed.

"No question in my mind," said Baby.

"Associating with."

Gloria winked at Baby with her blue eye. "Is that what they call it now? Associating with? I must've been in the jungle longer than I thought. You know, there's a tribe down there that has the most wonderful word for it. Let me see . . ."

"Never mind," said Grace. "Can't you people be any help?" Grace demanded. "I came here for advice."

"Just what kind of advice would you like, dear?" Baby asked as the Mr. Coffee gurgled threateningly from the corner. "I'm willing to give you all the advice you need."

"Ditto," said Gloria.

"Tell me what to do," Grace went on petulantly. "Tell me what's going on." She glanced at Gloria. "Read my future or something."

Gloria arranged an expression that was, she hoped, suitably maternal. After all, she was a little out of practice. "Make up your mind, Grace, I can read your future or I can tell you what to do. But I can't do both."

"Great," Grace sighed. "Just my luck to have somebody around who knows the future and won't tell me."

"Grace, don't be self-indulgent. This person is your mother, this person is not a parlor game."

"Thank you, Baby," Gloria said. Behind Grace's back, they grinned.

"Now," Baby went on. "Suppose you hold still for a minute and tell us what this Travis person has done besides not owning a suit. Come to think of it," she said, pouring coffee. "I really don't understand what he needs a suit for, anyhow. From what I gather, what you and Travis have got going doesn't really require suits, does it?"

"I am not talking about suits!" Grace thumped the

kitchen table with her fist. "I am talking about priorities! He has no priorities!"

"Don't do that. Your mother's coffee cake will fall."

"He's driving me crazy!" Grace burst out. "I am not ready for this."

"Mmm," Baby murmured understandingly.

"I see," said Gloria.

"I don't think my divorce is even final! I need more time —space. You know, to get settled. I still have stuff in boxes, for Christ's sake! I have to establish my life, you know what I mean? Find myself. I need a haircut."

Baby and Gloria nodded solemnly.

"To say nothing of the fact that I don't know what's going to happen if business doesn't get going at the mall. I mean, Maejean is doing very well, but what if she doesn't like the new line? What if it folds? Goes under?" Grace paused and stared at them.

"Oh, I hope not," Baby said. "Besides, from what I understand, things are going quite well at the store. Your mama and me went there ourselves and bought T-shirts, didn't we, Gloria?"

Gloria nodded.

"You see?"

But Grace did not. "Well, that's just the point, here. Anything can happen. Anything. The house could burn down. I like the house and everything, but I never had it in mind as anything permanent. I may just decide to move, you know? Get a condo."

"You might," Baby agreed.

"Not that I mind being here," Grace hastened to assure them. "I want to be. You know, for mother's sake and everything. And Mammy can always use someone to chat with, and keep an eye on Boo. She's getting on, after all."

"I knew she'd been talking to Iris Lee," Baby hissed over

her shoulder to Gloria. "It was that stuff about the suits."

Grace rattled on, breathless, oblivious. "The point of it is, I feel I would really be doing myself a disservice not to keep my options open, you know?"

"You don't have to tell me," Gloria concurred.

"Well, you see?" Grace gestured emphatically. "That's what I'm talking about. You did what you had to do, and you're a better person for it."

"Yes, indeedy," Gloria said and turned to pretend to check the cake again, just to hide her smile.

Grace took a deep breath and gazed at the ceiling where Travis Moseley's bullet was still lodged, a few inches from the light fixture. "There!" she cried, pointing at it. "Right there. We are talking about a man who shoots things!"

"Well, now Grace," Baby intervened. "As I recall, it just went off in the struggle. It might have been Charles T. who put the bullet in the ceiling just as easy as your boyfriend."

"He is not my—" Grace had to struggle to even utter the word, *"boyfriend."*

"Of course not, honey. A slip of an old woman's tongue," Baby assured her mildly. "Now, what is it you were telling us? About being a better person?"

"He's probably just using me anyway," Grace said righteously.

"Using you?" Gloria had momentarily lost the train of things as she was testing the cake with a broomstraw, the way Aunt Baby had taught her. "What's he using you for, exactly?"

"Gloria," Baby said. "Don't be obtuse. Sex, of course. He's just going to use her for his selfish gratification and toss her aside like a worn-out old boot, the swine."

Grace swallowed. "You think so?" she asked, stunned, then recovered herself. "Well, no. Of course not. I mean, I understand your point of view, Aunt Baby. But people

just don't do that anymore. I meant I thought he was just
using me to get the violin."

"Stradivarius violin," Gloria corrected.

"Cecil's violin," breathed Baby. "I'll always think of it
that way."

"Have you talked to him about it?" Gloria wanted to
know.

"No, and that's what makes me suspicious. He tried to
steal it, for God's sake! Then all of a sudden he couldn't care
less. 'Let Boo have it,' he says. 'Who needs a fiddle when
I got you?' I tell you, the man's whole attitude is revolting."

Baby smiled a little. "Well, I don't know if it's revolting,
exactly. Maybe you're overreacting."

"I am not overreacting!"

"Pardon me," Baby said. "I meant screaming."

"That did it," Gloria sighed resignedly, peering at her
cake. "It's an ashtray."

Baby frowned. "Maybe you could concentrate it back
up."

"There's an idea."

Grace paused, flustered. "Well, it doesn't matter anyway.
The violin is not the issue here. The issue here is that
getting any further into any kind of relationship with that
man is pointless. It doesn't make sense. There isn't any
future in it, right? Not with my whole life up in the air."

"Not that I can see," said Gloria, around another cigarette.

"So I just have to break it off."

"As soon as possible," said Baby, quite seriously.

"No point in prolonging the agony," said Gloria.

"Right," said Grace. "If I don't, someone is only going
to get hurt."

"Can't have that," Baby agreed.

Unexpectedly, Grace smiled. "You see? I knew it. I just

knew if I sat down and talked it through—with someone
who understood."

"We understand," said Gloria.

Still smiling, Grace began to gather up her samples. "Tonight. Over dinner," she decided aloud. "I'll do it then."

"Candlelight?" Baby asked.

Grace turned around on her way out the door. "You
think?" she asked.

"Hard truths are invariably made easier by candlelight,"
Baby assured her. "You want to be kind, don't you?"

"Well . . . sure."

"Then candles, trust me."

Baby watched the little red Carrera roar away from the
curb smiling like an aged seraph. "Lord," she said idly.
"That daughter of yours drives just like Maivis Johnson."

"Maivis who?" Gloria was withdrawing the coffee cake,
which had resurrected itself to some extent, but only on one
side, and came out of the oven looking more like something
from a child's science project than the mouthwatering con-
fection Baby's cookbook had promised. She sighed heavily.
Life in the jungle, in some ways, had been a little easier.
"Who's Maivis Johnson?" she asked again.

Baby stared at the coffee cake a minute before going on.
"Nobody," she said. "Just that life repeats itself, sometimes."

Gloria met her eyes and snickered. "Doesn't it just."

Baby, unable any longer to suppress her delight, began
to giggle also, until the two of them were like delinquent
schoolgirls, laughing till they cried.

"Gloria?" Baby said when she caught her breath again.

"Yes, Aunt Baby?"

"You owe me ten bucks."

Thirty=nine

IRIS LEE STRAIT got old overnight.

There were those in the town who said it of widows: Once the husband was in the ground, the wife wouldn't be long in this world. And Iris Lee Strait, much as her deterioration took people by surprise, wasn't proving any different. Clara Cannon put forth at some length on the subject at Maivis Johnson's funeral. Poor Clara had cried herself to sleep for three days in a row following Maivis's accident at the Safeway, and when she showed at the church she looked like a bad night walking. But Clara Cannon could bear what she had to, she staunchly assured everyone who cared to ask, and take what the Lord threw her way.

"Maivis Johnson was my truest friend in the whole world," she kept announcing, "and it's hard to see her go. But losing a friend ain't like losin' a man. I just wish you'd look at Iris Lee Strait these days and tell me I'm wrong. And with poor Ray Ed not two months in the ground."

Clara's audience could only nod their agreements. On those infrequent occasions, these days, that Iris made it away from her farm, folks hardly recognized her. It was not so much the new wrinkles, or the way the old ones had deepened. Nor was it that slightly careless way she combed her hair of late. No, it was something different than any of that that estranged her from the world. It was nothing more than a look, really, something in the eyes. Maybe folks hadn't seen it in Iris Lee before, but they knew the expression well enough. As though, inwardly, she were picking through old photographs, pausing to admire one, then another—that slightly bemused look of someone soon to die. The expression people wear as they begin to gather their lives close around them, going over the pictures in precious detail, afraid, somehow, that memories don't go to heaven, too. And Iris Lee Strait had that look these days. She had it all the time.

Since the Stradivarius had come to roost, the woman felt as if the sterling order of her conscience had been transformed into a kind of sinkhole, swallowing things with desperate speed. The world itself was slipping away, while from out of the depths, all the buried things in her heart rose up to walk and talk. For if it was true what Clara said, that Iris Lee Strait was a woman with her guts on ice and her secrets, too, something had happened in the past few months, something had happened and the freezer was broken down.

Iris Lee did the best she could against the change that had come upon her. She shoved treacherous, unbidden thoughts to the furthest corners of her mind and bundled up her wishes with strings spun of an old woman's caution. She told herself it was just Ray Ed dying that made her feel like this—or Gloria's coming home. Or maybe that Travis Moseley around the farm put her mind of things so long forgotten, his face being what it was. She lied to herself in the mirror in the morning, and lied to herself at night. And then, when the excuses and lies were running out, she got round to telling herself it was the secret alone that was bothering her so badly, and convinced herself that Baby, even after so many years, ought to be told. Only it was worse than that, finally. Worse than sleeping with her sister's husband. For from a distance of those many years, Iris Lee knew, finally, that she had done a worse wrong than merely bedding the man. She had loved him. And finally, she had watched him die.

For Cecil Moseley had come to her one last time that night, grabbing her out of the shadows of the barn when she went to feed the chickens after supper. He'd been drinking and wept as he begged her to understand.

"Come with me, Iris Lee. We could go to California— up north. Anyplace. God, Iris Lee—I love you. Just you."

Their eyes met in the dark and what Cecil had seen in hers made his heart, for one exquisite instant, go dancing in his breast. He crushed her to him, unable to speak.

She felt the scratch of linen on her face, caught the smell of laundry on him, and man.

"You love me," he whispered, burying his lips in her hair. "Oh dear god, you really love me."

"Yes."

"Come with me, then. We can go—" He broke off in midsentence as he felt her stiffen in his arms.

"No," she said. "I—I'm afraid."

His eyes were hot and urgent in the darkness. "It'll be

all right, Iris Lee. I'll wait for you. We'll go somewhere.
Somewhere where nobody knows us. It'll be all right."

Iris Lee looked at him. "Where?"

"Meet me on the cemetery road," Cecil told her. "Tonight."

She had only nodded at him wordlessly, not knowing
even then how to answer.

And she had come, finally, with a few dresses packed in
a carpet bag, her face hidden by a cloche hat and her coat
collar turned up around her neck. Cecil was waiting and the
sight of him whistling, looking up and down the road with
his bags and that fiddle and a shotgun for protection so
unnerved her that she'd slipped behind a tree watching
him, unable to leave that place. Unable to go to his arms.
She'd watched him for hours, watched his happiness turn to
worry and worry to fear as the long night passed. She
watched him without daring to move or breathe or think,
knowing that any action might shatter her secret heart
forever. That no matter what she did there would be no
returning. Then, finally, she watched as Cecil's worry
turned to fear and the fear at last to the understanding that
she did not love him after all. Not enough.

And she had watched him play that violin there in the
moonlight, the music covering the sounds of his tears. She
had watched the rifle and the decision in his eyes. She had
watched as he pulled the trigger, hiding in the trees.

She'd never said a word.

Forty

OLLOWING, ALBEIT HAPHAZARDLY, in her mother's footsteps, cooking was a skill Grace Ellen was coming on rather late in life. Having taken the plunge and invited Travis Moseley for his last supper, Grace Ellen in desperation had to recruit Maejean to come and help her in the kitchen. Dumping a man over a can of Campbell's and a green salad—candles or no—just hadn't seemed substantial enough to be taken seriously. And so for most of the afternoon, Maejean and Grace cooked for real: dressed chicken, potatoes, vegetables raided from Mammy's garden, biscuits, and, as the final, sweet farewell, chocolate fudge cake.

Grace frowned into a pot on the stove and then at Maejean, her face flushed from the steam.

"Are you sure I shouldn't have gotten a roast?" she demanded.

Maejean was meanwhile whipping up the cake batter like she'd been born to the task. "Sure I'm sure," she replied calmly. "Roast is too heavy. Chicken's better. Folks get more accomplished over a chicken leg than they get done over roast beef."

Grace peeked into the pot again, thought about stirring it just for something to do with her hands, and stopped again. "I guess you're right," she said. "Now that I think about it, red meat's too emotional. I don't want him getting emotional."

Maejean floured her cake pans. "Don't want that," she replied evenly.

Grace went on talking, though, for its own sake. "I hope he doesn't make a scene. Well—never mind—I won't give him time. We'll just get through dinner, get relaxed, and then I'll explain things."

"I meant to ask," Maejean said, idly licking the batter bowl. "Just what is it you're planning to explain?"

Grace looked surprised. "Why I can't see him anymore, of course. Why I can't make a commitment just now."

Maejean lit the stove. "Oh," she said. "That."

Grace began pacing. "You sound like you don't believe me."

"I believe you just fine," Maejean answered. "By the way, has he asked?"

"Asked what?"

"Asked you for . . . uhhhm . . . what'd you call it?"

"A commitment." Grace picked up a spoon. "No," she said. "But he will. I can feel it. They get that look."

"What look?" Davey appeared from somewhere in the back of the house, still damp from a shower, his hair slicked wetly back and tucking in his shirt.

"That look you got all the time," Grace snapped. "That vine-covered cottage, darn-my-socks and pay-my-bills look."

Davey glanced at Maejean. "What is she talking about?"

Maejean smiled a little. "Nothin'," she said. "Where're you off to?"

Davey avoided looking at anything. "Town," he said. "I got somethin' I gotta do."

Grace snorted derision. "Yeah, right."

"Go to hell, Grace," Davey growled.

"Children—" said Maejean. "Who is it, Davey? You got a girl?"

All at once, Davey smiled. More than smiled—he beamed, he glowed like someone had turned klieg lights on his teeth. "Yeah," he said. "I got a girl." And with that, he snatched up his car keys and was gone.

"Boy's got it bad," Maejean reflected.

But Grace was unable to concentrate much on her brother's follies, having, of course, more important things on her mind. "How do you know when zucchini is done?" she demanded.

Maejean untied her apron and sat down. "Tender but crisp," she instructed.

"What does that mean? That's like saying soft but hard."

Maejean looked at her. "Just cook it, okay? If it's green, men won't eat it anyway. Before Bubba went to the service I must've thrown out six hundred pounds of salad makin's. Should've kept a rabbit. You got any beer?"

Grace reached in the refrigerator and brought out a six-pack. "Here," she said. "You got any Pamprins?"

They exchanged.

"I put oysters in the cornbread dressing," Maejean said, swallowing. "They make it richer."

Grace looked concerned. "Oysters?" she asked. "Aren't oysters supposed to be an aphrodisiac?"

Maejean considered it. "Are they really?" she asked. "Here I've been eating cornbread and oyster dressing all my life. Can't say as I've ever noticed a difference afterward."

Worriedly, Grace peered at her chicken, considering its consequences. "You don't know Travis Moseley."

"Well, you could pick 'em out," Maejean offered. "Seems a shame, though. Why don't you just feed him real fast and then tell him—maybe the oysters won't have time to work."

Grace shrugged elaborately and popped a beer for herself. "I don't know what I'm so nervous about anyway," she said. "It's not like it's the first time I've dumped somebody."

"No," Maejean agreed. "It ain't."

"It's better this way," Grace said after half a can of beer.

"With oysters?" Maejean said. "I think so."

Grace looked at her. Now that she thought about it, Maejean hadn't seemed quite herself all day. "How's the store?"

Maejean shrugged. "Fine." There was a little pause, delicate and sad. "How's your daddy?"

Grace had commenced touching up her makeup in the shine from the dinner dishes. "Okay, I guess," she said.

"Is he . . . uhhmm . . . spending a lot of time at Baby's? With your mama?"

Grace paused with her lipstick halfway to her mouth. "Not really," she answered gently. The heart of Maejean Strait was as transparent as a raindrop, something that Grace had come to appreciate of late. "Baby says Gloria won't have him up there, and Mammy won't have her down here.

Between the two of them, I don't know how he stands it."

"Poor Charles T.," Maejean said sadly. "I can't help wondering. You know, if maybe I was too hard on him. You think?"

Grace met her eyes. Maejean wasn't weeping, but she might as well have been. "Doesn't matter what I think," Grace answered. "Why don't you go up and ask him your-self?"

Maejean blushed and hung her head. "I couldn't do that," she protested.

"Well, I don't see why not," Grace told her. "I'd go up there and make his mind up for him if I were you."

Maejean opened her third beer. Halfway through it, the idea of dropping in on Charles T. suddenly got more appealing. "You don't think he'd be mad at me?"

Grace shook her head. "I do not. You were getting along pretty well before Ma showed up. No reason you can't again."

Maejean admitted it was true. "But I don't know where I stand anymore, Grace. Maybe he's hopin' your ma will change her mind about him once her troubles are over."

Grace thoughtfully blotted her lipstick on a paper towel. "Well, if she does change her mind, it'll be a first," she said. "Besides, there's only one way to find out what Daddy thinks about you, Maejean, and that's to ask."

Maejean got to her feet, a trifle unsteadily. "Men," she said woefully. "Can't live with 'em. Can't shoot 'em."

They heard the low purr of Travis Moseley's car in the drive and Grace threw her makeup things into a nearby potted plant.

"Take the back door," she hissed at Maejean. "I don't want him to—"

Maejean looked puzzled. "To what?"

"To know you helped with the cooking. That way, it'd look like I went to some trouble."

Maejean took her beer with her. "You reckon Charles T.'s at home?" she asked, opening the back door and staring wistfully up the hill to the lights that shone from Iris Lee's house.

Grace was in a fever of impatience. "Of course he's home!" she said, pushing Maejean out the door. "This is the middle of nowhere, remember? Where the hell else would he be?"

" 'Bye," said Maejean, and headed up the half-mile of hill to Mammy's, her long legs moving through the pasture like a panther's in the dark.

But halfway up, she stopped, unbuttoning the top two buttons of her blouse and drawing deep, shuddery breaths. Too much beer, she thought dizzily, unsnapping the waist-band of her jeans. Too much beer and too much time passing by. Well, she resolved, she knew one man whose time had just run out. She meant to have it out with Charles T. Strait. Once and for all.

She got moving again then, inspired by the sweet, dizzying strains of music. Exquisite, shimmering songs that grew in volume as she drew nearer the house, the music filling her timid soul with the courage it needed, the sound going to her head like a pint of oysters. She untucked her shirt and shed it, then stepped out of her jeans in three quick movements. Boo must be home, she thought, smiling, feeling the first cool breaths of night on her skin. Not hard to find that boy these days, not since he'd got hold of that fiddle.

All a person had to do was listen.

Charles T. was sitting under the carport, reading the evening paper and allowing himself to wonder for the first time in weeks just what in hell was to become of him. He heard a little sound and squinted in the dark, trying to make out the lean alabaster form negotiating the barbed wire that kept the cows out of the yard. Slowly, as though he were witnessing some kind of explosion, he stood up, trying to make his mind accept that vision coming toward him, utterly dumbfounded as Maejean stepped out of the shadows and into the yellow light from the porch, naked as the day she was born.

"Charles T.," she called to him in a clear, unmistakable tone. "I want to talk to you."

Forty=one

I T WAS A NIGHT for loving, that was.

While Charles T. was busy relieving himself of his overalls and underwear, in order to make for more concise conversation with his unexpected guest, Travis Moseley was standing in the doorway of the little house at the bottom of the hill, watching his Grace from under the shadow of his hat, his face so full of the things on his mind that he dared not meet her eyes directly, but could only follow mutely as she pointed him toward a chair.

"I thought we'd eat right away," Grace told him, a little breathlessly. "Before everything's ruined."

Travis nodded and took his place at the table she'd set

with blue plates and candles and a artless centerpiece of chicory flowers that touched off a memory in him, just out of reach.

"Light the candles," she called from the kitchen, and he did so, producing matches from a pocket in his shirt, flipping open the book and producing a flame with one deft movement of his thumb.

He appraised her without speaking as she moved from cupboard to stove. She wasn't a woman who looked as though she belonged in a kitchen, yet she didn't look like she didn't, either. It was that quality in particular that disturbed him about her. Women ought to be more obvious —you didn't want to go to the trouble of forming an opinion about one just to be proven wrong. But watching her, Travis knew the futility of wishing different. Grace Ellen Strait wasn't someone you got to know all at once. It bewildered him a little, having so much feeling for someone he didn't know properly; it bewildered him still further to realize that, up until recently, such things as knowing his women had not been overly important. It made him cautious, such feeling, and quiet, too, for fear perhaps of being deceived. And yet Grace Ellen was no liar; she would tell you the truth with no provocation at all and, like as not, tell you more of it than you wanted to know. It grieved Travis a little, having a woman so full of answers. It made him wonder what his questions were, exactly.

He puzzled over it, watching and listening and marveling a little, while Grace hovered round the kitchen talking and stirring and checking a pot, and dropping things and talking and tasting and talking some more. The woman had a mouth like a she-cat in season, he reflected silently—moving all the time.

By the time she got dinner on the table, he'd learned her opinions on the weather; her Aunt Maejean with the bro-

ken heart; how Boo had progressed on that rattlesnake
violin and how she'd tried to get it from him and couldn't,
not even to steal it long enough to have its value appraised
by someone who knew how. In ten minutes' listening,
Travis learned all that and more—of the progress of the
new store in the mall, of how to cook zucchini (which he
loathed, incidentally), and the flower bulbs she'd planted
up the drive for the spring, parrot tulips and jonquils and
anemones. She talked incessantly of those things and everything else that came to her mind between topics. It occurred
to him that such a wealth of speech was unusual even for
Grace, and might indicate, in fact, that something was
amiss. But Travis saw no reason to try and pinpoint the
cause of her agitation, knowing that if he only kept still,
she'd come out with it eventually, especially at her rate.

The smell of chicken and oysters tickled his nose, and, as
soon as she'd taken her place at the table, Travis commenced to help himself, even to the zucchini, for fear of
offending her, figuring that if he covered it in gravy, it
might not be so bad. He covered the things with pepper and
salt and noticed the silence even before he had time to
consider it strange. Grace Ellen had stopped running her
mouth.

He had the first forkful halfway to his mouth before he
noticed that she, sitting in a chair just opposite, had begun
to cry—huge, welling, and, worst of all, utterly silent tears
that brimmed up and coursed down her cheeks so fast she
didn't even bother to brush them away.

He was completely floored. She'd never cried once in
their acquaintance, and he'd figured somehow that with all
her strength of articulation, she didn't have any need for
tears—that tears had been one of the sacrifices she'd made
in becoming so modern. So, for a moment, he could only
gape, his eyes wide and astonished, while two feet away, the

woman who might very well break his heart for real sat looking at nothing, weeping like she'd never stop. Given his feeling for her, the tears would have been enough to move him, but it was her silence that shook him to his bones. There were no words at all—only a kind of wet, tragical, sniffling as her throat and nose filled up with grief. If Grace Ellen Strait was too upset to speak, it meant things had gone critical. Slowly, he put down his fork, staring at his plate a moment before he could find words to put in his own mouth.

"Is it the zucchini?" he asked. "I don't mind it. Really."

Grace looked up and focused on him, utterly betrayed by his stupidity.

Travis licked his lips and got serious. Whatever this was, it went way beyond squash. He swallowed hard. "Grace, honey," he said, making an effort at calm for her sake, "What is it?"

But she could only shrug and shake her head, sobbing soundlessly into her napkin.

Travis leaned back a little in his chair, wondering that so many tears could be stored up in one head, especially a head as crowded as hers. His surprise was wearing off a little, though, and there marched in its place an impromptu parade of impatience and desire and frustration. And, trailing at the end, an obscure sense of guilt. Travis drew a deep breath. Since it was apparent she wasn't ready or able to tell him of the reason for such weeping he figured he might speed things along a little by guessing.

"Did somebody die?" he asked, almost timidly.

Grace wailed in such a way as to apprise him of his error.

Travis pushed his hat back up on his head. With Grace carrying on that way, it didn't seem right to feel like he had things to hide. "Are you sick?" he said, hoping maybe that she was. Sickness, at least, had cures.

"No!" she shouted, clearly annoyed at the callousness of the question.

Unable to take any more of this sitting down, Travis stood up and circled around to Grace's chair, hoping to quiet her somehow. His palms had begun to itch, but he ignored it. And still the woman cried.

"Grace," he said helplessly, feeling a catch in his own throat.

She stared up at him, her eyes liquid and weepy and so utterly without their usual defenses that Travis could no longer help himself, and reached down, drawing her head close and leaning it against his stomach, feeling her tears as they burned through his shirt.

When he managed to speak again, his voice was different, changed. "Tell me," he whispered. "Can't help if I don't know what the matter is." He pleaded a little, hoping at the same time that she wouldn't pull away.

Her voice came, muffled against the warmth of his belly, indistinguishable, grieving sounds.

"You shit," she said.

And so he could only hold her for a few moments, cherishing her the more. Until he realized with no little surprise that the damp nuzzling against his belly had a purpose behind it and that, through her still-falling tears, Grace had succeeded in undoing two of his shirt buttons with her teeth, and was working on a third. A virtue, he supposed wildly, the blood already rushing to his jeans, of having a small overbite. Shuddering, he felt her mouth on him— light, eager bites of hair and skin, tongue licking away any twinge of pain before it moved on.

Travis held on, afraid that any movement other than the abrupt swelling in his pants would ruin her urgent concentration.

When she had only the top button left to go, she turned her face to his, a heated, desperate light in her eyes.

"I don't know," she said again, soft and throaty. "I don't know what's wrong with me."

Travis pulled her up and into his arms, holding her achingly close, moving his mouth down over the poreless, perfumed skin of her neck in sweet, needful kisses. He paused and took her face in both his hands. Then, no longer unsure of himself, he kissed her—a long, slow affair that left them both gasping.

Travis Moseley looked Grace Ellen Strait right in the eye. And abruptly, he smiled.

"You don't know what's wrong?" he said, pulling her close, each and both relishing the sweet mystery that never quite gets discovered, that miracle that never quite runs out.

"Well, find out and shut up."

Take care of the women, boy.

Davey roared over the dark road toward town, his dead granddaddy's words alive in his mind. And he watched the road carefully, trying to pick some ectoplasm forming at the edge of a wood, some patch of fog that would rise up and speak to him, the way one had before.

"Take care of the women." Experimentally, Davey spoke the phrase aloud against the purr of the car's engine, and sighed. They made no more sense aloud than they did in his head.

It was Wednesday, and on Wednesday evening the Reverend Heck had Bible Contemplation classes, and his wife Luanne had Davey Strait. She didn't usually work at night, she'd told him, but she was putting money by for a mortgage. There was a new development going up in Queen City that had caught her eye. Davey had been convinced, initially, that such a statement was her way of encouraging his ardor, taking it to mean that she planned to leave the reverend for him. But after so many weeks of waiting, he'd found his faith in that potentiality beginning to flag. Contrary to popular opinion, hope does not spring eternal in the human breast. Sooner or later, young or old, we all reach a summit where killing and curing look pretty much the same.

Take care of the women, indeed. Try as he would, the words remained as mysterious as they had the night he'd first heard them, and Davey caught himself wishing, time and again, that his grandfather had the courtesy to be more specific. If the dead were going to walk and talk and give directions, it seemed the least they could do. And yet, the more poor Davey pondered the meaning, the more meaning eluded him. It had seemed a simple enough request on the surface of it, until Davey realized that there wasn't a female of his entire acquaintance who needed caring for, especially. Of course, there was always the possibility that Ray Ed had meant Gloria, having heard about her curse on the grapevine of the afterlife, but aside from immortality, Gloria seemed to have adjusted pretty well to life in Atlantis, much better, in fact, than anyone had expected. For a time Davey had visited frequently, just to make sure, but (as mothers will) she'd taken to reading his thoughts when they ran out of things to say to each other, and Davey had lately felt the need to cut down on such calls, not wanting, just then, to have his privacy invaded, mother or none.

It had to be Luanne.

Suddenly, after weeks of wondering, he knew. Take care of the women meant Luanne Heck and no one else. It excited him knowing that, it made him feel strong. As was their arrangement, he parked his car around the corner and stepped out into the night, whistling. And with the object of his desires in his sights at last, he chose the front walk for a change of pace, striding up the steps like a knight in an iron suit, sure of his reason to be there at last. She needed rescuing, was all. And Davey Strait, who loved her just as sure as he knew his name, was just the man for the job.

Luanne was already in bed when he got there, and saw something different right from the start. It made her smile inside. Davey Strait—too handsome not to be spoiled—a little bit lazy, a little bit scared, and more than a little in love, looked to her eyes like a boy turned into a man. Pity was, he couldn't be hers.

"Hi, hon," she drawled cheerfully and patted the place beside her. But Davey stood firm. Luanne sat a little further up and drew the sheets around herself, waiting for what she knew would come.

"We have to talk," Davey told her.

Luanne lit a Kool. "If you want," she said. "But folks can talk sittin' as well as standin' and naked as well as clothed."

Davey faltered a moment, then sat down to pull off his boots. She had a point. Just because he intended to rescue her from the life she was leading was no reason to scare her first. He intended to be firm with her was all, and by the time he was finished undressing, he noted, with some surprise, that he was. She reached for him, but he resisted.

"Talk first," he said, getting to his feet.

"Fine," Luanne said. "Talk. I'm listenin'."

Now that he had her attention, it took Davey a moment to find his voice. And when he did, the words that came out of his mouth so surprised him that for a moment he couldn't believe himself.

"I want to get married," he said.

Luanne stared at him, a little surprised herself. Usually it took them a little longer to get to the point. And then, usually it was jewelry or an apartment, or some promise of something. But not marriage. In seconds, though, she'd recovered her composure enough to reply.

"Really, Davey?" she asked calmly. "Married to who?"

Davey stared at her. "To you, of course. I want to marry you."

She lifted her left hand and wiggled her fingers so that the ring had time to register. "I'm married already, Davey," she said. "See?"

Davey began to pace. "I know that," he insisted. "I want you to leave him. Leave him and come with me. I got money."

"I do too, actually," Luanne saw fit to point out. "By this time, I probably got more of your money than you do."

"But Luanne, how can you stay with—with—what's his name again?"

"Harlan," Luanne told him.

"How can you?" Davey demanded. "He's a fucking preacher! And you're a . . ."

"Whore?" Luanne looked him full in the face.

"I didn't mean . . ." Davey blushed over his whole skin.

Luanne laughed. "Sooner or later, everybody's got to call things by their right names, Davey. I'm a whore. I'm a whore because I sleep with men for money and I like it."

Davey stared at her, and for one horrible moment she thought he would begin to weep. "Why did you get married?" Suddenly, he wanted to know.

"Because he's a preacher, Davey. I can't do this forever, I'll get old and ugly, but I'll still have Harlan. Harlan will get me to heaven, Davey. And I need to get to heaven when I die."

The tears did start then, hurt and helpless. But man's tears, nevertheless.

"I love you," he said, realizing that he hadn't said it before. He fell to his knees, not out of supplication or want, but only because he could no longer stand; the pain was too great.

She observed him, her green eyes distant and unknowable as ocean. "Funny how that don't change much, ain't it?"

She went to him then, throwing back the bedclothes and crossing the room, knowing no other way to balm the wound she had caused, and knowing, too, that men on their knees can be put to better use than talking and mouths to better use than hurtful words. She pressed herself against his face, holding him and rubbing his sweet, aching head with her fingertips, catching her breath sharply as Davey found her with his tongue and prepared to bury his pain.

"You don't love me," he murmured miserably, hiding his face against her wet skin.

And Luanne Heck only held him closer, holding his head so he would not see her green eyes glisten in the light, or be able to distinguish her tears from his own. She felt that sweet agony forming inside her, building, insisting, until her mouth began to move, forming words she could not say, all for the fear of going to hell.

Oh, Davey.

She came and her mind was one, whole, silent screaming.

That's not true.

Forty=two

BUT PERHAPS it was Gloria McSaxon, cursed with her insight and the wish to be kind, who knew more about love than any of them.

She was waiting on the verandah when Charles T. and Maejean drove up two days later, nervous in her heart and, as was her habit, penciling poetry to keep her mind off things. She was alone that morning, Baby having gone to the beauty parlor for something to lift her spirits. Gloria fretted over the page, unable to concentrate. She had known there was something in the wind for a number of days; every hour brought it closer. And yet, try as she would, she could not put a name to the sensation that tugged at her senses, real and foreboding as a shadow across the moon.

Gloria had come, over the course of her life, to think of her talent for prophecy as half a gift only. Despite her discipline and learning, despite the knowledge she had gathered on her travels round the world, the future remained a nonspecific sort of business, as cloaked in mystery as all the rest of life. Try as she would, she could never quite put together her sense of what was to come until, of course, it did. True, the woman had a certain talent for predicting the predictable, but anyone with eyes could do as much, and when Charles T. and the blushing Maejean climbed the steps and cleared their throats and prepared to break their news, Gloria couldn't help but be a little disappointed. She waited, though, hoping for some ring of confirmation in her heart and mind that these two represented the sense of change that Gloria was carrying around in her heart that day. But confirmation did not come.

Charles T. and Maejean stood before her like children after school, expecting their punishment for doing what came naturally.

"Gloria," Charles T. began in what he hoped was a firm voice.

Gloria sank down on the porch swing, indicating they should sit as well. "Why, Maejean," she said kindly. "You look lovely. Like you've turned over a whole new leaf."

Maejean colored up and look at her shoes. She had, in fact, taken special pains with her appearance that morning, if only to keep from being afraid. She had promised herself she wouldn't be jealous, but face to face with Gloria McSaxon, with her thick hair and amazing eyes, it was hard not to feel helpless.

Charles T. grinned, glancing at Maejean like a sailor at some new, uncharted shore, unable to believe the turns of fortune. When he looked back to Gloria, though, his face seemed to turn in on itself, contorted by the sheer weight of what he had to do.

"We came over here today because . . ." He broke off. Once he said the words, there would be no taking them back, and even though he was as ready to say them as he ever would be, it didn't promise to be easy. "Well," he began again. "There's no other way but just to come right out and say this, Gloria. Me and Maejean—well—"

"You want to get married?" Gloria filled in for him. Immortality and the propect of centuries notwithstanding, she was no more patient with Charles T.'s slowness of delivery than she'd ever been.

"You see, Maejean?" Charles T. smiled delightedly. "I told you she would know already. Gloria's mystical."

Gloria rolled her eyes. It grieved her a little when she thought of the men she had loved in her life. In retrospect, very few of them had much to recommend them. Still, she supposed idly, love makes simpletons of us all.

Charles T. shifted nervously. "Well, I wanted to ask you —you know—what you thought about it."

Gloria stared at him. "What I think?" she asked.

"Yes. Well, what I mean to say is—is it all right?"

Gloria stared past him out into the street. There was a long, low car parked at the curb opposite the house with a rack of bones behind the wheel. The sight inspired in her an overwhelming sense of grief, and yet, it was just a car. . . .

"What?" she asked, momentarily distracted.

Charles T. looked uncertain. He'd stayed up half the night hoping this wouldn't be difficult. He shifted his eyes to Maejean, wanting the sight of her to prove some inspiration. It did. "I want to know if it's all right with you. That Maejean and I get married, I mean."

Gloria frowned at him while keeping track of that car with her other eye. "Charles T.," she said patiently, in case he might have forgotten the obvious. "We haven't been married for twenty years."

"Well, I know that . . . but," Charles T. hesitated. "With you being cursed, well, you know. If you wanted us to put it off, I'd understand."

Maejean found she couldn't quite make the same claim. She stood up, shooting Charles T. a look that curdled his breakfast. Then instantly her expression softened. She figured that, having gotten this far with the man, it might not pay to press her luck.

"Charles T. is right," Maejean said, in an acquiescent tone that wouldn't have fooled the deaf and blind, "if Gloria here don't think we ought to get married, then we could just move in together."

Gloria raised an eyebrow. That Maejean had more guts than showed, to look at her. Good. She'd need them to love Charles T. for any length of time. She glanced across the street. The car was still there.

Charles T. stared from one woman to the other, feeling himself a lucky man, without quite knowing why. "Well, that's true," he admitted. "You, me, and Boo could take a house in town and get married some other time."

Maejean started. Somehow, her rosy visions of the future had failed to include Charles T.'s youngest child. "Boo?" she asked, stupidly.

"Of course, Boo," Charles T. told her. "I don't think we can leave him with Mammy. She's—" He interrupted himself, not sure of the word he wanted.

Gloria decided to help him out. Of all the unexpected pleasure of life in Atlantis, Texas, seeing Iris Lee Strait deteriorate at such an alarming speed was perhaps the most gratifying yet. Gloria may have been a mystic, but she was only human. "Incompetent?" she supplied brightly. "Old and senile?"

"Gloria, please," said Charles T.

"Sorry," Gloria replied and glanced at Maejean, who had apparently left her sense of humor in her makeup kit.

"I just think you could have mentioned it, Charles T.," Maejean blurted out. "It ain't right to just spring this on a person." Romance made Maejean less practical than usual.

Charles T. frowned, trying to ignore his own sense of alarm. "Mention what? Spring what? That I plan to live with my boy? A boy who needs me? Loves me?"

Gloria looked from one face to the other. This was proving more fun than she'd had for weeks. Not that she was jealous, precisely, or even that she cared one way or another how Charles and Maejean worked it out. But Gloria liked a drama now and then, even a little one.

Charles T. got up and began to pace the length of the porch, wondering whether he ought to feel betrayed. It had been awhile since he had been involved with women. He'd forgotten what they were like, how they could turn possessive in the blink of an eye. And just because a man wanted to do his duty, too.

"Look," he said.

"Look at what?" Maejean asked shrilly. "Near as I can tell, Boo is just fine where he is. He's got his fiddle and—"

"How is that fiddle, by the way?" Gloria interrupted, lightly. "Interesting piece of work, that. I wanted to meditate on it sometime."

Maejean glowered at her. "Shut up!"

"You can't talk to her that way," Charles T. threatened.

"Why not?" Maejean demanded heatedly. "She's the cause of all this. Why can't she take him? She's the boy's mother!"

"Excellent point, Maejean," Gloria put in. "And well taken, too."

"You mean you would?" Charles T. stared at Gloria.

"Insofar as that's possible," Gloria answered.

"You see?" Maejean cried, triumphant.

"There's Boo to be consulted, of course," Gloria went on leisurely.

"Consulted? I just know he'd love it here." Maejean gestured a little frantically at her surroundings. She knew she was talking too much, but she didn't care. Abruptly, she sank down in a wicker chair and commenced to cry. "Why was I born?" she asked no one, and was silent.

Gloria looked at her. It was a thing about new leaves, they didn't hold up if the wind got strong.

"I'll ask Baby," Gloria told her former husband. "But maybe Boo has other plans for himself."

Charles T. frowned. "Plans?" he asked bewilderedly. "Boo can't make plans, Gloria. He's—he's—well—he's not normal."

Gloria fixed him with her green eye glittering. "And you are a bigger fool than you look, Charles T. I like that about you."

Charles T. moved over to Maejean and commenced patting her shoulder. "It's all right, honey," he soothed her. "We'll get it all settled. Don't fret."

Gloria stared at them, thinking hard.

"It's just that he's my son!" Charles T. insisted over and over, "he's my child!"

Gloria shifted a little and the porch swing squeaked a protest. Twenty years, she reckoned silently, is long enough to keep a secret like the one she'd kept. Nobody human could ask for better. Besides, she'd promised that man salvation once, so long ago. Now, she supposed, was as good a time as any for him to get it. To be freed at last from those iron bands around his heart, freed of his regrets for all those things he couldn't have helped if he had tried.

So Gloria coughed a little to get their attention and then, when she had it, she paused. Predictable didn't mean easy.

She smiled a little sheepishly.

"Uhmm . . . technically, Charles T.," she said, directing herself to the one who was to be the most affected by such a revelation.

"That's not quite true."

Forty=three

AND SO IT WAS that the truth, as truth had a way of doing, came out.

Gloria McSaxon Strait had not, during the course of her marriage to Charles T., led an exemplary sort of life; she wasn't the type. Her affairs had begun slowly at first, like experiments, starting with the theory that she might be better off in the arms of another than her husband, and ending with the proof that she was indeed, as she had told them all so long ago, cut out for better things. Or at least, a greater variety of things than marriage and motherhood had to offer. Boo's real father, as it turned out, was merely the straw on an already overburdened camel's back. It was not such an unusual thing, she explained to Charles T. that afternoon on the porch, to have the folly of one's life suddenly illuminated by a perfect stranger. She had stayed long enough to see her unexpected pregnancy through to term, and long enough, too, to see that her baby Boo was, in many respects, just like his mother, doomed to an unusual life.

He could hardly have turned out differently, she explained. For his mother was a mystic and his father was a stranger who had, as it happened, wandered into Gloria's bed one afternoon while Charles T. was out working.

They were living in Shreveport then, she remembered, not wanting any more of life on the farm. Charles T. had begun his career as a teacher and was transferred there in the fall. One afternoon there came a knock at the door, and Gloria went to answer, clad only in her robe and a sense of despair. It wasn't her habit not to dress for visitors, but on that particular day, she recalled, she was behind in her routine, being too dispirited by the details of life as a housewife in Shreveport to make such decisions as going through her closet required. The children were in school, Grace in the third grade and Davey in the first. And Gloria was all alone. But not, as it turned out, for long.

The man standing at the door was like no one she had ever seen. He was selling, as people did in those days, encyclopedias, and the idea appealed to the woman, selling knowledge on the lay-away plan. And before she could think to stop herself, she invited the blond, blue-eyed salesman in the light-colored suit in for a cup of tea. They never spoke after that, but made love—on the sofa, on the floor, in the bathtub and the bedroom. They made love continually, knowing how little time they had—a whole long afternoon of it that no one, least of all Gloria, would live to regret. In its way, it was the perfect union, she reflected in

her confession, each knowing without question that which
was meant to be, each knowing afterward that it was done.
Fifteen minutes before the children were due back home,
Gloria had thrown on a housedress and her lover had put
on his suit, gathered up encyclopedias, and left, having
given one housewife, at least, a little piece of knowledge
she wouldn't ever forget.

"What a romantic story," Maejean sighed, when Gloria
was through talking. "Just lovely."

Charles T. stared at her, glad at last to have something
said that he might react to. "Maejean!" It was a cry of
protest.

"What?" she faced him, a little annoyed and dabbing at
her eyes. "It is a romantic story. Just like a French movie."

Charles T. sighed. He had no way of responding to all
this, no way at all.

Gloria was looking at him. "Charles T.," she said, as
gently as she could. "Are you all right?"

There was a little pause.

"Since you've asked, Gloria," he said. "I am not. I do
not, at this moment, know whether to shit or go blind! How
could you?!" He faltered then, the rest of his shouts dying
in his throat.

"How the fuck could you?" he asked again.

Gloria met his eyes without flinching. "I did," she said
quietly. "That's what matters."

He shot her a glance so full of torture and grief she
thought for a moment she'd been wrong to tell it all. Wrong
about everything.

"I ought to kill you," he said quietly, tears shining like
hatred out of his eyes.

"You ought," Gloria said, a little sadly. "But you can't."
There was a breathless silence. Restless, Maejean shifted in

her chair. "It's true, Charles T.," she reminded him. "That curse of hers."

Charles T. blinked once and the tension was broken, shattered like a piece of glass. He hung his head. "Sorry," he said.

Gloria managed a little smile. "Don't mention it," she told him.

They rose to leave then, and Gloria too, unable to sit still for anymore.

Maejean went to the car and left them standing together on the stairs, long enough to say their private good-byes.

"You said," Charles T. started to say and stopped, unsure if he really wanted an answer to the question forming in his mind.

Gloria looked up at him, near enough to touch. But he did not. "Boo," he said. "You told me he would be my salvation."

Amazingly Gloria laughed, as though the joke was somehow on her. "So I did, Charles T. And so he is."

Charles T. couldn't believe it. "I wish you'd tell me how!"

Gloria leaned against the porch railing and, for one shining instant, she was a girl again. His girl.

"Marry that young woman, Charles T.," Gloria said. "Love your children. You can do that now. Even Boo. You can love him all you want, and rest assured that whatever he is isn't your fault."

Charles T. looked at her, trying to take it all in.

Gloria smiled. "I'm telling you you can be happy, Charles T. What more salvation do you need?"

Halfway to the car, Charles T. turned back. He had one more question, one more thing on his mind, before he could begin to put it all to rest.

"That man," he said. "What was his name? Did you ever ask?"

Gloria stared at him, no longer a girl, no longer, it seemed, anyone he had ever known or loved, her face so remote he wasn't sure, at first, that she'd heard him.

Idly, Gloria tore a blossom from the wisteria and held it to her nose.

"He gave me his card," she said, looking back at that far afternoon. "It said, 'Travis Moseley, Senior. Salesman at large.' I think I threw it away."

Gloria seemed to shake herself awake then and smiled. "Don't worry, Charles T.," she said. "I'm sure it was just a coincidence."

Forty=four

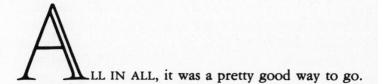

ALL IN ALL, it was a pretty good way to go.

It was, as people tend to say when they speak of the departed, all that she might have wished for.

On the morning that it happened, Iris Lee had awakened at dawn, if you could call that fitful tossing and wandering from room to room that she did during the hours of darkness sleep in the first place. But she had no choice, really. These days it seemed to her that it was only during the hours of night when she was herself anymore—only at night when she was most alive—and she hated to lose too much of that precious time in dreaming. It was at night that she prowled her house and farm like some old cat, compelled by something she could not name, something more a memory than any need to disturb those bones of hers. Her eyes were adjusted now to the darkness, meeting all she saw in the shadows with the same implacable expression in them, as though she was merely confirming to herself that nothing ever changed.

And like the eyes, the ears, too, were more alive in the solitary hours. There were nights when she could distinguish, out of the racket of wind and crickets, when she could hear with an insomniac's hallucinogenic clarity, the delighted cries that filtered through the open windows of the little house at the bottom of the hill, confusing the noise of love that Grace and Travis made with music in her mind.

Though they would have died to learn it, Iris Lee had been wide awake and peering through the bedroom curtains the night her son made love to Maejean on the lawn. She watched it all, from faltering start to shuddering finish, never wavering in her gaze, her old eyes locked on those two pale forms that thrashed together in the moonlight.

"It ain't so much," the old woman murmured to no one when it was done. "It ain't so much at all."

Boo had found her one night, down by the pond, weeping like a child and all but eaten alive by chiggers. He came out of the darkness like an apparition, holding his fiddle by the neck and staring at her as though he knew, without her saying anything, all about the burdens of aging hearts. He lifted her in his arms, light and insubstantial as a bundle of twigs, and carried her back to bed.

"Give it to me, Boo," she whispered, exhausted, as he leaned her back against the pillow. "The fiddle, let me hold it awhile."

He hesitated only moments, even as she was pulled further toward unconsciousness—even as she closed her eyes. Then he laid it down alongside her and the rattlesnake rattlers whispered their own lullabye.

But when she woke again, blinded by sunlight and rage, the bedclothes damp with weeping, the violin was gone.

And now it was morning again and she stood in her kitchen in her Sunday dress with a pocketbook to match, complete with stockings and her old lady shoes. She wanted to look right when she told her story. If she looked all right, then Baby would believe her.

At a quarter to eight, she went for the telephone, only to have it ring just as she touched it, making her pull away. She stared at the thing uncomprehendingly and it rang again, enough to convince her that the sound had not come out of her own mind, after all.

"Hello?" she asked, a little afraid.

"Mammy? It's Dearest."

Iris Lee closed her eyes. "Yes?"

"I just called to see how you were doin'," he said. He sounded kind. He was using the kind, distant tone that Iris had grown so sick of hearing in the past few weeks.

Iris Lee smiled a little. Even Dearest knew, then, how she was slipping away. Even Dearest, who normally gave no more thought to what went on around him than a day fly in June. It made her sad, somehow, that everyone could know and no one could help.

"I'm just fine," Iris answered him. "I'm going out."

He was instantly suspicious. "Where?" he wanted to know.

"I'm going to Baby's," Iris Lee said. "I got to tell her something."

Dearest drew a deep, thinking sort of breath. "Stay

there," he directed. "Stay right there and I'll come and drive you."

"No," Iris Lee said with a trace of her old strength. "I don't want you to come."

And she hung up and was out the door even as the phone began to ring once more.

Minutes later, Baby picked up a call at her house. "Yes?" she said brightly. She'd awakened with a sense of the right-ness of things that morning, as though it was Christmas and she expected a surprise.

"It's Dearest. I talked to Mammy a minute ago. She seemed to think she was going to your house."

Baby looked a little surprised. "Oh?" she asked. "Well, she didn't mention anything, but if Iris Lee says she's going to do something, chances are she will."

"Let me know, will you? I offered to drive her but she wouldn't let me," Dearest went on. "I'm at the store."

"Of course I will, if you want. But I'm sure she'll be fine, Dearest. Maybe she just wants to bring me some preserves or something. But I'll call you when she gets here, anyhow. Don't worry."

"All right," Dearest said, and hung up, a little disturbed. Something she'd said struck him wrong, but he couldn't put his finger on it.

Then he remembered.

Preserves?

Gloria was in the front room, staring out the window. There was that car again, the one she'd been seeing, the one nagging at her, that car with that skeleton of a man behind the wheel, pretending not to look at anything.

"That was Dearest on the phone," Baby said, coming

into the room. "He's worried about Iris Lee. Apparently, she told him she's coming to visit us."

Gloria tore her attention away from the car, startled. "She is?"

"That's what Dearest said," Baby went on. "I guess she must be feeling better, if she wants to come calling."

Gloria smiled a little. A lot of things might be said of Baby Sheba Todd, but she could never be faulted for a lack of optimism. "In that case," Gloria said aloud, "I'll go out. If Iris Lee is feeling good, I'd best not spoil her day."

"Well, that's true," Baby agreed. "You know, she puts me in mind of our own sweet mama at that age. Ornery as a snake, she was." Baby paused and stared at nothing. "Funny how things don't ever turn out the way you'd expect, isn't it? I always thought I'd be the one to, well—fail in my old age. Iris Lee was always so much stronger." Baby smiled ruefully. "I almost wish it was me. It must be so much harder for somebody like Iris."

Gloria had shrugged into a sweater. The morning was chilly, with the first breaths of winter in it. She turned back, though, and looked at the woman as though she was trying to commit her to memory, then went and embraced her for a long silent moment.

"Baby Todd," Gloria said, smiling through an unbidden mist of emotion. "There's nobody like you."

Baby nodded, neither flattered nor protesting. "You're right about that much, anyhow," she said, and patted Gloria's hand.

Gloria glanced out the window, suddenly resolved to go out and speak to that character in the car, whoever it was. But as though the peculiar figure had anticipated her somehow, he and his car had vanished, leaving only the empty street, quiet and shady and cool, and Gloria realized all at once that the car had never been there, that it had been a vision all along.

Baby might have dozed, no one was ever sure. They speculated that she heard those first stealthy footsteps coming up the porch under that arbor of purple flowers, heard too that slow, distinct click and believed it was something other than what it was, the snap of twig only, or the sound of the clasp on an old woman's handbag. They thought she must have heard something, if only that suspicion of sound as the front door swung inward, that she heard and rose to greet the sounds, thinking to meet her sister. No one knew for certain. No one ever would know that after Gloria left the house, Baby had never closed her eyes, but drifted, waking, into the last of her lace-edged dreams. A dream where she danced in a filmy white dress to the strains of a simple, old-fashioned waltz, music that had never once ceased sounding in her heart. It was the sweetest dream of all, that one she had at the last, of beauty and love and flowers that bloomed, never ending. It was the dream of the heart, that was—a strong, innocent heart that no loss could ever ruin, no wound would ever break.

And yet, when that undertaker of a man appeared in her vision, that horrific, shambling skeleton with his old man's gun, too heavy, almost, for lifting, she saw no threat, but only the agony in his eyes. The pain of love unnoticed. Baby saw him clearly and did not move from her place in the dream. The world only slowed a little, and she saw him as he aimed, saw and understood that sweet, brief flash of fire that bore a lover's bullet toward her chest.

Iris Lee was on the stairs and she heard it. She heard that sound that can never be mistaken for anything else. The world shattered to pieces. She heard it as though it wasn't over yet, but kept going on and on. And yet, for one exquisite moment, her mind would not believe the sound ringing in her ears.

She moved her feet and the spell was broken. She made for the open door and saw her sister being gathered up in the arms of the corpse that had been Ernest Earl Faxton. And then she saw it all. Saw the gun lying huge on the rug, saw the absurdly neat round hole just above her sister's heart—spouting red, too much of it ever to be stayed. And that was when Iris Lee began to scream. Sounds worse than those a gunshot makes, for these went on and on, gibbering agony that unreeled like string pulled taut enough to sing. Not-yet-not-yet-oh please-Jesus-not now-not *yet! Notyet not-yet!*

And inside, there were two on the floor. Ernest bent over his one chance at happiness, weeping and calling her name. Able at last to confess his heart because confession meant nothing anymore.

"I loved you," he insisted to the body in his arms. "It was only because I loved so much. Loved you so long."

And Baby Todd understood, those flirting, periwinkle eyes not yet closed, full to the last of the wonder of things.

"Why, Ernest," she said, and her voice was clear and calm and seemed to come from everywhere, like a spirit's.

"I love you, too."

Forty=five

DESTINY MAY NOT BE BLIND, exactly, but its eyes are almost surely in the back of its head. Only by looking backward can anyone see clearly the paths that were traveled; only then is the design of things in sight. And even at that, seeing is never quite believing, is it?

They buried Baby Todd and Ernest on the same cold day, Ernest having shuffled off his mortal coil just hours after his deed was done. The Beemish twins danced attendance over the proceedings, trying not to show their delight at the turn business was taking, and publicly, at least, doing pretty well. And the whole of Atlantis' population turned out for the doings—some to mourn the double passing, some to offer what comfort was possible, but most for the breath of scandal, old and fragile as a pressed corsage, that the murder brought to town.

Charles T. gave a eulogy and the rest of them wept, each not yet convinced that there wasn't something they might have done—dropped by, or stayed home or called up or known, just known somehow that Baby was to die. But they couldn't have known: no one in the family or even in the town could have known. Ernest Earl Faxton might have been crazy from drugs and disease, the people murmured on that cold afternoon, he might have been a killer, or he might have been insane, and there were even those who dared believe he might have been in love. Whatever the reason, though, it had died with the two of them, and if there had been some secret behind the reason, no one would ever know.

It was that notion of secrets that possessed the woman's survivors most, and for a time, it seemed, they were helpless not to tell what they knew. As if by going over what they'd done, they could better predict what was yet to happen. And so they told their secrets, each to the other, anxious to relieve their burdened hearts, figuring that such details might prove helpful if life turned out, as Baby's had, to end with little warning.

Having first gotten the question of Boo's father out of the way, and having, too, more life left to get through than the rest of them, Gloria McSaxon began, in those first empty days following the funeral, to take a kind of verbal inventory of her lovers and her past, names and places and times. And it was Maejean, her innocent ears burning, who heard her, as the two women went over Baby's house and packed her things away. Maejean proved the best of audiences for secrets such as Gloria's, being on the one hand not a little impressed by her exploits (Gloria had awfully round heels, for a white woman), while on the other hand Maejean could feel virtuous by comparison, thereby freed of any pangs of conscience she had about marrying Charles T.

It got to be like a child's game, this telling of secrets. Having heard Gloria's, Maejean's had seemed so mild—not worth keeping as secrets went—like fish too insignificant to fry. So, anxious to begin a new life with her conscience clear, she confided her single transgression from righteousness to Dearest one afternoon at the T-shirt store.

"When I was married the first time, to Bubba," she began in a shaky voice, "I stole money out of his wallet every time we had a fight. He'd go out and come home drunk and I'd steal every last cent and convince him the next morning that he'd spent everything." Maejean gestured around her. "Even before I got the inheritance money, I had a nest egg. It was Bubba paid for part of this place."

Dearest, somber-eyed, lit a thin cigar. "Serves him right," he said. "I know he's dead and all, but the man could hold a nickel till he wore it out."

It went like that, for a time. Charles T., after much soul-searching and deliberation, confessed to his children that he'd never been a fighter pilot, or even been to France. Davey in his turn confessed to Grace that he'd run out on a waitress back in Arkansas, and Grace, lying in bed next to Travis Moseley, confessed to herself that she'd been a coward all along. She took him by the shoulder and shook him awake, finding his sky-blue eyes in the dark.

"I love you," she told him matter-of-factly, and, with a silent apology to Baby Todd, went on. "And I think I want to get married."

Travis took the unexpected news with as much aplomb as he could, having wakened from a dream. He kissed her on the mouth and held her until she fell asleep again, and promised to himself that he would think it over.

And Travis Moseley, too, turned out to have a secret, buried so deep it could not come out by itself, but needed some help to be told. Help that came, less than a month later, from Boo and his rattlesnake fiddle.

It was at a birthday party, family birthdays being as inevitable, almost, as deaths. Gloria's was, as it turned out, within days of Iris Lee's and Grace, who was viewing such domestic occasions with a newer eye all the time, decided to throw them a party.

The evening did not promise to be as difficult as it first seemed, for Iris Lee had suffered a stroke the day of her sister's murder and had not been able since to speak or move very much, and thus could more or less be counted on to keep her feelings to herself. She had to be wheeled to the festivities in a chair, and was placed at the head of the table, the rest of them hoping she would see the honor of that much, at least. She sat looking at things no one else could see, through most of it, limp and forgotten as some ancient, abandoned doll.

Maejean, ever faithful, sat to her left, feeding the old woman with a spoon and leaning over to wipe her chin.

"I heard at the mall that they cleaned out Ernest Earl's house, finally," Maejean said at one point. "Clara Cannon told me."

Everyone stopped talking suddenly, as if that were important.

"She was picking up his things to sell at the next church sale. She figured when folks found out the things were from Ernest's, they could get a good price for them."

Davey went pale at this. He would never, he figured, get used to the workings of commerce. "Jesus Christ, Maejean," he said, by way of protest.

Maejean shot him a look. It was one more thing she truly loved about Charles T.; his children would not have to be raised.

"The point is, the sheriff says Ernest Earl kept a mummy."

Something flickered in Iris Lee's eyes, something that no one saw.

Grace stared at her. "Pardon me?"

Maejean nodded around a mouthful of roast beef. "Strangest thing. A mummy. Like King Tut. Only this one didn't have jewelry. Clara said they found this thing in his bedroom in the chifferobe. All in bandages. The coroner said it was a man, but he couldn't tell who." Maejean paused, looking from one face to another, experiencing the unfamiliar pleasures of center stage. "And that ain't all, either. Seems this old, old lady come up to the sheriff's office to claim the thing. Just showed up out of nowhere and said it was her son."

Travis Moseley was turning a little greenish.

"What did the sheriff do?" Charles T. asked.

Maejean shrugged and turned back to Iris Lee, who'd commenced to drool. "Gave it to her," she said matter-of-factly. "Said with the crime rate what it was, these days, he couldn't be bothered with crazies, too. Especially old ones. Besides, the deputy talked him into it, I guess. Said the old lady was a conjure woman from down in the thicket."

Travis Moseley turned from greenish to blushing red. But nobody noticed.

Finally, Dearest cleared his throat. "God," he reflected, shaking his head. "Mummies. Imagine being that crazy and nobody knowing it. What a life."

Opposite him, Gloria had closed her eyes. "Wait," she announced. "I'm getting an impression on this."

Charles T. shushed the rest of them with a wave of his

hand. "What is it, Gloria?" he asked in a voice that bordered on the reverential.

Gloria opened her eyes. "Nothing," she said in a disappointed tone. "Nothing at all."

Maejean leaned over to wipe Iris Lee's chin. "I believe I'll bring him roses sometime," she said. "Ernest Earl, I mean."

Grace stared at her, thunderstruck at such disloyalty. "What the hell for?"

Maejean glanced away from Iris Lee, just long enough to smile. "He puts me in mind of Valentino," she said, a little sadly. "Remember? And that missionary woman who brought roses to his grave. Way I see it, anyone who'd keep a mummy has to be afraid of being alone."

The rest of them sat silent. Maejean's statement struck them as so oddly romantic, so poorly thought out, that for a moment it was like having Baby Todd back amongst them.

After the supper dishes were cleared, Grace brought out a birthday cake she'd made herself, the candles lit and glowing.

"Happy birthday, Ma," she said and kissed Gloria on the cheek.

"And many more," Charles T. said heartily.

Everyone fell silent, not knowing where to look.

"Aw geez," said Davey miserably.

But Gloria only smiled, trying to recover from having the shock of such innocent intentions. "Never mind," she said. "Never mind."

And, as is the tradition of birthdays, she closed her eyes and blew out the candles, wishing to die with all her heart.

Then, from outside, came the sound of that single violin —the sound of some old hymn—sweet as syrup, sad as tears. And with that genius that was his alone, Boo Strait took matters into his own hands, presenting his mother with the only birthday gift that would matter anymore.

Travis Moseley stood up while the rest of them listened, hearing with his heart the real meaning of that song. He knew, suddenly, the secret he had carried around with him all those years of his life, too precious until this moment for telling, too real, now, for doubt.

Grace caught her breath to look at him. "Travis, what on earth is it?"

The last of that old hymn died on the wind.

"The conjure woman," he said. "My great-grandma. Icy Fee Moulder is still alive."

Forty=six

ESPITE TRAVIS'S not knowing where, precisely, to look for her, Icy Fee Moulder did not prove hard to find. But then, she was right where she had been all along.

Out on the old Moulder place, the signs had started slowly, over a matter of weeks. The signs had started and the signs went on—but the conjure woman did not see. The birds were first. They refused to sing in the mornings, out of that woods on the hill, scarlet cardinals and blue-black crows and silver-throated warblers, all fallen silent and waiting, as if they were afraid. But Icy Fee could not have noticed that much alone, not right away—she'd heard the sounds of morning for so many years of days that, when they were absent, she supplied them out of memory, not thinking anything strange.

She began to lose time after that, chunks of it, as she went for whole days without rest or nourishment, alone in the world with no one to touch or tell her when it was time to sleep. Sunshine and dark began to look the same to her, but she was a woman who had, by choice or circumstance or the placement of her stars, been forced to look so long into the shadow world of things that she couldn't be expected, really, to be able to tell the difference anymore. She tried, one day, to pick some flowers for her kitchen table, but they refused to come out of the ground at her touch and she could only stare, wondering, at those blossoms that fluttered in the wind, and think that she must be getting old.

Then, on the day before Gloria McSaxon Strait would come to her house in search of the only cure there is for immortality, Icy Fee Moulder began, at last, to weep. They surprised her, those tears. They were real enough, and wet, but she could not find any reason, really, to be weeping, her mind resisting to the last possible moment the meaning of her old body's grief.

Travis and Gloria came together that morning, Gloria in search of some remedy and Travis for his own sake, riding in a long, white car.

When she heard the sound coming down the road, Icy Fee felt real again for the first time in days. Someone coming to visit, she thought, somebody here. And when she was sure that the sound of that car was getting closer, when she was sure that it would stop for her, she stood up and smiled and straightened her dress, glad, after so long a time alone, for the company.

The woman standing on the porch as they drove up was impossibly, incredibly, old. Gloria and Travis exchanged a quick, startled look when they saw, needing to confirm that that shriveled, frail figure was indeed present in the flesh and not some hallucination. But Icy Fee never doubted them; she stayed on that sagging porch of hers as though she were growing out of it, waving and watching as they got out of the car.

As a gesture of respect, Travis Moseley took off his hat. Icy Fee smiled at him, seeing that handsome, golden-haired vision, allowing herself, for one whole, ineffably sweet moment, the pure luxury of her age.

"Cecil?" she asked him, in a cracked, disused voice.

Travis swallowed hard. "No, ma'am," he said.

"No," Icy Fee agreed reluctantly, after a second look. "No. I guess not."

Travis looked helplessly at Gloria, who in turn looked like she would shatter into pieces if forced to speak her errand there, so much hope had she invested in this gnome of a woman standing between them.

Travis's mouth had no spit left, but he tried again. "Do you—" he said. "Can you remember me?"

Icy Fee locked his eyes with her own, and he was held, swallowed in pale fire.

She worked her ancient lips. "You got a rash?" she asked him.

Travis felt as though he might weep for relief when she looked away again. "No, ma'am," he said. "But if you can, she—" he indicated Gloria, who had begun to tremble. "She needs a conjure."

The old woman glanced just once—so briefly—at Gloria, that it was all Gloria could do not to faint, so convinced was she of the futility of things.

Icy Fee tiptoed up and kissed Travis on the cheek. "Git," she said softly. "She'll maybe stay awhile."

Travis looked at Gloria, who nodded.

When he was gone, Icy Fee turned back to her guest, and Gloria saw that the old lady had begun to weep.

"Immortal," Gloria said, touching the front of her blouse, not knowing how much she needed to explain.

Icy Fee nodded and held open the screen door. "Only one conjure for that," she said and walked, delicate and slow, to the cupboards in the kitchen. "Only one cure."

Gloria stood in the center of the room, feeling lost and found at once. And she waited, asking the question in her mind.

But Icy Fee Moulder never answered. She found the one potion she sought in a dusty, ancient jar at the back and directed Gloria to put on the water for tea.

Gloria, meek as a child, set out two cups, but Icy Fee shook her head. "This is for me," she said and sipped, rolling the taste of it around on her tongue like spirits. Then, as though it were an ordinary day, Icy Fee began to tell her visitor of the bayou and the woods, and the plants that might cure or merely kill, depending on the quantity and which parts were used. She spoke of all the hidden things, and how to read the signs, passing on her secrets, lodging them all in Gloria's mind. It seemed to take forever, that instruction, though it also seemed to the bewildered Gloria that there was nothing to betray any passage of time, nothing but the words themselves and the dwindling number of swallows of tea left in Icy Fee Moulder's little china cup.

And then, at the last, when the tea was nearly gone, Icy Fee reached for those last few sips and her hand passed through the cup, contents and all.

Gloria stared, wide-eyed as a girl, and Icy Fee, not wanting her guest to be disappointed, did it again. And Gloria realized that there was something else, too, to betray the passing of hours that day. For the old woman sitting across the table was all but gone, fading to transparency, and that even was fading, dimmed and dimmer in those last few seconds, like she had never been, blowing away in the wind.

"Please," Gloria said, begging with her whole heart in her voice, insisting, though it was useless to try. "Please. Help me—you have to help me. I'm immortal."

And still she faded by degrees, like a dream in the morning, until only the eyes remained as evidence, pale and thoughtful and full to the last of fire.

"Gloria," and it was a whisper, only inside her mind. "Don't be stupid. Nobody lives forever."

EPILOGUE

GRACE WHEELED Iris Lee's chair into the sun, bustling around her with the efficiency of an experienced nurse, draping a dish towel securely around the old woman's neck for a bib and adjusting her position so that there wouldn't be a glare in her patient's eyes. Not, Grace privately suspected, that a little bit of sun in the eyes would make any difference to someone in Iris Lee's deplorable condition, but then again one never knows.

The ties of blood are strong and the ties of love are stronger still, and Grace went about the messy, impossible business of keeping the old woman alive with the same dedication they all did, there being, basically, no other way about it. And if there was some impatience showing out of the granddaughter's eyes that morning, a little exasperation in the way she tucked a light cover around the old lady's bony legs that were splayed out straight in the chair, like the tines of a divining rod, or if there was a note of harshness in Grace's tone as she began a bright, false monologue on the feel of the weather and the happenings in town—if those things were there, it wasn't anything special. It wasn't anything that any of the rest of the family hadn't experienced in the course of those many months. It was only the resigned, silent frustration of wanting it over, the purgatory of wanting to wake up one morning and look on a day and know that there wasn't a corpse needing feeding in the room nearby, a body covered in waxy skin and bedsores, waiting to be washed and changed and turned over, or propped in a chair like a piece of wood.

For Iris Lee had never recovered, even for a moment, from that day at Baby's house in town—never healed from that burst of blood that had happened in her brain at the sight of her sister dead on the carpet. She'd never gotten over those things and never would, nor her guilt nor her secret, either. In her mind she saw it again and again, saw that hole in the one heart that might have forgiven her, saw the passing of the one soul who might have understood how she, Iris Lee, had murdered Cecil Moseley sixty years before.

She was careful to look at nothing these days, but sat in her invalid's chair, paralyzed and terrible, unable, it seemed, to die.

But a family keeps on, regardless. And so they had. And it was Grace's turn to feed the grandmother because there was no one else, this day, to get it done. Charles T. and Maejean were finally on a honeymoon, heading toward

Alaska and the hope of cooler weather. Grace had had a postcard, she told the figure in the chair. The coolest-looking pines you ever saw.

And there had been a letter too, from Davey, who had packed up his things and driven back to Arkansas one day the previous January, to tie up loose ends, he said. And Boo had gone with him that day. He had laid himself down in front of Davey's car and wept until his brother relented, as brothers always do eventually, and taken the boy on one last ride away from that farm in Atlantis. It was all right, Davey assured them, he was reluctant to leave them all behind. Boo was playing electric fiddle along with Davey's band, the letter had said, so popular with women it was hard to keep him home.

Dearest was gone, too. Out of town with a lover who ran the fast-food franchise at the shopping mall, leaving Travis and the baby to mind the store, Travis having discovered some talent along with the birth of his child for earning an honest living. He and Grace weren't married yet, but they kept planning on it, assuming, of course, that things worked out.

Grace stirred the bowl of plain grits and milk and blew on them a little, so as not to burn the old woman's tongue. But it was no use, for hot, cold, or lukewarm, Iris Lee would not eat. Grace had only to get a bite in before it was spat back out at her, or simply rejected by lips and tongue, allowed to trickle down her chin. After a half-hour or so of this, Grace set the bowl aside and turned the chair so that Iris Lee could see her eyes.

"Tell me what you want?" she asked helplessly. "Do you want something different?"

Iris Lee blinked, hurt and afraid. Whatever it was, it wasn't the food.

Grace looked hard into those rheumy little eyes, nested in their yellowish whites, studied them, as if it were possible, just by looking, to tell what went on in the mind.

And there was a sound, unsure of itself, a gurgle turned to a whisper and died.

"What is it?" she asked again, unable to interpret such a development.

There was a long, agonized effort, then notes come from deep in the throat, like music.

Grace nodded. "Yes! A song—you want to hear a song?"

Iris Lee blinked, so long and slow it was like sleep. Then words—cruel and unformed.

"Die-e-e-eee."

Grace frowned and leaned closer. "Tell me, Mammy," she urged. "Tell Grace what you need."

Iris Lee stuttered and drooled and thumped the arm of her chair until she could make the rage in her mind turn to speech.

"Kill . . . muh . . . me. Please . . . kill . . . me. . . ."

Sighing and exhausted, Grace sank down on the stairs. That again. She picked up the bowl of food and stirred, lifting the spoon to the old lady's lips with a forced and pitying little smile.

"Don't be silly, Mammy," she chided softly. "Eat your grits."

And, from far down the hill, from the pasture by the pond, the wind began to sound like music, sighing through the trees.